THE TRAINING OF AN ENGLISH GENTLEMAN

I shivered helplessly, not just at the prospect of being flogged, but at being alone and naked and completely in a strong Lady's power. She uncoiled the whip from her belt, and cracked it in the air, and I moaned – it was a fearsome implement, fully six or seven feet long. Then she flogged me on the bare bottom.

I twisted my head to plead with her for mercy, the tears streaming down my face, but she announced that I was not to look at her. I glimpsed that she had her leather coat open, and her hand was between her thighs, at the crotch of her grey uniform skirt, moving gently as she whipped me.

By the same author:

MEMOIRS OF A CORNISH GOVERNESS
THE GOVERNESS AT ST AGATHA'S
THE GOVERNESS ABROAD
THE HOUSE OF MALDONA
THE ISLAND OF MALDONA
THE CASTLE OF MALDONA
PRIVATE MEMOIRS OF A KENTISH HEADMISTRESS
THE CORRECTION OF AN ESSEX MAID
THE SCHOOLING OF STELLA
MISS RATTAN'S LESSON
THE DISCIPLINE OF NURSE RIDING
THE SUBMISSION OF STELLA
CONFESSION OF AN ENGLISH SLAVE
SANDRA'S NEW SCHOOL
POLICE LADIES
PEEPING AT PAMELA
SOLDIER GIRLS
NURSES ENSLAVED
CAGED!
THE TAMING OF TRUDI
BELLE SUBMISSION
THE ENGLISH VICE
GIRL GOVERNESS
THE SMARTING OF SELINA

A NEXUS CLASSIC

THE TRAINING OF AN ENGLISH GENTLEMAN

Yolanda Celbridge

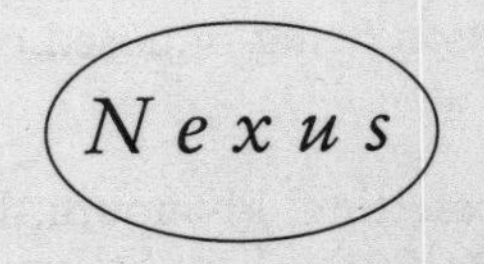

This book is a work of fiction.
In real life, make sure you practise safe, sane and consensual sex.

First published in 1999 by
Nexus
Thames Wharf Studios
Rainville Road
London W6 9HA

This Nexus Classic edition 2003

www.nexus-books.co.uk

ISBN 0 352 33858 X

Typeset by TW Typesetting, Plymouth, Devon
Printed and bound by Clays Ltd, St Ives PLC

Contents

Prologue

Shamed

I have always been an English gentleman, even though I did not set foot in England itself until the age of seventeen. Shortly after that I began to learn the taste for a woman's whip. It is a false commonplace that human males constantly struggle for power. In secret, they struggle for submission – to the female. Any man who ignores or resists enslavement to women is a fool, and no gentleman.

I was born in Italy: in the port of Trieste, which was then part of the Austrian Empire. When I was little, we moved to Tarvisio, in the Dolomites or Karawanken Alps, where the lands of the Italians meet those of the Germans and Slovenes. It was quite a confusing place to live, with all the political changes at that time, during and after the Great War. That was why we moved there: my dear father was a smuggler, to put things bluntly. He trafficked in anything, and sometimes in people, or false passports, or any sort of contraband that would travel by a variety of means: motor-car, bicycle, cart or even donkey.

At school, I was called 'donkey' because of my large penis, and in fact I was skilled at navigating the mountain passes with a mule laden with goods. However, throughout my boyhood, my penis excited interest in our boyish games, not least because, as well as its large size and girth, it is endowed with a curious birthmark, right underneath my prepuce, on my glans, which was in the shape of a crescent moon. At any rate, I was the one most often called upon to 'perform' in tests of manly prowess, and never disappointed, so that I acquired the extra nickname – 'cup of cream'.

My father said that my birthmark meant I was descended from a certain English knight, Sir Rogier de Prince, who had navigated these terrains on his way to the second, or third, crusade. Certainly, my sandy hair and fair complexion set me apart from my fellow-Italians. Hence my name became Italianised to Ruggiero Principe, although my birth certificate has me 'Roger', and I am properly known here in Surrey as Roger Prince.

My father was a fervent Anglophile, and helped many of the English officers who escaped from prison camps, or else were engaged on secret missions, during the closing stages of the Great War – the Kingdom of Italy fought with the British, opposing the Austrians, so that although technically Austrians, our loyalties lay with England. After the war, the territory of Trieste reverted to Italy and the defeated Austrian Empire was dismembered. It was then that my mamma tragically passed away in the influenza epidemic of 1918.

I always thought his story of my birthmark was mere fancy – my papa explained that it was passed on alternately to male and female – especially the part about inheriting great lands in England, but I came to believe it because I wanted to: the English officers we entertained were sterling fellows.

One way and another, we became quite rich, and had a villa on Lake Como, and a house in Venice, and so on. I always preferred the Alps – there is something so *English* about the Alps – all those maiden ladies with their water-colours, and earnest mountaineers with their woolly breeches! So, when the Great War was over, it seemed quite natural and thoroughly desirable to me that our new prosperity should despatch me for a year at Eppingham, one of the foremost English public schools, to complete my secondary education, at the age of seventeen. Afterwards it was assumed I should proceed to the University of Oxford.

Shortly before this, my father explained that there were certain financial matters he had to attend to, and he would have to absent himself for some time. Misunderstandings, was all he would say, and, in my innocence, I took him at his word. My affairs were provided for, with a trust fund administered by a firm of solicitors in Egham, Surrey, from which I should derive an income sufficient to my needs. We said goodbye, the villas in Venice and Como were sold, apparently to some Austrian Lady of Italian origin, and my father said he hoped I should realise my true nature as an English gentleman, for there was nothing left for either of us in Italy, and I should not expect to hear from him thereafter for a while.

It was with mixed feelings that I left on the train to London, via the English Channel. Excitement and uncertainty, surely, and also regret, for I had led a very happy childhood and adolescence, even though my acquaintance with the female sex was as yet minimal, except for the numerous fragrant Ladies my father had the custom of entertaining.

But there was one incident and the one unhappy memory of my childhood: though I was already sixteen, and a grown-up young fellow when it happened, it was most humiliating. And it is germane to my story, as the reader shall see.

I say that I did not learn the taste for being whipped by women until after my time at Eppingham; there, indeed, I was cruelly beaten, though not, unfortunately, by the sweet cruelty of women. But this one experience did lead me to taste a woman's whip, and for a long time I felt bitter at my humiliation, foolishly bitter!

It was shortly after the Armistice, and everywhere in Europe was turmoil, not least in our already confused little corner. No one knew which territory was going to belong to whom, and there were officials and troops in strange uniforms, militias and lawless bands, so that everything was uncertain. Nevertheless I continued to do my plodding work of transportation.

I was pulling a handcart on a familiar, isolated mountain pass, in deep snow, when I was accosted by a customs patrol wearing unfamiliar uniform, and speaking a language I thought was Slavonic. The handcart was not heavy, and I thought it might contain papers, or perhaps rolled-up paintings of old masters, but certainly no brandy or tobacco. At any rate, I was rather frightened. They wore heavy greatcoats against the cold, but I perceived that one of them was a female, though all I could see were her eyes under her fur hat. They took me to a hut of recent construction and hence unknown to me or I would naturally have taken another path. The Lady seemed to be in charge, and dismissed the others.

She was sheathed in a military greatcoat of black leather, with a fur hat and a scarf, yet I was not unaware of the supple curves of her body beneath, nor of her delicate female fragrance under the sweat and grime. Her eyes stared, piercing me, and they seemed angry and soft at the same time . . .

It was warm inside the customs shed from a stove. I assured her, truthfully, that I was ignorant of my cargo, and offered the usual bribe of the gold thaler I carried for that purpose, but she spurned it very righteously, and in anger. She barked in fractured Italian that I was to strip completely. I was terrified; she had a gun, and also a heavy whip coiled at her belt, like a horsewhip, beside the ungainly canister of an army gasmask. So, trembling in fear and shame, I obeyed. She left the hut to inspect my cart, leaving me naked.

When she returned, she said my cart was full of valuable papers, and would be confiscated, and I should be flogged as a spy, only my youth excusing me harsher chastisement. She said this quite casually, as though a naked flogging, administered by a female to a male, were quite natural. I was ignorant of any sort of beating, but did not plead for mercy, despite my horror of pain, since it seemed this *was* mercy. I shivered helplessly, not just at the prospect of being flogged, but at being alone and naked and completely in a strong Lady's power.

She ordered me to stand against the hot stove, which was painful enough in itself, and spread my legs. She proposed to beat me on the buttocks. She uncoiled the whip from her belt, and cracked it in the air, and I moaned – it was a fearsome implement, fully six or seven feet long. Then she flogged me on the bare bottom.

The first stroke cut me raw, and I gasped and squealed. The second was worse, and the third ten times that. I danced and wriggled, clutching the stove, as she told me not to move from my place, or more severe punishment should befall me. I could not imagine any punishment more severe, or any worse shame.

My head swam with pain, each lash of that fearful whip making my bare bum smart in horrid searing agony, such as I had never imagined could exist, let alone be applied to my body. I tried to count the strokes with stuttering teeth, but could not. The whip whistled in the air with dreadful meaning, and cracked mercilessly on my bare buttocks, snaking even more painfully, and with practised skill, down over the backs of my thighs.

I twisted my head to plead with her for mercy, the tears streaming down my face, but she barked that I was not to look at her. I glimpsed that she had her leather coat open, and her hand was between her thighs, at the crotch of her grey uniform skirt, moving gently as she whipped me.

At length I heard her pant louder and more hoarsely, and gulp as much as I gulped in my maddening pain. The whipcracks grew fiercer and more rapid, and I danced in my agony, squealing as the skin of my buttocks felt flayed from me by her lashes. I heard her cry out repeatedly, very softly, as though she was trying to stifle her own cries of pain, and then, with a gasping deep breath, she told me my punishment was over, and that I had taken five dozen strokes with that whip on my bare flesh.

I saw her look pointedly between my legs, a thin smile creasing her lips; I looked down, aware of a throbbing sensation that was not pain, and saw to my horror that my penis had risen, and had stood erect and clearly visible to my chastiser throughout my whipping! This increased my humiliation.

I was told to dress, and despatched red-faced and whimpering without my cart. It was now extremely uncomfortable to walk. My father was philosophical about the matter of my cargo – I did not admit I had been whipped – but I cried myself to sleep with bitter resentment at my humiliation. To be flogged – and by a woman! To smart so much under a *female's* whip seemed the greatest outrage to my male person.

And yet, when my smarting had subsided to a warm glow, I had to check myself from finding the sensation actually pleasant. I felt my ridged, puffy bottom and inspected myself in the mirror; I had taken a full sixty strokes with a *real whip*, more than many judicial punishments, and had taken it like a man! My buttocks were fearfully scarred and wealed, and dark mottled crimson streaked with ugly purple and black welts.

Yet, as I embarked for England still blushed with the marks of my punishment, I could not help feeling a certain pride in my endurance. I remembered the female aroma of the cruel Lady, the smell of her leather and her sweating boots, and the strange way she had rubbed herself between her thighs, as though my flogging had given her pleasure: and came to the conclusion that my beating had served some purpose, and that perhaps she had been merciful after all.

I shall not dwell on my time at Eppingham, near the pleasant town of Esher – suffice to say that in my year of education there, I received, and administered, beatings far more savage in spirit than my whipping by the mysterious customs Lady. My father had warned me that beating made an English gentleman – he was right, of course, but it is not beating from coarse and vengeful schoolboys that civilises a male. Because of the Great War, there was quite a shortage of senior boys, so that despite my inexperience, I was rapidly made a prefect.

But I was obliged to start off as the lowliest of 'new oiks', despite being nearly of university age. I was made to wear short trousers, and do 'fagging' duties, at which any imperfection was rewarded by the cane. Caning, official or unofficial, was frequently on the bare bottom or, if not, on thin shorts or pyjama bottoms pulled tight, which amounts to much the same. I took my beatings with a certain haughtiness, smug that my naked bottom had endured much worse, and from a female . . .

It was not the pain of the beatings I minded, so much as the humiliation of being beaten by other males, who I knew to be just as wicked and grubby as myself! We were beaten constantly, for the slightest misdemeanour, and with studied, casual indifference, as though our squirmings under the cane – which could be a dozen strokes or more – were of no account. I thought wistfully of my whipping in the Alpine shed, and how there had been a simplicity in the vengeful flogging I took from the female in leather – which did not entirely quench my thirst for some unspecified and unlikely revenge on her person. Yet even in her cruelty, she had somehow *cared* about me enough to thrash me.

Only once was a female involved in punishing me, and it was the headmaster's daughter, a pretty thing of sixth form age, usually glimpsed only from afar, who had caught me picking wild flowers which she insisted were 'hers'. She was (rightly) the apple of her papa's eye, and (again, rightly) could do no wrong; nothing would do but that I must be flogged, and that she must witness the punishment.

I was caned on the bare by the head prefect, the biggest and strongest boy in the school, and was given two dozen strokes with a four-foot yew cane; that sly and lovely slip of a girl watched bright-eyed as my naked buttocks shuddered at every stroke, licking her lips and counting them off. There is something about the cane, sinister and fearful: its slow, hissing malevolence raises ugly weals, yet with malign, almost ladylike precision, unlike the more painful yet somehow more generous lash of whip, tawse or even birch.

I squirmed and jerked as I was caned, my bare skin scorched at each stroke and smarting abominably, with a lump rising in my gorge and tears welling at my eyes. It was undoubtedly the worst caning I had taken at Eppingham. Yet I was aware of the pretty girl's eyes on my squirming bum and, to my horror, I felt a stirring as my penis rose! I could not help it – the dreadful pain seemed only to inflame my penis further. More specially, it thrilled me that a *woman* had ordained my punishment, that a *woman* was watching my naked flesh quiver under the cane.

When the two dozen were well delivered, there was silence, broken only by my gasping sobs. And then the pretty young girl spoke. Her eyes were on my shamefully stiff penis, until decency obliged her to avert her gaze. She was flushed and trembling.

'Disgusting!' she murmured. 'Give him the beating over again, please.'

As I lay in my bed that night, wretched and sullen at my humiliation, I could not help rubbing my raw bottom, and thinking of her . . . and my penis rose to full erection. I fell asleep almost happy, that *she* had wanted me punished, and to watch my agony, and that somehow my beating had given a Lady pleasure.

That was just before the middle of the Easter term and my year at Eppingham; a few days later, I was called to the headmaster, who was in company of the head prefect who had caned me. Most jovially, he told me that as a reward for my good behaviour and stiff upper lip and so on, I myself was henceforth to be a school prefect! We shook hands, and my caner said, 'No hard feelings, eh, old chap?' and, smiling, I agreed. To my amazement, I had no hard feelings, and I blurted that I had been glad of my caning!

Thereafter we became quite friendly, and vied with each other in the number of canings we could dish out to the junior boys, and the seniors as well – fellows with whom, weeks before, I had been comparing welts and brutalities, and now found myself administering the same cruel chastisements.

I was glad that my period of authority was so short, otherwise my enjoyment of caning others might have grown unseemly. I did take pleasure in caning, I must admit, and the feeling of power as I reddened a quivering bare bottom, but always I was dimly aware that there was something improper in my harshness: not that my fellows at school were undeserving of bare-bum caning, but that it was seemly and proper for them – as for me – to receive it from a *Lady's* hand.

1

Fresh to the Birch

I was to spend the summer before going up to Oxford at Virginia Lodge, the home of Major Dark, an old friend of my father's from the Great War. It was near the pleasant town of Virginia Water, at the boundaries of Berkshire and Surrey, an area which is sufficiently far from London to be the country, yet sufficiently near to be metropolitan. I should attend to my studies and be treated as one of the family, helping as needed in tasks on the estate.

As I waited for the motor-car to pick me up from the railway station, I had ample time to observe the Ladies of the town, without exception true flowers of English womanhood: wide faces and lips, rosy complexions, and blessed with a firm, thrusting ripeness in both bottom and breast. Or so it seemed to my young male eyes! They had blonde hair for the most part, curled and teased and bobbed; and as I watched the movement of their haunches, those ripe orbs swaying under satin, silk and muslin, I thought, as I still do, that there is nothing so delicious in this world as the ripe bottom of an English Lady.

Thus my pulses were already agreeably racing on that hot June day as the Dark family arrived in their gleaming Bentley to collect me, and I first set eyes on Miss Florence Dark. It would be wrong to say that Miss Dark was the first true love of my life, since the word 'love' has all sorts of soppy connotations. Rather, I was struck by a thunderbolt. Miss Florence Dark seemed to unite in her person all the beauties of Virginia Water, and of English womanhood in its entirety. She did not glance at me from her seat in the rear of the car; my adoration of her person was enhanced by the woeful certainty that she would never return it; that she gave not a fig for me, and was here as a chore of politeness; that the most I could hope for would be to act as her adoring errand-boy, if permitted.

I sat beside her on the drive back to Virginia Lodge. Her perfume, her nearness, the perfection of her creamy skin entranced me, and I felt a delicious, hopeless tickling in my manly parts. Her bosom swelled ripe and full; her croup matched her breasts impeccably, leading to powerful thighs and dainty slender feet. Her blonde tresses cascaded disdainfully over her wide cheekbones and strong brow, and her broad, full lips were set in an expression of stony indifference as she stared out of the window, away from me. She wore a suit of beige cotton, with white stockings and a white cotton blouse, buttoned severely to the collar, and her feet were shod in heavy, sensible shoes with a lovely golden buckle which looked like a little riding crop on a horse's saddle.

Her mother was similarly attired, though in sensible grey. She had lustrous raven hair, and a slightly tan complexion, with a pert, elfin beauty, very supple and fluid in her gestures, and seemed very young to be Miss Florence's mother.

I paid a clumsy compliment, that it was hard to tell mother from daughter, and Mrs Dark beamed in delight, though Miss Florence's stony expression did not change. Major Dark grinned too; he was a leathery, dapper man with an easy military manner.

'See, Flossie,' cried Mrs Dark. 'Our young man is flirting already!'

'He may be your young man, Mummy, but he is not mine,' she replied frostily. 'And please do not call me Flossie. It makes me sound like some sort of serving-maid.'

She sniffed, and stared out of the window away from me, as though the most interesting object in the world were a thousand yards distant.

Major Dark laughed, and said there was little danger of

her being mistaken for a serving-maid, as you couldn't get them nowadays.

'O, Daddy!' said Miss Florence, crossing her legs with a delicious swishing of cotton, and an equally delicious curl of her lip.

We passed through the pleasant rolling countryside, dotted with woods and mansions, and eventually, at the end of a winding, secluded lane, came to Virginia Lodge itself. The driveway took us past flower gardens, ponds and orchards, to a charming house that seemed part Elizabethan, part Jacobean, part Georgian, and much else I am sure, a testimony to our English genius for modesty and improvisation.

A pretty, if tousled, young Lady, who was addressed as 'Grubb', greeted us with a sullen curtsy and took charge of my meagre baggage. Major Dark explained that Grubb was a general factotum, who lived on the estate and 'did' for them.

'Hard to get male hands,' said the Major, mischievously, 'and I'm not sure I'd want them, given female aptitude for drudgery.'

'O, really!' cried Mrs Dark gaily, pretending to be cross, and Miss Florence's lips opened for a fleeting second in a heavenly sneer of amusement.

Grubb curtsied again, half-turning to reveal the ripe pears of her shapely and very large buttocks. She reminded me delightfully of the Ladies I had observed in Virginia Water, though a slightly more dishevelled version. Her face was smudged, her wide lips curled in an exquisite pout, framed by a rumpled mane of blonde hair streaked with pale fire by the sun. Her breasts were as massive as her rump, and the magnificent udders and croup might have seemed disproportionate in another female, except that her superbly muscled body carried their beauty quite effortlessly, even as they seemed threatening to burst from her sloppy, skimpy dress, that left her brown legs bare above heavy boots. She seemed like a mare, coquettishly proud of her animal beauty yet unsure how a Lady should present it properly.

I was shown to my room on the first floor, reached

through a maze of corridors and alcoves whose cobwebs spoke indeed of a dearth of servants. My room had a small four-poster bed of carved rosewood, a table, chair, water jug and wardrobe, porcelain chamber pot, and a bare board floor with an exquisite Persian rug. The bathroom was at the end of the corridor and, after my ablutions, I dressed for dinner. I was pleased to find the company dressed also, and that Major Dark paid me the compliment of wearing his military medals.

Mrs Dark was sumptuously dressed in a gown of dark crimson, with a low flounced front that left her pert breasts deliciously exposed, and pressed together by a subtle, unseen corselage into a lovely peach with a deep cleft. She was gay and flirtatious; her daughter cold, yet I was pleased – thrilled, to be truthful – that she had replaced her modest day clothes with a skimpy black silk cocktail dress, with narrow shoulder straps criss-crossed on a deeply plunging back, proving that her superbly thrusting breasts were unsupported by corselet or brassiere.

The magnificent breasts were much exposed, their cleft narrow like her mother's, but in no need of any support, so fully did they crowd the thin silk of her bosom. The hem came very high above her knees, revealing generous thigh, in black silk stockings. When she shifted in her chair, with her thighs exposed to my full view, I even spied a hint of bare skin, and the gleam of a golden garter strap in the curious shape of a crop and horse's saddle. I was ravished by the ease and indifference with which she moved her buttocks and crossed her legs, as though my anguished, longing gaze were of no more importance than a poodle's. A simple pearl choker adorned her swan's neck, and her blonde tresses were arranged in a chignon, with a few stray hairs tenderly kissing her brow and gleaming cheekbones, which were slightly rouged. How I longed to be one of those wisps of hair!

We dined on a handsome roast beef, with superb claret, and when the Ladies had retired to leave the Major and me alone with our port (served by Grubb in a fetching French maid's uniform, several sizes too small for her) we got to exchanging rather ribald anecdotes, and the Major reminisced about the 'old days'. After a while, he said that I must not mind Flossie and her ways.

She was nearly twenty-three years old, which, to me at eighteen, seemed vastly mature in years. The Major told me with a sigh that she still pined for one Greville, her sweetheart, who had been posted missing in Flanders in 1918. She refused to believe he would not return, and kept a guest room exactly as it had been on his last leave. Meanwhile, Miss Florence devoted herself to charitable works in the neighbourhood, and was out and about on her bicycle most days. He said that I must humour her a little, and perhaps my presence would draw her out in time from her self-imposed spinsterhood.

'I am away a lot on business,' he said. 'I try to get her to go to London, and get into Society – parties, and so on – but she won't go. So please bear with her, old man.'

The Major also explained to me that Dido – Mrs Dark – was not Florence's mother, but his second wife, hence the congruence of their ages, and this might have something to do with Miss Florence's attitude.

'Dido – Mrs Dark – was my nurse, you see, during the War in Mesopotamia, and afterwards, when I was convalescing back in Blighty. So fortunately her training enables her to take young Florence in hand when she is headstrong – so there is no reason why your stay here shouldn't make you as happy as it makes us, old man.'

I retired in high spirits – for an English gentleman to address another as old man betokens the fondest intimacy. Thereafter I settled into an easy routine at Virginia Lodge. Mealtimes in the day were informal, or not fixed at all. There were few tasks for me to do, since Grubb jealously guarded her competence at them all. The Major was usually away on his affairs; Miss Florence was out on her charitable tasks in the neighbourhood, and I would watch her with longing as those proud long legs pumped so gracefully at her bicycle pedals, carrying her away from me without a backward glance!

Mrs Dark, however, was at home most of the time, as

her passion was flower-gardening. She was always summoning me, or having Grubb summon me, to inspect some new blossom, upon which I had to deliver dutiful and enthusiastic judgement. One day she announced that she had planted a bed of Alpine flowers in my honour, and her twinkling eyes could not prevent her blushing faintly as she plucked a big red rose and put it in my buttonhole.

'The Alpine flowers will not blossom for a while, so in the meantime, you may have an English rose, Roger.'

I gravely informed her that the rose was not half as beautiful as its donor, and her blush turned fiery, as she acknowledged my clumsy compliment with a radiant smile.

Generally, I thought my life quite contented, and yet I secretly burned with desire to be noticed by my frosty, adored goddess, Miss Florence. How I envied her very bicycle, under the pumping of her thighs and buttocks, so sweetly swathed in her cottons, as I watched her depart every morning! As distraction, I immersed myself in study, aided by the Major's excellent library, the mark of a scholar and gentleman; or in walking rather aimlessly in the estate, each day discovering some new treasure: a folly, a grotto, a flowerbed, arbour or pond.

The land, imbued with her magical presence, became sacred to me, and every bee and flower were my fellow-worshippers at her shrine. One pleasant discovery, right at the edge of the estate, was a secluded lake, fringed with weeping willow and rushes. I made bold, on that hot day, to strip completely naked, and plunge into the fragrant waters, disturbing fish and birds and water-spiders with my splashing. The pleasure of swimming unencumbered by clothing is an exquisitely sensual one, and the caress of water on the nude body can easily come to seem the caress of a woman, so I closed my eyes as I swam and dreamt of Miss Florence – naked also, and our limbs entwined in the water! – and I must confess that, at these impure thoughts, my member rose to full rigidity, caressed by the flowing waters as though by Miss Florence's hands or thighs or breasts, and I felt a delicious unbearable tickling in my ball-sac.

It was not long before, to my surprise and delight, my

ball-sac gave up its cargo of manly fluids which had seethed within me these long weeks. It was as though I had made love to nature herself, or the water of life, and, though still virgin at that time, I felt that I had experienced something of a defloration. Thereafter I made my pilgrimage to the lake every day to pay my lustful homage to my imagined goddess, Miss Florence.

However, the more sap is drained, the more it rises. I was as passionate as ever, despite my daily aquatic relief. One day, I ventured into the shed where Miss Florence kept her bicycle, and was pleased to discover, amongst the bric-à-brac that even included a gasmask from the Great War, a set of dumb-bells, dusty from lack of use. I polished them up, and set myself to exercises, to burn off my lustful energy. Very soon, I found that my wiry frame began to expand with a respectable girth of hard muscle. In my vanity, I hoped that Miss Florence, at dinner, would make some remark! But she sat in her plainest, most modest frock, and took no notice.

Mrs Dark did, however, and found excuses to brush past my swelling biceps or even breast-muscle, with a little 'hmm' and a twinkle in her eye. I drew some solace from the fact that Miss Florence had tantalised me that once, with her breathtaking costume of our first dinner, since it persuaded me that, however dimly, she had thought me worth the teasing. It was Dido who shone at our little dinners, always in the most graceful yet daring gowns and décolletages. The Major confided over our port that he was well pleased with my presence, as it gave Mrs Dark 'a bit of zing, old chap', without elaborating on this mysterious comment, as though 'old chaps' would automatically understand. I nodded gravely.

In the fervid heat of that summer, I dreamed day and night of Miss Florence, and I saw her everywhere I went. I became obsessed with the things she had touched, or used, and of her purposes in doing so, and with what part of her sweet, sacred body. Everything at Virginia Lodge seemed imbued with her aura. And as for her clothing, it was the stuff of fantasy! Grubb had her lair in a ramshackle collection of outhouses some distance from the lodge, and I would make my way there and peek at the pennants of Miss Florence's gorgeous underthings fluttering to dry in the breeze: silks of black, white, navy or even scarlet, which tempted me to purloin them and carry them off to my own lair for my improper act of worship.

My attack on the weights grew more and more strenuous. I worked up fearful sweats, and took to exercising completely naked, imagining myself some Greek god in combat with the cold metal. After I was thoroughly lathered, I would don my sports clothing and scurry to the lake, to strip anew and perform my act of obeisance to the welcoming waters. Once or twice, in my fevered imagination, I thought I heard footfalls, or even glimpsed the flicker of a watching eye, but put it down to the heat and exhaustion. Major Dark and Miss Florence were after all about their business, and Dido's flowerbeds were far distant from the secluded lake.

One day, my schedule was running rather late. I had become engrossed in a book, and when I got to my exercises, the sun was already waning. It was nearly teatime before I was prepared to visit my lake, and I had just embarked on a final session of the punishing weight drill, when the door of the shed opened and a shaft of light fell across my sweating muscles. Panting, I had not heard the intruder approach, and dropped my weights with a fearful clang when I heard the cool fury of a Lady's voice:

'So this is what dirty little boys get up to.'

I turned round and saw that it was Miss Florence! Her breast was heaving, both from the exertion of her cycling and her rage at finding me in my immodest state, and her face was a livid red. Hastily, I reached for my shorts and shirt to cover myself, reflecting that since I had been facing the window, she would have seen no more than my bare buttocks. However, in reaching for my clothes, I was obliged to turn, so that there was no concealing from her my naked organ slapping against my thighs. I began to babble my lame excuses, as though I, not she, were the intruder, but her lip curled in angry scorn, which thrilled me more than she could have imagined.

'You worm,' she hissed. 'Touching my things . . .'

She stood with her arms akimbo, contemptuously surveying me.

'A smutty, smutty worm,' she murmured, her eyes wide and more serene as she enjoyed my abject embarrassment. 'How utterly pathetic you are. I suppose you do this all the time. Playing with yourself, I imagine, like a filthy little schoolboy.'

'No, Miss Florence,' I managed to gasp. 'I was only exercising. I didn't think anyone would come.'

'You know what happens to worms,' she said casually, and then ground her heel round and round in the sawdust.

'These weights belong to Greville,' she mused, with a faraway look. 'I should have polished them myself. Well, since you have done so, I suppose you may use them. Just make sure you bathe properly before dinner. You stink as all schoolboys do!'

With that, she parked her bicycle against the wall and, in a flounce of skirts, was gone. Panting and ecstatic – she had noticed my existence! – I looked at the bicycle that had so recently borne her precious body.

My organ rose rapidly, to aching stiffness, and I reached out timorously to touch the handlebars she had held, the pedals her dainty feet had trodden, the seat still warm from her pumping thighs! My member was so stiff I thought I should burst. Gingerly, I pressed the tip against one of the pedals, but the cold metal did nothing to dampen my ardour. Then, trembling, I pressed my lips to the bicycle seat, and began to kiss and lick the leather, still damp and fragrant from her panties and crotch. I drew the bicycle towards me then and pressed the saddle to my ball-sac, moaning in my fevered excitement.

Suddenly I was bathed in a shaft of light – the door opened wide – and Miss Florence stood once more before me! This time there could be no excuses.

'Why, you filthy, filthy brat!' she hissed.

There now seemed little point in trying to hide my

monstrous erection, which threatened to wilt in my terror. She grabbed me by the earlobe, and dragged me most painfully to the workbench, where she thrust my head down, with my bare bottom thrust in the air. I made no attempt to struggle or resist, and my organ stood stiffer than ever in my shame! There was a sheaf of bamboo poles beside the workbench, and with a swish she pulled one out, and whipped the air with it right beside my head.

'I am going to punish you, sir, for your disgusting behaviour,' she said coolly. 'I shall cane you, sir. It shall hurt dreadfully.'

'I am sorry, Miss!' I squealed.

'Not as sorry as you'll be after your caning, nor when I tell Mummy and Daddy about your disgraceful behaviour.'

'No, please!' I cried, in genuine distress. 'I shall gladly accept your punishment, Miss, but I beg you not to tell a soul! It is too shaming!'

'I am going to cane your bare bottom,' she said with relish, 'and you will be obliged to show the welts to the Major, and to Mummy, and I dare say to the serving girl, to compound your humiliation. I take it you have been caned bare before?'

'Yes, Miss, ' I moaned miserably. 'At Eppingham they were very strict.'

'Not half as strict as I shall be,' she snapped. 'And why is that horrid thing of yours still standing, like some hideous maypole? Reduce it at once, boy!'

She slapped my ball-sac with the tip of her bamboo.

'I regret . . . I cannot, Miss,' I moaned.

'Does a beating always excite you, then?' she said with scornful curiosity.

'Never before, Miss. But I have never been beaten by . . . by such a beautiful Lady before.'

'Don't think you can flatter me, worm!' she cried furiously, and swished her cane in the air again. 'On second thoughts, I shan't cane you just now. I am too angry with you, and won't let you have the satisfaction of a beating in anger. I shall wait until I can beat you impassively, with the disdain you deserve. No, in fact, I shan't cane you at all.'

'Miss?' I said, uncomprehending. 'Does that mean you accept my apology?'

I was unable to keep the disappointment from my voice. The thought of my naked buttocks squirming under my goddess's pitiless cane made the seed stir in my balls, and I thought for a moment that I should swoon and spurt just at that dreadful, ecstatic thought!

'I have no choice but to accept your apology, however worthless and insincere, and your promise to accept my punishment.'

'I do promise, Miss. Please cane me!' I cried. She grinned, a beautiful vixen.

'No, I shan't cane you. The cane is too good for you, boy. I shall birch you, on your naked bottom,' she whispered. 'A man's punishment for a smutty boy. It shall be when I decide. You must live in fear until then, and that anticipation shall be a delicious part of your punishment. And since I shall birch you in all tranquillity, I shan't be swayed by your pathetic cries for mercy, into giving you any. Have you ever been birched?'

Miserably, I admitted that I had not.

'It is much worse than the cane,' she said slowly, with gloating in her voice. 'You will beg me to stop, as Mistress Birch caresses every naked inch of your squirming, clenching bare bottom. And I shan't, not until you are reduced to pitiful squealing jelly.'

I began to wonder if my desire to submit to the cruelty of my goddess would extend to tolerance of the birch, a word which struck terror into my heart.

'To make your punishment more piquant,' she said, 'you shall fashion the birch for your own backside. I take it you have some idea what a proper flogging birch looks like?'

I nodded, with every appearance of wretchedness, but with my pulse racing in joy!

'You know where the birch grove is – there will be some fine new branches just now. So, in a few days, I'll administer your punishment. Mummy will be busy at the rhododendrons and fuchsias, and Daddy will be abroad on business, so I'll take you in the summerhouse by the lake. We shall be quite private.'

I jumped as I felt her fingers touch the bare skin of my bottom!

'Hmmm . . .' she said. 'I think you can take a good solid birch. Let us say eighteen rods, not a prissy dozen. That way I can birch you till you weep, and in the summerhouse there will be no one to hear. Bring me the birch when you have fashioned it, boy, and if it is not hard enough for my liking, you'll have to make it over, and make two birches, for your cowardice will earn you a second birching, the very next day! A proper birching, you see, quite exhausts one instrument. And if you are brave, well, I might forget to tell Mummy and Daddy about your filthiness.'

She paused in the doorway.

'You really think me beautiful?'

'O, yes, Miss, yes!'

She smiled thinly.

'Then your birching shall be that much harder . . .'

With that, she flounced her gorgeous tresses and stalked away without a backward look. In an ecstasy of passion, I rushed naked from the shed, not caring who saw me, and protected from immodesty only by my shirt clutched on my swollen member. I hurried to the lake and plunged in, and the first touch of the water – I imagined it her birch-twigs, caressing my organ! – made me spurt almost at once.

That night I could hardly sleep, and lay awake with pounding heart and rigid penis, listening to the excited chirping of the crickets, which in my fevered brain seemed more intense than usual. To be punished, at the hands of my goddess – my Mistress, as I now permitted myself to think of her! To be humiliated, birched on my bare bottom to sobbing helpless agony! I could imagine no greater terror and no greater happiness.

The next day, and the days that followed, our routine continued as imperturbably as always. Miss Florence took no notice of me at all, any more than she ever did, and I took great pride and satisfaction in the gravity of my demeanour, so much that Dido remarked on it. I explained that I was studying hard; in reality, I was in the birch grove, my trembling fingers selecting the hardest, juiciest branches for my own chastisement. But I made two birches: one, a veritable bush of twenty rods, four feet in length, I secreted in the birch grove, and presented my Mistress with another, a pitiable thing of only a dozen of the thinnest, feeblest rods.

'Please, Miss, I don't think my bottom could take any more – bare, I mean,' I whimpered.

As I had surmised, she became angry and said I had been warned, and had now earned two birchings. Then I fetched my real birch and duly presented her with the fearsome engine, my throat dry as I wondered if I had bitten off more than I could chew – but delirious with the joy that I should have my Mistress to myself for two sets of punishment! She swished the birch with a rushing, crackly sound, approved it, and told me to make a second like it.

Yet always a doubt nagged me – I knew I could take the cane, but the birch was an unknown quantity. And my Mistress was right – this dreadful anticipation did give a nuance of delight to my impending punishment, though perhaps not exactly as she intended. She could not possibly imagine that a young man craved a birching from her on his naked bottom – or could she . . .?

The day came; early in the morning, I made my way on her instructions to the little summerhouse. She was not there to greet me as I had hoped; rather, there was a note in her handwriting, in lilac ink.

'You shall attire yourself fittingly for your humiliation,' was all it said.

I looked around me. The summerhouse was sparsely furnished: a simple wooden ping-pong table, assorted chairs, and a sort of chaise-longue, on which was laid out a suit of clothing. It proved to be a schoolboy's uniform, neatly pressed and cleaned but somewhat dusty. I frowned, not sure what to make of this – it was clear she wished me to dress as a schoolboy for my chastisement. With a grimace, I stripped naked and began to put on the uniform, which fitted well enough, though it was a trifle small. There was a grey flannel shirt, a striped tie, blazer and school cap, and, to my puzzlement, a pair of short flannel trousers that came far above my knee.

There were no panties, which made rueful sense to me, since I knew she intended to administer the birch on the bare. I slipped on the shorts over my naked buttocks, where they fitted very snugly, although the bulge of my manhood was only accommodated with some discomfort. I trembled and blushed, feeling superbly humiliated: not only did she intend to birch me bare, but I was to be shamefully garbed as an 'oik', as we at Eppingham used to refer to junior boys. I worshipped my Mistress all the more for this subtle cruelty!

I heard her steps coming through the undergrowth, and then the crisp clacking of her shoes on the stairs. For an instant, my mind confused the sound with the cricket's chirping that I heard nightly. Then she appeared, icy and serene, her eyes and lips glinting in a Mistress's vengeful beauty. I leapt to my feet and stood trembling before her, head bowed and hands meekly behind my back.

'Take off your cap in the presence of a Lady!' she snapped, putting down a leather cricket bag.

I obeyed. She looked at the birch, which I had placed carefully on the table, and picked it up, stroking it with long, slender fingers tipped in green nail-polish.

'It'll do,' she said.

Somewhat to my surprise, she was not wearing her usual sensible daytime apparel, but was all in white, in a school Mistress's gymnasium or tennis kit. Her long, muscled legs shone bare and creamy, and ended in thick white cotton socks, adorably fluffy, I thought, with laced canvas rubber-soled tennis shoes. At her waist bobbed a short pleated skirt that covered her thighs scarcely halfway, and above this her narrow waist was swathed in a tight white blouse, damp with her perspiration so that, to my horrified delight, I could clearly see her bare breasts shimmering through the thin wet cotton. The imprint of her nipples jutted like gorgeous red strawberries on top of the luscious pastries of her teats, their fullness unadorned by any corselage or other support. The top two buttons of her blouse were carelessly open, revealing an expanse of ripe curved breast, and her hair swept back in a bushy, businesslike pony-tail.

'Gym kit,' she said briskly. 'Always best for a beating, as it helps me get a good run-up. Now, you know why you are here, boy, so let's get on with it. Trousers down, of course, and turn around, as I don't want to be disgusted and see anything I shouldn't. We've all morning, so we can make quite a meal of you.'

I obeyed; as I was unbuttoning my shorts, she rummaged in her bag and took out a pair of white kid gloves. But as she bent over, I could not restrain my lustful curiosity: her darling little skirt rode up over her fesses, and I saw that her own bum was bare! She wore no knickers – her peach was a vision of pure beauty. She heard my gasp of admiration and desire, and whirled round to confront me, letting her skirt drop. Her eyes were steely, but without anger, as though she had expended all passion in her first discovery of my wickedness, and the imposition of her harsh penalty. She nodded at me with dreadful wisdom.

'Peeking, eh? Only to be expected. You make a habit of looking at girls' bums, do you, worm?'

'O, no, Miss! I mean, that is –'

'Never mind. You'll take extra punishment for that little impropriety, you realise.'

'Yes, Miss,' I mumbled, hanging my head.

'Miss Cane can warm you up for Mistress Birch,' she said slyly. 'A tight three dozen, I think. Cheer up, boy, it could be worse. Although I can't think how . . . Now, knickers down, please, and bend over. I'll take you across the ping-pong table.'

I lowered my unbuttoned shorts to reveal my naked bottom, cupping my manhood rather inadequately in my palm.

'What!' she cried. 'No knickers! Why, you filthy, filthy whelp, that is the most disgusting –'

'But, Miss,' I interrupted desperately, 'there were none left for me to put on. And since I knew you intended to punish me on the bare . . .'

My voice tailed off feebly. I knew her scorn was just – a Lady's scorn is always just – and against my palm I felt the stirring of my penis beginning to rise.

'What is the most you have had from the cane?' she said. 'On the bare, I mean. On knickers it doesn't count.'

'Four dozen, I think, Miss,' I said.

'For being knickerless, you shall now take an extra three dozen,' she said coolly, 'making six dozen in all. Sets of a dozen, with a minute's pause – and that, whelp, is even before your proper correction begins.'

'As you say, Miss,' I murmured.

From her cricket bag, she withdrew a long whippy shaft of yellow wood, with a crook handle, and the tip splayed like a snake's tongue.

'I think I'll take you bare from the waist down,' she said thoughtfully. 'So, socks and shoes off too, and knot your shirt high up your back. It looks more tasteful that way. And I like to see a naughty boy dance on his bare feet as he is whipped.'

I obeyed, feeling the spiny wooden floor uncomfortable on my bare soles.

'You can bend over the table, now,' she said airily. 'That's what we normally – I mean, I think that will probably be suitable. And I'll get a good run-up – it must be thirty feet right across the room, so I can skin you properly.'

She said this quite matter-of-factly, as though I were no more than a fowl for plucking. I gulped, and my breath was hoarse as I took position, not in fear of the pain, although I did dread it, but in fear that I would blub and humiliate myself by being unable to take her punishment . . . the awful pain which is the mark, and the price, of sublime humiliation at a Lady's hands. I watched in awe as she slipped the thin leather gloves over her fingers, one by one, taunting me with her grace and power.

I bent over the table, my legs spread and my bum facing her, high up, and I clutched the sides of the table for support. The edge of the board bit into my belly-button. Despite my anguish, my penis stirred strongly, then rose in a smooth arc to its full throbbing erection. I could not disguise it from her gaze however much I shuffled.

She uttered an exclamation of disgust, and I heard her whistle softly.

'Good gr–' she began, then said, 'Ugh! Do you always get like that before a caning, boy?'

'No, Miss,' I said miserably. 'I can't help it – you know that.'

'We'll have to get rid of it, though.'

'Yes, Miss.'

'If you can't make her behave after Miss Cane visits your bottom, perhaps she should visit here too. We must have you seemly for Mistress Birch, mustn't we?'

She flicked the cane against the swollen bulb of my penis, right at the distended peehole, and I groaned a promise that 'she' should behave. She tickled my bulb for a while, looking down at it and breathing quite sharply, until she drew away.

'To business,' she panted.

She walked to the far corner of the room and positioned herself, crouched in a hunter's poise. I heard her swish the air with the cane in a few practice strokes, and gulped in fear despite my excitement and longing for her chastisement. Then her feet pounded across the floor, faster and faster; the cane whistled, and I jumped and clenched my buttocks as a streak of liquid fire suffused my naked skin. I clenched my teeth tight and felt tears spring to my eyes, and a fierce tightening of my gorge.

'O . . . O . . .' I heard my strangled sob, deep in my throat.

She laughed.

'That was nothing, boy,' she said. 'Any more blubbing, now, and you take the stroke over. Understood?'

I nodded frantically.

The stroke was repeated, right on the same welt, and then the third, and the fourth; there was pause for neither thought nor mercy, just the rhythmic clatter of her feet on the boards, followed by the agonising whistle of the cane, almost worse than the lash itself, and the stroke across my bare buttocks.

After the sixth or seventh stroke, my pain was so great that I seemed almost distant from it, and greeted the whistle of the cane, and its searing lash, with a kind of detachment, as though my squirming buttocks belonged to another being. My agony became a phenomenon, to be observed, noted, and even welcomed, and my heart beat with the pride that I, or the other, was bravely taking my Lady's punishment.

At the eighth stroke, I think, she asked me if it was tight enough, though without pausing in her beating.

'Tighter than I've ever had, Miss!' I sobbed.

'Good,' she panted, and delivered the ninth stroke almost at once.

'Gosh, Miss, I don't think a caning has ever hurt so much!' I blurted. 'Not even on the bare!'

'Wait for your next set,' she snapped, and proceeded to deliver the final three of the set without a run-up, and these rapid strokes had me hopping in my agony. She told me she would take a pause before the next dozen, and I could stand up and rub my bottom if I liked.

'You've coloured nicely,' she said. 'Six dozen will have you well crimson for Mistress Birch to complete the painting. But keep your back to me, boy, I do not wish you to disgust me any more than you do already.'

In truth, my erection, far from subsiding, was harder than ever! My whole bottom felt like a mass of red-hot coals, and, as I bent over and grasped the table edges for my second set, I imagined that it was her lips, not her cane, which had kissed me there. The second set began, and now I greeted the cane like an old friend. I was inured to the ferocious pain, and almost welcomed it, and the tears in my eyes were of gratitude that she, my goddess, had chosen to make my bum blossom. When the second dozen was complete, I knew I had taken it without a murmur, and accepted like a reward the cool touch of her gloved fingers on my naked fesses, stroking the puffy ridges and blossoms her cane had raised.

Nothing could soften my penis after that heavenly touch, and inwardly I resigned myself to endless, unthinkable punishment. At this thought, I groaned aloud.

'My, you are a funny boy,' she said. 'You don't cry out at my cane, yet you do at the touch of my glove! Still, I'm pleased with your skin, she is nice and blotchy, and Mistress Birch's calling card will be visible for quite a while, after she has paid her visit.'

I lost track of time; suffice to say that at each succeeding dozen with the cane, my bum squirmed more and more, and my joy grew at my utter humiliation. I longed for someone else – another Lady, perhaps – to witness my degradation, and the searing marks of my shame! But at last my 'extra' punishment was over.

Miss Florence produced from her bag a flask of tea, and a cup and saucer, and permitted me to serve her. Then she slopped the dregs of her tea into her saucer and placed it on the floor, indicating that I was to lap it like a kitten. Never has tea tasted so sublime as that saucerful, my glowing bum displayed in all her shame and my lips mewling in gratitude to my Mistress as she laughed at me!

It was time for Mistress Birch. Miss Florence picked up the instrument with reverence, and a gleam in her eye. She smiled with delicious cruelty as she ordered me to reassume my position, and said I should hold on very tight indeed. I was to spread my legs and bum fully, and I did so, shivering in the knowledge that my balls were now exposed; yet my penis still throbbed painfully hard at my belly. She said that she needed no run-up for the birch, whose kiss was a cosy and intimate thing, best enjoyed at close quarters. Nevertheless she lifted her flogging arm as high above her head as she could, before lashing my bare fesses with the swishing cracking birch rods.

What can I say to those whose bottoms have never tasted the implacable kiss of the birch? It is a thousand times worse than a mere caning. The cane delivers a sharp single stripe; the birch's girth covers the entire croup with her embrace, and that first stroke seemed to sear the whole expanse of my bare bottom like a thousand white-hot needles. The birch is indeed a caress, or a long, lingering kiss; the rods seem unwilling to draw away, but cling to the flogged flesh before they are dragged off for the next stroke. The pain is so intense, and so generously bestowed, that the buttocks feel they have been cupped in two giant palms of molten pain.

Now, my whole body jerked and shuddered at each stroke of that birch, and my knuckles were white as I grasped the sides of the table. I could not help but cry out in maddened torment at each lash, nor did my Mistress expect otherwise. I cried the more, because at each scream my lungs filled with the heavenly perfume of her exudations. I think – I hoped – that my cries of agony pleased her, for I heard her chuckle and click her tongue in satisfaction. I counted to twenty, then twenty-one, twenty-two, and then my smarting agony was so intense that I could count no longer, and my mind seemed to float from my body into a world of pure, glowing pain. I felt deliciously, ultimately, at one with my Mistress, the two of us all alone in my universe of pure agony.

I heard my shrieks – 'O! O! O, Mistress! Ahhh!' – as though from far away, and they were shrieks of adoration for her and her sublime cruelty. I knew that I squirmed for her and for her alone! She wanted to hurt me. She was mine, and I possessed her, and my penis and balls began to tingle at the joy of my submission. The birch strokes cascaded, on and on to forty or even fifty, and my balls ached with the glory of my wretchedness. Suddenly I could not restrain myself: my stiff penis jerked in spasm, and my cream flowed in a hot spurt from my peehole. My cries softened to whimpers, and my shudders stopped; so did the birching. Miss Florence said I had been birched sufficiently and might get up now. She panted so hard, and her face was so flushed, that I think she did not notice the evidence of my shame.

I did not get up, but flung myself at her feet, and began to kiss her shoes and fluffy sweating socks, licking and kissing her with my tears of gratitude. She took this in silence, and I peeped up, hoping, I confess, to gain a vision of the paradise that was her naked fount. But she had her skirt pressed tight and her thighs together. I saw little glistening rivulets of fluid adorning her soft inner thighs, as though she had peed, yet I knew that my Lady could not have done such a thing. The fluid was there, nevertheless, augmented as my worship of her feet continued. At length she gasped that I should rise.

'I knew Mistress Birch would get you modest,' she said, glancing with distaste at my now flaccid penis. 'You didn't take it badly, I suppose.'

'I was thinking all the time of the crickets chirping outside my bedroom window, Miss,' I stammered. 'Your footsteps, and the whacks of the beating – like crickets' noises, and that distraction helped me bear the chastisement.'

She laughed. 'We shall see how you fare under Mistress Birch's second visit. In the meantime, I shan't tell Mummy and Daddy –'

I blurted my thanks.

'– and neither shall you – Roger. It shall be our little secret. You really are a pathetic little worm, Roger, and little worms do get up to all sorts of mischief, but it is pleasing to watch them wriggle.'

'Yes, Miss,' I said humbly, and glowing with pride. She called me Roger!

'So, in your own best interests, I think that Mistress Birch will pay your bottom frequent and longer visits, and perhaps bring some of her interesting friends, too. And by the way, Roger, you are a silly worm as well as an insolent and pathetic one. There are no crickets at Virginia Lodge . . .'

2

Nude Flowering

If I was enchanted by Miss Florence before, my cruel punishment locked me in adoration of her. Her callous indifference to my person only heightened my ardour; at dinner, she was cold and reserved, her fiery green Mistress's nails now painted a modest pink. And she reverted to sneering at me as 'Ruggiero'. With what joy did I inspect my ruined bottom in the mirror! I hoped anxiously that my puffy, mottled flesh should not lighten before her anger was refreshed for my second ordained birching – and the many more I hoped for. There was a shy glint in my eye, and a smugness on my lips, on which Mrs Dark remarked; I said nothing. My weals were the secret gift of my possession by Miss Florence: a flogged bottom, as all worshippers of strong Ladies know, is an inviolate treasure . . .

My satisfaction at being possessed by my Mistress was much deeper than any lustful curiosity to make love to her, the very idea of invading her person seeming sacrilege. I found myself sad that her Greville was departed, and imagined him miraculously returning, with myself, shackled as her naked slave, serving the pair as they made lustful, happy sport before my eyes, their utter disdain for my presence being my ultimate happiness. In the meantime I resolved to let my bottom bear the marks of my Mistress's vengeance on the (male) world, for taking her loved one from her.

Two days after my birching, with my bottom still raw,

my Mistress intimated that it was time for Mistress Birch to call again. Once again I went to the summerhouse early in the morning; this time, my school uniform was dispensed with, and I was made to strip naked for my beating, and now from her cricket bag Miss Florence withdrew a length of heavy chain and shackles. Her nails once more were painted bright green; as she bound me, I wondered if her sweet, adorable toenails were the same.

She wrapped all my limbs until I could not move; looped the chain tightly round my balls and through my mouth, gagging me. She said I was to take seven dozen of the birch on the bare, and I could not have protested even had I wished to. The beating was far more painful, in that the welts of my first were still raw, but still my penis stood, and when she delivered the last vengeful stroke, I spurted my seed once more.

This time I knew she saw it but she made no comment, other than an anguished panting. I turned around and she told me to face the floor, but not before I had seen through my tears her fingers under her skirt, revealing her naked fount and her glistening streams of juices that trickled from her thighs where her hand rubbed her Lady's place. I waited, smarting and alone in my agony, until I heard her gasp very loudly ten or twelve times, and then, slowly, she unbound me, advising me to silence as to our activities, and promising that if I 'blabbed' Mistress Birch would next visit with unlimited severity.

'O, Mistress,' I sobbed – thrilled that she accepted my appellation of 'Mistress' – 'you know I shall blab, for I am such a weak worm, so I shall prepare for many stern visits from Mistress Birch.'

'Yes, Roger,' she gasped, her hand feverishly mopping her wet thighs with her skirt hem, 'I think you should.'

The world seemed transformed, as it is when one is 'in love'. Every leaf or flower or breath of air seemed full of my Mistress's radiance and the harsh beauty of her birch. It is most satisfying to possess a secret, whether guilty or joyful, and I suppose I walked with a spring in my step. At any rate, an event took place shortly after my second birching which would otherwise have seemed quite awesome, but which seemed now to be part of the natural, joyful order of things.

One morning, I was paying my customary visit to the lake, my ardour for the water's caress having in no way diminished since my bottom's entering Miss Florence's domain. I spent a blissfully long time swimming and splashing amongst the ducks and fish, then floating on my back with my floppy member across my belly and trailing in the water. The ducks paddled around it, imagining my bulb to be some exotic source of food.

Suddenly I was startled by a Lady's voice.

'So this is where you have been lurking!'

It was Mrs Dark, clad in a simple blue smock, and with bare feet and legs. She clutched a basket of rooted flowers, and had detached some petals to place prettily in her raven tresses.

I hurriedly sank down into the water to conceal my intimate parts, then stood on tiptoe, on the sandy bottom, with the water up to my nipples, and burbled a greeting. She smiled.

'Don't mind me,' she called. 'I am just collecting flowers, to see if any will transplant. I am glad you are making use of our estate.'

'I am afraid you caught me slightly unawares, Mrs Dark,' I stammered.

'Caught!' she cried. 'What a strange word! I have been watching you, Roger, and a very pretty sight it is. Do you think you are caught?'

'Well,' I said, red-faced, 'you have me at somewhat of a disadvantage. I mean my clothing is over there by your side.'

'So it is,' she said as though surprised.

'You wouldn't tease me, Mrs Dark?' I pleaded.

'You think I would tease you? And how, exactly? I insist you tell me.'

Such is the delicious wile of Ladies, inviting us to fashion the rods for our own willing croups!

'You could hide my clothes and make me a laughing-stock.'

'But why?'

'To make me do something I didn't want to,' I replied lamely, and her laughter trilled like sweet music.

'But I would never do such a thing, Roger,' she said. 'I should far rather make you do something you did want to.'

Her firm, pert breasts quivered as her body shook in her merriment under her thin smock. Without warning, she scooped up my clothes and scampered like a faun into the bushes, leaving me speechless and shocked. When she returned, she was flushed with amusement and pouted mockingly at me. She ordered me to resume my floating position, on my back, and said that I was silly, for she was a nurse, unaccustomed to false modesty, and well familiar with the human body.

I closed my eyes and obeyed, feeling uncomfortable as my member was once more exposed to her gaze, this time knowingly, so that my penis trembled and began to stiffen, rising from the water and quivering over my belly. I heard her stifle a gasp of astonishment.

I opened my eyes and saw her gazing at my awakening penis, which stiffened until halfway rigid. This is a position which seems to awaken lustful and mischievous curiosity in Ladies – they are menaced yet tickled at the same time – and Dido was no exception. She swallowed, composed herself and brushed her hair back, then put down her flower basket.

'It is such a hot day, Roger. Aren't you going to invite me to join you – or are you going to hog the water like a selfish male?'

I stuttered the commanded invitation. She at once lifted her smock over her head and gaily took it off. She was nude, and I stared at the perfection of her slender body, my penis stiffening all the while. The breasts were pert and hard, like pears, the belly flat, and the thighs rippled with sinuous muscle. Her mound swelled ripe and full as a little cantaloupe, with the big pink lips of her gash glistening in the sunlight. Her mound was shaven smooth as porcelain! My knowledge of female parts came from surreptitious study of medical photographs, and from sculptures and paintings of antiquity. The photographs always showed the Ladies to be endowed with bushy shocks of hair at their founts, and I had assumed the naked fount was confined to the realm of art; so it came as a surprise to see a 'real' Lady with shaven mink. I had not glimpsed Miss Florence's fount, only the back of her hand as she rubbed it.

Dido tripped towards the water on dainty feet, and lowered herself gracefully in, then began swimming in the opposite direction from me. I watched the gentle play of her back muscles, the scissoring of her thighs and the hard peach of her buttocks dancing in the water, and my penis now became fully erect. I reimmersed myself to shoulder height, and her eyes followed the prismatic image of my member, refracted by the crystal water. She burst out laughing, her voice so musical as to melt any timidity.

'It looks as if you have two cocks, Roger!' she cried, taking me aback with her forthright language. 'Or are they giant fishes nibbling your balls? Don't be bashful, sir – nudity is the friendliest thing. And what indecorousness can happen with all these ducks watching?'

I accused her of teasing me, and she emitted a peal of laughter, then cried that I should race her, and struck off at a fast swim towards the far end of the lake, her body darting in the water like a shiny fish. I lumbered in pursuit; my swimming, while adequate, was not as expert as Dido's, and she reached the far bank well before me. She stopped and turned to look, the water lapping at her breasts and the big brown nipples standing up hard like pebbles.

Laughing at my clumsy progress, she lifted her arms to beckon me in mockery. Yet habit dies hard, and my erect penis, accustomed to the caress of the water, now had a vision of naked female loveliness to hasten my fulfilment. It was not long before I felt the honeyed tickling in my balls. I spasmed and a jet of seed spurted from me, clearly visible as it trailed in the water.

'O!' I cried. 'O . . .' and then gasped as my lips collided with her naked breasts.

'I see only a little fish now,' she said, staring down at my softened member, and took me by the ears. 'Haven't you ever seen a Lady with nothing on, Roger?'

I blushed fierily, and stammered that I had not. She laughed, and kissed my lips.

'Don't be embarrassed!' she murmured. 'Your shyness is so pretty. So I suppose that means you have never been with a Lady either?'

'No, Mrs Dark.'

'Roger, we are naked together, and you must call me Dido. So, Roger, you are a blushing virgin . . .'

I mumbled something about marriage, and she said, 'Yes, marriage', as though she had said 'yes, parlour-maids'. Then she said that she was naked and alone with me, and admitted that she had teased me, and I must now do the thing which I really wanted to do. I was aghast and foolishly asked her what she meant.

'Why, picking flowers for me, of course!' she cried, and nimbly darted from my embrace to swim back to our shore.

When I emerged at last, she was sitting cross-legged and nonchalant on the bank, so that I could see the spread lips and pink flesh of her open gash. She affected not to notice that my cock almost at once stiffened to throbbing hardness, except when I made a foolish attempt to cover my immodesty with my inadequate palms, which made her tinkle with laughter, that I was so bashful. I asked her for my clothes, and she made the coquette, putting her hand on her chin and pouting that she had quite forgotten where they were.

'Pick those flowers over there,' she ordered, 'and perhaps I shall remember. You don't mind, Roger?'

I did not mind; I was in the power of this sweet flirtatious minx, even though she was another man's wife, and her power was different from the dominant power of my Mistress. This power was expressed in the open flaps of her naked gash, which seemed to stare at my erect cock like a glistening shiny eye. I said that a gentleman must serve a Lady, and retreated from her with my cock facing her, so that she should not see my flogged bottom. She noticed at once, of course, and commanded me to turn round and squat on all fours to pick the flowers, with my bottom to her, for the modesty that I seemed so concerned with.

Her lightness and gaiety suddenly made secrets seem unimportant. I knelt as ordered, and showed her my wealed bottom. At once, I was rewarded with a loud, and I think genuine, gasp of astonishment; she told me to forget the flowers and come to Nurse.

I was to show her my horrid wounds; she put me across her knee, as though for a spanking, and my belly pressed to the firm smooth skin of her bare thighs, with my erect penis wedged against her hip. She began to stroke my bum with cool and dainty fingers.

'Such horrid welts!' she cried. 'How . . . who did this to you?'

'O,' I said, thinking of a desperate lie, 'it was my last week at school, Mrs – I mean , Dido – and I was caught, ah, breaking bounds, you know, and smoking too, and cheeking the chaplain, and having a naughty French magazine, and for all those crimes at once, I got what they called a royal beating, that is, thirty strokes of the cane.'

In fact, a 'royal beating' at Eppingham was only twenty-four strokes, but I did not wish to boast that I had taken a double royal beating, for picking flowers.

'Two and a half dozen! Were you flogged on the bare bottom, Roger?' she whispered breathlessly. 'It looks like it.'

I said I was.

'Such a cruel school. I'm not sure if I can believe it . . .'

Her fingers lingered in my furrow and began to stroke me tenderly, but quite playfully. The fingertips brushed the pucker of my bumhole, which sent a strange and delicious tickling through my spine. She noticed my little wriggle, and also that I did not protest, but even spread my bum so that my bumhole widened a notch, and her fingers continued to play there, delving deeper until I was wriggling quite hard and her fingertips were actually inside my cavern itself.

'You were caned on the bare at school, Roger?'

I said this was so.

'Always on the bare?'

'Mostly,' I replied, with a little moan of pleasure as her fingers tickled inside my anus.

'Were you ever beaten completely bare, Roger? I mean, nude, for shame?'

Her voice trembled, and I answered yes, guessing that this was the answer which would please her. She gave a little purr of curiosity, and her tickling of my anus intensified.

'How awfully cruel,' she murmured. 'I have heard that at some schools there are mass floggings – a row of boys, all naked and whipped on their bare bottoms. That must be horrid.'

'Yes . . . yes,' I moaned.

'And how many strokes, for such a beating?'

'Up to twenty-four, and never less than eighteen.'

I felt a wriggling of her hand beneath me, and noticed that she had begun to rub herself, as though absentmindedly, on her shaven fount. Her stroking of my bottom grew lustful – there is no other word – and now she had the full length of her index finger poking inside my bumhole as she rubbed her own sex, without pretence of absent-mindedness. Suddenly she snorted, then laughed.

'You are naughty, Roger. You are making it up – those are birch marks, not cane marks.'

I blurted that if I made it up, it was to please her.

'No, it wasn't,' she said firmly. 'It was to protect another – the guilty party who laid this cruel blossom on your poor innocent bum.'

She held up a finger, with a fleck of green nail polish.

'I found this lodged in one of your cruel welts,' she said mockingly.

Before I could respond, she began to rub my nates with flower-petals, and roots, and some of the soil that clung to them. She said that a good nurse knew the healing properties of nature, and I admitted that the balm was indeed soothing. Then she turned me gently over, so that my stiff cock was pointing to the sky, and the bulb almost touching the hard cups of her nipples, and began to garland my penis with flowers!

She took the hairs of my own mink and wound them round her fingers, then braided flower petals into them, so that my bush looked like a girl's hair. Then she garlanded my head with flowers, and finally snipped a long pink tulip and pushed the stem right into my peehole! To do this, she pulled back my prepuce to its fullest extent, revealing my whole naked bulb, and making me start in sudden discomfort.

'What a pretty birthmark!' she cried, staring at my crescent moon. 'It must be good luck!'

And her lips brushed the skin of my bulb, right on my birthmark. She laughed and said I looked like a pretty flower garden, and she must pick herself some flowers from my garden.

'Some Ladies, Roger, can never have enough flowers,' she whispered.

With a lithe swivelling of her body, she straddled me, and pressed the tip of my throbbing cock lightly against the engorged lips of her gash, seeping with shiny fluid.

'And I must have this one for my collection,' she said.

She arched her back and I marvelled at the suppleness of her body as she curled forward and plucked the tulip from my peehole, then put the stem in her own mouth, all the while holding her trembling quim-lips against my cock. She righted herself and almost at once I groaned as I felt my shaft slide deep into her hot wet slit. I felt the muscles of her quim fasten powerfully on my cock and begin to suck and pump me, even as she did not move her hips, but with a sensuous writhing of her belly. Gradually, her haunches moved, and she began to rock up and down on my belly, her quim still sucking on my shaft as it moved in and out of her gash, my peehole thrusting right to the tip of her womb at each deep thrust.

'I am a busy bee, Roger,' she gasped fiercely, 'and I want all the honey from those balls. I saw you spurt in the water – it was so lovely and I know you have more for me, young man. Thrust into me, Roger, fuck me with that lovely big cock until I can't take any more pleasure. Split my gash, Roger, fuck me, Roger, O, fuck me so hard . . .'

I was astounded to hear such language from a Lady's lips, yet found it immeasurably exciting, and began to thrust my buttocks in time with her own, grasping her squirming arse-globes as they writhed and danced on my belly slippery with her gushing love juices. I found the weight of her body on mine very exciting, too, and felt that I was submitting to this Lady just as much as I had submitted to my Mistress, Miss Florence. Dido was obviously accustomed to being in full control of any male that pleasured her, and I relished my role as the tool of her satisfaction, my cock simply an engine of delight, as though my mind and person were concentrated in my giant organ throbbing and bucking inside her slippery tight gash.

Her breasts bobbed like sweet little cakes; I put up my hands and grasped the stiff nipples, which seemed almost to dwarf the breasts themselves, and squeezed the lovely little bullets, kneading and pinching them, to make her whinny in pleasure. Her hand delved between the spread gash lips, feeling my sliding cock, and grasping the engorged little bud that I saw nestling between her quim lips. Gasping in a paroxysm of joy, she began to rub her bud very vigorously, almost pummelling it with hard slaps of her excitement.

With hooded eyes, she looked down on me, and asked if her masturbating excited me. I gasped truthfully that it did. It was strangely exciting that such was the stimulus of my own manhood, she was driven to seek still more pleasure in touching herself.

'That is my clitty, Roger,' she gasped, 'the home of every joy and pleasure to a Lady. We masturbate quite as much as you boys, you know – more, for we can do it again and again without ever becoming sated.'

Dido was right; we bucked until she had climaxed three times, before her nurse's expertise would finally permit my aching balls and numb cock to deliver their bounty of sperm into her wet, throbbing womb.

Her milking of my cock was expert. Whenever she

sensed from my shivering that I was close to spasm, she would rest from bucking, and place her fingers around the base of my shaft, cupping the balls too and squeezing them very tight, so that my ardour, but not my stiffness, diminished somewhat. Then her sweet writhing would begin over again, and I watched her frig her stiff clitty more and more vigorously until she began to groan, then cry out, and finally she howled and her belly fluttered as she sobbed 'O! O! O!' and came to orgasm. Her love juice on my balls and thighs was a hot, oily torrent, and I dipped my fingers in her shivering swollen cooze, and put some of her fluid in my mouth, licking it all up, to her cries of excitement and pleasure.

When she finally did permit me to deliver my spurt, I cried out helplessly, as though my whole body were a lake of honey. Then we nestled, and she told me that she was a very special nurse. I laughed, and said she had given herself my compliment.

'No, I mean it seriously,' she said, propping her elbow on my flaccid shaft. 'I have a special appetite, you see.'

She flicked the tender bulb of my cock.

'For this cock, Roger, for all cocks. Some Ladies are made so – don't be shocked. When I was an army nurse, in the field hospital in Mesopotamia, I was good at dressing wounds, bandages and splints and so on. But I learnt that men can be wounded in other ways – in their pride. When his flower does not blossom, a man is not a man, and to make war, he must be able to make love. I learnt that a woman has such simple and beautiful power, to make those flowers blossom and take her own pleasure while doing it . . . the pleasure of her own power, Roger. So I watered those flowers with the juices of my own cooze, and nurtured them back to strength. That is where I met Major Dark. Twelve cocks in one ward, to be nursed into strength and life and beauty, all at once, one after the other – and his was the twelfth! A complete success. So you see, Roger, there is no limit to the love and tolerance of a man to whose virility I hold the key.'

She began to tickle my balls, as though idly, and I chuckled, my cock trembling and swelling a little.

'I have your cock in my power, haven't I?' she murmured.

'Yes, Dido – and gladly so,' I answered with complete truthfulness.

'But I wonder who has your bottom in her power,' she mused. 'At least, I don't wonder. It was Florence, wasn't it? The truth, now.'

I protested that I was sworn to secrecy.

'I might have known,' she said. 'I guess the truth, Roger, and assure you that my stepdaughter shall pay for her impetuousness.'

She took the tulip which had adorned my peehole, and pushed it right inside her sopping gash. She writhed with her belly, then invited me to retrieve it. I did so, marvelling at the soft wet velvet of her Lady's place that had so recently caressed my cock, and when I retrieved the flower, soaked in her juices, she took it from me and put it in my mouth, and told me to swallow it as a promise that our little tryst would remain a secret. I swallowed it. There were so many secrets at Virginia Lodge, and now I was one!

She rose suddenly, and grabbed my hand, leading me to the water, where we bathed again. Now she said that there might be further trysts, as I was in her power and had swallowed her juices; but I might not initiate these trysts, nor ever make reference to them, and must await the pleasure of her summons. I happily agreed to this.

'The minx shall pay for her insolence,' she murmured, half to herself. 'But I have another little secret to share with you, Roger. I saw you in the birch grove, fashioning your birch, and when you weren't looking I added a rod of my own.'

3

A Mistress Disciplined

That night, I lay restless, naked in bed and stiff of cock, my mind swirling with joyful thoughts of my bare body the prey of stern Ladies. I was now part of an intrigue of Ladies' secrets! The sounds of the crickets were much louder and angrier than before. Unable to sleep, I decided to make a foray and see these strange creatures for myself.

I dressed and crept barefoot into the garden, where the rhythmic slapping noise was quite loud and seemed nearby. I delved into the bushes and proceeded towards the corner of the house, but the noise seemed now to recede, as though the bushes muffled rather than revealed its source. I stepped out of the shrubbery and there, on the corner, was Miss Florence's room, the light on but the linen blind closed; inside I saw two silhouetted female figures. I knew that was the source of the sound, and that it was no cricket.

One of the figures was standing, holding an implement of some kind. The other was visible only in posterior, and seemed to be bending over, to present her fesses to the first. The outline of clothing was visible on both figures, but the submissive one presented the smooth outline of thighs and bottom that must be bare; one portion of clothing was ruched up on her back, the other lowered to her knees.

The standing figure presented herself briefly in profile, and I recognised Dido's dainty chin and pert breasts. She lifted her implement, a rod of some kind, and brought it down swiftly a dozen or more times on the outstretched fesses of her companion, making just that thin slapping crack which in the distance I had imagined to be a cricket's chirp. The humiliant female made a tight, groaning sound, 'Mmm! Mmmph! Mm!' as though her lips were restrained by a gag.

'Sssh!' hissed Dido.

'Mmm . . . mm mm!' moaned her victim, and I could not stay my recognition that the voice was Miss Florence's.

There was a pause, and another dozen strokes were delivered to Miss Florence's bared buttocks, which, even at a distance, I could observe twitching in her discomfort. She moaned again, and Dido urged her to silence.

'You know you want it, bitch,' she hissed.

Another set of the rod followed, then a pause, and by now Miss Florence's moans had faded to a low, anguished sobbing – but the whopping continued unabated, with Dido the picture of calm. I peered more closely – the implement of chastisement seemed none other than a bamboo pole, like the one Miss Florence had first proposed for my own chastisement. I thought, ungraciously, that my Mistress was getting away quite lightly. I could not imagine what drove my proud Mistress to 'want it', as I, a humiliant male, wanted it. Yet the thought and vision of her naked buttocks bare for a whipping made my cock stiffen and my balls tingle.

At length, Dido lowered the pole out of sight, and her arm began to thrust vigorously, at which Miss Florence's moans grew to yelps. The spectacle ended for me when Dido sank to the floor, her head at Miss Florence's belly and crotch; after a few moments, during which my Mistress sobbed loud and her buttocks quivered like jellies, Dido's arms rose and her fingers fastened on the nipples, then drew the sobbing Miss Florence down towards her. There were muffled groans and quick, yelping cries, but the two Ladies did not reappear, and I thought it seemly to depart, with my curiosity satisfied, and pleased in my possession of yet another secret.

The knowledge that my Mistress herself had bared her goddess's globes for chastisement, whether just or wilful, did not diminish her in my eyes. On the contrary, I knew that the next time her wrath obliged me to bare my own bottom to her birch, I should take her strokes in tender sympathy, and the knowledge that my squirming was the means of avenging her own. However, my deflowering by Dido led me to see things in a new light, as one does: a Lady – specifically my Mistress – was still a mysterious and magical creature wrapped in furs and silks, except that I now knew what delights lay under her adornments. Ladies sometimes complain that gentlemen 'undress them' with their eyes – given their beauty, it seems to me ungallant not to.

I had half-witnessed a scene of submission, and resolved to complete the satisfaction of my curiosity by the time-honoured if inglorious means of the keyhole. I knew I should be punished if caught, and thus reasoned to myself that I was playing fair. Besides, the prying eyes of my two Ladies had discovered me in an immodest state, and I thought myself entitled to pry into their secrets in return.

Accordingly, the next night I crept to the door of Miss Florence's room, concealing myself beside a suit of armour which the Major had brought back as a trophy from the Middle East. The corridor was lit by the eerie gleam of the moon; I heard rustling and pacing noises from Miss Florence's room, and at last there was a noise from the staircase. Dido approached, wearing a crisp and dainty nurse's uniform, starched blue skirt and white blouse, with lovely black stockings that gleamed in the moonlight, a coquettish white bonnet, and sharp high-heeled shoes. She carried two bulging cricket bags.

She knocked softly on Miss Florence's door, and entered without bidding. I heard them whisper, the door was locked, and in no time I had my eye at the keyhole, of generous antique dimension. My member at once trembled and began to stiffen. Miss Florence was almost naked.

She wore a corset of pale pink satin, with a frilly lace top that did not cover her breasts, but left them bare, and thrust them up like melons, with the buds of her wide cherry nipples deliciously stiff and tense amid their pimpled areolae. Her long colt's legs were sheathed in gleaming silk stockings, pulled up very tight almost to her fount, and of pure alabaster white. They were secured by pink garter straps to a pink suspender belt of frilly lace, which left a sweet downy strip of belly skin bare under her corset, with the big cleft of her navel visible, like a lovely second gash.

She wore pink shoes, too, with sharp points and heels of a height I had never imagined before, and which made her thighs and calves ripple and shiver deliciously as she balanced. Her fingernails were varnished green . . . and her fount was naked to my gaze. Not shaven bare like Dido's, but a lush hillock of golden curls, so ripe and thick that I longed to be a mouse scampering amidst her tresses. Beneath that, her fount-lips glistened pink and swollen and wet . . .

On her bed was strewn an array of clothing far removed from her sensible daytime attire. There were skimpy corselets and nighties and petticoats in livid hues, and a rainbow of stockings and panties, all in shiny satin or silk. And there was the most delicious pair of pink silken panties I had ever seen, which she must have just decided to remove, to surprise her visitor with the submission of naked fount – for the crotch was damp and stained. She had evidently spent time in selecting her garments, for she whispered:

'Do I please you, Dido?'

Dido answered that if Miss Florence pleased herself, that was well enough.

'But you make yourself a frilly little Lady for me, Flossie, even when you know I shan't join your devotion to Sapphism, and only act as a nurse, to please you, and, I hope, to correct these juvenile tendencies of yours, by sating them.'

'Juvenile! If only I could lead you to despise the male as I do,' murmured Miss Florence.

She lowered her head and bit her lip, and I saw her eyes moisten.

'Well,' said Dido briskly, 'you may remain corsed,

Flossie, as I see it is tight enough to be suitably painful, but you shall remove your shoes and stockings, and suspender belt. I am going to practise my splints and bandages on you tonight, before I play cricket with your naughty, naughty bare bottom.'

At these words, Miss Florence's face brightened, and she hastened to obey. She fumbled with her garter straps, and unhooked the suspender belt, then rolled the silken stockings off each smooth bare leg till they were little piles at her ankles, and in a delicious fluid motion kicked off shoes and stockings at once; I wished her dainty bare feet should kick me thus as I lay bound before her, and make me catch both shoes and stockings in my mouth! I now saw that her toenails were painted the same green as her fingers.

The revelation of her Sapphism came as a surprise, but made her infinitely more desirable in my eyes, because she was now truly unattainable! And her beating of me, a male, seemed infinitely precious because her contempt was sincere. She really did despise me! I could not fathom the absent Greville's role in this, except to wonder if he was a polite fiction, to disguise her true Sapphic nature. At any rate, my Mistress now revealed herself to me as perfection itself, an object of unconquerable adoration.

That lush mink was denied for ever to my lustful scamperings; that velvet wet gash would never caress my rampant cock, should I even contemplate such impudence. And when I next bared myself for her chastisement, and she called me filth, and worm, and suchlike, I should have the giddy, morbid satisfaction of knowing she really meant it, and that any flicker of affection on her part could not remotely be interest in my person. It was my squirming and my pain which interested her, and nothing else – and at this electric thought, I felt as though my balls would spurt there and then.

I watched Dido unpack her bags. She withdrew rolls of gauze and bandages, and several thin wooden splints; a large syringe attached to an enormous translucent rubber bulb, like a pear, and finally her bamboo pole. She ordered Miss Florence to clear her bed, and as my Mistress dawdled, folding her things neatly, she hissed and called her bitch, and Miss Florence petulantly brushed all her clothes in a heap on to the floor by the window.

Then she had to lie down on her back, with her arms and legs stretched out, so that I had a vision of her beautiful cooze-petals, spread to show the glistening pink flesh within, as though for my eyes. Dido proceeded to place a splint along her left leg, and bind it tightly in thick bandage, all the way up to the moist swollen quim lips. It was evident that her treatment by a nurse excited my Mistress. Dido bound her foot as well, and then repeated the procedure with the right foot and leg, licking her lips as she worked.

She splinted and bound the arms, and the shoulders down to the teats, with the corset a vivid pink slash between the two white mounds of bandage. Miss Florence was unable to move her arms at all, and her legs only stiffly, like a broken marionette.

Dido grinned in satisfaction at her work, then picked her up like a doll, and flopped her over on her belly. Her trussed limbs twitched helplessly. Dido pulled the feet away from the bed, so that her legs hung over the floor, quivering about a foot from the carpet. Then she fetched a long leather thong, and bound both ankles, pulling them down and lashing them to the feet of the bed, and ignoring Miss Florence's squeals of pain, muffled by the pillow into which her face was pressed. Her thighs were splayed wide, with her furrow and cooze open to my view; I looked in awe at the thickness of her mink, the lush curly hairs ascending from anus to cooze in an unbroken forest.

Dido took her syringe and filled the rubber bulb with hot water from the tap at the pretty porcelain sink. Then she added a phial of purple liquid to the water in the bulb, and set the device aside, on the Jacobean oak sideboard, for the purple to suffuse.

Without warning, she plunged her hand deep into Miss Florence's crevice, from behind, and the trussed body jerked as Dido began a vigorous rubbing of her quim lips. She put two, then three fingers inside Miss Florence's gash, and twisted her hand so that her thumb frotted the clitty. Miss Florence squealed in shame and discomfort, but her buttocks tightened and pressed on Dido's probing hand, as though to make her frot harder.

'You do like a Lady's firm touch, don't you, you little pervert?' said Dido gaily – ignoring the fact that my Mistress was superbly taller than her, and indeed myself.

'Yes . . . O, yes, Dido,' moaned Miss Florence.

'But we can't let perverts go unpunished,' added Dido thoughtfully.

'Please, no,' murmured my Mistress, squirming on her bed.

Abruptly, Dido ceased her frottage, to a moan of dismay from Miss Florence, and applied her wet fingers to the nozzle of the syringe until it shone moist with Miss Florence's juices.

'Pity that young man of yours didn't attend to you properly, in cooze!' said Dido roughly.

'He is no bugger,' cried Miss Florence, 'even if he does like –'

Her words were cut short as Dido parted her fesses and thrust the glistening tube brutally into her anus, to her very root, and causing Miss Florence to wriggle and shriek in anguish. Her splints cracked and clattered at the writhing of her body. Then Dido lifted the filled bulb and squeezed: there were bubbles, and a rushing sound, as the fluid was injected into Miss Florence's anus shaft.

She lay coughing and groaning, with little hiccupping sobs, until Dido said she could evacuate. Miss Florence strained, there was a hissing noise as her belly and buttocks writhed, and the bulb was filled again in thick purple spurts from her bumhole. Dido repeated this operation four or five times until, finally, she ordered Miss Florence not to evacuate, but to hold the cleanser inside her shaft, while she fetched a washbasin. When this was positioned between Miss Florence's bandaged feet, she removed the tube from the anus and told Miss Florence to close her legs; then she lifted her bamboo pole and began to flog Miss Florence's naked fesses very hard, warning her all the while that she must hold it in.

Miss Florence moaned pitifully; her buttocks clenched hard, both at the pain of her vivid weals which soon criss-crossed her naked flesh, and the effort of holding her cruel hygienic cargo within her. Dido positioned herself slightly to one side of her victim, or patient, and put her hand squarely under the writhing cooze-lips, finding the clitty and frotting it as vigorously as she flogged the buttocks.

'O! O! I can't bear it!' sobbed Miss Florence, after she had taken five or six dozen lashes. 'Please let me gush!'

Dido refused, and delivered a further fifty or so strokes, until the bare bottom was gleaming as livid and purple as the liquid she held inside. It was only then that Dido delivered two or three swingeing final strokes, and her fingers became a blur on my Mistress's clitty, and she finally gave permission; then Miss Florence arched her back and howled loudly in her spasm of climax, as the purple fluid gushed from her bumhole into the basin at her feet, mingling with the river of gleaming quim oil that sparkled on her bandaged thighs.

Dido removed her fist from Miss Florence's gash, and sank to her knees, careful not to crumple her skirt. She pressed her lips against the distended nubbin of the clitty, which I could glimpse standing swollen and wet amid the mink-curls. She kissed the clitty, then licked it with a flickering tongue, all the while with a disdainful little smile on her lips; then she took the nubbin between her teeth and bit very gently, making Miss Florence jerk and writhe.

Dido began to suck and chew on the raw swollen pleasure bud as though it were a lollipop! Miss Florence's loins wriggled and heaved in her maddened joy; suddenly, cruelly, Dido stopped her caress and began to spank Miss Florence's livid purple buttocks with her palms, very hard, so that my Mistress buried her face in her pillow, sobbing at her new frustration and pain. The slaps on her bare squirming fesses rang through the corridor, and I thought myself not unjustified in having imagined them crickets' chirping . . .

Dido's hand slipped beneath her own skirt.

The spanking ceased after over a hundred firm slaps to Miss Florence's wealed bare fesses, and her hand balled into a fist, which invaded the wet gash, pumping in and out of the writhing slit as Dido's other hand moved more and more vigorously beneath her skirt. Her face was set in a grim, determined frown as, despite her professed disdain for Sapphism, she masturbated both her own gash and her patient's. Love juices gushed from Miss Florence's squirming quim, and I saw Dido's stockings dampen with moisture from her own, as she panted now in the pleasure of her masturbation.

Her skirt rose, and I saw her own fist thrusting into her knickerless quim, now glistening with her love oils, as her thumb pummelled her own clit. Dido's belly heaved, and her gasps grew as loud as those of her patient in bondage; suddenly she withdrew from Miss Florence's quim, and thrust her shining fingers into the wrinkled pucker of the arsebud: two fingers, three, then, to my amazement, her whole hand balled into a tight fist, which she slid in and out of my Mistress's cruelly distended anus, as she screamed and writhed in her bandages. I knew she reached orgasm once more; to the music of Miss Florence's screams, Dido howled and writhed in her own spasm as she fist-buggered my shrieking Mistress.

'Well!' said Dido briskly, and panting only a little, as she stood up and smoothed her uniform. 'I think it is a nice night for a ride, my Sapphic bitch . . .'

Miss Florence was released from her bondage and stood sobbing and naked, but for her soiled corset, before her nurse. Dido slapped her bare breasts roughly. As though practised in the drill, Miss Florence at once squatted on the floor with her thighs apart as though to pee. Dido unfastened the large brass door-key from its chain beneath my eyehole, and attached a long pony's rein to the loop of the key, then thrust the key firmly inside Miss Florence's gash, and ordered her to hold tight.

My Mistress pressed her thighs, and her belly tightened as she held the key and rein inside her slit. Dido flicked the rein, and Miss Florence knelt on all fours, naked but for her pink corset, now outdone in colour by her livid puce buttocks, and padded awkwardly towards the door. The black blotches amid her crimson welts on the tops of the buttocks waggled prettily as she moved towards me, and reluctantly I retreated to my hiding place, whence I watched the pair emerge from the bedroom and proceed at a hobble towards the stairs.

'I don't like your treatment of Roger,' I heard Dido say as they descended. 'For a Lesbian, you like to tease him too much.'

'Tease him!' cried Miss Florence. 'I despise him. And I want the impudent brat to hate me for it.'

Nothing could possibly soften my rigid cock after my Mistress's sweet words.

'Then, I think, twice round the grounds, my Sapphic pony, and a dip in the lake to cool you off,' said Dido as they left the building.

The coast was clear and any thought of impropriety vanished as I followed my stiff cock into my Mistress's chamber. I crept in, to smell the sweet perfume of lust and gaze at her clothing rumpled on the floor. My disturbance of the disarray would go unnoticed; I knelt in adoration, and lifted an armful of silken underthings, pressing them to my face, and drawing deep breaths of ecstasy.

I heard rattling noises below, and pulled the shades a fraction to look down. Dido sat in a little jaunting car, holding reins and a long whip, whose end she cracked prettily over the naked buttocks of my Mistress. Miss Florence was tethered by her quim-plug, and also by a harness clamped to her nipples, with a metal bit forcing her mouth open and holding her tongue down. Her arms were fastened behind her back, both with handcuffs of studded leather, and by a brace that pinioned her upper arms together in a leather sheath. Her head was clamped in heavy blinkers that forced her to look straight ahead. Apart from her harness and pink corset, she was otherwise apparently nude.

Dido flicked the rein that held the key in her slit, and Miss Florence jerked into action, pulling the cart with her breasts and quim. Her rein tightened and the cart lurched forward, and Dido's whip cracked fiercely across her bare buttocks, making her whinny in her gag like a pony. She raised her knees high in a trot, almost up to her pendulous breasts, and now I saw that her feet were shod in heavy surgical boots strapped all the way up her calves to just below her knees, with soles and heels of thick iron slabs about eight or nine inches in height. She had to keep her legs very straight, so as not to topple when these cruel hooves crashed to the ground at her every step.

I listened and watched as the pony and trap disappeared into the moonlit night. Certain that no one would suspect my visit to the dishevelled chamber, I pressed my nose and lips to the moist bedspread where my Mistress had writhed in her ecstasy; kissed every patch of floor and cloth dampened by her love juices; then, trembling, kissed her stockings and corselets, and put her panties and scented shoes to my mouth and nostrils. My balls ached with desire.

I could not help myself, such was my frenzy. I stripped off my clothing and stood naked before her rainbow of scented silks and satins. I selected a petticoat, and slipped into it. I rolled silk stockings on to my legs, regretting my horrid male hairiness – until that delicious moment when her stocking tops clung to my thighs like a Lady's fingers, seeming to clasp me in cool embrace just below my balls.

Blushing at my shameful foolishness, I put on a lacy brassiere, which of course flopped empty in front of me, then stuffed it with stockings to make a full breast. Then I laced a corset painfully tight, then completed my robing with skirt, suspender belt, blouse, jacket and scarf, and squeezed into a pair of high shoes that were deliciously small and painful.

Finally, I inspected myself in the mirror. My breath was heavy and my face flushed, and I resisted the temptation to search for her rouge and powder, whose disturbance might be noticed. With trembling fingers, I reached for the pair of wet pink panties, the flimsiest, gauziest creation, which she had removed before Dido's arrival.

I kissed the place where her quim and bumhole had touched, and slipped them up over my stockings. I pulled the lovely pink panties tight over my balls and throbbing cock, very high, in order to encompass the whole of my organ.

At last, with the silk stretched painfully, I managed to get my cock covered, with the thong biting into my furrow. I was fully encased in my Mistress's beauty! My balls and cock felt godlike, so tightly and painfully sheathed in my goddess's panties. I thought my penis should be a rock for ever. I could not bear the thought of having to remove them.

I sat on the bed, relishing my shame, and the spectacle I should present to my Mistress if she returned, and almost wanting her to, for I knew that savage punishment would await me, a birching more severe than anything I had yet contemplated! Birched, and in full bondage, and gagged to stifle my screams of real agony – such was my reverie.

Thus I daydreamed until I heard the clatter of the pony and trap returning. Then my cold male reason took over. Too many secrets or revelations in one day would not do. I saw Dido halt her pony, with my Mistress dripping wet and shivering from her immersion in the lake. She was sobbing through her wet bridle, her shoulders and buttocks a glistening mass of livid new welts.

Rapidly, I divested myself of her clothing, and threw it back in its heap on the floor. Their loan would be undetected, but in my haste I forgot – no, in truth I could not bear to leave – the precious pink panties of hers that clasped so sweetly. I dressed rapidly, and gained my room before the Ladies returned, still wearing her panties. I fell on my bed, quite exhausted with my surreptitious happiness, and dozed off, thinking that I would in due course find a way to return the panties without my Mistress's knowing my secret. Unless, I whispered to myself as I was halfway to sleep, I really wanted her to know . . .

4

Wringing Wet

The next morning, my two breakfast companions were as correct as ever, with not a hint that anything unusual had ever taken place amongst any of us. This continued for the days thereafter, and though I carefully washed my Mistress's pink panties, I dawdled over their return, partly because I was uncertain how to go about it, and partly because I did not wish to part with my precious trophy; gradually I began to think she would not notice at all. How wrong I was to think that any Lady should fail to notice the absence of an undergarment!

The third morning after my theft of the panties, Miss Florence announced portentously to Dido, over breakfast, that her favourite knickers were missing. She said that the slut Grubb had probably spoiled them or lost them from the laundry, or more likely stolen them. At any event she must be punished.

'Florence!' said Dido mildly. 'Does our guest need to hear such things?'

'It is a matter of law and order,' insisted Miss Florence, without looking at me, 'and doesn't concern him. I've spoken to Grubb. If she hasn't the panties, or an explanation, or both, by this evening, then I'll thrash her. The slut is well due a thrashing on that impudent bum of hers.'

'You forget, Florence,' said Dido, without looking at me, 'that, as acting head of the household, I must give my permission for such a thing, and I absolutely forbid you to thrash the girl. She might take umbrage, and leave our service! Especially after . . . well, she cannot help having such a big bum, even if it does make you jealous.'

Miss Florence glowered, and brushed a sliver of boiled egg from her chin.

'I'm sure the knickers will turn up,' said Dido cheerfully, 'don't you think so, Roger?'

I blushed too! I stammered that such things usually turned up, and Grubb was quite innocent in the matter. My Mistress turned to me, and stared fiercely.

'Are you calling me a liar?' she snapped.

'Why, no, Miss, of course not,' I blurted.

She rose from the table, and her eyes glinted into mine.

'I rather think you are, Ruggiero,' she said sweetly.

I took my leave as soon as possible, and went back to my room, where I removed the precious panties from under my pillow. I felt sorry for the unfortunate Grubb, and envious too, since I wanted my Mistress's lash for my own bottom.

I made my way down to the cluster of shacks by the stream, where Grubb had her abode and workplace. Beside sheds and laundry hut and her cottage was a hayloft, cluttered with sacks of potatoes and farming implements, while the ground was strewn with cartwheels, rakes, and other rural items in no apparent order. Laundry fluttered from various lines, according to their weight, with the Ladies' frillies the brightest and most enticing.

The confusion of Grubb's domain suited my purpose: I intended to drop the panties so that they seemed to have fallen by accident, yet not so obscurely that they would be overlooked. I heard Grubb busy in her wash-house, with the sound of cheerful whistling and the clanking of a mangle. I did my best to walk quietly, but the confusion of the terrain, and the sharp senses of a Lady, betrayed me.

'Is that you, Major?' came Grubb's cry. 'I thought you were still away – but I'm always ready for you!'

It was useless to try and hide; I stuffed the pink panties in my pocket and stepped forward into the sunlight. Grubb was carrying a basket of wet laundry under her arms. I saw her eyes on my fumbling fingers, and feared that she might have seen the bright pink of the panties. But then her eyes rose to my face.

'O! Sir!' she cried.

Grubb was naked to the waist! She wore only a thin green skirt, soaked with suds, that clung wetly to her powerful thighs and moulded her large buttocks like quivering flans. Her bare breasts were frothy and glistening from her washing, as they perched like bulbs on top of her pile of clothes. The massive teats were criss-crossed in a lovely little pattern of tiny veins, like a sculpture in marble. The nipples were big and conical and pointed cheekily upwards like little chimneys. The hour-glass beauty of her frame – the slender, almost pencil-thin waist, adorned by such splendid teats, and such a peach of a bottom, seemed almost out of kilter, yet formed a harmony and rough beauty which, I confess, had my penis twitching and tickled my balls, even in my embarrassment.

She made no move to cover her breasts, but rather cast her basket of washing aside and stood to inspect me, hands on hips and breasts swaying gently.

'Well, sir!' she said, with a ravishing smile. 'I expected the Major – but of course you are all boys together, and I'm glad you've come at last. Shy, were you? No need, sir . . .'

I mumbled something about looking for the summer-house and getting lost, and Grubb frowned and clicked her tongue, with an impish smile.

'You mustn't be shy, sir, nor must you mock. You know where the summerhouse is, and I know where it is, and it ain't here. All that is here is me, and it's me you've come for.'

She took her nipples between her fingers, and squeezed them into fruits. With a giggle, she ordered me to approach, and said that every lad in the neighbourhood would assure me she gave good service for a good price. Numbly, my cock stiffening despite myself, I went towards her, smelling her rough animal perfume.

'What'll it be, sir? A tit-fuck? A suck? Five shillings for

a tit-fuck, seven and six for a suck, and a shilling a dozen if you want to spank my bare bum first. The Major hasn't spanked me for quite a while,' she added coyly, her eyes on the bulge of my manhood.

She whistled.

'You are a real gentleman,' she murmured. 'I don't mind if you want to . . . you know.'

I stammered that I had no money. I was close to her, enchanted by her perfume and the big marbled teats just inches from my face. I felt her hand brush the tip of my straining penis.

'You can owe me, sir,' she whispered, putting her tongue out and licking her lips. 'What's it to be?'

I thought, fleetingly, of Dido – had she not said that flowers were there to be picked? Grubb's fingers were rubbing my bulb as she unbuttoned my trousers. She was a few inches taller than me, and, by standing on tiptoe, she pushed her stiff cherry nipples right on to my lips, with my nose pressed in the warm, soft cleft of her breasts, that seemed to smother me in their sweetness. I groaned in dismay and delight; I could not resist a Lady.

My naked cock burst free, and her fingers clasped it.

'God!' she cried, and swiftly disengaged her teats from my face, then knelt to take my swollen hard bulb between her lips.

She licked my peehole and sucked me with swift pigeon-like motions, until I stood hard as a rock. Panting, she lifted her head, and said there would be no charge this time, for she wanted me to sample all her wares.

'But you must spank me bare, sir,' she added, and faintly I agreed to do whatever she proposed.

In an instant she had me naked, my cock gleaming in the sunlight, and her tongue busy flicking on my shaft and balls.

'You are a gentleman, sir, so you will be fond of bumming,' she whispered. 'Normally a bumming is ten shillings, or a guinea for bumhole and cooze, but it shall be my treat, sir.'

I protested my innocence of bumming, but she said she insisted on both her holes feeling my cock.

'I've never seen one so big, sir,' she said. 'And I'm curious to see if she'll fit in my bumhole. Is that what all foreign gentlemen have?'

I protested that I was English, or as good as made no difference, and she gave me a big smile as her lips fastened on my throbbing bulb, like a girl with a butterscotch ice cream.

'I hope she'll fit,' she mumbled. 'Few of the village lads can afford ten bob for a bumming, so it's only the Major, usually. I won't lower my prices any, that would be cheapening myself, you see.'

'O, Miss Grubb,' I moaned, as her tongue lathered my stiff cock.

'You called me Miss! O, thank you, sir!' she cried in genuine delight. 'Only the Major does that.'

She rose, and clasped my cock between her teats, which she began to rub eagerly around my member, the nipples frotting each other, and actually meeting between my cock and belly, enclosing me like a roll. My helmet protruded to her chin, and with long lapping strokes her agile tongue began to lick my peehole. Her breasts artfully drew my prepuce fully back, and she gasped at the moon of my birthmark.

'You must be a wizard,' she exclaimed, forgetting to call me sir, as she licked the shiny little crescent.

The soft teat-flesh caressed my balls and cock, sometimes playfully engulfing my whole bulb as she rubbed, and after a minute of this gentle frigging she released my throbbing member and knelt. She pulled my stiff shaft down to her lips, and opened them like a bird of prey, then seized my bulb in her mouth, licking and squeezing and pecking. I clasped her tousled blonde head and pressed her to me.

Her mouth suddenly and voraciously descended almost to my balls, and I felt my peehole touch the back of her throat, as though I were enveloped in a silky wet cooze. Her head began to bob up and down as she powerfully sucked my cock.

'O, Miss,' I gasped, 'you are moving too fast for –'

She chuckled mischievously and said 'mmm' as a drop of sperm emerged at my peehole, turning to a flood as my bucking member discharged into her throat, and I writhed as my honeyed spasm shook me.

She withdrew her dripping mouth, licked her lips, and swallowed two or three times, saying 'mmm' again.

'You certainly are a heavy creamer, sir, and I bet there is plenty left for my holes. That's why I brought you off fast. Now we've plenty of time till the next spurt. Haven't we, my sweet?'

She addressed these last words to my cock itself, and began to stroke my balls, licking the softening wet shaft of the penis until it began to stir and tremble anew. Then she looked up with wide bright eyes and asked me if I weren't going to take her skirt up, and put her over my knee for a spanking on her bare.

Dazed, I allowed myself to be seated on a rock, and accepted the sinewy cargo of her body across my thighs. I sensed that it was somehow wrong for a male to inflict pain on a Lady's body – yet wrong to disobey a Lady's command. My dilemma was resolved when she pressed my fingers to the hem of her skirt and tugged it up, indicating that I should rip the garment from her bottom and reveal her bum bare for spanking.

'I like being taken, sir,' she shivered, and I had the pleasant feeling that I was the one being taken. I obliged her. I pulled her skirt up quite roughly, which made her sigh in satisfaction, and revealed her naked peach. The beauty of those firm, creamy orbs made my cock stiffen fully again, and I gazed in wonder at the marks of previous beatings, like a pretty patchwork of chastisement mottling her pale skin.

Gingerly, I began to spank her bare buttocks with my palm, my member rock-hard and nestling in the fold of her belly, shrouded by her billowing skirt, which eddied delightfully at each spank, like the sail of a ship. She urged me to spank her harder; I did so; harder again; again; I obeyed until I was genuinely spanking the reddening bare bum with all my might, and she wriggled and purred with little gasps of satisfaction.

After several dozen hard spanks, her bum was dancing a pretty crimson, and my thighs were moistened by a warm trickle of oil from her squirming fount. I felt the lips swollen and squashing against me under her heavy thatched mound, and the hard little button of her clitty eagerly frotting against my bare skin. The nubbin was surprisingly and deliciously large, like a miniature cock; I had a sudden fantasy that I was this squirming Lady, her bare nates my own, and it was her firm palm spanking my own bare . . . I understood why my Mistress called my cock 'her', and began to see that a Lady must enjoy her submission to spank and whip just like any male.

Grubb's wriggling grew more intense as her bare bottom was suffused with darker and darker crimson, and her whole body shuddered as she squealed and rubbed her belly and teats against me like a playful kitten. Her cooze was quite wet and dripped over my thigh as she rubbed the hard bud of her clitty against me. I must have delivered over a hundred spanks, and her bottom was deliciously puffy, when she groaned that I was very cruel not to 'bring her off' with a proper poking.

I ceased spanking; she did not rise, but crouched on the ground and put her face in the earth, then with both hands clasped her buttocks and drew them apart, to reveal her furrow and blossoming anus pucker, which nestled in the very hairy thatch of her wide mink like rose petals. She pulled at the wrinkled pink whorl until it parted like a little mouth, and ordered me to give her a 'proper shafting'.

I was, I confess, nervous; I had of course heard of the practice of bumming, but that a Lady should so wantonly and so naturally demand it . . .!

'Come on!' she cried. 'Your cock in my bumhole! Lovely and tight, sir, better than gash!'

A Lady's wish or command must always be obeyed! Nervously, I placed the tip of my bulb against her pucker, which jumped and clutched my peehole! I pushed into her a little way, feeling her cavity very tight, but she moaned with satisfaction and relaxed the anus, sucking me into her as she thrust her bum against my haunches. I got halfway,

I think, into her tight elastic shaft when my penis came to a halt, as though meeting an immovable obstacle.

But she writhed and spread her fesses wider, and sucked with her bumhole on my squeezed cock, and suddenly she gasped, her anus gave way, and I plunged right to her root in a magical rush. Her anus fitted my cock like a glove many sizes too small, but deliciously snug, and she said 'mmm' in pleasure when I stammered this to her.

My prepuce was drawn painfully back to its limit, and I lay still for a while, afraid that, if I moved, my organ should split her tender hole. But she wriggled and squeezed more, and begged me to poke her hard. I began to thrust; my cock sank into her hole, almost to my balls, and she groaned as I thrust harder and faster, her anus squeezing and sucking me as though to eat me. Her bumhole was like a pump, and I felt that hard as I might buck, with my thighs slapping loudly against her own, it was really the Lady who was bucking me. I wanted, suddenly, to punish her for her impudence, and recommenced spanking the squirming bare nates so lovely and red before me.

'O, yes!' she howled. 'Harder, harder, poke me till I burst. Split me with your cock! I've never had such a monstrous thing in my bum! Spank me raw, sir, make me dance for you and give me all your spunk in my bumhole!'

Despite her passionate invitation, I felt that Grubb was artfully controlling my cock and the precise moment when I should spurt, which was not to be before her own spasm. She raised one hand and began to masturbate quite vigorously and openly as I poked her bumhole. In such a short time, I had become used to the fact that Ladies liked to masturbate shamelessly. And, sauce for the goose being sauce for the gander, I confess that I was now possessed of a wicked curiosity to know myself what joy could be obtained from this unusual coupling she called 'bumming' . . .

I spanked her harder and faster, her bottom now quivering like two huge strawberry jellies, and her bum's pressure on my thrusting bulb and shaft made me cry that I would spurt shortly, and could not help it. At that, she began to moan in loud breathless yelps; her fingers blurred as they rubbed her clitty, and her bum writhed and squeezed until I thought she should milk me of my last drop and trap my cock inside her for ever. Her squeals turned to howls as she convulsed in the quivering of her own spasm, and, at the same moment, my seed rushed from me and spurted right against her anal root.

'O, sir!' she gasped. 'O, master! O, O . . .!'

Even after I had stopped flowing, she continued to milk me with her bumhole, and my rush of pleasure gave way to a soft and agreeable sensation of warmth, like a second, but less intense orgasm. She continued to masturbate her clitty for a little while longer, and then her fingers snaked through her furrow to clasp my balls, stroking me tenderly. I bent forward and licked a bead of sweat at the small of her back, and sniffed the ripe fabric of her bunched dress. Slowly and gradually, she relaxed her sphincter and permitted my softening cock to leave her service; my will had no part in the matter. She pushed my bulb from her anus with a plopping sound. Delightfully, I felt myself the plaything of this new, rough maid!

Footsteps rustled on the path; Grubb started in fear, and hissed that Her Ladyship was coming – I presumed she meant my Mistress. Sure enough, I heard her voice.

'Grubb! Come here, you slut!' cried Miss Florence.

Grubb motioned me to bury myself in the straw in the hayloft. I obeyed at once, forgetting my nudity in my haste. From my hiding place, I watched Grubb lower and smooth her dress, before scooping up my clothing in a bundle.

Miss Florence appeared, dressed in sober grey, and brandishing a riding crop.

'What are you doing, Grubb?' she barked.

'Laundry, Miss,' said Grubb.

Miss Florence pointed accusingly at my bundle of clothing.

'Who were you calling master just now?' she said slyly.

'Why, the new master brought his clothes for cleaning, Miss.'

'Couldn't he have left them in the laundry basket? I dare say he wanted to ogle your big teats, girl. Haven't I told you to dress properly?'

'It is so hot, Miss,' Grubb whined.

Miss Florence snorted that male things had better be kept separate from nice things – and then she demanded to know where her pink panties were. Grubb's professed ignorance made my Mistress furious. She knocked my clothes from Grubb's arms, into the muddy residue of a puddle. Then she slapped Grubb's bare breasts five times with the back of her hand, making them wobble and quiver, and become flushed a slight, delicious pink.

Grubb took the beating, but her eyes moistened and her lips curled in anguish, and she cried out that Her Ladyship was unfair. At this, Miss Florence lifted her riding crop and dealt Grubb three savage lashes right across the nipples.

'Naked like a whore!' she cried, and began to trample my clothes into the mud, as though they, or I, were the guilty party.

'Now you have some cleaning to do!' she cried meanly.

I saw a tell-tale sliver of pink silk peeping from my trouser pocket as she kicked! At once, Grubb scooped up my clothes again and fled into her laundry hut, sobbing piteously. She placed my clothing in a basket, out of harm's way, and I wondered if she had in fact seen the panties, and was now my accomplice. Miss Florence stormed after her into the shed, leaving the door flapping open.

I watched with growing unease. Miss Florence took Grubb by the hair and pulled it cruelly, telling her it was her last chance to confess her wrongdoing. Grubb squealed that she was innocent, and my Mistress pushed her head down to the ground.

'Please, no, Miss!' shrieked Grubb. 'You know Mrs Dark was cross, the last time –'

A hard slap to her face silenced her protest.

'Mrs Dark is not at home, slut,' Miss Florence hissed, 'and I have you all to myself. Present your bum for whopping.'

Miss Florence picked up her riding crop and ripped

Grubb's dress from her waist, revealing her bare bum still glowing from my spanks.

'Your croup is red!' cried my Mistress. 'Who did this, you slut?'

'I . . . I sat on some sharp rocks in the sun, Miss,' moaned Grubb.

'Those are the marks of fingers!' cried Miss Florence.

She stuttered that she had been hot for spanking, and so had spanked her own bottom! Miss Florence snapped that she would teach Grubb to be a slut and a liar, and lifted her crop high. She brought it down fiercely on Grubb's pinioned bare buttocks, leaving a fearful welt. This stroke was followed almost at once by a second, a third, and the strokes continued unabated, whirring like a hand flicking through a pack of cards. Grubb's wealed, puce buttocks were bare beacons of agony, the only respite in her squirming yelps coming when Miss Florence paused to rest her arm.

I was speechless with fear and indecision, but I sensed that my appearance, far from calming my Mistress, would only increase her vengeful fury, and that she would deny me the joy of taking the punishment on myself, but make me witness the further correction of the helpless maid.

Even as she twisted and shuddered under the lash, Grubb steadfastly refused to alter her story. My Mistress was panting hard as she whipped, and her face was flushed, with a dreamy savage look in her eyes as they focused on Grubb's writhing bare. At last, I could be still no longer and rose from my hiding place, covering my stiff penis with straw in an absurd instinct of modesty; when, suddenly, Miss Florence let out a long wail of frustration and fury.

'Damn you!' she hissed.

She knelt between Grubb's quivering thighs and put her face at her furrow, then with an eager tongue began to lick the dripping lips of Grubb's gash!

'You filthy slut,' she moaned, 'you dirty, dirty beast.'

She licked Grubb's swollen cooze until the trapped maid began to shiver and mewl in her turn. I saw her clitty throbbing stiff and glistening under my Mistress's avid tonguing, and Grubb began to gasp in pleasure. Miss Florence's tongue moved to Grubb's anus bud, which she licked as fervently as she had the clit, getting her tongue inside to a depth of an inch or more, and poking the maid's bumhole as though her tongue were a cock. Grubb writhed and sighed in ticklish joy, and her thighs clasped Miss Florence's head. Then, Miss Florence lifted her body a few inches, and took one of Grubb's ankles from the ground, leaving her balanced on one leg and supported by her straining arms.

She took Grubb's bare foot and lifted her own skirt, then pressed it against her own white panties, and began to frot the toes on her Lady's place, which rapidly became stained with her quim's moisture. Her other hand delved into Grubb's open gash and she got her whole hand inside the wet slit, as her tongue continued to lick and poke the tender bumhole.

Her white stockings were smutted in the mud, and one of her garter straps snapped open, but she did not seem to care. Grubb was now flexing and bending her toes against my Mistress's quim lips, their swollen petals clearly outlined against the darkening wet sop of her stained panties, and I saw that Grubb's big toe was deftly frotting my Mistress's clitty.

'O . . .' moaned Miss Florence, 'O . . . you wicked slut . . .'

She pushed Grubb's foot inside her panties, so that they slipped down her thighs, and I saw her magnificent mane of mink-curls sodden and glistening with her copious juices as the maid's foot now frotted her naked fount. Grubb too, moaned in anguished joy; the fingertips of one hand were flicking the distended bulbs of her own stiffened nipples.

'O . . .' cried Miss Florence, louder now, 'O . . .'

Suddenly her belly convulsed, and her cries grew to a harsh staccato yelping as her teeth fastened on Grubb's distended pink bum-wrinkle, and her tongue flickered, the lips covering the maid's anus with harsh kisses as Miss Florence shivered and moaned in her orgasm. She rested for a moment, panting harshly, before lifting her flushed face.

'Spanked yourself, you say?'

'O . . .' moaned Grubb, still caressing her swollen nipples, 'O, yes, Miss . . .'

'And why do I taste sperm in your bumhole, slut!' cried my Mistress.

Grubb answered only with a low, despairing moan; Miss Florence rose, kicked off her sopping knickers and stockings, and wadded them into Grubb's mouth.

'You disgust me,' she snarled. 'Look how you have soiled my underthings – make sure they come back spotlessly clean, or else it is the lash again.'

She waved her hand, as though throwing aside some smut or piece of mud, and strode away, leaving Grubb to recover her dignity.

'As for you, Roger,' she called back, 'wherever you are hiding – just be glad that I don't feel like punishing you today!'

She knew! My heart felt chill; I rushed from my concealment and covered Grubb's breasts with soft kisses.

'You poor girl!' I cried. 'Such cruelty from your Mistress!'

'Why, it is nothing, sir,' she laughed, rubbing her fesses with detached curiosity.

She stooped and picked up two shiny, tinkling objects which my Mistress had dropped in the dirt, and held them up with a gleeful smile. They were half-crown coins.

'Nothing that Milady's five shillings won't cure,' she said.

Then she said I should wait as she washed my soiled clothing, and the sun would dry them in no time. I seemed to have little choice but to agree, and watched the rippling of her bare back and arms, and the delicious rhythm of her breasts swaying, as she lathered my things, then hung them up. There was a flash of pink; she had washed the panties, too.

'Well, sir,' she said, wiping her hands on her bum, 'we have a little time before your things dry. And there is something that five shillings will not cure.'

She calmly stepped out of her dress, and advanced on me, nude as myself. She grasped my cock, which was already stiffening, and pressed the bulb into her big fleshy quim lips, and my peehole right against her hard nubbin. Using my cock as her tool, she parted her legs and began to masturbate.

'My cruel Mistress got herself off, but not me,' she panted. 'And you, sir, haven't had me in cooze yet. Unless you want to watch me frig, and spurt your cream over my belly as I come. Rather inside, I think.'

I needed no encouragement to obey her gentle orders. She laid me on my back, on the hard ground, and mounted me as Dido had done; like Dido, she bucked and writhed until my organ was raw and maddened with a longing to spurt, and like Dido, she knew how to make me draw back from my spurt so that her own belly could heave in orgasm three times before she milked me of my sperm. I spanked her fesses as she bucked, but they were only playful little slaps to urge her on, and not a real chastisement.

I spanked her breasts too, at her insistence, as she waved them flapping over my hands, teasing me with their immense whip-reddened beauty, as she gaily frigged her clit. Her hand flickered vigorously in her gaping wet gash that streamed with her love juice as she bounced on my aching haunches, until the practised and unrelenting masturbation of her clitty brought her to her final, sobbing orgasm. As she rose, she said that her tit-spank made her hot for 'another doing', and soon . . .

In a rather callow fashion I assured her that I should visit when I had some shillings to my name.

I walked unsteadily back to the lodge, filled with contentment and foreboding at the same time. I heard my Mistress bustling within and, too late, I realised that my laundered shirt was streaked with the pink from her panties! I rushed to my room, not knowing if I had been spotted, or if I had, what level of punishment she would decide to award. And in fearful contemplation of my inevitable whipping, I spent the rest of the day in utter bliss! With the shivery thought that if a maid could get such pleasure at her bumming from a master, perhaps the reverse was also true.

5

Pink Panties

I met Dido in the grounds, and she rather curtly informed me that we were to dress for dinner. Accordingly, I put on my best white tie and tails, thinking myself rather grand, but all fancies that a mere male can aspire to beauty were abandoned once I entered the dining-room. Dido and Miss Florence stood by the fireplace arrayed like goddesses, both in revealing gowns of the most sumptuous velvet: Dido in purple, and my Mistress in black. Both had ample breast-flesh exposed by very low-cut fronts, and with hourglass figures that I thought surely must be corsed. Miss Florence's breasts were thrust up like tempting ripe melons, and the swell of her buttocks was so smooth and firm that I could not detect the line of her panties.

The robes of both Ladies buttoned rather daringly right up the front, and Dido's was open to well above the knee, revealing black silk stockings, which went rather gaily with her purple. As she moved, there was a momentary vision of stocking top and even garter strap.

Both had sparkling chokers, heels of the highest, spikiest leather, and I saw that Miss Florence, on her own black silk stockings – sheer rather than Dido's discreet fishnet – wore an ankle bracelet in gold, which was in the shape of a riding crop and saddle.

Dido's hair was done in curly ringlets which cascaded over her naked shoulders like a forest of dark fronds, while Miss Florence's was swept up in a magnificent and regal tower like a pagoda. I burbled some florid and clumsy compliments. My Mistress was unmoved, but Dido laughed prettily and told me I would gain no indulgences with my continental charm.

Then Grubb entered, wheeling a trolley of champagne and tit-bits, which were served to us standing by the fireplace. She looked quite lovely, her splendour increased by the obvious discomfort of her frilly maid's uniform. She had a little black skirt, white lace apron and bonnet, with heels as high as my Ladies'. The uniform was much too small for her: her breasts bulged alarmingly from the unbuttonable top of her blouse, and the little pleated skirt rode up to show the stocking-tops and the soft swell of the mound above, cased in skimpy black lace panties which allowed tufts of her ample mink hair to cascade down her thighs like tendrils. Her cheerful face was set in a demure mask of dutiful submission.

Grubb was not a great success as a serving-maid. She spilt drinks, upset plates, and stumbled on her teetering high heels. We smiled indulgently, and Dido entertained us with the gossip of her day in town, and visit to the hairdresser's, and prattled about mutual acquaintances, saying she had had the pleasure of running into Mrs Mantle and had invited her to tea, being invited in turn to the forthcoming meeting of the Virginia Water Progressive Ladies' club, for a talk by the noted thinker, Dr Alice Arbiter, on the subject of 'Law and Order'.

I noticed that my Mistress was silent about her own daily routine, and the good works amongst the unfortunates of society, and reasoned that she found these too distressing for us. I reflected how strangely this household mirrored our society as a whole: I was the only male with three delightful females, we all behaved with the utmost decorum, yet all of us were privy to secrets about the others. The real, and most delicious, secret being that none of us (so I supposed) was quite sure exactly which secrets the others possessed.

We moved to the table, where Dido insisted I sit in the Major's chair, as I was now master of the household in his absence. Grubb served our dinner and, as always, her cooking made up for her shortcomings as serving wench. There was a fine claret to accompany a monstrous crusted creation she called 'Berkshire Pie', golden and steaming and smelling very succulent. This was divided into three portions by the garnish of a different flower: a tulip, a rose, and a dandelion, perched on the crust. I got the dandelion. Grubb withdrew, leaving us to our meal, and I saw that at the centre of each portion was wedged a large black object. Dido informed me that a Berkshire pie was a confection of beef, rabbit, venison, and a 'Berkshire oyster' to give it zest. A Berkshire oyster was a Thames oyster, but wrapped in the testicle of a stag, and this delicacy was to be swallowed as the *pièce de résistance* at the end of the pie.

As we ate, Dido asked Miss Florence if she had solved the mystery of the missing knickers. She spoke quite unconcernedly with her mouth full, and Miss Florence answered also as she chewed, which surprised me. She said that Grubb had not provided her with a satisfactory answer, and begged Dido's permission to thrash the slut black and blue – this within Grubb's hearing in her adjacent pantry.

Dido took rather a large gulp of claret, spilling some on the damask, and said that seemed rather drastic.

'Are you sure Grubb is the culprit?' she said, spitting out a rabbit bone.

'Who else could it be?' asked Miss Florence, her mouth stuffed with pastry crust whose juices dribbled down her chin.

Neither Lady paid me any attention.

'The cane, then, I suppose,' said Dido.

'At least four dozen, Mummy, perhaps five, or even six,' cried my Mistress.

'It is the job of the master to punish the servants,' said Dido thoughtfully, 'and I suppose Roger will have to do it in this case – a very serious one indeed. Don't you agree, Roger?'

Now, they both looked at me with gimlet eyes.

'Why, yes,' I stammered. 'Theft of intimate garments – most serious, Ladies.'

'Roger will flog her, then,' said Dido, her eyes gleaming. 'I suppose she had better be strapped down, or she will thresh too much. He is a strong young man.'

Both Ladies shifted, and crossed their legs, and I noticed that more of their buttons seemed to have come undone, so that I had a delicious, fleeting glimpse of pantied mounds and silky garter straps over lovely smooth thigh-skin peeping between the stocking tops and panties – that sacred, mouth-watering ribbon of skin!

My insufferable male smugness had not yet been thrashed from me, and I hope it never will, if it assures continued thrashings from a stern Lady! My reasoning was thus: I should prepare the hapless Grubb for chastisement; lift the rods over her bared bottom; ascertain secretly from her where she had replaced the panties; at the last moment, insist on a final search of those premises.

Grubb would be spared and vindicated, and my statesmanship honoured! I should then confess privately to my Mistress that I had been aware of Grubb's misdeed, and had replaced the panties myself, to chivalrously save her Lady's bottom – thus, doubtless, earning myself a severe birching from my wrathful Mistress, for my pride.

'Whatever miscreant has the Lady's knickers in her possession,' I blurted, my mouth full of pie, 'deserves the severest, merciless thrashing! A paltry six dozen scarcely suffices!'

Dido fixed me with a glacial look.

'Did you speak, sir?' she said. 'I did not hear you with your mouth full.'

I was mortified! I blushed fierily, and was rewarded with a brief glance of the utmost scorn from my Mistress. Dido sliced into her Berkshire oyster, her knife cleaving the leathery testicle to reveal the succulent pale oyster within. She forked it into her mouth, and chewed vigorously, the juices dribbling down her chin and on to her bare breast, where she made no attempt to wipe the stain. My Mistress followed suit, and both Ladies, their mouths crammed, expressed their approval.

My turn came, and I cut into my Berkshire oyster, the

outside flesh giving way easily enough, but my knife met with resistance from the inside. I looked down, and stared aghast. Both Ladies froze in mid-mouthful, gazing at me with glacial frowns. Speared to my fork was no Thames oyster, but the pink panties of my Mistress!

I was speechless for a cold, electric minute. Then I managed to smile, and babble that it was a jolly good trick at my expense, and I appreciated the English sense of humour. No one else was laughing, least of all Grubb, who surveyed me with arms folded, frowning from her pantry door.

'I see no trick, sir,' said Dido. 'I see a thief in possession of my daughter's stolen panties.'

'You cur!' cried Miss Florence. 'To make a joke of something so precious!'

'But surely the joke has been played on me,' I protested, in a futile, indeed insulting, attempt to influence the determined Ladies with reason.

'I believe you opined, sir,' Dido continued, 'that whoever was in possession of the stolen knickers deserved the severest punishment.'

Her lip now curled in amused pity.

'A paltry six dozen scarcely suffices – those, I believe, were your words.'

'But – I didn't mean – are you suggesting –' I blurted.

'I am not suggesting anything, Roger,' said Dido. 'In this house, we use the English language to mean what we say. Your possession of Miss Florence's panties is a fact. And the possessor of the panties must be punished, as you have demanded.'

'The worm must wriggle!' cried Miss Florence, and I shivered.

'Since my daughter is the aggrieved party, it is her right to insist on retribution,' said Dido mildly, 'as she apparently does. And since you, as acting master of the house, can scarcely be expected to undertake your own chastisement – though stranger things are known to happen – the task falls to me, I think. With your permission, of course.'

How sweet Ladies are! They could not know I had committed the theft, but it was my fault nonetheless – the trick played on me was somehow my fault – and since I was artfully invited to agree my own punishment, my beating too would be my own doing! I tried to look pained, with wounded dignity, as I agreed to my chastisement, and conceal my true delight: I should be flogged by a Lady, before others, and their glorious cruelty would be all the sweeter for its injustice.

'On second thoughts,' said Dido, 'it would pain me too much to flog my own house guest, however vicious his conduct. I think I shall delegate the task to my daughter – assuming you agree, Roger.'

I nodded in utter humiliance.

'O, very well,' said Miss Florence fussily. 'Grubb is still under suspicion, Mummy, but whatever unfunny practical joke this wretch was attempting, it has backfired, and the biter is bit!'

Suddenly, both Ladies laughed uproariously in my face. Then, quite coolly, they ignored me as they discussed the method of my chastisement. It went without saying that I should be caned, and on the bare, but Miss Florence insisted on the 'special cane', and Dido agreed.

'That will make his bum smart awfully,' Dido said. 'Are you sure a swift, sharp birching would not suffice?'

'If the male doesn't squirm to my satisfaction, Mummy, I shall consider the birch as *well* as the cane. Remember what the male said – punishment should be merciless.'

'Yes, he said that,' said Dido, nodding sagely. 'And luckily I am here as nurse, to make sure he can take it.'

Miss Florence said eagerly that a serving slut would take her flogging quite naked, so I should do the same. Dido objected to this, on grounds of modesty, and it was agreed that as extra humiliance, I should be obliged to wear the panties I had purloined, to cover my private parts, but that they would be pulled down to leave my bottom bare for the lash, and prevent them being spoiled by the cane.

'You may strip naked, Roger, and don the pink knickers,' said Dido.

'What? Now?'

She nodded.

'This minute.'

Dumbfounded, I stripped off my garments, as the Ladies – though not the stony-faced Grubb – looked decorously away. I put on the precious pink panties, smelling them moist and oily, and just like an oyster, as though Miss Florence had worn them only recently. This thought caused my member to rise to full throbbing stiffness, and I covered her as best I could with the pink silk, while leaving my fesses naked as instructed. I turned to face the Ladies, and even though my hands were cupped in front of my manhood, my immodest state was obvious. I heard both Ladies stifle gasps.

Then I was instructed to bend over and touch my toes, in the school position, while Miss Florence fetched the special cane. This proved surprisingly easy to locate, for it was kept in the dining-room sideboard on top of the Dresden china. I looked up and saw a special cane indeed, or canes. To a stout central handle of braided leather, about two feet in length, were fixed four separate wooden canes, about two and a half feet in length, and half an inch thick, with wickedly forked tips. I shuddered, and gulped, knowing they would weal my bare fesses abominably.

'I shall beat him to jelly, Mummy,' said Miss Florence.

'If you must,' said Dido.

Dido positioned herself in an armchair before me, with her thighs and Lady's place right in front of my face, and her legs scornfully crossed to give me a tempting peek of her stocking tops and the sweet distant mound of her panties, which were purple silk to match her dress. Her suspender belt was purple, too, and the black stockings seemed a deliciously sluttish variant on this harmony of colour. For a moment, I had a peek of a purple satin corset, pinched very tight and ridging her belly-skin. The points of her shoes poked inches from my face, as though she were planning to stroke me.

I felt Miss Florence's cool fingers in the waistband of her panties, pulling them further down to reveal my bottom fully bare. As she pulled them, my erect member suddenly popped from her mooring, and waggled stiff and naked to their gaze.

Miss Florence exclaimed in disgust, while Dido raised one eyebrow and suggested she fetch the ice bucket, as the panties were obviously not strong enough to contain such ardour.

Grubb wheeled over the drinks trolley and placed it under my belly, and my cock was buried in the freezing ice bucket! There was a hole at the edge of the lid, for the neck of the wine bottle, and it just fitted over my cock, so that the lid could be buckled shut, and imprison her. Despite my pain, I was still rampant and erect.

I heard Miss Florence draw a deep breath and the rustle of her robe as she lifted the canes. The four rods whistled, and I jerked fiercely in pain as their lash seared my naked buttocks. I could not restrain my squeal of agony; the canes spread as wide as a birch, but bit deeper.

'No noise, Roger,' said Dido pleasantly. 'You must take it like an Englishman.'

The second stroke lashed me; I did not cry out this time, but could not help gasping as the impact seemed to drive the breath from me. It touched me at the same welts as the first, and hurt infinitely more. My bum clenched and wriggled in my smarting. Dido lit a cigarette, and calmly blew smoke in my face. The third stroke took me; I felt my bum squirm helplessly, and Dido coolly uncrossed her legs, and let her robe fall beside her thighs.

'There is quite a difference between the idea of pain and the reality, Roger,' she said. 'Between the longing to submit to a Lady, and what that submission entails – a public beating! Before other Ladies, with your bottom bare and squirming like a maggot, and your proud cock on ice! Stiff upper lip, my boy! And no squealing!'

With that, she poked the toe of her foot right inside my mouth, almost to the back of my throat, wiggling it gaily and advising me to suck on it in submission! Trembling in pain and bliss, I did so, smelling the juicy aroma of her sweated stockings.

She laughed daintly; I tried to count the strokes; at the eleventh, I could no longer keep track. My eyes blinked to stem my tears, and my lips clenched as violently as my bum shook, to stop me crying out with the rising of my gorge at each harsh, efficient and degrading stroke. So great was my pain that I almost forgot the ice that burned my still erect penis. At each thudding stroke to my jerking bottom, the glasses on the trolley tingled merrily.

Dido's legs shifted again, replacing one foot with the other in my mouth, and through my tears I saw her open her thighs slightly – and to my astonishment, I saw the full swelling of her mound under her tight panties. Slowly, she pushed the thong of her panties aside, to reveal the bare fount, gleaming and freshly shaven, with the ripe quim lips swollen and glistening with the love juices that seeped from her open gash!

Her oil trickled sparkling down her thighs and moistened her lacy stocking tops. Then her fount was covered from my view, by her hand, which began to rub there in a slow, luxurious motion. As Dido watched me writhe in the agony of my beating, she was masturbating. And as she masturbated, her cruel caress of my mouth with her sharp shoe became more luxurious. Her hand trickled with her gash-juices; she moved her ankle and twisted her foot so that now I was forced to mouth her painfully spiked heel, that ground between my lips as though she were crushing an ant.

'I think you are doing rather well, Roger,' she said, taunting me with her open frottage.

This delicious sneer of approval stiffened my cock unbearably.

'There is probably a lot worse to come,' she said lazily, 'for you insisted on merciless, didn't you?'

'Y . . . yes, Mistress!' I gasped, in sudden pride. 'O! O! I must take a Lady's thrashing, at her pleasure.'

'Pleasure? Why, disciplining the male requires skill and hard work,' she chided. 'But it has certain . . . satisfactions, for a Lady.'

I could now see her flicking the stiff bud of her glistening wet clitty, and she parted her thighs wider, still grinding me with her heel, and grinning at me in amused disdain. Suddenly, my pride swelled as did my cock. I was thrilled to afford a Lady her exquisitely cruel pleasure, and grateful for her scorn. My bottom flamed and I squirmed more and more helplessly in my agony, joyful that my humiliance pleased two cruel Mistresses.

At each stroke, my legs now jerked straight behind my body, and I kicked wildly; Dido wondered aloud if I shouldn't be tethered or held down. I felt a strong pair of hands clamping my ankles and smelled Grubb's perfume.

'I'm glad to assist, Miss,' she said eagerly. 'There is nothing nicer than watching a wicked fellow's bare bum smart under a Lady's just lash! I'm the innocent one. There was nothing the matter with my pie, I assure you!'

So, even Grubb betrayed me, and I felt myself truly the victim of some conspiracy of sorceresses. Yet in that shame was my greatest delight: to be flogged and humiliated, held down by a serving wench, while a Lady coolly and disdainfully pleasured herself at my torment, made my pain seem glorious. And now, after dozens of those vicious cane-strokes, my plateau of agony was reached and my bottom writhed to please my Mistresses.

'He's colouring nicely, Miss,' said Grubb, and I heard myself gasp, through Dido's crushing heel-leather, my thanks for the compliment!

My head lolled down under the trolley, and I could see my Mistress's legs and Grubb's body behind me. Miss Florence's robe was unbuttoned up to her navel, revealing a delicious waspie corset in black metal-studded silk, that must have been unbearably tight on her skin, and thrust her breast-melons up superbly – and I saw her pantied mound. Grubb held me with her hands, but knelt with her face up to my Mistress's gash, and had her head squeezed between her bare thighs, with her lips on the panties, at her cooze.

The maid drew my spread legs suddenly together and held them with only one strong hand, though I needed no holding and could not resist. With her free hand, she delved beneath her frilly knickers and maid's skirt and began to masturbate, as her tongue flickered on the sopping wet crotch of Miss Florence's panties. Then I saw Miss Florence's hand descend to the panties and lower them, so that Grubb's chin and lips were buried in her luxuriant mink-hair, and her tongue busy between the shining wet quim lips, darting at the big distended button of the clitty.

'Tell me, Roger,' said Dido, panting slightly as she stroked her own clit, 'have you any other offences you wish to confess? One punishment shall purge all.'

I blurted out everything. Under the merciless rhythm of my Mistress's caning, I confessed to my intrusion into her room, my purloining the panties, robing myself in her clothing, in my adoration and longing to feel her aura. Dido said that, as a nurse, she had encountered many males who liked to be robed as Ladies, and found it rather charming.

'Though not,' she added severely, 'when law and order is offended.'

At that she breathed very heavily, and her fingers twitched at her gash, sinking deep inside the wet oily slit and quite pummelling her stiff clitty, and I saw that she was almost at climax. Suddenly, my beating faltered, the cane-strokes grew more haphazard, and I looked to see that Miss Florence's legs were shuddering at the flicking of Grubb's tongue on her naked clit, while the maid's own buttocks, well revealed under the flimsy skirt, were churning and writhing as she herself strongly masturbated. Honey welled in my balls, my cock trembled and throbbed; I breathed the heady perfume of three lustful Ladies, and the wafting odour of their stockinged feet, scented sweetly with their exudations.

'These other offences may be taken into consideration,' gasped Miss Florence, 'and a single punishment cover all. This punishment will therefore continue with a birching on the malefactor's bare bottom, without pause for relief from his caning.'

At these words, Dido sighed, then panted and groaned;

her heel kicked and bucked in my open mouth, I saw her fount gush with love oil, and her belly began to heave, as she cried out in her orgasm! My Mistress too began to squeal softly; her juices gushed on her fine black stockings, and over her ribbon of bare thigh, as Grubb's tonguing grew fiercer, and then she, too, convulsed in her spasm, followed closely by the maid herself, whose vigorous frotting had puddled the floor with juices from her own gash. I knew that, once released from my icy trap, my own balls would not be long in spurting.

My three tormentors were a picture of lust unsated, and when Ladies are lustful, they become something more than Ladies. I was ordered to rise, then roughly seized by my Mistress, and forced down to lie on my back. Miss Florence ripped her panties from my ankles, then forced up my legs, so that my thighs were pressed against my chest, and my balls and throbbing cock exposed. She pinioned me in this position, by squatting with her thighs on the backs of mine, and her feet on my shoulders, bathing me with their ripe odour.

Little folds of sweet soft flesh were pressed from her strained corset. Her swept dress tickled my naked balls; I was utterly helpless, swathed in her robe and her perfume. Grubb removed her knickers entirely, and squatted full on my face, wth her oily, sweating quim and anus pressed to my lips and nose. I felt her gushing love oils on my chin, flowing from her in a torrent. Almost at once, Dido had found a birch, a huge sheaf of crackling rods, and handed it to Miss Florence.

'No, Mummy,' said my Mistress politely, 'it is your turn. Shall you give him the Turkish birch?'

She lifted her robe, to bare my erect manhood.

'Very well,' said Dido. 'If you think he deserves it. For your information, Roger, the Turkish birch is something I learned in Mesopotamia. It is like an ordinary birching – the east of Turkey is very rich in superb, strong birch trees, around the lakes of the Caucasus, especially – except I am going to birch your naked balls.'

Smothered by Grubb's sopping quim and buttocks, I

could not protest. I jerked as though to struggle free, and whimpered in my throat, but the crushing weight of the Ladies' bodies trapped me completely. My attempts to struggle seemed to excite them, and Grubb began to writhe on my face, with the oils gushing more copiously from her quim and almost choking me. And from my Mistress's cooze, too, poured a generous stream of juices, which trickled hot on my thighs and belly, and dripped on to the throbbing bulb of my cock.

Dido picked up the birch and thrashed the air.

'This will hurt most horribly, Roger, as you can imagine,' she said. 'But you are a very wicked boy and have earned it.'

The birch swished the air and cracked smartly on to my buttocks, just below my balls. The pain on my naked skin was agony, yet, in my dread of what was to come, I scarcely reacted. She took me again, right on my skin already purpled by the fourfold cane.

'Missed,' she said.

Again and again, she birched my bare bum on exactly the same place, and my tears mingled with the streams of the squirming Grubb's love juice. I felt as though I were flayed alive, as if the caning had robbed me even of the tender portion of skin by which my bottom could resist the cruel kiss of the birch. As I squirmed helplessly, Grubb shifted and pushed the swollen bud of her clitty right into my mouth, against my tongue, and, as I gagged, my tongue flickered desperately against its throbbing stiffness, making her moan with delight as she pressed her bum to my face to crush me all the harder.

'Frig me, you slut,' hissed my Mistress. 'Come on, do me on my clitty.'

I felt Grubb's arm move, and then my Mistress's body began to sway as she pinioned me, and she moaned, 'O yes, do my clitty, she's so stiff, bring me off, you dirty bitch . . .'

'Missed,' said Dido again, in mild surprise. 'Dear, dear.'

I must have taken over forty strokes with the birch, and my bare nates were on fire with pain, yet still my balls were untouched.

'This time,' said Dido, panting harshly as she herself masturbated in time with my flogging. 'This time . . .'

The birch swished, and landed on my balls! But in mockery, crueller than any whipstroke. She laughed as she gently tickled my straining ball-sac with the tips of the birch. This was followed by a flurry of strokes to my bare bum, that had me squealing and writhing. Then there was another tickle of my balls, and one to the bulb of my cock, and then another flurry to bum.

'You naughty, naughty boy,' she murmured. 'We must have proper law and order . . .'

I felt Grubb writhe on my face, my Mistress too groaned as her clitty was diddled; there was a pause in the birch strokes, and Dido herself pressed her naked sopping cooze-lips to my balls, sitting hard on them and squashing them as she writhed on my ball-sac, pressing her clitty against me in sharp, deft strokes. One fingertip began to stroke my straining peehole, causing me an excruciating tickling in my cock and squashed balls, and I whimpered and moaned as I felt my cream rise.

Then all three Ladies panted more and more harshly, their several writhings grew fiercer on my trapped body, and I was drenched in their flows of oily warm cooze-juice. Dido's finger drummed on my peehole; I felt a drop of seed, then another and, finally, I could restrain myself no longer, and my cock throbbed and jerked as I spurted my entire bounty of hot cream all over her waiting fingers. My cries, muffled by Grubb's squashing buttocks and quim, were joined by the sharp wails of pleasure from each Lady, as they shuddered on me in their own spasms.

At length, I was permitted to rise, dripping and sobbing, to find my Ladies demure and smoothing their robes, inspecting me as though I were some vermin who had crept in. Dido gave me my Mistress's panties to wipe myself of my shame; when I had done so, I knelt and kissed my Mistress's shoed and ripe-scented stockinged feet, and handed the garment back to her. She allowed me to kiss and lick her feet for a while in submission, as Dido wondered how my bum had got so awfully black. Then my

Mistress scornfully brushed away my hand holding the panties.

'O, that old rag!' she cried. 'You may dispose of that, I've no use for it!'

My white tie and tails felt awfully silly as I sat down again for Grubb to serve pudding.

Dido put her lips to my ear, and whispered, 'She is a very naughty girl – Flossie, I mean. Headstrong, you know. Why, I observed what happened with Grubb and you, and her unapproved punishment. We must have words in private, Roger, and discuss how best to discipline the naughty girl. She's too much of a handful for me! A male's hand is needed.'

I was quite dumbstruck, and could only nod politely.

'I did admire you, though,' she whispered. 'Taking it like an Englishman, to indulge the silly harlot.'

Then she spoke aloud, as Grubb committed yet another error and spilt the pudding.

'I was most impressed by your honesty, Roger. I mean, confessing that you like to wear a Lady's things. Grubb, as you see, is quite hopeless, and Mrs Mantle is a very strict guest. Now I have solved the problem of who shall be maid when she comes to tea!'

6

Maid in Frillies

'There!' cried Dido. 'You are as pretty as a picture, Roger. Isn't he, Florence?'

A faint smile curled on my Mistress's lip. Dido gave me permission to inspect myself in the mirror, and I saw a strange creature who fussed with garter straps and flounces and ribbons; smoothed her frilly little skirt, which promptly bobbed up again, nervously inspected sheer silk stockings, and wobbled on perilous high heels. The brassiere of my corselage bulged with flower petals plucked by Dido herself, and lush sandy tresses from my perruque cascaded over my starched white blouse. I looked doubtfully at the protruberance of my male organ beneath my petticoat, skirt, and apron.

'I'm not sure, Mistress,' I said doubtfully.

'Nonsense!' cried Dido, clapping her hands in delight. 'And call me Miss, now that you are a proper maid. Mistress is for males.'

My bottom still smarted fearfully from the episode of my 'Berkshire pie', although, in the few days since, my relations with my two Ladies had been one of the usual cool cordiality. They had not alluded to my chastisement, even though aware, from my grimaces, of the discomfort I felt even in sitting down with them to dinner. Yet there was a slight tension between the two Ladies, and I was mindful of Dido's words concerning Miss Florence's imperfection.

A submissive male is as glad as any other for a pause between the thrashings his bum has merited, and I was glad of this respite, as well as being apprehensive about my role as maid for the service of the guest Mrs Mantle. I felt like a toy or plaything of these two Ladies, still in silent conspiracy to mock me, despite their own disagreements: the sensation was not disagreeable to me.

'There is nothing to be worried about, Roger,' said Dido. 'If you are discovered – what then? The trick is mine.'

'Ours, Mummy,' insisted Miss Florence.

Her gaze rested on my prominent bulge.

'Yes, that horrid trick,' she murmured.

Dido made me lift my skirts. My naked cock sprang into view and, thrilled by my exposure in Lady's dress, I felt her rise to a throbbing stiffness, and blushed heartily. Dido took an ice-cold serving spoon and tapped hard on my peehole several times, then proceeded to tap all the way down my shaft like a railway engineer, until she attended to my straining balls. The shock of this cold impact had the desired effect of softening me, and she laughed and said it was an old nurse's trick.

Now she took a roll of bandage, with a thin wire running down the middle, and wound it very tightly round my cock-shaft, causing me to wince. The balls, too, were enveloped, until my manhood was a tight, wired package. She then took a roll of pure wire and wrapped the cock a second time, to just below my helmet, drew the wire down through my furrow, across my anus bud and up to my waist, where she looped it in a belt, or harness. My cock was thus pressed tightly in my crevice, with my helmet in my furrow! It was quite painful, and I said so. Miss Florence smiled wide, and Dido said I was swaddled in a 'gaffe', and my cock would pass for a big Lady's mound, like Grubb's.

She said I was to have a treat, and produced the pink knickers which had caused me so much distress! She slipped them on me; my bandaged cock did indeed look like the swelling mound of a well-formed Lady.

'Pink knickers under black and white is rather naughty,' she said impishly, 'and will give Mrs Mantle a shock.'

I looked at myself again, and felt very strange – I was quite attractive! I was demure and pretty, the very picture of submission. I teetered down the stairs to the pantry, where Grubb was busy with cakes and scones; she looked at me with a grin and promptly touched the bulge of my cock, or fount, and said, 'Who's a pretty maid, then?'

'Do not be facetious, Grubb,' I replied.

'Eh?'

'I mean . . . O, Grubb, do I look all right? Is my hair proper, my skirt not too short or too long? My stockings smooth? I am so confused, and you mustn't tease me!'

'You'll do,' said Grubb, tapping my mound very mischievously, as it made my bound cock tingle and swell – only a little, but most uncomfortably.

The doorbell chimed; I heard the loud 'Hulloo!' of Mrs Mantle's voice. I rushed to open the door, with a curtsy, and she swept past me without a glance, to be greeted by my Ladies.

'I'm in the mood for tea,' she boomed, after I took charge of her coat and gloves, again without scrutiny of my person. 'Had to thrash a stable boy, the idle whelp – thirsty work.'

'On the bare, Mrs Mantle?' said my Mistress sweetly. 'I do hope so.'

'Only way with a male,' said the newcomer warmly. 'Have to keep 'em on their toes – as it were.'

She laughed heartily at her own pleasantry.

Soon I bustled in with the tea things, was introduced as 'the new skivvy, Ruggiera', and blushed genuinely when Mrs Mantle pronounced me a 'pretty little thing'. She was a handsome Lady, imposing in the manner of the English gentlewoman, ripe of breast and croup, over which swirled a modest but fetching summer frock and jacket in light brown cotton, but with boots and spurs, and a riding crop that dangled at her waist so naturally as to seem part of her.

Her hair was short and bobbed, framing a well-tanned face whose handsome bones spoke of easy authority. Her age was perhaps mid-thirties, and she was superbly youthful for it. I fussed around her in my service of tea, doing my best to adopt the posture and movements of a submissive maid. Despite this, her rude healthy perfume caused my member to tingle in excitement at her closeness, and I had to concentrate on things other than female beauty, to avoid embarrassment. But as I grew more confident in my role, I was thrilled that the postures of submission seemed to come naturally to me, and I was accepted as a true maid.

It was only then, I think, that I first realised the true beauty of femaleness, that is, freed as I was from the strutting arrogance of my male self, and introduced to a world of smiles and hints and glances and little flutterings of the eyes . . . the world of subtle femininity, in fact. I scraped and bowed and averted my gaze in shy humiliance, and so active was I in my new role that I gave way to that very feminine foible, of becoming flustered. When confused, males become belligerent and stupid, but Ladies become flustered, throwing their confusion back on their confuser.

A serving-maid, unfortunately, has limited gain from being flustered. What occurred was trifling – it may, or may not, have been fate, as females are fond of interpreting events – at any rate, I spilt some tea and a scone containing raspberry jam and clotted cream all over Mrs Mantle's frock. A Lady would ensure that the whole thing seemed Mrs Mantle's own fault; as a mere serving wench, I was not allowed that luxury.

Dido affected surprise and embarrassment, Miss Florence sneered and tossed her head in contempt; only Mrs Mantle approached the matter in a businesslike fashion. It was agreed that her outer skirt must be washed and dried in the sun. Opining that we were all 'gels' together, she unconcernedly stepped out of it, revealing her pale muslin petticoat beneath, with a fetching frilly hem, and the skirt was transported to Grubb for cleaning.

She slapped my bottom, not unkindly.

'This gel,' she said briskly, 'shall of course make amends. It is a matter of law and order amongst the serving classes, who must be taught propriety. Mantle says so, and I agree.'

I flushed and bit my lip, in genuine shame at my clumsiness. I did so want to be a proper Lady! I mumbled my excuses (in Italian, to make me seem more helpless) and Mrs Mantle said that a foreign gel was doubly in need of lessons in English manners.

'I think she needs a whopping, Ladies,' she announced to Miss Florence and Dido, who tried to hide the gleam in their eyes. 'You do whop her, don't you?'

'Why, yes, Mrs Mantle,' they said both at once.

'Please do our house the honour of attending to our maid's chastisement, Mrs Mantle,' said Dido sweetly.

'Well, then!' cried Mrs Mantle, unhooking her riding crop. 'Bend over, you naughty slut! I take it she understands bend over?'

Dido said 'she' understood it very well.

I bent over, sniffing a little, and touched my toes. I was trembling. Mrs Mantle pulled up my skimpy skirt and petticoat, to reveal my pink-knickered bum, upon which she remarked that they were too pretty for a maid, but supposed it was the foreign custom. She pulled the knickers up very tight into my furrow, so that my buttocks were almost completely exposed.

'Since she's your gel, I won't thrash her on the bare, for modesty,' Mrs Mantle pronounced virtuously, 'but with knickers pulled well up, it's the same sort of thing. And then you save on knickers, as they don't get shredded by the crop. Don't gels these days go through a lot of knickers! At least, my Bernice does. Rarely bother with the things myself. Mantle says he prefers the wind whistling through the rigging! My, what a pretty bum! Bit small for a gel's, but well marked, so I dare say she is no stranger to whopping after all.'

Dido agreed that 'she' was well accustomed to the lash.

'Then a half-dozen dozen will put a pretty blush on her,' said Mrs Mantle with relish as she lifted her crop. I saw that it had a metal tip in the shape of an 'M', like a branding iron, before it descended on my bared buttocks.

I winced as the first cut took me very hard; again at the second, harder still; the third maintained the same force, as she found her flogging rhythm. The metal tip of the crop added a painful zest to a beating that her strong muscled arm already made painful enough, and I could not stop my buttocks from clenching, and, as the lashes rained on my helpless bare bum-skin, from squirming quite dramatically. Since I was a girl, this went unchided, as did my high squeals and the tears which moistened my cheeks as I sobbed under the harsh whipping.

'Yes – most pretty bum, just like a boy's,' said Mrs Mantle as she paused to help herself to a cake, the consumption of which in no way inhibited the force of her beating.

I took my prescribed six dozen from her smarting crop, in tearful writhing distress, and afterwards bowed low and curtsied to my chastiser, whispering '*grazie, signora*'.

'Well, she does have some manners,' exclaimed Mrs Mantle, and produced a silk hankie with which she wiped away my tears.

'There, there, dear, you'll be a good girl in future, won't you?' she murmured, stroking my bare, wealed bottom for quite a long time, and I saw that her face was well flushed. Then she drew up my knickers properly, and smoothed my skirts for me, saying that those knickers looked rather familiar. Her hand was trembling; she stroked my bottom through the thin knicker silk, and I stayed in position so that she could do so. Suddenly she went 'hmmph!' and smartly withdrew her caressing hand, to smack into a whole plate of cakes, that spilt over her muslin petticoat!

Her blush deepened.

'I suppose that was no one's fault but mine,' she said with a frown. 'But I suppose you'd better clean this petticoat too.'

I led her to the scullery, which Grubb had absented to attend to the top-skirt. She stepped out of her jam-stained petticoat, quite unconcerned at her nudity, and handed me the garment for cleaning. She wore no knickers underneath it. 'Can't go back to tea starkers,' she said, 'so I'll just stay and watch.'

I washed her petticoat carefully in the basin, but unable to keep my eyes from her huge curly mink which she displayed quite unashamedly, as though I did not exist. Lolling with thighs apart in the small armchair, she lit a cigarette and puffed contentedly, idly stroking and scratching the curly bush at her fount. Her croup beneath was very large and firm, with muscled rider's thighs.

'I confess,' she mused, through a blue plume of smoke, 'that I do like thrashing a juicy bare bum, my pet. Especially a male's, when I make them blub and wriggle. The serving classes need it just like Ladies and gentlemen, and it is a most proper exercise.'

I murmured that it was my duty as a wench to serve a Lady in all things.

'But you can't enjoy being thrashed,' she said. 'Only boys like that . . . or some.'

I answered that if my squirming girl's bottom pleased a Lady, then it was also my pleasure.

'Hmmph!' she said softly after a while of smoking. 'Perhaps you'd like to visit my home on your day off, maid. Your bum is juicier than most gels', and . . . my purse is not unkind.'

I curtsied and said that would give me great joy. Then I wrung out the petticoat and went outside to hang it in the sunshine. When I returned, Mrs Mantle told me that as we waited for it to dry, I should polish her boots. I knelt and applied myself to the task with brushes and cream, my bum wiggling in the air, and as I worked, I felt the lazy tickle of her crop in my pantied furrow.

'Such a pretty, pretty bum,' she mused. 'Yes, I insist you call on me, Miss. You must be quite lonely, in a foreign land. No young men . . . alone at night, and diddling yourself a lot, I suppose. You know – all of us do it – rubbing yourself, maid, for pleasure and company . . .'

'Sometimes other girls are better company, Madam,' I said.

I looked up and smiled, but cast my eyes down when I saw Mrs Mantle's hand cupping her Lady's place and gently rubbing. She told me softly to continue my work and keep my bum high, and I obeyed, feeling my own member stiffen painfully in her bonds at the thought that the sight of me caused this Lady pleasure.

She was tickling herself at her mink as though it were the most natural thing in the world, and I affected not to notice, even when she announced that a good 'diddle' was the heartiest pleasure, especially amongst girls, and she told her Bernice not to be ashamed of diddling herself, as all young girls, with their lustful instincts, did it tremendously. When I had buffed the leather, I applied my tongue to her boots, and licked them to a gleaming shine, lifting her surprisingly dainty feet and licking the soles and heels as well.

'I know where I have seen those knickers before,' she said suddenly. 'I recognise the stitching – they belong to my daughter Bernice! How on earth did you get them?'

I replied that they were a gift from my Mistress.

'Ah! Florence and Bernice go riding together – must have got switched by mistake.'

I looked up, and saw that Mrs Mantle's fingers were actually inside her gash-lips, and that her thighs and bum were writhing gently in her chair as she openly masturbated! She smiled at me quite gaily.

'Gels frig a lot. It is the country air – and I am a country gel. Come, Ruggiera, admit that you do it too.'

I blushed and smiled, but said nothing.

'Frigging your clitty every night, eh? It is healthy and natural, my maid. And your bum's so pretty, why, the sight of her red and wriggling under my crop made me quite juicy myself! And I am not in the habit of avoiding satisfaction. Pull your knickers up high, there's a dear – that bare bum squirming and jerking so beautifully . . . O! O! Beating, even just the thought of beating, gets me excited. I don't care if you mind. Ahh . . .'

Silently, she took my hand and drew it to her wet gash, placing my fingers against her clitty, which was stiff like a delicious little acorn under her forest of curly mink-hairs. I did not resist, and she shivered at my touch.

'Good girl,' she whispered, stroking my wig, 'good girl . . .'

I plunged my face between her naked quivering thighs, and drank her juices as I tongued her clitty very fast and firmly! She shuddered and moaned loudly.

'But you, Mistress, have not been a good girl, have you?' I said slyly, feeling a rush of daring, as I paused for breath.

'Why, you impudent – O, lick my clitty, maid . . . don't stop!'

'I mean, spilling the teacakes like a clumsy schoolgirl! Does Mr Mantle never take the crop to your bum when you are a naughty girl?'

'Me? A naughty girl?'

Then she giggled, panting hard.

'Yes . . . O, O yes, he does, you sweet slut. Sometimes I am quite a naughty girl indeed. But that shall be our secret, if you please.'

My hand snaked around her furrow and found the stiff pucker of her anus, where I inserted my index finger to the depth of an inch, and began to tickle her.

'O! O!' she cried, her magnificent bare croup squirming on my hand. 'You are the naughty one . . . that is gorgeous and wicked. Tickling my bumhole! Such a giddy thing!'

'We are all gels, together, *signora*,' I whispered. 'Aren't we?'

'Yes . . .'

'And sometimes, we all need our bottoms whopped. Even a married Lady.'

'Yes . . . yes, we do . . .'

She moaned louder and longer, and with fervent strokes of my tongue, my finger now buried fully in her anus and thrusting like a little penis, I made her gasp and wriggle as her quim gushed with fragrant juices over my lapping mouth, and brought her to a shivering, whimpering climax.

'O yes! Lick me, whop me . . . O, yes . . .' she cried, her fingers clutching me to her.

Afterwards, I tidied myself and fetched her petticoat which had dried satisfactorily, then mopped the oily juices that bathed her thighs and fount. The bushy tresses of her mink were quite sopping, and I squeezed them to wring them like the petticoat. Now she turned round, and I saw the full magnificence of her naked croup, the peach well marbled with crop marks, and the faint imprint of 'M' all over the naked fesses. She saw my glance, and blushed.

'I shall indeed call on you, Mistress,' I said with another bow, 'if I am of a mind to. That is, I think, when Mr Mantle is away, and gels can be gels . . .'

I touched her naked buttocks, and she shivered, sighing.

'Some bums are so beautiful that whopping is almost too good for them, Madam,' I said. '*Almost* . . .'

'You promise you'll come soon? Promise, maid?' she whispered.

I looked at her levelly, said nothing, but lowered my eyes. She slipped half-a-crown into my pink panties, and pushed it into my furrow.

'Our little secret,' she said with a blush of shame.

Mrs Mantle departed very subdued after her tea, leaving my Ladies to exchange polite but frosty smiles. Dido said she had overheard Mrs Mantle admire Miss Florence's pink panties on my bottom, and that they were very like her daughter Bernice's . . .

'If they *are* yours, Florence,' she said. 'What secrets simple knickers may contain!'

Miss Florence blushed fiery crimson, and swept from the room.

'You did very well as a Lady's maid, Roger,' said Dido, 'despite your slight mishap. Do you think you were punished enough for it, though?'

'That is for you to know, and me to find out, Mistress,' I said, curtsying as prettily as I could, which made Dido clap her hands in delight.

'O!' she cried. 'You are perfect as a Lady's maid! As a Lady!'

'Does that mean I am to continue to serve you as maid, Mistress?' I murmured.

'That, Roger, is for me to know, and you to find out,' she whispered.

One evening a few days later, as I was about to dress for dinner, there was a rap on my door. I was naked, and before I could call out, Dido opened the door and entered, carrying her nurse's bag. She put the bag down and held a mischievous finger to her lips, then took from it a lovely muslin dress in yellow, with lemon bows and ribbons and flounces at arms and hem; a matching corset and panties in paler yellow, and a pair of yellow high-heeled shoes!

'I thought you might look nice in a different colour,' she said casually. 'And yellow is a very progressive colour, you know, for after dinner we are going to the meeting of the Virginia Water Progressives. Strictly ladies only – so you must go as one of us.'

She reached down and touched my penis.

'Is your poor petal still sore after her binding as a maid?' she said.

Before I could assure her my 'petal' was not sore, she continued, 'She looks all raw. It is hard being a Lady! But I have some lotion for her.'

She made me lie on the bed, with my cock towards her, and by now I was stiffening rapidly, especially as she lifted her pleated blue skirt to reveal her shaven fount unadorned by knickers. She pointed to the wet lips of her gash.

'The lotion is here, Roger,' she said. 'It is time to pick your flower again, so that you won't embarrass yourself by standing up amongst all the Ladies this evening.'

She took hold of the shaft of my cock and began to rub vigorously, at the same time tickling my balls with a gossamer touch. I groaned, and my shaft throbbed stiff.

'You *are* a naughty girl,' she panted, now rubbing her own clitty, which stood dark and stiff amid her swollen quim lips.

Suddenly, she straddled me and sank down heavily, her open thighs crushing my balls as she plunged my cock inside her to its hilt. I felt her slit gush with oily love juice; her skirt swished and caressed my flesh as she masturbated blatantly and energetically, slapping the tight little clit-bud with vigorous caress of her fingertips. She bounced and bucked on me with fervent strokes, her buttocks slapping my thighs, until very shortly she groaned, her belly fluttered and heaved, and she cried out, 'Yes, yes! I'm coming! Yes! O . . .'

And as suddenly as she had mounted me, she was off me, leaving my cock throbbing raw and stiff and unsatisfied!

'There!' she gasped, her eyes heavy with lust. 'I needed that! No preamble, Roger, no honeyed words and poetry and suchlike. A stiff cock, no matter whose – my dripping gash – and fuck! It is so wicked and exciting, and so very necessary.'

I buried my head between her thighs, and sucked the juices from her open gash.

'But we can't leave your poor petal like that,' she cooed, shifting me, and at once fastened her lips around my bulb, licking my peehole and pressing my shaft with her mouth until with equal suddenness, I spurted in her throat, watching her bobbing motions as she swallowed my cream.

'Both of us done!' she said, wiping her lips with her fingers and licking them. 'Don't clean off my juices, it will make you smell more like a Lady. But before you dress, I have a lesson to teach you, so that you may better understand our Ladies' deliberations this evening.'

I thanked her and said my cock was hers to use as she pleased.

'And Grubb's too?' she said with a wry smile. 'I saw you, Roger – your lovely, brutal maleness, as you poked the maid. And I had such a lovely frig while I watched – quite spoiled my stockings with my quim juice, you naughty girl!'

I protested that I had acted to please the maid, and Dido said that girls did naughty things to please, and must still be punished for it. She reached into her bag, and I asked if I was to be thrashed. She ran her fingers tenderly over my wealed bum, and said that I had thrashing enough for a while, and that I was to squirm for her in a different way.

'Mrs Mantle didn't really make you squirm that day, maid,' she said, 'but now I shall. When I watched you poke that poor maid's bum with that dreadful *thing* of yours, I thought you do not yet know what it *really* feels like to submit as a Lady. After this, you will be well versed and able to understand our concern for the proper control of the male.'

She drew from her back a long, shining hygienic appliance.

'This, Roger, is known as a dildo,' she said.

I peered closely; it was a device of two black rubber cylinders or prongs, shaped like males' cocks, and strikingly similar in dimension and shape to my own! She ordered me to turn on my belly, and spread the cheeks of my bum so that she could see my pucker. I did so, trembling in genuine alarm.

'You mean to poke *me* in the bumhole, Mistress?'

'Yes.'

'But I've never . . .'

'I don't believe you. Deceitful girl!'

'I swear!'

'Then it will be all the more painful and humiliating, Roger,' she whispered. 'You do want to wear your pretty new dress and knickers and everything for me, don't you?'

'O, yes!'

'Well, then!' she exclaimed, as though settling the matter.

She stroked the massive rubber shafts of the dildo, and smiled. Then she unfastened her skirt completely and laid it aside, her arse-globes gleaming as I watched. I turned my head in horrified fascination as she took one of the prongs and parted her quim lips, played at the wet channel of her gash and at her nubbin with little sighs of contentment, then firmly thrust the black shaft all the way into her slit, with a sigh of greater contentment.

She strapped the device by a cord around her waist, so that the second prong stood up from her gash like a giant penis, framed prettily by her garters and stocking tops, and the bare flesh beneath. She had her shoes on and playfully lifted her agile leg to poke one heel inside my spread bumhole! It hurt terribly. I groaned, and she laughed rather scornfully, saying a mere Lady's heel was nothing at all. She wriggled the heel very deep and painfully inside my anus, and, despite my squirming and discomfort, I felt my cock stiffen hard.

Then she scissored her thighs and brought up her other

leg and, to my horror, I felt her second pointed heel join the first, squeezing beside it deep into my anus, so that my bum-skin was stretched in agony, tight as a drum! Vigorously, she poked my bumhole with both heels; I howled in anguish, but my penis throbbed and my balls ached with welling sperm as though my erection was about to burst me . . .

Dido bum-heeled me most severely, until I was squirming in delicious pain, and she said that was only a foretaste of a proper bumming. She put her fingers to her quim and soaked them in her love juice, with which she oiled the shaft that was to penetrate me. To be penetrated, and by a Lady . . . such a fierce yet thrilling word. I whimpered to her that my bum had never been poked before. There was a slithering plop as she removed her heels from the elastic clutch of my bumhole.

'Protest all you want,' she said lazily. 'It shan't do you any good.'

'I merely advise, Mistress, I do not protest,' I said with as much dignity as I could.

'You might soon,' she said.

I gasped and yelped as I felt the huge cold tip of the dildo burst into the tender opening of my bumhole. She laughed more, and said that was only an inch. Then she pushed very hard, the dildo slid into my groaning shaft, and the pain was indescribable.

'O, it's worse than the birch,' I moaned. 'Please, Mistress, please . . .'

'Please, what?' she asked, and I realised that I did not know.

The prong seemed stuck; she ordered me to relax my bum muscle, which I did as best I could, but her thrusts only seemed to increase my bumhole's resistance to the invader. I moaned that it was no good, and she wouldn't fit (I thought of the horrid shaft as hers!) but she snapped that I had buggered Grubb to the hilt, and my anus could take it too.

Suddenly I gasped, not in pain but in relief that was almost joyful, for, as if obeying an unspoken command, my anus suddenly yielded to her, and I felt the huge dildo sink in one giddy plunge right to the root of my belly. It was the same rush that I had felt when my own cock was inside Grubb's bumhole: a sudden joyful submission to pain and fullness.

If I say the pain was indescribable, then so was my joy. I had submitted in the most degraded fashion possible to my Mistress, and was helpless under her rule. To be buggered! The ultimate terror for any male, yet – under a dominant Lady – the ultimate joy!

Her haunches began to buck as she poked me in the bumhole, even harder than my attendance on Grubb's willing arse-shaft.

'Hurt much?' she panted.

'You'll split me, Mistress!' I squealed. 'O! O! How it hurts!'

She chuckled and flicked the tip of my stiff cock, saying casually that a bum-poking usually made a male spurt. I could scarcely believe it, yet there was a tickling in my balls, stranger than anything I had known. Suddenly, she withdrew without any warning, her dildo making a plop as it emerged from my bumhole, and at once ordered me to turn round and lie on my back, with my thighs raised, just like a girl for poking.

'Buggery is not normally done in the missionary position,' she said, 'but I like to see the tears on a male's face.'

Straddling me, as a male would a compliant female, she inserted the prong again, and this time it slid into my anus with no resistance at all, rather a grasp of welcome. My cock lay hard against my belly, and her own fount banged against my stiff balls as she slapped and thrust into me. I could see the naked stiff bud of her clitty rubbing against her own dildo as it slid in and out of her gash, oiled by her copious flood of love juice that moistened my balls and cock. There was a dribble of saliva at the corner of her slack open mouth as she buggered me, that trickled prettily down her chin.

'O! Please . . .' I moaned again, unable to help it.

'Yes, Roger?' she gasped.

'Please . . . don't stop,' I whimpered.

She grinned fiercely.

'Now you truly are a girl,' she hissed.

Her hand squeezed the shaft of my cock, while her thumb caressed my peehole, and she began to rub vigorously up and down. As she powerfully buggered me, her hand stretched my prepuce back to its fullest extent in one swift motion, which made me cry out in surprised discomfort, yet her whispered desire to see my cock and birthmark in full nudity was very thrilling. She rubbed my cock, drawing the prepuce right up and back with each stroke, as the pounding pressure of her shaft drummed in my squirming, clenching bumhole, now squeezing the dildo as if to suck my Mistress further into me. The tickling in my balls grew unbearably sharp, and I gasped that she was going to make me come.

'Come, Roger, come for me,' she cooed and, at that, my cock bucked and I spurted my cream into her waiting fingers, my voice howling in the sweetness of my spasm. She did not cease her arse-fucking, but put her glistening fingers to her lips, and licked my sperm, then to her clitty, where she rubbed herself with my cream and suddenly, with fierce, practised strokes, masturbated to her own shuddering orgasm. With one final and conclusive thrust into my bumhole, my ordeal of submission was at an end.

Now I lay groaning and feeling utterly drained as she removed and wiped clean her dildos, dressed herself, and repacked her nurse's bag. Briskly, she said it was time to dress in my new yellow things. She corsed me very tightly, then said she must bandage my cock, but less harshly than before, as my yellow skirt was not so skimpy as the maid's frilly. It is lovely to be dressed as a Lady, by a Lady! She made sure that my stockings and panties were smooth, my skirts proper, and my wig straight. This was covered by a lovely broad summer bonnet, and, when I looked in the glass, again I saw a new person. I said to Dido that it must be wonderful to be a female, and become a new woman with every change of clothing, and she said she felt sorry for us poor drab males.

'We females can be a million different women, but you can only be one thing! Except when you dress up for theatricals – which is why males like playacting.'

She tapped my cock.

'Happily, that one thing is the most important . . .'

Suddenly, her face darkened and she ordered me to place myself over her knee. Bewildered, I obeyed and took position, whereupon she drew down my new yellow knickers and began to spank my bare bum with neither ceremony nor explanation.

'Damn you, Roger,' she moaned, 'damn that cock and that bum . . .'

I wriggled a little, but her spanking was furious rather than hard, even though it extended to nearly a hundred and fifty slaps, so that I smarted quite a lot when she ceased, and I looked up, to see tears in her eyes.

'Mistress!' I cried. 'Why ever did you spank me? Have I offended?'

She stroked my reddened bum, and bent down to kiss it, then lick my balls, before carefully drawing up my knickers again.

'O, Roger,' she whispered, 'you wouldn't understand. Your Mistress Florence thrashes you because she hates men. An imperfection for which I intend to make her smart one day.'

'Thrashes me? But I assure you . . .'

'Don't pretend, boy. There are no secrets in this house, and I know what you have been about,' she said wryly. 'My trouble is that *I* don't hate men at all . . .'

7

The Naked Truth

Dinner passed without incident; my Mistress Florence was her usual indifferent self, and did not deign to notice my pretty yellow costume, although Dido bubbled with compliments; even Grubb in her ill-fitting frillies simpered a little enviously. I took Miss Florence's normality as the greatest compliment, as it meant my robing was accepted, or at least that nothing could dent her superb contempt for me. She did make one or two acid remarks about the imminent meeting of the Progressive Ladies, and how all unseemly males could profit from a lesson in law and order.

Dido drove us to the meeting, which was not far away, in a rather grander house than Virginia Lodge. We parked in front of the mansion, and our door was opened by a young liveried fellow of about Miss Florence's age. I was going to wish him the time of day in the English 'maty' fashion when I realised he was leering concupiscently at me! I blushed and smoothed my skirt, and entered the house with quite ladylike hauteur.

Imagine my surprise when we were greeted by our hostess: none other than Mrs Mantle! She was quite different from our last encounter; now, arrayed in stunning simplicity in a little black cocktail dress, with thin straps over her bare shoulders, she looked scarcely older than her daughter Bernice, who accompanied her. I gulped, fearing she would recognise me, as I was introduced as Miss Carpaccio, daughter of one of the Major's continental business friends; but she did not – such is the power of female raiment. I found that if I spoke very softly, almost whispering, and tightened my throat, I was able to make my rather deep voice twist into a kind of female contralto. Bernice, down briefly from her college at Cambridge, was quite unlike her buxom and well-muscled mother; she was dark of hair and pale, or artistic, of complexion, tall and willowy like a lovely slender sapling, and quite towered over her mother and myself, and even gave an inch or two to Miss Florence.

I could not help but notice her figure, skimpily cased as it was in a cocktail dress just like her mother's; her breasts and bum were curious, pointing out quite pertly from an otherwise reed-like frame, and the bum in particular looked juicy and tempting, like two hard apples on the slender but sturdy legs and thighs which rippled intriguingly. I detected no sign of undergarments, and the nipples stood out quite clearly, like porcelain eggcups turned upside down.

Miss Bernice cast a quizzical eye over me, possessed I dare say of the curiosity that women share with men about the female body. I did a good imitation of a Lady: preening and primping, and shifting nervously, and patting my bum and dress hem, and it was not at all an act.

There were about six Ladies, all of whom were cordially introduced, and all dressed as though for a dinner or party. These being progressive Ladies, we were served wine. This was served by the grinning, though now rather sheepish, lad who had opened our car door, and whose name it seemed was Denton. Mrs Mantle barked at him as she would at a parlour-maid; I gathered that Mr Mantle was not present, and Mrs Mantle had decided to give the female staff the evening off. We made small talk, and anxiously awaited the arrival of the great Miss Alice Arbiter, a very progressive Lady indeed, since as well as being a renowned thinker and academic, she was also very rich.

Miss Arbiter eventually made her appearance, throwing her coat to the male servant with every appearance of disdain; she was greeted with ooh's of delight. Her manner was gracious; she even addressed some words to me in fluent Italian, informing me that she owned property in Venice and at Lake Como. Certainly, she struck me as a very imposing person: tall as Miss Bernice, yet with muscled sinewy grace, and with a shock of fiery blonde hair, bleached by the sun, that recalled Grubb's. It was done in a lovely forest of ringlets, and I now knew where Dido had the inspiration for her own 'Grecian' look.

If all the others were dressed up, Miss Arbiter was dressed down; that is, she wore only a simple grey smock of thin cotton, rather like a Roman toga, with sandalled feet on bare legs. Her dress, though it swirled loosely, did nothing at all to hide her figure – I should say voluptuous, but that would be doing discredit to the word. Her breasts were firm, jutting mountains; the croup, orbs of muscled strength and full rounded beauty. It was evident that under her dress she was naked, except for some kind of girdle or belt at her waist. Her nod to fashion, however, was the sandals: not simple peasant shoes, but intricately strapped, ribbed and jewelled affairs of dainty morocco, on heels as high as those of Dido or my Mistress!

She accepted a glass of wine and toasted the Progressive Ladies of Virginia Water, and progressive Ladies in general, with a slight Australian accent: I was informed that Miss Arbiter had extensive interests in the Antipodes and travelled a lot. Her forthright tones went well with her openness and ease of manner. She mentioned that Australia was a very exciting melting pot, with settlers from all sorts of places, especially Italy.

It was very hot, and the French windows were open; outside was the unmistakable sound of crickets, upon which I mischievously remarked. Mrs Mantle informed me that this part of Surrey was quite infested with the creatures! Miss Alice Arbiter scoffed that for crickets it was necessary to visit the outback of Queensland, where they were brutes as big as shoe boxes.

'And you should see them fuck,' she said quite casually. 'It is like all-in wrestling.'

There was a frisson of progressive excitement at Miss

Arbiter's casual but elegant use of this word. Mrs Mantle said that they were honoured by her visit and looking forward to her lecture, and Miss Arbiter scoffed again.

'Lecture!' she exclaimed. 'That implies a power relationship between the lecturer and the lectured – but we are all girls together, and may exchange views openly and freely. I will, of course, make some introductory remarks to get the ball rolling.'

With that, she stood up, and with one swift motion, pulled her dress over her head, and stood before us completely naked, except for a studded leather belt, coiled around her bare belly! There were little murmurs of mischievous astonishment, coupled with admiration for her daring and her superb physique.

'I always lecture in the nude,' she said simply. 'In Australia, where I lecture at various progressive institutes, we have the climate for it: more important, it helps me to think, and absolves me from any of the folderol of academic rank – caps, gowns, and such rot. Male inventions all, a pretence of authority. My words, Ladies, are my only authority, my person naked as my spirit. Women should not fear being nude amongst themselves, nor should they fear to express their affection for each other – the caresses of Ladies are often more sensuous and tender than the brute pokings of an inflamed male.'

I saw Miss Bernice's eyes narrow and her lips curl in private satisfaction. However, I could not help contemplating Miss Arbiter's nudity with an unfeminine interest and, despite my cock's light binding, felt a stirring in my shaft and a nice tickling in my balls. Clothed, she impressed; nude, she was superb!

Her long, slender legs rippled with hard muscle, and the delicate slabs of her thighs were set apart, with a gully between them, giving her the aspect of a rider. Her mound was shaven bare like Dido's, and was deliciously plump like a pastry, with dark quim lips almost wine-coloured, and the button of the surprisingly large clitoris quite visible, like a proud jewel; I reflected that was perhaps why she shaved there, to show herself off. The breasts were truly hillocks, jutting deep and wide without need of support, and the creamy, tan flesh topped by big round nipples that stood up like red apples. The flat belly held a pleasingly extruded navel that poked out like a smaller fruit to match her nipples, with an adorable little whorl at its centre. Her buttocks too were tan, as though she sunbathed naked, and swelled like a peach of perfection, with a very wide furrow that allowed a peep of her large dark pucker, made more vivid by the complete hairlessness of her Lady's place.

She began to speak, her voice soft yet compelling. Law and order, she said, was the most burning topic of any society, since it was to do with keeping rascally males under control, so that women were let get on with their work in peace: work that included enriching their minds and their bodies unhindered by male stupidity. It seemed that most of the crime and stupidity in the world were due to males, or rather to the lack of taming which males were not given. She deplored the decline in corporal punishment, and said that whipping was a sound and just punishment for almost any misdemeanour, and – cutting short an interruption – for females as well as males.

The problem was that when proper punishment was inflicted by males on other males, it did not have the correct effect, provoking resentment and hatred instead of submission. For a male to be truly tamed into docility, his punishment – that is, flogging – should always be at the hands of a female, whose gentleness would impart itself to his flogged body even as he writhed under her just lash. As a lecturer in jurisprudence, and a landowner too, she put her principles into practice, and any of her hands who was guilty of slacking, idleness, or any misdemeanour, knew he could expect a naked flogging in public, on both back and buttocks from his Mistress: not before his comrades, but in front of all the womenfolk.

At this, she touched her leather ceinture; it uncoiled as though by magic, and the progressives gasped.

'I never travel without my stockwhip,' said Miss Arbiter, cracking the fearsome implement loudly in the sunlit evening air. It was a good six feet long, a massive, gleaming tongue with a tip splayed into three smaller tongues, and with metal studs along its length. The Ladies shivered in excitement, and Miss Alice Arbiter smiled with her panther's white teeth, and said a Lady never knew when she would have to deal with an imperfect male . . .

She proceeded to tell us of all the matriarchal societies in history, when there were no gods, only goddessses, and no kings, only queens, and that everyone was the happier for it. All the time she stroked the oiled leather of her stockwhip, as though eager to demonstrate her principles. Everything in life was about power. The brutal power of the male served merely to destroy, like a battering-ram; a Lady's power was to enslave, dominate and entice by subtle wiles, to the enrichment of enslaver and enslaved.

Mrs Mantle said proudly that she whipped Denton, the stable-boy, whenever he was slovenly, and he willingly accepted his humiliation; Miss Arbiter nodded her approval.

'Whip or cane?' she said.

'Riding crop, usually,' said Mrs Mantle, 'though sometimes my husband's cane.'

Miss Arbiter said that the implement scarcely mattered, and even a hand-spanking would suffice, since the main point was the humiliation of the male, and pain the means of conveying it.

'It is all a question of communication,' she said. 'My nudity is a form of communication, for example, to show I have nothing to hide. I wonder which of you Ladies has something to hide . . . I mean, something intimate and disgraceful, which you had never thought of confiding.'

There was a rustle, as stockings and dresses shifted in a lovely swishing of silks. Miss Arbiter looked searchingly at Mrs Mantle, who blushed, and whispered that sometimes, when *she* was naughty, Mantle caned her on the bare bum. Eyes glittered; the rustling of thighs and bottoms grew more animated as, one by one, the Ladies confided their innermost secrets. There were tales of unusual positions for the act of love; of beatings received and administered to willing or unwilling buttocks; Mrs Norringe, a handsome Lady of Mrs Mantle's age, confided that she was poked in the bumhole quite regularly, and enjoyed it.

'Well and good,' said Miss Arbiter. 'I love a good bum-poking, myself, from a male with a big cock – or a Lady with interesting toys – but was your poker in your power, Mrs Norringe, or you in his? That is the question for progressive Ladies . . . But our Italian guest has not spoken.'

Blushing, I confessed that my bottom was no stranger to the rod and I had frequently been whipped on the bare.

Miss Arbiter said that it was not much of a secret and that most Ladies could say the same.

'But, Miss,' I said coolly, staring her in the eyes, 'I enjoy it, and crave nothing more.'

I saw Dido smile, and Miss Arbiter too, but my Mistress reacted with a frown.

'Really! That won't do!' she muttered under her breath.

Then her lips tightened in a fierce grimace, and she stared at me and nodded, indicating clearly that anything my bottom had experienced at her hands would be as nothing to the beating I might expect in future.

Miss Arbiter brought up the question of diddling, stroking her naked fount quite lustfully as she did so and even, I saw, flicking her large, and now slightly stiffened, clitty once or twice, with a little smile on her lips. She said that all females masturbated – she did, constantly – but it was something our repressed male society forbade to be discussed. One by one, the Ladies shyly admitted that they, too, diddled, quite frequently and copiously. Bernice Mantle yawned, as though these stories were of scant interest, and Miss Arbiter pounced on this, and asked if her set at Cambridge were accustomed to such openness.

'Why, yes, Miss,' said Bernice, with a dazzling smile, as though to indicate her infinite tolerance of her mother's fuddy-duddy friends. 'Sometimes we beat each other for a lark – I have beaten, and been beaten.'

'And diddling, Bernice? Your mamma is a progressive – you may speak openly.'

Mrs Mantle flushed, as though there were a limit to her progressiveness, but Bernice said calmly that with modern science, and methods of thwarting nature, a modern Lady had little need of diddling, as there were so many virile males around. Miss Arbiter said sternly that the social whirl might be a lark, but that corporal punishment was serious. Then she smiled and said gaily that it was a pity there were no males to practise on.

'Mummy,' said Bernice airily, 'didn't you say that the boy Denton was well due a thrashing?'

Mrs Mantle flushed, but her eyes glittered.

'Why, yes,' she said, 'but I was waiting for your father to return – he likes to watch, to see that I do not get carried away.'

Miss Arbiter's eyes glittered too, and she said there was no danger of that, in such respectable company.

It was agreed that the servant Denton should be summoned to take his due punishment there and then. The heat and perfume of the garden, and the combined scents of our bodies, conspired to create lustfulness; it was agreed with clapping of hands that the male Denton should serve as an example, and that his chastisement should be undertaken by several progressive female hands. He was sent for, and after his first shock, then lustful glances, at Miss Arbiter's nude body, stood sullenly as the purpose of his presence was explained; his protests were stifled by Mrs Mantle's explanation that if he refused punishment now, he should receive it thrice over from Mr Mantle's much harder arm.

Mrs Mantle said severely that she always flogged him naked, and this flogging was to be no exception. Denton sighed and agreed, and stripped himself bare, secreting himself with absurd modesty behind a sofa, to emerge completely naked, and his rather large organ stiffening noticeably at the sight of Miss Alice Arbiter's nude body. I even saw the gleam of a sly smile at his lips, as though he expected some immodest reward for his flogging. His smile disappeared, as did his erection, when Miss Arbiter expertly flicked her whip and caught him right on the shaft of his stiffening organ, which promptly softened and hung as sullen as his flushed face.

The young man was ordered to bend over the sofa, with his legs splayed, and a towel was placed underneath his private parts. In this position, he was forced to listen, his face growing paler, as the Ladies discussed the extent of his punishment and the implements to be used. Everyone wanted a go; Mrs Mantle brought her crop, which my own bottom had tasted, and a selection of canes, and said that the boy rarely took less than five dozen. Miss Arbiter cracked her whip again, and said that his punishment would be all the sweeter if the Ladies cared to make themselves at their ease, and flog him nude as she herself was, so that their aim and severity, and sense of glorious female freedom and power, would not be distracted by thoughts of spoiling their clothing.

'We must know our own bodies,' she said, 'and being nude with each other is a step in relishing the power of those bodies – and our power to make the naked male suffer and squirm before our beauty. Women are nude, my friends – males are merely naked.'

This suggestion was greeted with mischievous delight, and Mrs Norringe was the first Lady to eagerly strip herself, and stand as bare as her victim, with Mrs Mantle's crop in hand.

Her breasts wobbled deliciously as she delivered a dozen to the male's bare bum. He clenched his buttocks, and screwed his face in a frown, but did not make any noise of distress. When her set was finished, Mrs Norringe was quite breathless and her face was flushed; I saw that her generous forest of mink-curls was glistening and moist. She made no move to don her clothing, saying that it was so hot, as Bernice Mantle took one of her mother's canes, and stripped as though it were quite natural to her.

I admired her slender body and the mink which grew like a little forest between her thighs, stretching all the way up her flat belly to her navel, and below, hanging in lovely tufts well below her bare bum, like an unkempt bird's nest. My cock tingled as I saw the toughness in that willowy body, and wondered of her true relation, and pantie-swapping, with Miss Florence. Her caning of Denton was severe and, I suspected, with some personal grudge in her fierce strokes to his bare, for now he began to whimper softly.

'That was very tight, Miss Mantle,' he sobbed when a dozen had marked him.

Bernice's eyes glinted; her forest too gleamed wetly, and the lips of her quim protruded quite swollen from her tangled mink-hairs.

My Mistress, jealously perhaps, insisted on taking the boy next, but would not undress to more than her scanties. I gasped as she cast off her summer dress, as did all the others, and even Miss Arbiter; Miss Florence's body was constrained in the tightest of corsets, in turquoise satin, that acted as panties as well, and had garter straps for her pale silk stockings. The shiny corset just covered her nipples and was strapless, so that the full mounds of her breasts were squashed up like two luscious melons of creamy bare skin. Her heels gave her added height, and she truly seemed to me an avenging goddess as she selected the longest and hardest of Mrs Mantle's canes, and lifted her arm fully before cracking it across the male's bare, and already reddened, buttocks.

Now he squealed in genuine anguish, and Miss Arbiter told him sharply to be quiet. Miss Florence did not even look at her victim as she caned him, as though prior use had made her disdain him, but stared hard at me, as though making clear that, in her mind, it was my bottom she flogged. This knowledge made me pant with longing; my cock stiffened most painfully under her tight bandages, and I blushed. Miss Florence smiled grimly, knowing I understood her.

'O! O!' cried Denton after over a dozen on the bare from Miss Florence's cane. 'That was tight, Miss! Haven't I had enough, now?'

Before Mrs Mantle could answer, there was a sharp crack, and the full thong of Miss Arbiter's leather stockwhip slammed on the male's puce buttocks, causing him to jump and squeal. Miss Arbiter shut the French windows, and made sure the room door was locked. There were little glistening trickles of juice on her thighs.

The hot, lustful air affected us all; I knew that my throbbing cock would likely burst from her bonds, and dreaded the embarrassment. As the Ladies stripped to administer chastisement, the person of the flogged male, and his varied offences, seemed almost forgotten. Clothing was strewn willy-nilly, and Ladies cooed in glee as they tried each other's things on, including their silky undergarments; how I regretted that I could not join in! Dido herself stripped quite naked and administered a brief but severe caning to the male's now quivering nates, and she looked at me too, but grinning slyly. Her eyes glanced at the towel concealing his member, and at my own crotch, and I looked; his strainings and shiftings, I saw, were to conceal the hugeness of his erection!

There is something so artless and beautiful about a room of perfumed, half-naked females, swapping clothes in delicious intimacy. I avoided catching Denton's eye, to conceal the fact that we felt the same . . . to be amongst women, intimately, is to scent the holy of holies.

But I looked at his bare bum, now squirming most heartily, and wondered if I looked the same under my Mistress's lash. Suddenly, I regretted not having enjoyed my canings at Eppingham, for I saw that a squirming and purpled bare bum is an object of seemly beauty. I saw that Miss Arbiter was rubbing her naked fount-lips quite openly as she licked her lips and grunted in satisfaction at every weal to the male's bare; certain of the stripped Ladies did the same, fingering themselves while blushing and sighing nervously, but gradually following their teacher's example and openly masturbating at the spectacle of the flogged male bottom! How I longed to abase myself, before female eyes, under Miss Florence's contemptuous whip! My cock strained stiff in her bonds.

Suddenly, all bright eyes were on me; Miss Arbiter said sweetly that I must take my turn, and that I must be awfully hot in my pretty yellow clothes; furthermore, she guessed that others would like to try my frock, my blouse, perhaps my underthings too, and it would be selfish to deny them that pleasure. I stammered that I had never thought of taking pleasure in wielding the cane.

'Then it is time you did, Signorina Carpaccio,' Miss Arbiter said tersely. 'You must gain the self-knowledge of your own power over a male.'

I protested that I had not always been whipped by males, but mostly by females, and Miss Arbiter smiled thinly.

'So that is what you crave?' she said. 'Then beating a male shall be all the more fulfilling. Imagine that this helpless naked arse is the arse of all the males who have ever whipped you, signorina. Or imagine it to be your own arse, if you prefer.'

She grinned maliciously at me, and I blushed, wondering if she suspected! I said that I preferred to remain dressed, to sighs of disappointment. Then I took the cane still warm from my Mistress's hand, and positioned myself in front of Denton's bare. I lifted the cane to its full height, and brought it down as hard as I could, to be rewarded with a frenzied spasm of bum-jerking, and a tortured squeal from the young man's throat.

'No squealing,' ordered Miss Arbiter. 'Miss Carpaccio's dozen has now become two dozen, boy.'

I heard him gasp in anguish as I continued the beating as hard as I could; I was reminded of my own schooldays, obliged as prefect to beat other boys at Uppingham, and my feelings of guilt at so brutally expressing my power. Now, I had the same exultation, but no guilt; Denton's hard penis told me that he felt the same awe in submission to females as I – as any proper male. I beat him so hard that I quite forgot myself, and went well beyond the ordained two dozen, while the Ladies clapped in delight, and openly masturbated their well-moistened quims. Miss Arbiter was a swift teacher, and liberty a swift lesson.

I saw that Mrs Mantle and her daughter had both remained nude, and this caused them no embarrassment, for all eyes were on that squirming male bottom under my merciless cane-strokes. His legs jerked straight behind him as I flogged, a pretty touch and indicating his extreme agony, which caused ooh's of appreciation. I found to my dismay that my erection continued to stiffen, not in appreciation of his maleness, but of his helpless nudity, and my power over bare buttocks! Through my sweat-blurred eyes, I imagined those squirming nates to be my own. With every cut, I longed for my Mistress's cane . . .

At last, his beating was over, and it was time for Miss Arbiter to deliver his final chastisement with her stockwhip. I turned, flushed and panting, and to my horror felt my member completely stiff and suddenly bursting from binding and thin panties alike, to stand in ominous swelling beneath my frock! I flushed in embarrasssment, and strove to cover myself, but did not escape Miss Arbiter's eye. To make matters worse, in my exertion, the flower petals which formed my false bosom had become loose, and now from the front of my blouse emerged a cascade of pink rose petals.

'Well!' said Miss Arbiter. 'Pink on yellow, a pretty combination. But not as pretty as that!'

She tapped my straining erection under my dress with the handle of her stockwhip. Her perfume beside me was savage and sensuous, and my member could not soften.

'No wonder you did not wish to undress . . . *young man*!'

There were gasps of dismay and astonishment, but I noticed few hands were removed from sopping wet minks. Miss Arbiter smiled, and said she thought the boy Denton had taken enough. Denton was allowed to stand, and looked at me and my erect penis, eyes burning in puzzled resentment. Obeisance not to women, but to a male! I shivered, fearing some future revenge. But now I feared the reward for my deception.

'Good heavens!' said Dido mildly. 'Signorina! Or Signor . . .? Major Dark will have to do some explaining. Still, he does look rather pretty, doesn't she, Miss Arbiter?'

'He!' cried Miss Arbiter, with a suspicious look at Dido. '*She'll* look much prettier when *her* arse is thrashed to the bone!'

There was a chilling silence, broken only by my own whimpers. Miss Arbiter cracked the full length of her stockwhip, snaking it almost to the windows.

'Well, Ladies,' she said, 'it seems we have a male to demonstrate the methods of progressive discipline after all.'

She looked me in the eye, and roughly squeezed my throbbing cock through my dress. 'I mean the real methods,' she said loudly, then whispered to me, in Italian: 'which will make you scream for mercy – unless you have any objection, Signorina.'

Her animal perfume, and the angry, lustful scent of her wet quim, dizzied me, and my rampant stiff cock spoke for me. Numbly, I shook my head.

I was powerless to resist the firm hands of Miss Alice Arbiter as she contemptuously ripped my pretty yellow things from me, down to my panties and stockings; then these too were torn down, and I stood shamed and naked in front of the females. My cock stood rampant as Miss Arbiter stroked the thongs of her stockwhip. She raised her sandalled foot and poked me painfully right on my balls; I gasped in my distress, and at the quivering of her ripe muscled thigh flesh as she pressed her sharp foot against my tender place. The Ladies smiled, and I saw Bernice place her arm in proprietorial fashion around the corsed waist of my Mistress, who did not resist the caress.

Miss Arbiter's toe flicked suddenly, and slapped the gleaming bulb of my cock. I groaned, and fell to my knees before her, mumbling my pleas for forgiveness. Her high sandals glimmered before my moist eyes, and I began to lick and suck the toes and the heels too, and licked the soles beneath. My humiliance to her person strangely comforted me like an old friend, and she accepted it in silence.

'The male knows his place,' she said. 'He shames himself willingly.'

Her whip slithered across my bare buttocks and shoulders, its caress like a snake's.

'I beg you, Miss . . .' I blurted.

'He begs!' sneered Miss Arbiter.

'Not for mercy, Miss,' I stammered, 'for I expect none. I beg for just punishment, and the forgiveness of Ladies.'

She reached under my perruque and pulled me sharply by the earlobe, then forced my head down over the sofa, still warm from Denton's bum. I felt eager hands grasping my wrists and ankles, forcing my limbs apart. Then Miss Arbiter's palm was on my bare bum.

'I see our maid is no stranger to welts,' she said thoughtfully.

Then she asked if I were quite comfortable. I said I was most uncomfortable, and she clicked her tongue in approval. It is said that emotions have a scent; in her, I smelt lust, and I smelt vengeance . . . and suddenly longed for *her* to whip me.

I winced as the first ferocious lash of the stockwhip on my bare buttocks slammed me against the chair, and made me shudder in pain. The leather whip was as heavy and stinging as any cane. There was not the sharp cane's smarting, nor the crackling embrace of the fearsome birch, but somehow the worst of both combined. The second and third lashes whistled in the air and cracked across my naked fesses, making me clench in unbearable agony as the tongues seemed to coil around my thighs and buttocks, right into my furrow, searching out every crevice in a hot embrace of searing pain.

Tears sprang to my eyes, and I bit my lip to stop the cries welling in my gorge. Each lash of that dreadful whip on my bare nates seemed infinitely worse than the one before, and I could not but squirm in helpless agony as firm hands held me immobile by wrists and ankles. Through my blurred eyes I saw a sea of bright smiles, and hands stroking naked founts like reeds in the breeze.

At the twenty-third or twenty-fourth stroke, I could not help letting out a long, strangled moan of despair. At this, Miss Arbiter said the whelp must be gagged, and shamefully, with panties. Eager hands stretched out their garments, and Miss Arbiter selected two pairs, both sodden with quim juices, and wadded them brutally in my mouth.

'A fine spectacle,' she said. 'I'm wet between the legs, my friends. I trust you are.'

There were murmurs of delighted assent.

'Law and order is for males,' drawled Bernice, her hand stroking my Mistress's quim through her turquoise satin, which was dark and damp. 'Liberty is for females . . .'

Miss Arbiter handed the whip to Mrs Mantle, who, clad only in a shimmering short petticoat, with her firm breasts bouncing in her exertion, continued my lashing as vigorously as before. I must have taken over forty strokes; Miss Arbiter positioned herself in front of my face, and with slow, deliberate movements, masturbated contemptuously as I squirmed and writhed in my agony. I saw her thighs gleaming with trickled love juices, and, following her example, all the other Ladies openly pleasured themselves, Dido the most eagerly of all. Bernice's fingers had crept beneath my Mistress's fount gusset, and her murmurs of decorous reserve were silenced by a rough slap to her corsed breasts.

'Silence, slut,' hissed Miss Bernice to her friend and riding companion, and Miss Florence bowed her head. There were thin rivulets of shiny love oil trickling from the swelling of her gusset, where a shiny tuft of wet mink-hair peeped.

Miss Arbiter, above the cooings of lustful pleasure, explained that masturbation, or 'frotting' as she called it, was the highest expression of female freedom, and delightfully enhanced by the spectacle of a flogged and shamed male. Her belly shuddered – her fingers whipped her swollen dark clit – as she frigged herself to a moaning, shuddering climax, in open view of all!

There were mmm's and coos of joy as the enraptured Ladies followed her example, and now all begged for a turn with the stockwhip. The whipping progressed to my shoulders, striping me cruelly and making me jerk to a different dance; then low down the backs of my thighs, which hurt cruelly and had me jumping on my tiptoes. Through my gag of wet female panties, I squealed in unbridled agony. The whip's tongues snaked at my furrow, cracking on my squirming bumhole, which hurt fearfully, and brushing with terrible promise the hard skin of my strained ball-sac. My legs were held firmly splayed; my balls and the shaft of my cock were open to any punishment for my crime of maleness.

Suddenly, Miss Arbiter announced that I had taken eighty-eight strokes from her stockwhip; she retrieved the implement, and said she would make it a round century. Her lashes were stronger than any of the others', and now my howls were scarcely muffled by my gag, which was wet with my streaming tears. My body jerked and writhed like a puppet as her whipthongs caught me again and again, for that last, vicious dozen, on just the same spot right at the smarting centre of my fesses. My cries of pain almost, but not quite, drowned the moaning of females in the raptures of their frotted orgasms . . .

'He's purple,' panted Bernice, 'almost black. How pretty, and how just!'

At the hundredth, Miss Arbiter said my flogging was complete and removed my gag, to leave me sobbing and spluttering in my spasms of pain. Yet my cock still throbbed in my delicious humiliance, and Miss Arbiter, snorting, took hold of my balls and squeezed them quite painfully. I looked up, hopeful of release.

'Thank you, Ladies,' I sobbed, 'for my just chastisement.'

Miss Arbiter laughed.

'Why, Miss,' she sneered, 'you may thank us for your whipping, but your chastisement is far from complete.'

8

Stable Lads

'It seems that flogging makes your dick stand up,' said Miss Arbiter as I stood naked and ashamed. 'Or perhaps she can't stand up any other way. At any rate, you look like an animal, and the stable is the place for animals.'

She flicked her whip, quite gently, so that it curled around my balls, placing me under arrest in a sort of lasso. Then she ordered me to crouch on all fours, and jerked the whip, obliging me to follow her. Suddenly, she flew to the door, tugging my balls quite painfully, so that I moaned; in a swift motion, she unlocked it, and pounced on the kneeling figure outside. It was the servant Denton.

He had been spying through the keyhole, and, with a snarl, Miss Arbiter caught him by the earlobe. His penis was exposed and I saw that his own erection was as proud as mine. Miss Arbiter heaped scornful insult upon the shamefaced wretch, and told him that he evidently had not been taught a proper lesson. Miss Mantle clucked that he brought disgrace to the house, and Miss Arbiter had her authority to chastise the boy as severely as she pleased. Thus, we formed a cortège: myself hobbling as best I could behind Miss Arbiter; Denton, loping in pain as his ear was pulled; and the Ladies murmuring behind us, their clothing in varied states of disarray. Only Bernice and Miss Arbiter retained full nudity, and Bernice drew Miss Florence along with a finger crooked in the gusset of her satin corselet.

We arrived at an empty stable, like a barn, and with various rural accoutrements which Miss Arbiter said would serve our purposes amply. She handed her whip to Miss Bernice, who amused herself by flicking it idly, sending little tremors through my tethered manhood. Miss Arbiter ordered Denton to extend his arms. He did so, with a faltering erection, and Miss Arbiter slapped a length of heavy chain around his wrists.

Then she fastened the chain through a pulley in the ceiling and, with powerful muscles, pulled the male up until his toes only brushed the ground. He was whimpering and groaned loud, as Miss Arbiter ripped the shirt from his back, and pulled down his trousers to sag around his ankles, his shame causing much laughter. He was bare, and hovering on painful tiptoe, and his penis had gone quite soft, dangling like a big cucumber on his downy thighs. Miss Arbiter laughed and said that he should be punished for his spying, and, if he was to dangle like a boy, then he should be punished as one.

'What do you think the punishment should be, Miss?' she said to me.

I stammered that it was not my position to say.

'At a public school, prefects would cane boys for spying, on the bare buttocks,' said Mrs Norringe suddenly.

Her pretty face gleamed with cruel desire.

'The Italian miss is no boy, but an animal,' said Miss Arbiter. 'And I dare say the stable lad has never been to school. Perhaps it is time for some, after we break this animal, and turn her into a man.'

Miss Arbiter bound four heavy horseshoes to my hands and feet, forcing me to hobble clumsily. Then she found an old husk of corncob, stretched my buttocks apart with the fingers of one hand, and brutally thrust it deep into my anus, making me squeal and wriggle in distress. Everyone laughed, and she ordered me to hold my bum plug inside me.

She retrieved her whip and uncoiled it from my balls, then amused us all by lashing my buttocks fiercely and sending me hobbling in a circle round the trembling body of my fellow-miscreant. This degradation kept my penis hard, and Miss Arbiter sneered, but I sensed that none of the Ladies was displeased.

'He makes a fine pony,' said Dido, 'so why don't we harness him properly, and race him?'

I felt a heavy harness strapped on my back; my mouth was filled with gagging bit and bridle, and blinkers were flattened right over my eyes, so that I was blindfold. My bridle was attached to reins, and now I felt them tug, urging me to hobble forward. The corncob in my bum hurt abominably, but I obeyed my command.

'Stay, boy!' cried Miss Arbiter. 'We shall race him. Mrs Dark, please go first.'

I felt Dido's dress brush my thighs as she mounted me, then her naked quim fastened around my neck. She was surprisingly heavy, and I sagged somewhat, until a flurry of strokes from the riding crop lashed my bare bum and made me whinny, just like a real pony. Dido's fount was oily wet, and she cried 'Giddy-up', plying my bum with frequent crop-strokes as I hobbled as fast as I could to carry her round in a circle.

'Why, a sheep could go faster,' said Miss Arbiter scornfully.

Dido's perfumed thighs and bum were replaced by a different Lady, whom I imagined to be Mrs Mantle from her odour. She whipped me most fiercely, and I raced around the barn quite furiously, to escape the dreadful burning strokes to my bare. Panting and sobbing, I heard the Ladies clamour to race me, and, one by one, they mounted and whipped me on until I was lathered in my own sweat and the copious fluids from the naked founts that slithered on my back. I gasped at the sudden weight of not one, but two bodies!

I knew it was my Mistress, her moist satin gusset pressing the small of my back, while the hairy bush of Bernice's wet mink clutched my neck. As I was whipped, I felt hard taps on my bum plug, searing my tender anus in strokes of agony, as my Mistress amused herself at my degradation. Groaning, I made my circuit, and the whipstrokes of my Mistress achieved my fastest time. She was pronounced winner. Miss Arbiter asked me if I felt shamed to be treated thus in public, and I whinnied and sobbed that I did. Then she took off my blindfold and told me I was to drink. I looked up; Denton's face was pale and his eyes wide as he gaped at my humiliance, and my standing cock.

I was unyoked, but now Miss Arbiter held a gleaming implement in front of me, and I gulped in real fear: it was the curving blade of a scythe! The bum plug remained in my anus, but now a dog's collar was fastened to my neck, and to it the handle of the scythe. The handle of the tool pressed against my back; the blade fitted snugly in my furrow, and curved underneath my balls and cock, where its tip shone just at my tight bulb.

I groaned in torment, knowing that if I made a false move my agony hereto should be nothing. The razor-sharp blade tickled my balls, but I was powerless to do more than the faintest trembling. Miss Arbiter took a sheaf of bamboo canes from the corner, and said my chastisement now should of needs be more subtle; as I drank, I should be beaten separately on each fesse, by volunteers – which was all of them – while she herself should attend to Denton's miscreant body with her stockwhip.

My drinking was this: each Lady was to lift her skirt, and reveal to me her bare fount, the gash lips spread at my mouth, and I was to tongue each one of them on the clit, so that her juice flowed into my mouth. All the time my own buttocks would take the heavy bamboo, while Denton would take a flogging from Miss Arbiter's whip. She explained to Denton that his punishment depended on the length of time it took my tongue to bring each Lady to orgasm, with no subterfuge. Every female belly had to writhe, and every gash flow with the juices of unfeigned pleasure. So if Denton suffered from my laziness, I was to blame for his pain.

I was to kneel, underneath him, with my mouth at waist height, and Miss Arbiter then bound the bulb of his flaccid cock with a thin length of wire, just round the base of the glans, and very tightly, so that he shrieked, the wire biting just under the prepuce which she pulled all the way back from his glans. The other end of this wire was fastened to the hilt of my scythe, just at my own balls, so that any movement or swelling of Denton's cock should lift the scythe to my balls and cause me the worst agony.

The first lash of the stockwhip echoed in the barn as the leather cracked on Denton's already wealed fesses, causing him to shriek. He was ordered to take his punishment in silence. The first quim was eagerly presented to my lips, and I began to tongue the already distended clitty, without looking up to see its owner. My mouth was bathed in a gush of fragrant love juice, and I licked frantically, hearing little moans of pleasure, and feeling the loins shift and wriggle around my pressing mouth, until, to my relief, the Lady shivered and sighed, then cried out sharply a dozen times as I brought her to come.

Her place was at once taken by another, and I did the same thing; all the time my bum smarted at the twin lashes of two bamboo canes, one caressing each of my fesses, and over it was the harsh crashing slap of the leather stockwhip on Denton's bare, so that, as his body trembled, I felt the scythe shiver against my naked balls.

Yet my erection was firm; my tongue found the rhythm of pleasuring the naked gashes presented, and I licked in time with the bamboo that flogged my bare. I recognised Miss Bernice's gash, because of her huge and luxuriant mink, whose hairs straggled against my nose and lips, although her love juice was less copious than the others'. She was followed by her mother, whose mink was that part of her person where she most resembled her lithe daughter, and whose torrent of quim oil quite surpassed her.

Finally, it was my Mistress herself who pressed herself to me, and she still wore her satin corselet, though the gusset was sopping with her oily quim juice. I had to tongue the protruding stiffness of her clit through the satin, and I knew this was a contemptuous game on her part, to make me take longer, as my own bottom quivered under my bamboo thrashing, yet unable to do more than quiver, for fear of the scythe's blade against my balls.

'O! O!' I heard Denton's anguished wails. 'O, hurry, man, damn you! Make the gashes come, sir! O, I can't take it! Please! Mercy, Miss!'

But the thong of Miss Arbiter's whip cracked pitilessly against the young man's bare, wriggling body, his squirming conveyed to my own cock through the shivering scythe blade. I heard Miss Florence gasp, and her loins began to writhe . . . Then she cried out, the crotch of her corselet dripped with her juices, and my tongue could feel the clitty throbbing as though begging for relief. I fastened my teeth on the distended nubbin and began to chew through the satin, making her writhe and scream out as, finally, she erupted in her spasm of pleasure.

I felt a stirring at my cock; the scythe moved, pressing against my balls and shaft. I looked up, and saw Denton's bare body a mass of black and blue welts, from shoulders to buttocks, and that his cock was stirring.

I wailed; Miss Arbiter ceased her flogging, and pressed her own shaven quim to my mouth, muzzling me, but not to make me lick her. Rather, she wished to pinion me in place. Unable to move, trapped by her fragrant naked belly, I glanced past her rippling haunches to see the flogged body of Denton, and his cock rising fast. The scythe was razor-sharp against my balls, pressing closer and closer as his stiffening cock raised it. I whimpered and sobbed into the perfumed hillock of Miss Arbiter's mound, begging 'please . . . please . . .' and, as I yelped in pure terror, she laughed aloud and pulled me to my feet, loosening the horrid wire that bound me.

'O, Miss!' I cried. 'That was crueller than any whipping!'

'Then you shan't mind another,' she said smugly, 'for I think Denton's risen cock has earned him his revenge. You took such a long time in pleasuring us . . . he is quite raw.'

Denton was released from his pulley, and stood before me, his cock now as stiff as mine, and the same tears of agony streaming on his cheeks. But there was fury in his eyes.

'Your fault!' he said. 'My lashes . . . your doing, sir! Scoundrel!'

Miss Arbiter threw him one of the bamboos, still warm from my wealed fesses, and told me to bend over, just as schoolboys did.

'A little play-acting,' she said. 'Denton, you shall be the prefect and punish this whelp for his impertinence – a hearty three dozen on the bare.'

I looked at the faces of my several Mistresses (as I now thought of them) and not one failed to grin her approval. I saw that my Mistress had her fingers trapped in Miss Bernice's naked slit, and was obediently masturbating her, on Bernice's direction, though Miss Florence blushed a little at her friend's open dominance. Bernice urged her on with hard little spanks to her satined bum. Miss Florence looked at me and nodded that I should obey, and I bent over and touched my toes.

'You impudent bugger,' spat Denton, 'you nasty prying pervert, sir!'

I felt the bamboo again on my bare nates, much more painful than before, for it landed across both buttocks at once, and I sensed the harsh savagery of a male hand behind my beating. I had taken such punishment at Eppingham, without protest or murmur, and was resolved to do so again. The strokes rained on me, not very expertly but with harsh force.

'Squirm, you bugger,' hissed Denton. 'Wriggle your arse for me.'

But I did not wriggle, though my bummed corncob hurt terribly at each stroke. I stood panting at the pain of the caning, but determined to take it like a man. Under a male's beating, I felt my cock soften and shrink to limpness, and Miss Arbiter noted this with disapproval. I looked round and saw that Denton's member was hard as rock as he flogged me! But I took the three dozen without squealing or squirming, and he threw down his cane in disgust. My cock now dangled fully soft, and Miss Arbiter said there seemed only one way to get me in correct position for my true punishment.

'Admit that you liked being buggered by my corncob,' she sneered.

I sobbed that it was too humiliating, and at that she exploded in fury. Now, I was to receive a *real* beating, and confess the truth – that I loved buggery.

Miss Arbiter ascended a ladder. My ankles were trussed, and I was hoisted to the ceiling so that I hung upside down, with my legs splayed and each ankle fastened far apart. She now roughly withdrew my corncob, which hurt, and replaced it with the thick long knob of the scythe's handle, thrusting it brutally into my anus to almost its full depth. It was not painfully gnarled like the corncob, but its very smoothness seemed more brutal because of its menacing size, and the ease with which it penetrated my tender membrane. I squirmed and squealed, and in response she spat on my balls.

Then she fastened a thin wire very tightly around my balls and my flaccid cock, knotting it to the same point as my chain, but leaving it with some slack. I was given a rope to hold, and this was hoisted as well so that my body dangled at an angle, with my bottom exposed for chastisement. But to my horror – if I let go of the rope, I should fall to vertical, that is, upside down, and the wire binding my balls would snap tight as any executioner's noose.

Whimpering, I clutched desperately to the rope as each Lady delivered a whipping with the stockwhip to my bare buttocks; my body flailed the air as the leather seared my naked bum-flesh, and each woman gave me over two dozen with the lash. At the same time, Miss Arbiter, from her perch on the ladder, gleefully and savagely buggered me with the scythe handle, thrusting it to my root with hard cruel strokes, and making my anus seem as though its walls would burst from the shaft, thicker than any cock or dildo I could imagine.

All the time I clung to the rope, tears of shame and terror streaming down my face, as my bumhole squirmed in the agony of my cruel buggering. Yet my tortured balls tingled – and by the end of my flogging, my penis was fully stiff and throbbing, the peehole staring at me balefully like an eye. Miss Arbiter slapped my balls, and asked me again if I confessed to loving buggery.

'By a strong Lady – yes, Miss!' I wailed. 'I do confess!'

She squeezed my throbbing shaft, slapped my balls and

peehole, and then unfastened me. She withdrew the shaft from my bum, and, taking the surprised Denton by his ear once more, forced him to squat and part his buttocks, then pushed the scythe handle right into his own anus. His squeals caused me vengeful pleasure, but it was short-lived; Denton was trussed with ropes, and thrown sobbing on to the ground to watch as I myself was seized by many hands and a heavy chain wrapped around the entirety of my body, except for my cock. I was made to lie on my back, immobilised by the chain, and my cock and balls standing stiff and helpless.

Miss Arbiter lifted the sharp heel of her sandalled foot, and ground it into the bulb of my cock, making me squeal in pain. Then she tickled my shaft with her heel, before spiking my balls with it, pressing gently, yet hard enough to have me moaning in terror. She moved her shoe so that it bridged my manhood, her toe and heel straddling my balls, and then stood on me, crushing me with her full weight, so that her instep pressed cruelly against the ball-sac and shaft of my organ.

I sobbed and tried to wriggle under my blanket of chain, but at the same time felt a delicious tickling surge in my cock, which throbbed harder than ever. Miss Arbiter withdrew, and her place was taken by Mrs Norringe, her delicate shoe crushing me in the same artful way, as if she were fully experienced in the crushing of males, with all her weight on my balls, though she was much lighter than Miss Arbiter. All the Ladies gleefully followed suit, and Miss Florence crushed me harder than anyone, grinding her heel most cruelly against my balls so that I shrieked in pain, my cock still rigid.

I was left to lie there, gasping, until Miss Arbiter fastened a metal 'sperm clip' over the shaft of my erect cock, and told me it would prevent me spurting until I had properly served my Ladies. Then she squatted over me as though to evacuate. I saw the lips of her gash glistening swollen and fat, with the huge distended acorn of her clitty throbbing like a vengeful weapon. She lowered herself on to my throbbing cock, and began to bounce hard up and down on my loins, pleasuring her clitty with practised flicks of her fingers, until she had bucked herself to a mewling, groaning climax. And afterwards, she relieved herself upon me in a hissing, contemptuous stream. I felt wretchedly ashamed, not at my golden bath, but that my cock was nothing more than a tool for her masturbation.

I was straddled by every progressive Lady, all of them bucking and writhing on my sore tool as they used me for their pleasure; my Mistress pulled aside the gusset of her satin corselet to reveal her naked swollen quim lips and, as she mounted me, her friend Bernice pressed her own bare gash into my Mistress's face, obliging her to suck and lick at her clitty while she bucked on my cock. When my Mistress had groaned and squealed in her own climax, the positions were reversed, and, while Miss Bernice rode me like a horse, her own lips glistened as she chewed on the gash of Miss Florence, kneeling above her with the rivulets of juice flowing prettily down her bare quivering thighs.

I had lost track of time, and heard owls screeching in the stillness of the summer night; yet I did not want my submission to end. Miss Arbiter observed that Denton's cock was softening, and said that the problems with disobedient males was to get them to stand satisfactorily together. Accordingly, she released me from my chains and handed me the bamboo.

'Perhaps a male can beat some stiffness into the boy,' she said curtly, and I stood above the trussed buttocks of Denton, and began to flog his bare darkened arse, quite as strongly as I would have flogged a miscreant boy at Eppingham.

As I beat him, Miss Arbiter squatted and took the corncob and began to move it rhythmically in and out of his bumhole in hard and shameful buggery. He squealed and wriggled quite shamelessly and, as I approached my third dozen, I noticed that his cock was stiffening once more; by the end of the three dozen, he was fully erect.

Now it was Dido who took the lead. She purred with pleasure and squatted over the stable lad's massive shaft, fastening a metal sperm clip to its base, like my own, then sank its entire length into her bumhole, lying back on his trussed body and grasping me by the wrists. She pulled me towards her and greedily grabbed my stiff cock, then plunged it into her gaping wet slit, so that I filled her.

'Fuck me, Roger, fuck me hard,' she whispered, and I began to buck in and out of her, while her bum writhed on Denton's shaft in her anus, and her nimble fingers flicked her clitty to throbbing hardness.

It was not long before she shivered and sang in her heat of orgasm; her place was taken by Mrs Norringe, whom I fucked with equal vigour, the cock-clip effectively dampening my balls from their urge to spurt. Then Mrs Mantle laid herself on Denton's shaft and inserted it into her quim, lying down to face him, and instructed me to take her in the anus. I did so, and she wriggled quite beautifully with Denton's cock in her slit, as I buggered the sturdy bare matron until she too had climaxed once more.

As Mrs Mantle squirmed on the lad's shaft in cooze, with my own cock strongly buggering her, Bernice squatted on Denton's face and sat with her full weight on his mouth, ordering him to tongue her anus while she masturbated 'for real pleasure', and placed four of Miss Florence's fingers inside her slit to thrust powerfully in and out, to the rhythm of my fucking and her own clit-frotting. It was strange feeling another male's stiff cock separated from mine only by the thin membrane between a Lady's slit and bumhole, and I felt a sudden friendship for the lad, as though we were both soldiers in service together.

As I fucked, my bum jumped again as enthusiastic Ladies spurred me with cane-strokes to my bare arse. They cut me dreadfully, yet in the mechanical pumping of my loins the pain seemed a distant tickle. Suddenly, the positions were reversed; I was pushed on to the dirt, and my raw arse squirmed as Mrs Norringe mounted me and drove my shaft deep into her elastic moist bumhole, while Denton pumped at her cooze with his clipped cock, urged on by caning to his bare bum.

My eyes were covered by the sweating, perfumed thighs of another Lady, I was not sure whose; then she sank her cooze right on to my mouth and nose, the hairy anus tickling me as she writhed on me and frotted herself, making my eager tongue thrust in and out of her dripping slit. I heard her voice: it was Mrs Mantle, and she gasped that my tongue was as sweet as my bottom, so adorable in Bernice's pink panties when she had beaten me.

'I recognised you, dear Ruggiera,' she said, 'and I am so pleased such a pretty girl has such a pretty cock.'

There was a snarl from her daughter Bernice, directed at my Mistress.

'What! You gave my panties to . . . to this *male*?'

I heard a slap and a squeal. Miss Florence protested that I had taken them from her room, without her consent, as a souvenir. This made matters worse.

'He was in your room? You ungrateful bitch!' cried Bernice, and Mrs Mantle rose from my face to cover her own in alarm, as I saw her daughter writhing in the dirt and covering her friend with kicks and slaps.

'Bitch . . . bitch . . .' she cried, ripping at the turquoise satin of Miss Florence's corselet until it hung from her in shreds, and her magnificent teats flopped naked and defenceless in the dirt, reddening as they were mercilessly pummelled by her friend's fists.

She ripped the last shreds of the garment from Miss Florence's crotch, and stuffed the sopping gusset in her mouth to gag her squeals; then, with her foot pinioning my Mistress's neck in the dirt, she seized the bamboo and began to flog her bare bum, which squirmed helplessly under the rain of harsh strokes.

'Six dozen should punish you, slut,' she hissed, 'and when I get you alone, there will be six dozen more with the crop, and then you'll ride your pony bare bum, with no saddle . . .'

Pitilessly, she flogged the bare bum of my Mistress, who wriggled and squealed through her gag, yet seemed to make no move to escape the clutches of Bernice, who had her by the hair, pulling it tightly as she beat her bottom.

She went well beyond the six dozen, and there were murmurings of disquiet at this harshness amongst Ladies;

Miss Arbiter, however, surveyed the spectacle with a flickering hand at her wet quim. I looked at her hand as she masturbated, then at the faint sprouting of stubble on her shaven fount, and then to her mane of blonde hair, cascading over her forehead as she groaned in her own pleasuring, and frowned. But my attention was distracted by Dido, who leapt forward and stayed Bernice's flogging arm.

'Enough!' she cried. 'My daughter is –'

Bernice thrust her contemptuously away.

'Your daughter is nothing but a frilly little bitch,' she said, 'a lesbic whore who relishes the whipping of a stern Mistress.'

'That stern Mistress should be me and no other,' said Dido. 'And I think even Miss Arbiter will agree that Sapphism can go too far.'

Miss Arbiter's response was interrupted by Dido's firmly grasping Bernice's naked limbs and pinioning them. Then she forced the protesting caner down to the dirt beside my Mistress.

'Please, Dido,' whimpered Miss Florence, 'I deserved my flogging . . .'

'And flogged you shall be,' hissed Dido, 'when we get home. But not before this bitch has tasted proper submission.'

She grabbed both myself and the lad Denton by our stiff cocks and swiftly unfastened our clips. Then she made Denton lie beneath the squirming naked woman and forced her down on his cock so that it plunged into her gash, burying his balls in the furry tuft of her mink. She pushed Bernice's thighs up so that her ankles were at her neck, and guided my cock to the quivering pucker of her anus. I tickled her bud for some moments while she squealed in protest, until Dido herself sat with naked gash on Bernice's face.

I thrust my cock deep into her bumhole and began to fuck her vigorously, as Denton below me was poking her in quim, lifting his arse from the ground and thrusting into her with short, hard movements.

With new fire in her eyes, my Mistress squatted to avenge herself on her cruel friend, and pushed her head under my pumping thighs so that her lovely mane tickled and caressed my naked balls. Then she opened her jaws wide and began to bite Bernice's bare bum, very hard, leaving vivid teethmarks and drawing yelps of agony from her buggered paramour.

Bernice wriggled and squealed under Dido's bum as the juices flowed from her quim, down Bernice's chin, and Dido began to pleasure herself with her fingers on her clit, panting harshly. As I buggered the Sapphic Bernice, Dido leant forward and kissed me wetly full on the lips, holding me there as she unfastened my cock-ring, and then Denton's. I felt my honey well in my balls and, with a loud groan of anguished ecstasy, I spurted my sperm into the writhing lesbian's anus; at the same time Denton cried out as his own seed bathed her quim. Groaning, we withdrew, our raw cocks finally softened, and leaving Bernice sobbing and shuddering on the ground.

But now, Mrs Mantle, skirted in majesty, took her by the ear and said she had shamed her friend and guest, and when she was little, she had taken her over her knee when she was naughty, and now she was to get a big girl's punishment. Furious, she took her naked daughter and lifted the bamboo, its ends now split by its forceful use, and dealt a hard blow to Bernice's fesses, already livid with Miss Florence's crimson teethmarks.

She made Bernice stand and bend over 'in schoolboy's position', touching her toes, to receive a vigorous three dozen on the bare with the split bamboo, so that by the end of her chastisement, Bernice was bruised and wealed dark crimson, and her squirming made the Ladies gape in dismay. Yet I noticed that, as the Ladies held themselves for comfort at this cruel spectacle, their hands crept to their founts, and gently rubbed and caressed each other with little gasps of satisfaction; Dido clasped Mrs Norringe most lustfully, with her nurse's hand gliding in and out of her wet gaping gash, as she took Miss Arbiter's trembling hand and rubbed it against her own swollen clitty.

Miss Arbiter continued to frot herself, her lustfulness overcoming her unease at Mrs Mantle's disdain for Sapphism. When Bernice's flogging was over, my Mistress clasped her to her quivering bare breasts, and said she was sorry, and Bernice must cane her and bite her all over her body to make her pay for it, and make her ride bare bum, to hurt, and she promised Bernice a gift of her own most precious panties, to wear for ever and ever . . .

Bernice kissed Miss Florence's breasts, and chewed the stiff cups of her nipples, biting them quite hard, to my Mistress's whimpers of pleasure, with her hand fevered between her naked quim lips, and said that she had deserved her punishment, for being such a beast.

Outside, an early cock crowed; the first glimmerings of dawn brightened the sky. This seemed a signal for the progressive Ladies to make themselves decorous once more, grinning shyly as they robed themselves, daintily smoothing rumpled underthings and dresses, with some playful dispute as to whose knickers belonged to whom. Mrs Mantle gravely thanked Miss Alice Arbiter for her most interesting exposition, and I found myself next to Denton. We watched as Miss Arbiter accepted her thanks, while tenderly stroking Bernice's flogged bare bum.

'Sorry about that, sir,' he said rather shamefacedly. 'I got carried away. Does your bum hurt awfully?'

I said it did.

'Mine too,' he said. 'But it is sort of warm and glowing . . . it's not half bad, really. Is it true what you said – that you like being flogged by a woman?'

'Yes,' I said. 'There is no greater pleasure, Denton. Think about it – about yourself . . .'

'Women are funny creatures,' he said with a grin, rubbing his bare wealed bottom, and turning to show me his bruises.

I did the same, and he whistled in admiration. Then we shook hands.

'Men too,' I said.

In the car going home, Dido said she thought Miss Arbiter most impressive.

I said one thing puzzled me.

'And what is that? Her forceful manner?'

'No, her hair. It is lovely and blonde, but when my face was close to her Lady's place, I saw a little stubble sprouting where she had shaved, and it was dark; and there was a little hint of dark hair at the roots of her head.'

'Never mind, Roger, the main thing is, I was right – you do look lovely in yellow.'

'Miss Arbiter was right, too,' purred my Mistress. 'Our girl does love being buggered . . .'

9

A Birthday Treat

It was my Mistress's birthday! Happily, it took place on a delicious summer morning, when the orchards and brooks sparkled in the bright sun, and the humming of bees and birds made England seem the rosiest place in the world. A surprise awaited Miss Florence in the summerhouse, and I was permitted to accompany her there. Her haughty moue could not conceal her girlish excitement at her surprise, and this was suited by her dress, a lovely silk purple frock with mauve stockings, as pretty as the flowers which garlanded our path. Yet her girlish appearance did not hide the dominant female within; dominant towards me yet I had seen her 'frilly' side with the lesbic Bernice Mantle. Which was play-acting, I wondered?

Dido, in surprising contrast, wore a black leather: thinly cut blouson, tightly buttoned even on this balmy day, and very short bum-hugging skirt with black seamed fishnet stockings and lovely high heels, patent leather I think, like a schoolmistress intending to deliver a stern lesson.

The summerhouse was in darkness, and Dido told Miss Florence to enter first for her surprise. Excitedly, she disappeared into the chamber. Suddenly there was a loud whooshing noise, and a squeal of outrage from my Mistress. Dido smiled broadly, and followed me into the summerhouse. In the shuttered gloom I saw that Miss Florence's ankles were pinioned by the jaws of, I guessed, a mantrap – padded, yet immobilising her cruelly. She shrieked and sobbed at her humiliation, and even in shadow I discerned her proud face burning with rage. On the table stood a birthday cake with two thick pink candles.

'Didn't you find your cake?' said Dido amiably. 'Thoughtless girl!'

'Release me, you horrible bitch!' wailed Miss Florence.

'What a naughty and imperfect thing to say,' Dido continued. 'I don't think imperfect girls deserve release – do you, Roger? Not until they have pleased me by purging their imperfections.'

I did not protest that her imperfection was caused by Dido's trap in the first place.

'You bitch,' hissed my Mistress, sullen now rather than furious. 'And as for your whelp –'

'Roger is our guest and acting master of the house,' said Dido, 'and shall not be insulted. Now, Miss, for a long time I have been aware of your misdemeanours: the matter of Miss Bernice, and your shameful conduct over the pink panties, in which you embroiled our guest; your treatment of Grubb, against my express command; and others. Your general attitude, Miss! I dare say you know you deserve punishment, and that the punishment shall be whipping – witnessed properly by the acting master.'

'I'll tell Daddy!' cried Miss Florence.

'Do, if you will,' said Dido mildly. 'But revealing secrets causes others to be revealed, Florence, and you know our bargain. Now, do you wish to respect it, and submit to your long overdue chastisement?'

To my surprise, Miss Florence burst into tears, and snuffled piteously that she accepted.

She hung her head, mechanically smoothing her rumpled pretty dress, and shunning my gaze. Dido ordered her to remove her clothing. Miss Florence sighed and pulled her dress over her head, to stand nude save for her pretty mauve stockings, lace-trimmed silk panties, and matching suspenders.

'The panties, too, Miss,' said Dido. 'Do you think you are going to escape a beating on the bare, just as it's your birthday?'

Tearfully, Miss Florence rolled the silk panties over her

thighs, revealing the thick hairy forest of her mink, whose curls sprang joyously out when freed from their tight silken sheath. She allowed the panties to rest on the jaws of her trap. Now, stripped to stockings and heels, she raised the succulent moons of her bare bum to our gaze. The swelling mauve heels of her high shoes gleamed like little mirrors of the orbs above, where the downy hairs at her furrow stood bristling in her fear, like grasses, above her goose-pimpled flesh. Her head hung in shame, and her arms dangled limp at her sides.

Without ceremony, Dido pulled down a coarse rope from a pulley fixed to the ceiling, and grasped Miss Florence by the wrists. She pulled her arms high behind her back; Miss Florence's head was pressed to her thighs. Dido bound her wrists with the rope, then hoisted her arms high above her back and fixed the rope in that position. Her golden tresses hung helplessly dishevelled over her face, to mask her anguished eyes.

Dido then fetched other, thinner ropes from the cupboard, and looped one around the shoulders and breasts, and under the armpits, then around the backs of her thighs at her knees, thus folding her down. A separate rope bound her knees tight, and another her elbows, suspended over the small of her back; finally, Dido wadded Miss Florence's own silken panties into a moist ball and pushed it into her mouth. Miss Florence groaned through her gag and tears of shame trickled down her cheeks. Then Dido produced the gasmask I recognised from the shed – it was a horrid thing of glass and mouldy rubber, dusty and cobwebbed, and she fastened it tightly round my Mistress's head.

'Happy birthday, Flossie,' said Dido. 'There will be a lovely cake after your surprise . . . which you shall commence, young man, if you please, with a vigorous spanking of her bare bottom.'

When a Lady says 'if you please', it is the sternest of commands. I felt powerless to disobey. I looked at the helpless bare bum of my Mistress, trembling so beautifully, and her breath muffled and hoarse under the gasmask, through whose smutted glass her eyes peered wide and frightened. I admit that, shamefully, my body stirred in desire. I lifted my hand to deliver her spanking. The soft, smooth buttocks shivered like petals in the breeze at the first crack of my palm on her naked skin. A pretty pink blush appeared almost at once, and Dido urged me to make my spanks harder.

I obeyed because I desired to obey and, as I saw her bare arse-globes redden and begin to squirm and shiver under my spanking, I slapped her with all my force. I was aware of my stiffening cock, and of Dido's wide eyes upon my bulge, and felt a sudden surge of anger that I was used for her cruel game. I spanked and spanked those naked quivering globes, wishing to punish them for their shameless nudity, and for their crime of arousing me. I wanted to make my Mistress squirm for so easily humiliating herself before me!

'Wriggle, would you?' I hissed, as my hand slapped bare flesh. 'I'll teach you to wriggle.'

'Make the bitch squirm!' Dido cried.

I repeated this to Miss Florence, calling her 'bitch'. Dimly, I was aware of Dido's movements behind me: her hand delved beneath her leather skirt and rubbed eagerly at her mound, as she frotted herself at the spectacle of Miss Florence's shame. I rained spanks on the thighs as well as the fesses, and left livid finger-marks at the soft thigh-flesh just by her stocking tops, each spank rousing a squeal of anguish. Her whole body shuddered, the legs jerking rigid in their trap, at the force of my cruel spanking.

Eventually, after I had delivered well over eighty spanks, Dido called a halt. I saw that the tops of her stockings were moistened by glistening juices from her fingered cooze. She whispered that I was very masterful, and I blushed as she looked straight and shamelessly at the swelling of my erect cock. I replied that I only wished to serve Ladies, and please them.

'You do,' Dido murmured, and her eyes focused on Miss Florence's own stockings, which were moistened too by glistening trickles of her love oil.

The cupboard creaked open again, and now Dido

produced a long yellow cane, of about four feet, and with a wicked snake's tongue. She swished it low in the air, causing Miss Florence's mink-hairs to flutter, and chuckled that a sound spanking warmed the bitch for a proper surprise. Then suddenly she brushed my swollen cock and said she commanded the master to put himself at ease.

'All your clothes off, sir,' she purred. 'The spectacle shall be prettier.'

Ashamed of myself, I stripped naked, feeling embarrassed at Dido's lustful eyes on my throbbing cock as my bulb brushed across my belly. However, I felt more at ease, both in nudity and at my new humiliance: no longer master, but naked at a stern Mistress's bidding. She ordered me to kneel right beside Miss Florence's croup.

Suddenly, the yellow cane flashed, and there was a loud crack across my Mistress's bare bottom. She jerked and squealed, her fesses clenching madly.

'One,' Dido murmured.

Miss Florence moaned, her muffled voice lifting in a question.

'No, I shan't tell you how many you are to get, Florence,' said Dido pleasantly. 'That is part of your lovely surprise.'

She dealt another stroke to the same place; Miss Florence howled.

'Two,' said Dido. 'Just two, so far! Don't waste all your breath, my dear, you'll need it for the hundredth.'

I was aghast; my face was inches from the red streaks on Miss Florence's clenched peach, the perfume of her sweat and fear powerfully arousing me. The thought of a full one hundred such strokes on my Mistress's precious skin made me tremble, yet also stiffened my cock to rampant hardness. Dido saw and understood my excitement, for she bent to squeeze my penis even as she lashed Miss Florence's buttocks a third time.

Twenty strokes were delivered on the bare before Dido paused. She lifted her skirt; her knickerless fount and her thighs were awash with the juices from her quim and, with a sigh, she began to frot herself quite shamelessly as she stroked the marbled bare skin of Miss Florence's wealed croup. Her gash lips were spread wide and wet, and the bud of the clitty trembled as she rubbed herself. Panting and flushed with pleasure, she took my hand and clamped my fingers between her thighs. Then she recommenced the beating.

Only our harsh breathing disturbed the silence of the dusty summerhouse, and over it the dry whippy whistle of the cane as it landed over and over on the clenched, squirming buttocks of my flogged Mistress. My hand was bathed in Dido's trickling cooze-juice as her thighs rubbed me against her gash to the rhythm of her caning. From time to time, I felt her sharp leather toecap tickling my balls, and tapping my bulb quite painfully. Her whole body swayed like a sapling tree as she put all her force into the caning, and counting through pursed lips all the time: 'thirty-nine . . . forty . . . forty-one . . .'

Suddenly, there was a loud snap and the tip of the cane, about eight inches, broke off on Miss Florence's bum-skin!

'Bother!' said Dido. 'Obviously, her bum is too tough for mere caning.'

Now she ordered me to fetch a birch from the cupboard, playfully instructing me to proceed on all fours and fetch it in my mouth like a cur. My progress to the cupboard was accompanied by two sharp cane-strokes, one to each fesse, which made me squeal in hurt surprise, and smarted painfully. The birch was very large and bushy, and little twigs broke off in my mouth as I presented it to Dido. She took it from my lips and swished it inches from my face, grinning. Then she touched my own bare buttocks with it, slithering the twigs across my skin, and tapping my balls with her toe.

'Still hard?' she murmured. 'Let us see if Florence's squirming will dismay you, Roger. Just imagine your own bum under birch . . .'

Suddenly, she raised her arm and delivered a crackling, swishing lash with the birch right across the livid red moons of Miss Florence's croup. Her entire body stiffened and her buttocks clenched. As the birch slid from the naked skin, a new, passionate welt was visible.

'One,' said Dido again . . .

I watched in horror as my Mistress's already glowing buttocks were darkened to puce by the cunning lash of the birch, her twigs seeking every crevice and every fold of skin for merciless caress. I was ordered to stand. My hand was placed firmly at Dido's fount, my fingers now on her stiff throbbing clitty and her free hand cupped my balls, her fingers straying to my stiff shaft. My command was to stroke her as she birched. I did so, and at each birch stroke, coupled with my caress of her nubbin, she whinnied in pleasure and squeezed my balls hard, even as my Mistress's tormented and streaked buttocks writhed in unthinkable agony. I could not intervene; Dido had me in her power and obliged me to frot her clitty hard, as well as thrusting three fingers in and out of her wet gash; she panted and sighed in cruel, lustful delight.

The birching continued for over an hour, the strokes uniformly severe. Miss Florence was a quivering jelly of sobs and tears, her naked buttocks livid and puffy, streaked with black. Over fifty strokes of the birch had swished her bottom. Now, Dido opened her dripping cooze-lips to release my hand, and she let go of my balls. She ordered me to fetch the birthday cake from the table. As I went to pick up the cake, I saw that my sobbing Mistress's thighs were a lake of her own cooze-oils.

The cake itself bore its two candles, which, close up, I saw to be inordinately huge, and sculpted from icing sugar, in the shape of two male cocks: the candles were dildos. Furthermore, the sculpted prepuces were cleverly shown drawn back from their bulbs, to reveal a crescent moon on each helmet, in replica of my own birthmark. Dido prised Miss Florence's clenched fesses apart, to reveal her wet quim and tight bum-pucker, and invited me to present her with her cake . . .

I placed the tips of the candles against my Mistress's bumhole and gash, and she spread her buttocks as though accepting their admittance. Dido moistened the candles with oil from Miss Florence's own quim and, when the shafts were gleaming, I pushed them neatly into each gaping hole, so that both anus and cooze were filled to the hilt with hard sugar. The body of the cake protruded from her wealed buttocks like a flowering growth. Dido ordered me to kneel, and begin eating.

When I was on my knees, she pushed my face into the cake, and said she hoped I liked ginger. I began to chew – the cake was indeed delicious – and Dido joined me, then I felt her stroking my balls, with words of encouragement for a hearty appetite. She replaced my fingers at her fount, and told me to masturbate her as I ate; I obeyed, and her thighs were as moist as the succulent cake.

We devoured the cake, our faces pushing the dildos into Miss Florence's holes as we did so, and making her squeal, until our lips met at the scented furrow of my Mistress's sticky bum. The candles thrust in her holes were beginning to melt, and rivulets of liquid sugar joined her cooze-oils to gush down the backs of her thighs. Together, Dido and I lapped eagerly at the sugar dildos, drawing them out of the holes with our teeth, and exchanging sticky kisses as we slurped at our syrupy cooze-pudding.

Her little shivers and moans as I frotted her told me she would come soon, but, as I licked and sucked the sweating, scented crevice of my Mistress's buttocks, I was in heaven at this new obeisance to her person. I chewed her pucker and fount-lips very gently, licking and kissing as I sucked the sugary juices, and my tongue crept up the hot bare flesh of her bum-globes, shivering at the puffy ridges etched by the birch, as though by this caress I could kiss her flogged bottom better.

Then Dido squeezed my balls, indicating that I should rise, and said Miss Florence must not be left out of her own treat.

'Sugar in quim is one thing, but cock is another,' she said. 'Roger's spunk is welling in these tight balls, and his cock is just the pleasure to rid you of those distressing lesbic tendencies. Attend to the bitch, Roger, if you please . . . your cock in her bumhole.'

My protests, and those of Miss Florence, were silenced by a vicious slap to my ball-sac. Groaning, I placed the tip of my erect cock against Miss Florence's pucker, and began to push into the sticky bumhole. She moaned through her gasmask, and shook her head violently. I hesitated; furiously, Dido ripped the gasmask and panties from her.

'Well, slut?' she demanded.

'Yes! Poke my bumhole,' sobbed my Mistress, gasping, and her face smutted from the filthy gasmask. 'I cannot be shamed further. Poke me as hard as you like. My birthday treat!'

She laughed bitterly. Yet I had no choice but to obey, or rather, I wanted no choice. I thrust my cock into her elastic anus, and felt her walls give way to my pressure. There was the briefest resistance halfway down her shaft, and then she groaned and gasped fiercely, and her anus yielded to me completely, the tip of my cock sliding in deep, to nuzzle her belly's root.

I began to thrust vigorously into her tight soft bumhole, my balls slapping against the furrowed weals on her buttocks and thighs. Suddenly, my thrusting became a frantic bucking as I felt Dido's cane sting my own bare! The yellow cane lashed me like a streak of raw fire, smarting most awfully, and I could not help crying out.

'O! O! Dido! Mistress!' I gasped.

'Who is your Mistress, Roger?' said Dido sweetly as she caned me.

'Not I!' cried Miss Florence. 'I'll take his cock and spunk in my bum, because I've no choice, but he may not call me Mistress!'

To be thus denied hurt me more than any bare-bum caning, and, resentful, I resolved to punish my Mistress, and make her submit by my brutal bum-poking, so that she would agree to be my Mistress! As Dido's hard caning lashed me on the bare, I slammed my cock again and again into the squirming anus.

'Is this part of your secret bargain?' I gasped.

'Don't pry, you whelp!' cried Miss Florence. 'O God, how it hurts! You fuck so deep . . . O! O!'

In a fury, I began to spank her bare nates once more,

trying to leave the imprint of my fiingertips on top of her livid bruises from Dido's birch. I spanked her as I fucked that tight velvet bumhole, which caressed my thrusting cock like the silkiest glove, until at last my balls could not hold back, and I too cried out as I delivered my hot spurt to the innermost belly of my wriggling Mistress. She emitted a long, choking sob as my cock softened and I withdrew from her twitching sticky shaft. Dido's eyes were diamonds of lust.

'I shall lick the spermed moon, master,' she whispered, and took my cock in her mouth.

With deft flickers of her tongue on my peehole and soft caress of fingertips on my aching balls, she coaxed my member back to stiffness. She squatted with her thighs wide beneath her upturned skirt, and her fingers deep in her wet pink gash.

Master! I looked down on Dido as she tongued me and for a moment forgot my enslavement. I pushed her roughly to the floor. My bum smarted so painfully from her caning that I could scarcely stop my fingers trembling as they picked up her birch. She struggled gamely, with fear in her eyes, but I held her neck down.

'Squirm for me, Miss!' I cried.

In rapid succession, I gave her two dozen strokes of the birch on her bare bum; when her skirt drooped over her skin, she pushed the hem up for me, though she squirmed and wriggled in great pain as her buttocks puffed and mottled with a forest of crisp red lines.

'O! Roger! O . . .' she squealed.

Her taut fesses clenched madly, and her body writhed as I added strokes to the backs of the thighs and the very rim of the top buttocks. For balance, my own bum was pressed right against the face of my trapped Mistress, with her long tresses dangling and soothing my wealed bum-skin; suddenly I felt her wet, firm tongue licking my furrow.

'Mmm . . .' moaned Miss Florence. 'Flog the bitch harder, master . . .'

I obeyed in silence. I flogged Dido on the bare, until the birch was almost denuded of twigs, and her arse-globes flamed raw. I saw rivulets of cooze-juice gush from her fount down her quivering thighs and pooling on the floorboards beneath her. I could not restrain myself; I let fall the birch, seized Dido by the haunches, then drew her up to my balls, with my bulb touching her wriggling furrow. I rammed my cock into her body, plunging at once right to the hilt into her silky wet gash, and slammed my belly against her fesses as I brutally fucked her from behind. She cried out long and loud as I thrust. My own bum-cheeks were spread, and Miss Florence's tongue probed my pucker, tickling me deliciously until she was an inch inside my anus. I paid no heed to Dido's squirming cries of protest.

'You'll pay for this! O . . . O! Yes! You'll pay . . . yes! O! Roger!'

I clenched my buttocks to trap Miss Florence's tongue, and bobbed her head up and down as my bumhole was deliciously tickled.

'So cruel,' moaned Dido. 'Yes . . .'

There are moments when delicate lust is overwelmed by cruel passion. I was aware that revenge would be visited on me by my two outraged Mistresses: yet my animal desire ignored the future. Or perhaps invited my punishment . . .

The mottled welts of a birch on a Lady's bare bum seemed then the most gorgeous sight in all creation! – and Dido's pretty bum-blush soon had my balls tickling with honey and aching to spend. Dido's eager fingers were frotting her clit as I poked her.

'O! You'll split me!' she cried. 'Ooo . . .'

And I knew she was bringing herself to come. I could not hold back, and as the first jet of my spunk washed the neck of her pulsing womb, she howled and shuddered in a fierce orgasm. The frenzied tickling of Miss Florence's tongue in my bumhole added a delicious pleasure to my spasm of climax. I let Dido fall roughly to the floor, where she lay in a bundle of quivering wealed flesh, her fingers still masturbating, and her quim gushing with copious love juices. Her skirt clung to her sweating belly, and I was afforded a full view of her fount and bum. I chuckled in cruel satisfaction – and this was my undoing, for a Lady is not mocked. Dido looked past me, with blazing eyes, to Miss Florence.

'*You* helped him!' she sobbed.

She rose shakily and manipulated the trap to release Miss Florence, at once kicking her savagely in the fount and felling my Mistress to the floor, where she lay squealing and clutching herself. Dido fell on her and began to pummel her breasts and belly, using her knee as a battering ram against the portal of her quim, and sinking it hard between the fluttering gash-petals. She punched and scratched the melons of Miss Florence's bare breasts until the big nipples were as raw and red as her own flogged bum. It was a dreadful sight – yet my cock stirred and rose to half-stiffness as I contemplated this naked female savagery.

Miss Florence squealed and tried to ward off the blows of her vengeful stepmother, but made no real attempt to evade her thrashing. Neither did I attempt to rescue her: content to see vengeance meted between females for their crime in arousing me so! My cock was ramrod stiff by the time Dido, panting and sweating, got up from Miss Florence's squirming body, and began to kick the quim lips with her toe-points, at the same time kicking and crushing the breasts with her other boot, making them quiver like jellies.

I took Dido by the bum, and now it was her turn to squeal; I pushed her to the floor, with her head at Miss Florence's cooze and her own fount above Miss Florence's face. My Mistress sank her teeth into Dido's fleshy wet cooze-lips, and she screamed! In return, she plunged her face into Miss Florence's own gash and began to chew and bite quite ferociously, her teeth fastening on the distended pink clitty, which caused my Mistress's bum and haunches to buck and lift in the air to her piercing squeals of anguish. I lowered myself on to Dido and parted her buttocks, and this time the tip of my throbbing cock parted her arse-petal, and I sank my shaft fiercely into her squirming tight anus.

'O! O!' she squealed, then, 'Aah . . .' as her bumhole's

resistance gave way and I plunged fully inside her arse-cavern.

My peehole and bulb were snug at her belly's root, and I began to poke her vigorously in the anus, my thighs cupping Miss Florence's face and my knees resting on her coverlet of golden hair, trapping her head. The two Ladies began to coo and moan as their biting of quims turned to tender tonguing, and soon they kissed each other's cooze-lips like lovers kissing on the mouth. Their tongues flickered on swollen red clitties, wet with juices that flowed from their gaping quims.

My poking slammed Dido's face against Miss Florence's fount; I leant over Dido's back and grasped my Mistress's ankles, drawing them towards me so that her legs arched over her stepmother. Then I shook off her shoes, and took her stockinged feet, in sweating mauve silk, into my mouth, and sucked them hard as I poked Dido's pulsing anal shaft. I bit through the damp silk and had her bare toes in my mouth, filling my nostrils with her sweet ripe scent. My tongue probed the fruity wax between her lovely wriggling toes, and my joy increased the force of my bum-poking, until Dido was squealing in delighted submission to my thrusts.

Suddenly, Dido's anus tightened on my cock like a vice and I could not budge. I waited for her spasm to subside, still licking my Mistress's toes, but then Dido rolled over, toppling me sideways on to the floor, with my cock still pinioned by her bumhole. Miss Florence rose, wiping her dripping mouth, and fetched the mantrap, holding it beside Dido's quim. She reached into her stepmother's furrow and with a groan, prised the locked buttocks apart, releasing my cock, which plopped out still stiff and throbbing and my balls aching to spurt. With a vengeful smile, Miss Florence snapped the trap over my cock, only an inch from my balls! I cried out in panic and shame and promised them anything if they would release me.

'O, you will do anything for us, all right,' said Miss Florence. 'Won't he, Mummy?'

Dido knelt heavily on my shoulders and Miss Florence

on my ankles, with the trap locked on my stiff member and hurting dreadfully despite its padding. With two heavy female bodies pinioning me, I was deliciously helpless . . .

They flipped me on my belly, squashing my cock most painfully, and drew back my arms and legs so that my wrists met my ankles above my bum. Swiftly, a thong bound me and was looped to the ceiling pulley; dazed, I could offer scant resistance. They pulled up the rope from the ceiling, suspending me like a crab in mid-air, with my balls swollen to bursting as they brushed the teeth of the trap that held my cock. Miss Florence raised her shredded stocking and tickled my balls with her bare toes.

'Revenge, Mummy?' she purred. 'He made us do such wicked things!'

'Long and slow revenge,' said Dido.

The two females exchanged kisses on the cheeks. Then they looked thoughtfully at my trussed body. There were whispers; Miss Florence fetched a length of copper wire and a short bushy birch.

'It'll have to be the short birch, Mummy,' she said.

'Yes,' said Dido. 'For a proper Turkish, when we've warmed his bum.'

I gasped as the wire was looped around my exposed balls and tightened fearfully, then it was strung up to the ceiling pulley.

Miss Florence giggled.

'They are just like tomatoes!' she cried.

'And a good target,' said Dido, placing the birch beneath my ankles, above my splayed fesses.

She held the birch with both hands and brought it down sharply on my fesses. It could not travel far, but smarted, the more so as the first stroke was followed almost at once by a second and third. My birching sounded like the furious beating of a cake, so rapid and harsh were the short, quick strokes. I gasped and squealed, my buttocks clenching as best they could, though in my dangling crab position I could not press them close, and the restraining wire on my balls prevented my body from any but the smallest shivering. Dido delivered the birch for ten minutes or so, after which tears were streaming on my cheeks, and I sobbed uncontrollably; then she handed the implement to Miss Florence, who birched me even harder.

'Take that, you filthy boy,' she hissed. 'That . . . and that . . .'

'Please! Enough!' I cried – foolishly, for this pleading spurred her to greater ardour, and Miss Florence's birching lasted longer than Dido's, a good fifteen minutes I think.

I could no longer count the strokes, and my teeth were chattering in the fright and confusion of my searing pain. Dido stroked my strained balls, murmuring that they would make a lovely sight under a real Turkish birching.

At last my flogging stopped; my croup seemed a lake of liquid fire. Yet now I felt the twigs of the birch tickle my balls. It swished high in the air – I tensed, tried to plead at last, but could only croak in a broken sob – and suddenly the birch was stayed.

'O no!' cried Miss Florence. 'Daddy! He wasn't due back until . . .'

Dido peered through the shutters.

'Painting! At his easel!' she said. 'Well . . .'

'Do you think he heard?'

'Grubb as his model – some classical subject, I suppose – naked, too, the slut!'

Breathlessly, the Ladies conferred and decided to exit through the rear window facing the lake.

'Wait! My dress!' cried Miss Florence.

'No time! Look, Grubb's coming!'

Dido began to scramble through the window, awkward in her tight leather costume, and presenting me with a view of her bare wealed arse-globes under her drawn-up skirt, which would normally have rekindled my desire. With a vengeful look, my Mistress slapped my swollen balls, making me yelp, and then followed her stepmother. Her purple dress lay abandoned behind her. Grubb now entered through the door, admitting bright sunlight; she was draped in a filmy white toga.

'The master sent me looking for you, sir,' she said

nonchalantly. 'I'm modelling a goddess for his picture. D'you think I look pretty?'

'O, Grubb,' I gasped, looking at the ripe swirl of her fesses beneath the flimsy cloth, 'you are the prettiest goddess in the world.'

I meant it. Her deft fingers casually freed me from my bonds as though she were merely untrussing a roast of meat. Then she picked up Miss Florence's dress and draped my loins for modesty.

'Now you are decent, sir. Pretty as a girl! Not that the master would mind. What a nice purple dress of my Mistress's! It quite matches your bum, sir, if I may be so bold.'

Clutching the dress to my bruised haunches, I stepped out after her and blinked in the sunshine. There was Major Dark, in a white linen suit and wide floppy hat, sitting serenely at his easel.

'Delighted to see you, old boy,' he said, and instructed Grubb to reassume her nude pose. He did not comment on my strange attire, nor the evidence of my body's ordeal, except to say he hoped I was having fun. He prattled about his visit to Italy, the glories of classical art, and said that Grubb was a superb model.

'Womanhood – soft and curved, with just the right hint of brutality, old man.'

He gave me some tea from his flask, which had a welcome drop of brandy in it, and then said he expected I planned to have a swim in the lake. I blurted that sometimes I did so, and he told me to go ahead, as I was sweating so. I might leave my clothing – we were all boys together, apart from Grubb, and nudity shamed no one here . . .

On that sunny day, everything seemed suddenly normal again. Like a newly freed slave, I cast off my frock and scampered naked across the grass to plunge into the lake and somehow cleanse the marks of my chastisement. When I emerged, dripping, the Major said that I had been up to mischief, judging from my bottom, and hoped I took it in good sport.

'Sometimes girls get a bit carried away,' he said, 'but it

is all in fun, and I believe you gave as good as you got, Roger. My girls need a good seeing to – both of them.'

I began to stammer some foolish excuse, that a gentleman must always obey the command of a Lady, but he put his finger to his lips. 'I saw everything, old man. Even made some pencil sketches . . . You are a good model too, being so well equipped. I can see why the Ladies both want you and resent you!'

'They seem to have some devilish pact, or bargain, sir.'

'The secret!' he laughed. 'Why, Flossie is my adopted, not my real, daughter. Dido knows, but Flossie doesn't know that I know she knows, and Dido doesn't know that Flossie knows that . . . well, women's secrets are complicated things, old man! Usually they aren't secret at all, except in the imagination. As for *my* secret, I get a great pleasure from observing your activities with Dido and Flossie. There! It is such a lovely feeling to see women made happy with such a well-endowed young man. As though I were making you a gift to them . . . And you are such a decent chap, Roger, I can't thank you enough.'

We made our way back to the lodge, and the Major told me not to let 'the girls' know that I was privy to their secrets.

'Like Flossie's birthday – after that vigorous seeing-to, she must be looking forward to her next one, in a month or two, I dare say. That wasn't her real birthday! She decides to have one whenever she feels like a surprise. Don't forget to dress for dinner, old man.'

I went up to my room, my heart glowing with happiness just as my birched bottom glowed. I was considered a *decent chap*!

10

Prometheus Bound

There were so many secrets in this house. Since Miss Florence's birthday, both females showed a certain coldness towards me, or rather a slyness, as though they had some further mischief planned for me. I took to spending time with the Major, on his painting expeditions, and usually accompanied by Grubb, who served as model for an impressive variety of classical figures, most of them nude. The Major feigned to excuse his fondness for painting, saying it was to balance the Ladies' passion for the theatre.

'Haymarket, Strand, Shaftesbury Avenue – they can't get enough of it, old boy. Females are fascinated by dressing up, and the mischievous possibilities of pretending to be someone else.'

Grubb was happy and artless in her nudity; I supposed the prospect of immortality removed any hint of prudery. One day, the Major casually asked me if the spectacle of Grubb's nude body – she was posing, I think, as Helen of Troy – excited me. I blushed, and said it would be dishonest to deny it.

'That is healthy,' he said, 'even though, or perhaps because, she is a lusty serving girl. You are perhaps unaware that Dido has expressed a desire to paint – envious, I dare say, of my own modest talents. Of course I approved – watercolours of churches and cornfields and suchlike are a fitting pastime for a Lady. But I am afraid she has her eye on stronger meat, as it were. She wishes to invade the preserve of male artists – classical themes and, specifically, the nude – the male nude. I am rather old-fashioned, but it is unwise to oppose a Lady's will, old man.'

I agreed heartily and sincerely, and he smiled.

'Dido would like *you* to model for her, Roger.'

I stammered that I should be honoured.

'She has in mind the figure of Prometheus – you know, the chap who offended Zeus by giving the gift of fire to humans, and was bound in chains for his impudence. Of course, the binding would be for show – silken cords, or something,' he added quickly.

'Of course.'

'There are other themes,' he continued, 'which I myself should like to paint, and in which you might be useful. Apollo and Daphne, for example – Daphne was the nymph ravished by the god in a birch grove by the River Orontes. Dido, of course, could portray Daphne with *full* realism. I hope you understand, as one chap to another.'

'Why . . . yes, if you like.'

'I do like, Roger. You see, the virtuous state of marriage sometimes needs a little spice, to remind the partners that they are more than mere companions. For a married gentleman to see his wife as a young, animal being, pleasured by a virile young male – such as yourself – can be . . . very stimulating.'

I replied that I was guest at Virginia Lodge and bound to oblige, and the Major smiled broadly and said it was agreed.

'And a little rehearsal might be in order,' he added. 'I observed your prowess in the summerhouse on my girl's birthday, with great pleasure. But there is even greater pleasure in observing with the Lady's consent, knowing that her play-acting is as much for her spectator as her companion . . .'

Thus it was agreed that I should serve Dido's body and her husband's lustful curiosity. But nothing was said about this matter for a few days, to my frustration, and I found that my visits to the soothing waters of the lake resumed as the marks on my bottom faded. At dinner, I began to drop hints about the delights of artistic modelling, and how male as well as female vanity was tickled by the prospect of posing, or pretending to be someone else.

'O, men are always play-acting!' sneered my Mistress as we ingested a delicious sherry trifle of Grubb's fabrication.

Dido, between mouthfuls, at last mentioned her project of Prometheus, as though it had just occurred to her – the sly minx! – and I leapt in to suggest myself as model.

'I suppose he would do, wouldn't he, Florence?' she said.

'Unless we can find a *real* man.'

'Do you think Mrs Mantle would release Denton from his duties?'

Miss Florence laughed scornfully; emboldened, I proposed my greater suitability than the unschooled Denton's, and my posing as Prometheus was grudgingly agreed, female wiles as usual making it seem my idea all along. The Major clapped his hands and said that we should all proceed to the library, for petits fours and liqueurs, and celebrate with a game of cards, although I did not at the time understand how cards were a celebration of anything. However, I have learnt that our English manners are based on hint and euphemism, so that a 'card game' may be anything desired . . .

The Ladies were to precede us to the library and set out the card table, while the Major and I relaxed over a glass of port. After some small talk, which avoided art, or women, we made our way up to the library and entered a charming room scented with rich leather bindings and decorated in a rococo style, with a powder-blue ceiling replete with naked nymphs and satyrs. The only lighting came from three blue candles which gave our game an air of agreeable mystery.

Dido and Miss Florence were already seated at the table, with the cards laid out, and beside it a trolley with cakes and liqueurs, and cigars for the gentlemen. The card table itself was low, and looked very ornate and very rococo indeed, and, on peering more closely, I saw with surprise that it was the figure of Grubb herself. She was clad in her frilly maid's outfit, with her skimpily knickered arse-globes pointing right at my eyes. She crouched on hands and knees, with her ramrod back covered by a green baize cloth. The Major nonchalantly took his seat at Grubb's head, and I at her bottom, and I knew the distraction of her fragrant orbs would rob me of any small distinction I possessed at card-playing.

It was agreed it would be a 'good jape' to play for money, and then, as none of us seemed to be carrying coinage, that it would be an even better jape to play instead for articles of clothing; every point lost meant a garment discarded, and, as the Major pointed out most reasonably, that would be a blessing to losers on this clammy night. Now I observed that Miss Florence wore an outdoor coat, hat, gloves, and even a cape. And as the game progressed, with her as dealer, I formed the awful conclusion that she was a cheat.

I cannot even remember what the game was – some intricate form of poker, I think. At any rate, it soon became clear that Dido and I must vie for the title of worst player. She lost hand after hand; primly, she took off her white kid gloves one by one, then unfastened her crimson robe, and let it fall to her ankles, revealing herself sheathed in a white satin waist cincher, white lacy bra and suspender belt, and silk stockings to match.

She put up a playful argument that her brassiere should be counted as two garments, since it covered two separate parts of her, but the Major opined firmly that her bosom was one item. However, Miss Florence sided with her stepmother and, for a short while, Dido played with one breast deliciously bare, the other half-covered by her brassiere cup whose sister dangled at her belly. Eventually, it had to fall, and her bare breasts gleamed in the sultry candlelight, the nipples visibly hardened as though caressed by unseen lips.

Miss Florence, for appearances' sake, dealt herself one or two losing hands, and jettisoned her cape, hat and scarf. By that time, I was wearing nothing but my trousers. Dido was in stockinged feet, her cincher had come off, leaving lovely harsh pinch marks on her belly, and her suspender belt was lost, leaving her stocking tops loose around her thighs. The Major too lost heavily, and was down to his grey silk drawers. Dido said he looked very pretty, and Miss Florence dealt her an abysmal hand, so that her left stocking had to go.

I found the sight of a Lady with one bare leg, and one stockinged, very exciting. My excitement was increased when she lost again, and with a sigh rolled down her right stocking, and then, losing once more, she defiantly pulled down her panties and sat proudly nude. With a chuckle, she draped the panties on the bulge of my cock which I had been vainly trying to conceal.

My own losing streak continued remorselessly; soon I was barefoot and sitting in only my panties, with Dido's, cheekily and at her insistence, perched on top of my straining erection! The moment came when I lost my last garment; feigning nonchalance, I rose, tugged my waistband over my bulb, and lowered the garment, freeing my erect cock to the amused inspection of all.

Even Grubb, from her perch as our card table, shifted a little to twist her neck and peek. I had to hold my cards high to avoid my helmet, which Dido obligingly adorned with her own white silk panties, and their soft caress made my member strain even harder. Her silk was still fragrant, and slightly soiled, from her Lady's place, and the scent of her quim and bumhole made my already feeble concentration ebb quite away.

Miss Florence smiled thinly as she dealt; the hand was reduced to Dido and myself, and I beat her, upon which she impishly apologised that she had no more currrency. Miss Florence snapped that she could forfeit the *use* of her discarded garments, to the winner of the hand. She smiled at me rather nastily. The implication was clear: my Mistress wished me to robe myself in Dido's things . . .

So it continued; now I was winning, and, piece by piece, donned Dido's stockings, her brassiere and cincher, which pinched abominably, and finally her petticoat. But when I made to don her panties, she refused, and lifted up my petticoat and skirt to keep my organ in view.

'I will not have my intimate thing sullied by a male organ,' she said with prim hypocrisy.

'Then how will you pay?' said the Major, beaming.

Dido opened the lips of her fount to show her glistening pink gash.

'These flaps are yours, Roger,' she said, 'but you must take them still attached to me . . .'

The Major nodded his approval, smiling with suppressed eagerness. I saw that his own cock was stiff as he inspected his wife's naked fount, like a wonder entirely new to him, and my erect penis trembling inches from her gash.

Dido rose, her eyes on my engorged shaft, and parted her legs as she bent over Grubb's body, showing me her fat quim lips swollen and gleaming wet with love oils. I stood and positioned myself beside her bare bum, and my bulb touched her glistening gash lips. I looked at the Major for approval, and his smile broadened. At that moment, Miss Florence retrieved from her cape a braided leather quirt about twenty inches long, studded with silver pins, and gravely handed it to me.

The Major nodded once more.

I lifted the crop high over Dido's buttocks, and lashed her on the bare quite hard. She quivered and sighed as a thin red blossom appeared on her skin.

'Harder,' she whispered.

I whipped her again and again, and her bum quivered like a flan, the bare skin reddening and my cuts ridging her to puffy swellings. Now her fingers were at her husband's cock, freeing it from its silken surround, and her lips fastened on it. I continued to lash her naked bum and she sucked her husband's cock vigorously, with frantic little bobbing movements of her head and shoulders.

Her quim teased at my peehole and I could no longer restrain myself; I threw off her petticoat and, naked for her service, put my helmet two inches within her quim lips, then, with a single hard thrust, plunged my cock to the hilt inside her velvet wet slit. My peehole slammed hard against the sucking hard neck of her womb.

I began to buck fiercely, and Dido moaned, panting, as

her lips sucked and pummelled her husband's cock. My crop-strokes to her bare grew fiercer with my poking, and the silver pins raised pretty crimson welts all over her squirming backside. I varied the angle of my beating, so that the quirt took her on the haunches and the soft skin of the upper thighs, where the welts were very livid, and her moans became real squeals of pain.

I glanced at Miss Florence, who sat rigid, her face flushed, with her skirt and petticoats up over her stockinged thighs and her hand moving in sensuous rhythm at her yellow silk panties: as she watched my flogging of her stepmother, she masturbated openly. She frotted herself most vigorously as my quirt cracked on Dido's bare, and my own buttocks trembled in the rhythm of my poking. Dido's haunches moved to my thrusts, her quim silky and wet as she squeezed my stiff cock, and I knew I must spurt within her very soon.

Suddenly, my Mistress rose and lifted her skirt and undergarment, wrapping them above her waist; then stepped out of her stained yellow panties and began to frot her naked clitty. After a dozen or so strokes to the distended bud, she gasped and grabbed my quirt from me, and applied it to my own bare bum, lashing me even harder than I had lashed her stepmother, who groaned in protest at the cessation of her beating. My bum began to smart fiercely at my Mistress's lashes, but any protest was stilled by my welling ecstasy inside Dido's squeezing, sucking gash.

Miss Florence had the toe of her boot between Grubb's buttocks, at her furrow, as she whipped me, and I saw from the rippling of her powerful thighs that she was poking the poor maid in her anus, scarcely protected by the flimsy panties. Grubb's knickers were sopping wet with love juice, and Grubb did not protest as Miss Florence's sharp toecap eased the thong aside to expose her naked gash, and began to toe-frot her swollen red clitty. Now, Grubb's moans of satisfaction joined ours. Her bum shivered, the big pale moons staring at me as though beseeching a spank; the cards, then the baize cloth, slid to the floor.

‘Spurt in her, worm!’ Miss Florence hissed as she flogged me. ‘Abase yourself!’

I began to rain spanks on Dido’s bum with my bare hand as I poked her. My own bare buttocks quivered and smarted most severely at Miss Florence’s merciless flogging, but all of a sudden it ceased; she snarled in an anguished mewl of frustration, and I felt her hands grasp my shoulders. Then her weight was on me, and I felt her naked quim rubbing against my glowing bare bum-cheeks. Copious hot love oil flowed from her gash on to my wealed bottom as I felt the stiff clitty dart up and down my squirming furrow.

I braced myself, to take all of my Mistress’s weight, and my poking of Dido was perforce heavier. The strong flow of her love oil down my bum and thighs, the tickling of her swollen clitty, and Dido’s powerfully sucking quim, made my cream well in my balls and I exploded in a howl of ecstasy as I spurted hard and full into Dido’s grasping womb.

Dido released the Major’s still rampant cock, and rose, making Miss Florence slide gently to the floor. My cock was gently released from Dido’s velvet wet glove of pleasure. The Major stood, and Dido pressed her face into his chair, with her thighs and gash still parted for fucking. Miss Florence’s fingers played with my balls and soft cock, quite tenderly, teasing them back to trembling hardness, as the Major plunged his cock into his wife’s shaft, where my cream mingled with her own love juices. He began to fuck her most vigorously, slapping her wealed thighs as one would a pony, and she whinnied for him.

‘Poke me, fuck me!’ she cried. ‘Ride me and buck my hole! Make me squirm for a worthless slut! Yes, another man’s cock has fucked what is rightfully yours! Split my whore’s gash! Fuck me till I scream! Yes, yes, O yes . . . !’

‘You are a buttered bun!’ cried the Major. ‘Your slit oiled by another’s cock! Take that! And that! Squirm, you filthy whore!’

He spanked her hard while bucking her very forcefully, and she squealed and writhed in pain, real or pretended.

Her hand crept between her gash lips and she began to frot herself as her husband poked her, and it was not long before her whinnying grew to the squeal of a long, shuddering spasm, which was echoed by her husband.

'O! O!' they cried together. 'O, darling!'

My cock was stiff at my Mistress's frigging; I saw that Grubb had her panties at her knees and was frotting her own naked slit. Miss Florence pushed her toe-point between Grubb's gash lips and kicked gently for her to stand up. Grubb did so; her eyes met those of her Mistress in unspoken agreement. And suddenly I found myself pinioned and obliged to lie back on the floor, with my cock standing.

My member was not long exposed. First, my face was covered by a fragrant, sopping quim and thighs which pressed down heavily on my head and began to rock back and forth, drenching me with quim juice and forcing a stiff clitty between my teeth, for my tongue to give pleasure. I was unsure whose bum and thighs crushed me so, whether Grubb's or Miss Florence's, and this uncertainty added to my excitement.

Suddenly my cock was sheathed by a wet gash, my haunches were clasped by powerful thighs, and the bum and gash slapped heavily up and down on my belly as the velvet slit poured love juice over my balls and grasped, sucking, at my raw bulb. Both heavy bodies crushed me mercilessly in divine submission; I was a tool for their animal pleasure. To be ravished with the Lady sitting on top, and in control, is pleasure enough – to be 'queened' as well, that is, sat on by another Lady's intimate parts, is beyond ecstasy. My female garments were squashed and sopping wet with the juices that flowed from my users . . .

As the two bodies threshed more and more, and bounced with painful heaviness on my face and balls, all the while anointing me with copious torrents of hot juices, I felt the cream well in my balls once more. Firm fingers stroked and squeezed my ball-sac, and above me I heard cries and gasps of my Ladies' orgasms, as I felt the passionate writhing of their bums and thighs squashing me brutally in their anguish of pleasure; it was enough to release my own sperm-flood, and I spurted once more, my bucking cock discharging nectar while my throat bobbed and I swallowed the love oil which soaked my lips. And with it, I tasted a powerful flow of hot liquid that was not love oil . . . and knew it was Grubb whose slit my cock had poked, while my tongue had pleasured my queening Mistress . . .

The candles had guttered out, leaving us in moonlight. My bra and underthings were soaking wet. I heard my Mistress laugh scornfully, and her voice coo: 'Frillies do suit the whelp, after all, and I am sure it is the only way I can stand him . . .'

The following day was chosen for my debut as model, and I obediently carried Dido's paints and easel for her to the summerhouse, beside which was a rocky outcrop thought suitable as Mount Olympus. By coincidence, the Major had to absent himself on business, so the party consisted of myself, the two Ladies, and Grubb carrying chairs and boxes. On Dido's command, I stripped to the nude, and felt completely modest, my role being as artist's model rather than lustful tool. Dido said I looked delightfully innocent, adding that this would not do for Prometheus . . .

I placed myself atop the rock, while Dido set up her equipment and Grubb brought a pile of filmy golden cords for my binding. Dido ordered me to lie down and adopt the 'crab' position and, when I hesitated, she chided me that it was all for show and I must not be scared of chastisement.

I lay on my side, with arms and legs stretched behind me. I felt my wrists and ankles loosely bound, and there was a slight stirring in my exposed member as I began to relish my submissive pose, artistic or not. Miss Florence finished the knot, and saw my cock still soft, and said she supposed my docile organ betokened obedience. Gaily, I replied that it did, and suddenly I gasped as she swiftly replaced my featherweight cords with a binding of the hardest leather thongs.

My wrigglings were useless; Miss Florence smiled cruelly as she showed me the pile of light cords was fake; there was only one golden cord, and the rest of the pile was heavy thongs. I looked at Grubb for comfort and was rewarded with a mocking simper, then protested feebly to Dido that she had told me not to be afraid of chastisement.

'Exactly. I didn't say there would *be* none.'

The three of them lifted me up in strong arms and with surprising agility, hung me by the ankles from a tree branch, and Dido sighed, and said painting could wait.

'That was show as well,' she said. 'I am more interested in revenge for your several insolences, Roger. To spoil my daughter's birthday – to bugger the serving girl – to fuck me in front of my own husband! You are a very wicked boy.'

She balled her fist and punched the helmet of my cock like a prizefighter, and my shaft rose stiff but helpless, casting a shadow like a sundial. It was agreed that I was a male pig, and must be made to snuffle like a pig.

Grubb unfurled a coil of copper wire, then began to wind it around my balls and the shaft of my cock, until my whole manhood was cased in a tight metal corset, leaving only the helmet bare. She pulled down my prepuce roughly, all the way to its root, and delivered a teasing kiss to my crescent moon. The wire was noosed around my balls, and Grubb tightened it, then stretched the wire taut and fastened it to a tree stump. She twanged it like a violin string, which sent painful shivers through me.

Miss Florence was wearing her purple flowered dress; she lifted the hem and reached to her panties, white silk rather than the mauve ones, and whose crotch was well stained by previous emissions as well as a fresh moist patch. She pulled off her panties and wadded them into my mouth for a gag which she fastened in place with a leather strap round my neck and chin. Dido said I made a very pretty Prometheus.

'You will remember that Prometheus brought mankind the gift of fire,' she said.

Then she took three candles from her box and lit them,

passing one to each woman. They squatted beneath my wired balls, holding the candle flames beneath me until the wire gradually heated, and I began to squirm in growing discomfort.

'No! Please!' I cried, but my pleading made them laugh more. My balls felt roasted, and tears of pain flowed down my cheeks. I called them witches and sorceresses, and cried out that they should flog me as hard as they liked, for no flogging could be worse.

'You heard the pig,' sneered Dido, and snuffed out the candles. 'We obedient witches must do his bidding.'

Sobbing like a schoolgirl, I felt my wrists loosened so that my torso plummeted down and I was hanging upside down by my ankles. My head was barely six inches from the ground. My wrists were spread and fastened to staves, hammered into the ground; while my ankles were separated, and slid in separate knots along the tree branch, so that my naked body was splayed upside down in the shape of an X. My attempts to whimper were stilled by Grubb's jerking the hot wire noose around my balls. Then Dido fastened my head in my Mistress's filthy gasmask, stifling, yet still sweet from her own breath. Dido lifted a heavy leather implement which I recognised.

'You are right, Roger, we are all sorceresses,' she said, 'and Miss Arbiter is one of us. She has kindly lent me her stockwhip for your renewed training. Now, my sisters, we witches are always nude to dance around our sacrifices . . .'

The three dropped their summer dresses and stood naked, then began to moan in an unearthly chant, clasping hands and dancing around my trussed body. Their breasts bobbed prettily, and they stopped from time to time to garland each other with daisies, dandelions, and kisses. A ring of dandelions was looped around my wired ball-sac, and dangled mockingly as I shivered. Dido took a letter from her box, and waved it in front of me.

'There is some news for you, Roger!' she said, taunting me.

Then she lifted the stockwhip and lashed me across my back and buttocks, making me jerk in pain. She dealt another stroke, slanting the other way, and continued to beat me in this criss-cross fashion for an age. My arse-globes and shoulders burned worse than my cock and balls, and for all my pitiful clenching and flailing, suspended helplessly in mid-air, could not escape the searing pain of her whiplashes. Grubb and Miss Florence demanded their turns, and received them, so that my flogging continued without pause in the sunny glade, sweat and tears dripping from my face to puddle the ground. I saw other puddles, too, where quim juices dripped from the slits of my naked tormentors, now frotting each other as they laughed at my whipped body.

'It is bad news, Roger,' panted Dido, masturbating as she knelt with her haughty gash right before my eyes.

Behind her, Grubb danced, tweaking and tugging at her huge distended clitty amidst her furry bush of wet tangled mink-hair.

'He's purpling nicely on the bum,' said Miss Florence, frotting her spread gash. 'How just! He'll be as black as a cinder when we drown him.'

I groaned, unable to believe my ears. Grubb said that they mustn't drown me before I had been punished enough to beg for it as an end to pain, and Dido agreed. The sun sank low as my remorseless flogging continued; I was unable to control myself, fearing that the final whipping would at last be delivered to my balls. Curiously, despite my terror, the hot wire maintained my penis hard, and Dido said an erect male was a fitting sacrifice for witches.

'I am afraid, Roger,' she said, 'no one will miss you. I shall tell the Major you had to return to Italy, and he will be happy to have Denton butter my bun in your place.'

'Denton has a fine cock and likes bum-fucking,' said Grubb thoughtfully.

Dido and Miss Florence giggled in unison.

Dido fetched a thick branch and placed it above my anus, then poked it straight into my bumhole, with excruciating pain, and began to poke me in the arse. Dido continued her flogging, striping me low on the buttocks, and I thought I should faint at this double agony. All the witches shrieked with glee.

I admit that, in our previous sport, I had indeed thought we were play-acting; but now the play was truly sinister, and I reflected on my situation, alone and trussed naked and helpless, flogged by witches, far from home . . . It is at such moments that the darkest fears assail the sunniest disposition. What if play-acting were at an end? Then, a surge of hopeful desire reassured me that this was their cruellest and most subtle play-acting of all, and my cock throbbed mightily! Dido placed her swollen clitty an inch from my eyes, rubbing and stroking herself, and addressed me, as though it were the clitty herself speaking.

'You have only to speak, Roger, and your pain will end. That is, nod your head in agreement.'

The lash, wielded by Miss Florence, continued to stroke my quivering buttocks as Grubb buggered me with the tree stump.

'Just curse all women as witches, Roger,' she said sweetly. 'Say you hate females, and will never again worship gash or clit, nor take a Lady's whip. Nod to agree, Roger . . .'

Her masturbation was powerful and hypnotic before my wide eyes. Furiously, I shook my head in the negative, trying to groan the word 'Never!' through my gag.

Grubb rammed the tree stump right to the hilt inside my squirming anus and began to twist it around, causing me to writhe in unspeakable agony; Miss Florence cracked the stockwhip right around my buttocks, to lash my inner thighs, a kiss away from my balls.

'I ask again, Roger,' said Dido. 'Nod yes, that you damn all women.'

Again I shook my head in violent refusal. My whipping and cruel buggery continued for some minutes, and again Dido squatted; I was delirious and half fainting with pain, and, as she repeated her sombre request, again I refused.

'Well!' cried Dido.

My whipping abruptly ceased, and I felt the wooden dildo harshly pulled from my raw anus.

'He won't play-act!' said Miss Florence crossly.

Dido rose and, still masturbating, placed her fingernail

at the ridge of my glans, where she began to move it round and round my bulb as though to cut me. At the same time, my Mistress's fingertip began to rub my peehole, and Grubb returned to my arse-pucker, but now with tender, tickling fingers. My honey welled in my tickling balls and, with a groan, I spurted, all over my Mistress's and Dido's hands, with Grubb cupping a palm below my balls to catch some sperm. The three witches rubbed my spunk over their naked breasts and quims, moaning again in their unearthly chant. Then, without a backward glance, they picked up their clothing, without donning it; nude, and their hands caressing each other's bare bottoms, they walked silently away over the grass.

I hung there for hours, dozing and sobbing in my gasmask, cheered only by its taste of my Mistress. Gradually, the sun went down and my wealed body shivered in the cold. I felt utterly wretched and bewildered; suddenly, in my half delirium, I heard female voices. I looked up and saw Dido and Miss Florence, prettily attired in their evening robes.

'Why, Roger,' cried Dido, 'what curious games you get up to! It is lucky we came to fetch my painting things, or we should never have found you.'

Gentle hands released me from my mask and bonds, and I was clothed in a silk white petticoat of Dido's, then half-carried back to the lodge, with Grubb in the rear, bearing the easel and painting equipment. But I saw that there was now a picture covering the canvas! There I was, bound and whipped by three naked witches, my bare buttocks and back quite livid with stripes, and labelled 'Masked Prometheus' . . .

Grubb, dressed in frillies, served me a whisky as I relaxed in the Major's armchair, and Dido and Miss Florence fussed over me. I clung to my silk petticoat as though it were protection against further revenge; then I was dressed in white stockings and panties, a corselet and my yellow robe. I smiled gratefully as Grubb buckled my yellow shoes and complimented me that white underthings went very well with yellow. She brought me the letter Dido had earlier waved, on a silver tray. Miss Florence and Dido took their seats beside me, like girls eagerly awaiting a bedtime story, and Grubb said that she would call dinner very soon.

I opened the letter, and found it a summons from the firm of solicitors in Egham, who were entrusted with my financial affairs. It seemed there was a problem over the income from my trust fund, and I was to call on their Miss Porritt before – I looked at the date, and it was only a week hence.

'You are probably poor all of a sudden, Roger,' said Dido gravely. 'That is how I interpret the letter. And of course you cannot stay here if you are poor . . . at least not as a pampered guest. You shall have to find a job! I may be able to assist you.'

I looked at the date of the letter, and found it had been sent two months previously! Dido and Miss Florence burst out laughing at my discomfiture; but it is hard for a fellow to rage at a Lady when wearing her pretty frock and underthings.

'You knew all the time,' I said bitterly. 'You kept me here for your . . . your play-acting, knowing that this thing hung over me all the time. Well, Ladies, all I can say is, I am pleased you have had your revenge for whatever affront I am guilty of, and hope your cruel chastisements and teasing have given you pleasure.'

'Yes, Roger, they have,' said Dido. 'But cheer up – you have plenty to look forward to. Our play-acting is not over, and our revenge is not even begun . . .'

11

Tug of War

Dido briefly explained my future: I was to be a servant at Mrs Norringe's rest home for Ladies of the theatre, by the river at Chertsey.

'You will have to work hard, Roger,' she said. 'Mrs Norringe is firm but fair. Oxford seems impossible, unless you can sort out your finances with Miss Porritt but, who knows, it could be your entrance into the theatre! No more of *my* chastisements for your poor bottom for a while, but don't worry, Roger – it *is* only for a while . . .'

She kissed me on the cheek upon our arrival, the imprint of her lips like warm honey. I watched the car speed away from Mrs Norringe's mansion and felt curiously alone, with the Thames sparkling in the near distance at the end of tree-fringed lawns. I knocked on the front door, and after a moment it was opened by a young man who was dressed in a kind of schoolboy's uniform: grey woollen shorts, cut very tight and high, a grey shirt and striped tie, and woollen knee-socks with black boots. Under the shock of tow hair, the face looked familiar.

'Denton!' I cried.

'Hello, sir – or I should call you chum, I suppose,' he said with a cheeky grin. 'I've gone up in the world, as you see – I hear *you've* come down a peg.'

He admitted me to the spacious hallway, like that of a grand hotel. There were potted palms, tapestries and drapes in bright pastels, paintings of the nude female, which I recognised as Major Dark's, and everywhere a heady female perfume.

'I'm sure you'll like it here,' he said, patting a thick black notebook at his belt. 'I'll take you to Miss Owsley – she's our housekeeper.'

I remembered Miss Owsley a little, as Mrs Norringe's silent companion at the meeting of the progressive Ladies. We entered a comfortable sitting-room with the accoutrements of an office, as well as leather chairs and a well-filled bookcase, and a rack of instruments of discipline – on open display. The window looked over the lawns to the river, where there was a little bathing cove shrouded by trees. Miss Owsley entered, dressed quite differently from before.

'This the new drudge?' she said, and Denton nodded. She dismissed him and inspected me.

'Signor – or signorina!' she cried brightly. 'I remember you from Mrs Mantle's do – a drudge of taste, but very naughty – I shall have to discipline you extra hard!'

'Drudge?' I stammered. 'I thought – I mean, I wasn't sure –'

Her bosom swelled. Close up and not dressed in country clothes, Miss Owsley was young, I realised, perhaps of an age with my adored Mistress. Her breasts stood very pert, sheathed in a tight white blouse and cupped in a lacy black brassiere which was perfectly and delectably visible through the thin cotton. The blouse had short sleeves, cut almost to the shoulder, and she wore gloves, or rather gauntlets, thin black leather that came up over her elbows and half covered her biceps.

Her legs were long and coltish, swathed in black silk, and made longer by quiveringly high black heels, with long toe-points. Her nether garment was not a skirt, but what is called a culotte, that is, a pair of shorts in the same black glove-leather, very tight and short at the crotch. This charming garment was cut so high that it soared over her hips like butterfly's wings, revealing a good portion of her garters and stocking tops, frilly lace like her brassiere, and even a glimpse of her suspender belt and black knickers. Her hair was short and pleasingly bobbed at her chin, and her aspect was enticingly boyish, thus powerfully feminine.

'Well, that's enough chat!' she said brightly. 'Trousers off, drudge!'

'I . . . I beg your pardon?' I blurted.

'Don't beg for pardon here, boy, for naughty drudges get none. Trousers off and let's see bum! Footwear too, and knot your shirt up over your back before you take position.'

She picked up a long cane from the rack, inspected it with delight, as though seeing it for the first time, and swished it in the air. Her smile was wide and white, like a beast's.

'New boys start with a free whopping,' she said. 'Twenty on bare.'

'Chastised, before I start?' I said, regretting my impudence almost at once.

'Perhaps Dido didn't explain – naughty girl! This is a creative and therapeutic establishment, for females only . . . with males to serve. Your whoppings are noted in your paybook, which you carry at your belt, and every time a Lady thrashes you, you get a penny-ha'penny per stroke taken. A drudge who is popular and obedient can soon amass pounds – why, Denton has been with us only a few weeks, and he is already quite flush. It is good you have a penchant for robing yourself as a female – some of our Ladies like being served by a boy-maid . . . and thrashing a male in frillies.'

She added that all canings at Mrs Norringe's were taken on the bare. Numbly, I stripped as she commanded, excited despite my fears. I felt powerless in the presence of a new, forbidding Mistress, and my penis stirred. Miss Owsley gasped and blushed a tinge of delicious pink.

'Well! I'm sure you'll be popular, Roger. I wonder if we have a restrainer big enough . . . Meanwhile, let's see if a crisp bare caning can't teach *her* to behave!'

I bent over and took position, touching my toes, and heard Miss Owsley kick off her shoes.

'I get a better run-up with my shoes off,' she said. 'You may make yourself useful and clean my shoes as I beat you, with your tongue of course: inside and out, and don't forget the heels.'

She placed her shoes at my mouth. They were fruity with

her odour, and I began to lick eagerly, feeling my cock stiffen to full hardness as I served her. I felt the tip of her cane brush my furrow and tickle my exposed anus bud.

Then she took a few steps backward, and I heard her feet thumping as she ran at me; the cane whistled and cracked fiercely across my bare buttocks; my croup jerked, and I bit her shoe-strap.

'A nice blossom,' she said. 'I can see birch marks there, Roger – Dido and Florence, I suppose? And Eppingham – you must have had a lot of bare canings there.'

'Yes, Miss,' I said. 'Oo!' as the second lash stroked me, and I felt my fesses clench.

'Come, Roger, that is only two,' she said gaily. 'Eighteen more. O, and don't twitch, like a good boy, or I'll give you the cut over again. Understood?'

'Y . . . yes, Miss,' I blurted.

The third and fourth strokes brought tears to my eyes, but I stifled my cry of pain and forced my quivering bum to stay still.

'Yes,' she said, 'some of our Ladies like to birch – it is very therapeutic for them. So if you can take that like a man, you should make plenty of shillings. There! There! And there!'

Each exclamation was accompanied by a rapid cane-stroke with no run-up – my bottom was seared in pure agony and my teeth tightened on the leather of her shoe as I tried not to cry out. I set myself to licking her shoes clean, as instructed, and yet the eighth stroke, after a longer run-up, was so hard that I could not stifle a long, low moan deep in my throat.

She said I must take that one again, for blubbing. I heard her feet thump, and the cane caught me in exactly the same weal. I jerked and shuddered, but managed not to clench my burning bum. She clucked her approval.

I panted and gasped louder as the beating continued, hard and remorseless, and my tongue and lips worked fervently on her shoes, until the leather, fragrant from her feet, was gleaming wet. At last, I had taken the twenty-first stroke, and she paused, panting.

'You stripe well, Roger, and take it well too. I have overlooked the sweet little twitches which a well-flogged bum cannot help. So, you have earned for twenty – two shillings and sixpence!'

I felt her cool fingertips running on my ridged fesses. Then they slid below my furrow and brushed my balls straining tight beneath my erect penis.

'Nice and puffy,' she said, breathing heavily. 'I'll let you earn another shilling . . . eight more, if you can take them.'

'You do cane tight, Miss.'

'Would you like them?' she murmured.

'I need them, Miss.'

The further eight strokes had my teeth chattering. They were pure agony on my raw buttocks, and I was afraid to leave teethmarks in her shoe leather. When I had taken the eight, she said I might rise, and I leant sobbing against her desk, as she stroked my bare, panting, and with her fingers quite openly feeling the lower shaft of my erection.

'Hmm . . .' she said. 'I'll call Denton in a moment – he shall be your guide. You'll put on your uniform' – she gestured to a neat pile of grey on her sofa – 'but there is the matter of your restrainer. All drudges have to wear it, to prevent unseemliness. But you *are* rather unseemly – you missed roll-call, when the boys are ploughed. I'd better plough you now, so that I can fit your restrainer.'

Briskly, she grasped the bulb of my cock and drew back my foreskin fully, then squeezed me tight and began to rub vigorously up and down. At the same time, she stroked my smarting buttocks with deliciously cool fingers.

'Come on, Roger, there's a good boy,' she whispered, tickling my anus bud.

Her hand then cupped my balls; I felt my honey tickling and, almost at once, she brought me to a heavenly spurt, catching my sperm in her cupped palm. I turned and stammered my thanks; her smile of approval was like a bouquet of flowers. She put her hand beneath the hem of her culotte, and from her black panties took a little silk handkerchief, mauve like Miss Florence's own panties, and wiped her hand, before replacing it at her crotch, where her fingers remained quite a long time, moving gently, before she said 'hmm!' and removed them, smiling and flushed.

Then she explained that roll-call every morning was accompanied by the hygienic operation I had just experienced, known as 'ploughing', to make sure the drudges did not become rampant in the course of their duties. Then their manly parts were locked in a restrainer, the key in Miss Owsley's possession, and of the Mistress of Discipline.

'It is a mysterious fact that tanning the bare bum frequently causes males to stiffen, as you did, Roger,' she said.

From her cabinet, she took a metal cup, or pouch, fastened on a waist-thong that was to snake through the furrow. She eyed my softened member, and said this one was the biggest and might do. It fitted tightly around my balls and shaft, and she snapped it shut. There was a peehole at the end, and the device was not quite painful, but certainly uncomfortable.

'You'll get used to it,' she said, tucking the key into her stocking top.

Then I had to dress in my uniform, while she entered my tally in my new paybook.

'Twenty-eight strokes, at a penny-ha'penny a stroke, nets you three shillings and sixpence, Roger!' she trilled. 'I won't deduct anything for the privilege of licking my shoes.'

Then she rang for Denton, to show me round my new home and workplace.

I found myself warming to Denton; at Mrs Mantle's his servant's livery had given him airs, while at Mrs Norringe's, the drudge's uniform somehow made him more affable. He explained to me our various drudgery: cleaning, laundry, and so on, but that our main task was to serve the therapeutic needs of the Lady guests. When summoned, we had to jump to it. Apart from that, we were free to amuse ourselves, but might not leave the grounds without an 'exeat'. Denton said that there were half a dozen of us 'fellows'; we took meals together, except when excused by a Lady's service, and shared a dormitory. It was very strict – there was no escaping roll-call, or ploughing.

'I expect Miss Owsley has already ploughed you as a new boy?' he said nonchalantly.

Blushing, I admitted she had.

'And you've got your restrainer. I can see from your walk.'

'It's awfully tight, Denton. And the way your peehole, I mean your bulb, sticks out of the restrainer and rubs against your trousers, is rather uncomfortable.'

He said there was a reason: the friction of wool on the naked glans – he called it 'your shiner' – numbed the nerve endings, and so made a fellow slower to spurt.

There was a distant cry of 'boy' from a female voice, and the sound of thumping feet.

Shortly after, there was a crisp sound of cane on bare skin, and a muted 'O! O!'

Denton smiled.

'A beating can be administered on the spot, by any Lady you serve, with cane or tawse, but for more than two dozen, or for any birching, she has to make an appointment via Miss Crouch, the Head of Discipline. She reports to Miss Owsley, who reports to Mrs Norringe herself. The rules are very fine . . . in theory. Sometimes they are overlooked in the heat of the moment.'

He grinned wryly and rubbed his bottom.

'But a shilling is a shilling . . . If you are given an appointment you must note it in the diary section of your paybook, and be punctual. If you are slack, you get the beating twice over, without payment. If the Ladies like you – I mean your bottom, old man – you'll find your appointment book well filled. And if you want, after a whopping, you can go to Miss Crouch for ointment, which she smears on your bare bum. It is quite effective, but she charges fourpence. *I* don't bother.'

I asked if any of the Ladies required therapy to their own bottoms. Denton replied that our sister establishment near Egham catered to Ladies in need of submissive therapy: the 'Eghamites'. I remarked on how many Ladies seemed to be theatrical, and he replied glumly that he had never met one who wasn't.

We came to the little secluded cove on the river, cluttered with driftwood and old tree trunks, and I saw a number of Ladies with parasols. All were nude. Denton said that Mrs Norringe, on the example of Miss Alice Arbiter, encouraged the healthy practice of naked sunbathing. The Ladies raised their heads and eyed us and, promptly, one of them summoned me – 'the new boy!'

She was the same age as my Mistress, I guessed, and exuded rude health, so that I wondered what drove her to seek therapy. Her hair was a pretty ash blonde, smooth and shiny, in the latest boyish style, and clung to her head like a bathing-cap with sweet little curls dancing under her beringed earlobes. Her breasts and bum were smooth and swelled quite tautly, and between her rippling thighs rose a furry forest of mink-hair that reminded me of dear Grubb's. She introduced herself as Mrs Chomley, ascertained my own name, and then handed me a bottle of smelly lotion which she said was for suntanning, a mixture of olive oil and grapefruit juice. I was to rub her body with this potion.

She turned on her back, and I knelt down and began to rub the mixture into her shoulders, then her belly. She ordered me not to neglect her 'titties' , which she said were very sensitive to sunshine.

Her breasts were large and conical, very pert for their generous size, and topped with big cherry nipples, like little tents, that stiffened abruptly as my fingers brushed them. She murmured that I should rub the oil well into her 'nippies' and squeeze them to make sure it was absorbed. The little domes stiffened very hard at my probing touch, and she sighed. Then she instructed me to attend to her thighs, and not to forget her mound, which she called her 'jungle'. Her fleshy quim lips peeped prominently beneath the tangle of silky curls, and here too my fingers were instructed to attend carefully, kneading and pummelling her Lady's place until she was well soaked in the oil and, I realised, with secretions of her own. My fingers could not help brushing the bud of her prominent clitty, and she sighed louder and parted her legs.

She directed me to her thighs and calves, and I made her gleam with the oil; then her dainty feet, the toenails lacquered bright pink like her fingernails. As though by accident, her toes brushed my crotch as she shifted, and I was glad of the pouch of my restrainer, to conceal my uncomfortable stiffening. The touch of her lovely feet had me straining quite painfully inside my cock's casing.

I complimented her on her suntan, deliciously marred only by the marks of bra and suspenders on her flesh, and she snapped that I should speak only when spoken to.

'I'm too indolent to whip your bum just now,' she said, 'but you will kindly attend to my own, and in silence.'

She rolled on to her belly and spread her arse-cheeks so that I saw her little anus bud winking at me in her deep furrow. Trembling, I applied the lotion there, allowing my fingers to tickle her, and she squirmed a little, with soft moans of pleasure. Once, she clenched her bumhole and trapped my fingertip for a playful moment. And when I was released, she did not turn round, but continued to writhe very gently on her towel, and I saw that the cloth was moistened with a little pool that seeped from her fount. Without looking at me, she dismissed me, saying I was not a bad drudge, though too talkative.

Denton was similarly employed; almost at once, I was beckoned by another Lady for the same service. She was Miss Task, slim and elfin, with a handsome, mischievous face. Her muscled thighs and arms were sportive, and the pert slabs of her breasts and bum were like pliant rubber under my fingers. Her hair was long and curly, a shiny russet, and I saw she was graced with a very thick mink, which, unlike the other Ladies', bore no evidence of trimming, but grew luxuriantly like a broad, matted lawn. She wore huge tufts of fragrant, sweaty hair at each armpit, as though daring anyone to comment on her boldness.

'I suppose you've been ploughed?' she said in a loud voice, as I rubbed her back.

I blushed and admitted that I had.

'And are you heavy? I mean, a heavy creamer? Do you spurt a lot?'

I stammered that I had no means of comparison; she twisted, and grinned at me.

'I bet you have,' she said. 'I certainly do. I shall make a point of attending roll-call. I like heavy creamers,' she added reflectively as she settled back to resume her sunbath. 'I like making boys cream in their restrainers when I birch them, and their faces blush just like their bare bums . . .'

At the end of the cove, under a cluster of branches, sat a Lady who observed us with haughty interest. She sat cross-legged, with one big toe between her bum-cheeks, and the other at the lips of her shaven fount, the lips pierced by a golden ring, and her palms upwards on her knees. Denton whispered that this was Mrs Holbein, the unofficial drama Mistress. Her skin was the colour of teak, her features African and delicately Nilotic but with long green oriental eyes, and she beguiled me.

Squatting, her figure seemed a perfect hourglass, the breasts full silky udders that surpassed even Miss Florence's in girth, or even Grubb's; topped by big brick nipples, each of which was pierced by a dangling golden nipple clasp, in the shape of an apothecary's serpent. The thighs perched on a croup matching the breasts in their oval perfection, and her head was a dome, shining and completely shaven like her fount! She was the very opposite of the gaily hirsute Miss Task. Curled beside her on her towel was a pile of shiny human hair, like the perruque I myself had worn, but black in colour.

We approached at the summons of her crooked little finger. She looked at me coolly in the eyes, then at the bulge of my restrainer, and ordered us both to remove our shirts and shorts. We were to go into the river and fetch her some pondweed. We obeyed, forbidden only to remove our restrainers, and plunged into the muddy river. The water tightened the leather thong holding my restrainer, making it bite my furrow most uncomfortably. When we returned with armfuls of bulbous weed, Mrs Holbein told us to give her a 'plant rub'.

We pinched the bulbs to release a sticky sap, and rubbed it into Mrs Holbein's bare body as she squatted. When we had done her belly, she lifted herself into the air on her fingertips, the belly muscles tight as a drum, so that we could attend her thighs and bottom, and the lips of her fount, swelling like a mouth of gleaming chocolate. To complete her treatment, we had to wrap her entire body in the long strands of weed. I could see that Denton's cock was stiffening like mine. Mrs Holbein said that pondweed had a lustful effect, and laughed that we must be very uncomfortable.

'Especially your crescent moon, boy,' she said to me, her eyes on my glans as it strained through the restrainer's peehole. 'It is very lewd to wink at me.'

'I assure you, Madam –' I began.

'Don't compound your impudence, sir,' she said smoothly. 'I think a beating is in order. You . . . and your accomplice.'

I watched Denton bend over her knee and receive a bare-bum spanking, quite glumly, as a mere spanking would earn him only a shilling, no matter how many slaps he took. He took over seventy – his naked fesses were writhing and well reddened as the Lady's firm hand spanked him, and as usual my curiosity was mixed with embarrassment at watching another male chastised on the bare buttocks. The other Ladies felt no such embarrassment and clustered to observe, their breasts bobbing as they laughed at his distress. I turned away from the spectacle of Denton's squirming bum, but Mrs Holbein sharply ordered me to look, as Denton manfully held back tears of humiliation at the harsh spanking. He was finally released and permitted to cool his bottom in the river; now it was my turn.

Mrs Holbein flicked my glans, right on my moon, and I shivered in awkward surprise.

'Lewd,' she murmured. 'But enticing . . .'

Then I felt her powerful hand on the back of my neck,

and I was pushed down between her thighs, with my bottom in the air. I smelt the powerful odour of her gash, suffused with that of her medicinal weed. She thrust her toe between my lips, tickling the roof of my mouth. She told me to suck firmly.

The first spank cracked against my bare bum, very hard. Then they came in swift flurries of half a dozen, a brief pause, and another flurry. I felt myself squirming as though under the cane, for Mrs Holbein delivered the hardest hand-spanking I had ever felt. I dutifully sucked on her bare foot, tasting her ripe fruity aroma, and she warned me not to bite whenever I jerked at a particularly harsh spank to my thigh or even the tender base of my ball-sac. The attendant Ladies cooed in mischievous appreciation.

Suddenly, Mrs Holbein paused for longer, and I thought my spanking over. I knew I had taken well over a hundred hard spanks. But she said my rude moon was still ogling her. She ordered me to lift my bum higher and spread my cheeks wide. I did so, then felt a hard finger pushed right into my bumhole, to its full depth, where it wriggled and stretched me to make room for two more, and my anus felt filled to bursting. Her sharpened fingernails pricked my channel like an eagle's talons, and tears of shame and distress filled my eyes. Denton emerged from the river and give me a startled look.

Then my spanking recommenced, Mrs Holbein holding me up by the fingers in my bumhole like a puppeteer, and twirling me round to show off my reddened backside. I moaned in my humiliance as I sucked and licked, not just her proffered toes, but the creamy skin of her whole velvet foot. The weeds began to slide from her body, and I felt the slimy strands slither across my back and bottom. Her thighs were bared too, and my skin touched hers. My cock throbbed most painfully in her restrainer and my balls tickled, aching to spurt. Her skin was so creamy, silky smooth, and her smoky perfume so sweet!

Her fingers poked me harder and harder in my bumhole as she spanked, and my squirming drove me to press down on her thigh, until the skin of my exposed peehole touched her just by her gash! At each spank, my glans was rubbed against her thigh – my balls ached and tickled so – I could not restrain myself and I groaned, with little panting yelps of joy, as the spunk spurted all over her dark smooth skin.

This went unnoticed, since my back and buttocks were turned, and Mrs Holbein discreetly wiped my cream into the juices that already prettily seeped from her quim. She hissed that I was a dirty whelp and continued to spank fiercely. Miss Task cried that the others should have a turn, and Mrs Holbein hissed dismissively. She continued to spank me for ten long minutes, then with a plopping sound, wrenched her fingers from my anus, and said I had been spanked enough.

'He's lovely and raw . . .' murmured Miss Task.

I looked up and saw the circle of nude Ladies, each of them well moistened at their founts, as though the spectacle of my shame and the gay ease of their own nudity excited them. Painters have often portrayed groups of naked females, in a sylvan setting, as both innocent and lustful at the same time, as though nudity in green nature reveals their feminine essence most profoundly. So the ebullient Miss Task insisted they have a game.

'Very well,' said Mrs Holbein smoothly. 'I challenge you to a tug of war – my boy versus yours, first to give is the loser, and five shillings on the . . . the outcome.'

'Five shillings!' cried Miss Task.

'Not game?' sneered Mrs Holbein.

'Done!' cried Miss Task, and turned to Denton, producing a hairpin, with which she unlocked his restrainer, explaining that the game required bare cock.

'It is against the rules,' said Mrs Chomley.

'Bugger the rules!' said Miss Task. 'Anyway, Miss Crouch goes to Egham today.'

She proceeded to open my own restrainer, and there were gasps as my naked cock flopped out, only to tremble and rise again at the Ladies' inspection. Denton's cock too began to stir, and he glowered, being somewhat smaller than me. Mrs Holbein took hold of my balls and squeezed, to arrest my stiffening. Miss Task did the same to Denton.

'Wait till we are ready,' Mrs Holbein told me, puzzlingly.

I had a good idea what this shameful contest was to be, and my fears were confirmed when Mrs Holbein explained that we would be frotted until one of us creamed, the male who held on to his spurt the longest being the winner. Mrs Holbein would frot Denton's cock, and Miss Task my own. Mrs Chomley was appointed judge, to ensure 'fair pulling'. Miss Task laughed, and squeezed her champion Denton quite hard on the balls, to dampen his ardour. I perceived that the odds favoured him; I had just been inflamed by my spanking, whereas he had had time to cool off in the river; and it was observed my cock had risen the harder on being freed from her restrainer. Only Mrs Holbein was smugly aware that my balls had already spurted.

We took our places, blushing and trying not to look at each other, as we were inspected by the gleeful naked assembly. Most of the Ladies stood on my side, where I could see them, and began to rub their breasts and quims quite lustfully in my gaze, to stimulate me into coming faster, as they had bet on Denton . . .

I felt Miss Task's hands on my own balls, not squeezing but caressing and gently tickling me to erection. Her fingers tenderly drew back my prepuce, revealing my moon, which caused further exclamations, and Mrs Chomley said the tug should begin.

Miss Task's touch was pure heaven! Her fingers stroked my peehole and glans, delicately touching me like a butterfly, and then suddenly squeezing my shaft and vigorously rubbing it up and down five or six times before recommencing the caress of my helmet.

'Don't hurry, Roger,' she whispered, 'you can take your time in coming. I love to frot you so, love touching your big stiff cock, she is so beautiful! When you are ready, you can spurt your cream for me. I don't care about winning, I just want to touch and stroke your handsome cock as long as I can. My, how stiff you are! What a lot of cream you must have for me! I can't wait for you to splash me with it, all lovely and hot and sticky . . . just like my wet cooze. Do you know how wet you make me, Roger? I'm really sopping as I feel your cock tremble for me. How I should love to cane your bare bum . . . yes, cane her till she's purple! Your bottom bare and squirming so prettily as she smarts under my cane . . . all puffy and wealed and helpless. How you'd hate me! O! I'm so wet, thinking of it.'

I moaned and felt my cock stiffen rock hard, trembling at the thought of the devious Miss Task thrashing me bare. I looked round and saw that Denton's member was enclosed in the dark envelope of Mrs Holbein's fingers. She winked at me – that I had already spurted was our little secret, but so deft was Miss Task's touch, so sly and honeyed her words, that I dreaded disappointing my sultry new Mistress; my endurance was not helped by the spectacle of the nude females before me, openly masturbating, with wide streaming gashes, and pinching their erect nipples, blowing me little pouting kisses to spur me on. I groaned and panted desperately, feeling my cream gather in my balls.

Denton too was panting harshly, with his cock rigid and trembling, and Mrs Holbein had his prepuce pulled all the way back, and was frotting quite vigorously, with deep strokes on the glans that had him gasping and shivering with pleasure. She whispered in his ear.

'No licking!' cried Mrs Chomley as referee.

'Or, better than the cane, Roger, the birch!' whispered Miss Task. 'Just think . . . my birch kissing your bare bum till she squirms, all black and blue! Think of that, Roger, and you shan't come. Your Mrs Holbein won't birch you, she's no cash spender, although she's the richest woman in Curacao! I suggested this contest as a way of helping her out, discreetly, when I lose! So just think of my birch lashing your bare, Roger, and for extra shame, a big fat hard dildo pushed right up your anus, hurting you so dreadfully as I bugger you and thrust in and out and fuck you in the bum till you squeal . . .'

I almost did squeal as my knees turned to jelly at my lustful longing for just such treatment from this artful

Lady, the perfume of her lithe naked body filling me as her supple fingers frotted my throbbing cock. I saw that Mrs Holbein was now frotting Denton with utmost vigour, whispering, 'Come on . . . come on . . .' her looks of encouragement holding a delicious veiled threat if he failed to oblige her.

'O . . .' I moaned, 'O . . . I'm going to . . .'

Mrs Holbein frotted Denton with her fingers a blur. I felt the honey tickle my balls and knew I could not hold off my spurt – and suddenly, to my relief, I heard Denton's anguished yelp as a great jet of cream spurted from his peehole over Mrs Holbein's flickering fingers, and she beamed victorious.

'O! Don't stop, Miss!' I cried to Miss Task.

'Of course I shan't stop, you wicked boy,' she cooed, and rubbed my shaft now with utmost force, but with sudden disdain; in seconds, I convulsed in a spasm, and my jet of seed spurted powerfully over her fingers.

'It seems I have lost my wager and must pay Mrs Holbein her five shillings,' said Miss Task loudly. 'And now my dear friend can afford to give you a proper caning. But I am cross with you, boy! I meant what I said about birching your bare, and buggering you . . .'

She stroked my naked buttocks, and I shivered.

'. . . no matter how much it costs me.'

Suddenly, we were interrupted by a loud female voice, which came from a figure all in nurse's white, who appeared at the top of the grassy knoll overlooking us.

'Ladies!' cried the newcomer, her white skirt flapping like a seagull's wings.

'Why, Miss Crouch!' replied Mrs Holbein.

12

Strict Teatime

The ladies stood still, covering their founts with their palms, all except Mrs Holbein and Miss Task, who stood in defiant nudity. The newcomer approached us angrily. I thought her very young to be Mistress of Discipline, lithe and muscular, with trim, taut buttocks swelling proudly against her matron's skirt, and pert breasts that heaved prettily in her indignation. Her hair was snow-blonde, almost white, and cropped in a mannish bristly style like an American 'crew-cut', which gave her an appearance of hard and athletic femininity.

'Unseemliness!' she cried. 'I am gone moments, and return to find . . . unseemliness!'

'Only sport, Miss Crouch,' drawled Mrs Holbein.

'It was Mrs Holbein's idea!' said Miss Task slyly.

Mrs Holbein looked scornful and shrugged. 'I admit it,' she said.

'The drudges will be chastised, of course,' spat Miss Crouch, 'but decent behaviour cannot be expected of *males*. Ladies merit serious correction.'

She jangled the keyring at her belt, which nestled beside crops and canes, swirling at her waist like an extra skirt.

'Here and now?' said Mrs Holbein.

'Yes, Madam. You know the rules, accepted – and paid for – by all of you. You will please replace your perruque, decently.'

Mrs Holbein fixed her black wig on her head, so that its tresses swirled across the swelling dark tips of her nipples;

then affixed a slightly smaller hairpiece to her shaven fount, covering almost all her lower belly. She smiled at me, and murmured that it was a Lady's conceit to adorn herself with her own hair. She bent over and touched her toes, presenting Miss Crouch with the ripe orbs of her bottom.

'How many, Miss?' she purred.

'Twenty-four, Mrs Holbein,' said Miss Crouch, selecting the longest cane from her belt, and flexing it, with a smile of cold satisfaction.

'And the drudges?'

'A dozen each – unpaid, of course.'

'Then let them go free, Miss. I'll take their punishment,' said Mrs Holbein.

'Four dozen!'

'Yes. With a minute's pause between dozens, if you would be kind.'

'Well!' Miss Crouch exclaimed.

The full soft melons of Mrs Holbein's breasts swayed gently as she spoke, her nipples brushing the grass. I could see her quim lips swollen amid the tangled thicket of her fount-wig, and the gleaming hard bud of the clitty.

'I have often wondered if you would not be happier at our sister establishment at Egham, Mrs Holbein,' said Miss Crouch drily.

She lifted her arm; her bosom swelled, her croup tightened, and I shivered. She lashed Mrs Holbein's bare buttocks with the cane, very hard, and a dark streak of crimson blushed the ebony flesh. Another stroke followed, to the same weal, and another, mercilessly fast. Mrs Holbein's buttocks quivered and I heard her gasp, and her hung teats trembled against the leaves of grass. Her chastiser licked her lips and delivered the fourth stroke, high at the top of the fesses, which made Mrs Holbein clench her buttocks and groan.

Miss Crouch's muscles rippled awesomely as she flogged. I could scarcely stand the spectacle of a proud Lady's humiliance, even willing, though her companions watched excitedly, and I saw fingers creep to naked gashes for discreet frotting; every one of those gashes sparkled wet with the juice of lust. Denton was blushing, as ashamed as myself, but neither of us looked away. The cane whistled and cracked on Mrs Holbein's quivering bare, to a dozen, at which point Miss Crouch panted that there was a minute's pause. Mrs Holbein rose and rubbed her striped buttocks.

'My, it smarts!' she gasped. 'You cane tighter than ever, Miss. It must be the fresh air.'

Miss Crouch's eyes flashed, and she looked at her watch until the minute was up. Then Mrs Holbein reassumed position for the second set, Miss Crouch now varying her strokes to weal the bare fesses in a criss-cross pattern, with hard slashing strokes to the underside of the buttocks, and the sides of the thighs, almost at her hips, where the welts were even more livid than in the soft meat of the croup's centre. Mrs Holbein's teeth gleamed white, her lips stretched in a rictus of agony.

'What are you Ladies staring at so timidly?' cried Miss Crouch. 'Be thankful you are not at Egham!'

This advice did nothing to stem their lustful frotting, nor their thrilled murmurs. Miss Crouch had delivered twenty-one strokes, and said that the last three would be tightest of all. The cane was a blur as she swished the clenched buttocks of her shivering prey, and then the ordained two dozen was complete.

'But now for the drudges' punishment,' she hissed.

I fell to her knees and begged her to give me my punishment – and Denton's too, if she wished – and spare Mrs Holbein's croup further weals. She silenced me, and Mrs Holbein cried that she was ready and willing to take her further flogging.

The third set duly began; Mrs Holbein was quivering very hard now as her lashing proceeded, and I saw Miss Crouch was sweating profusely, her unsupported breasts clearly outlined as they shook quivering against her damp blouse; the nipples stood erect like little houses, and sweat plastered her nurse's skirt to her evidently knickerless bottom and fount, where a darker patch of moisture overlay the dampness of her sweat. Despite my horror at Mrs Holbein's agony, my cock was quivering once more.

Miss Task masturbated quite openly, her eyes shining with gleeful lust as she observed her rival's humiliance, and she smacked her lips in time with each stroke of the cane on Mrs Holbein's shivering brown buttocks. Mrs Holbein did not bother to rise for the final pause between sets, but urged Miss Crouch to finish her. Miss Crouch now lifted the cane with both hands, her body itself a whiplash as she dealt the final dozen to Mrs Holbein's bare fesses. I saw that there were tears glistening on her cheeks, and felt a longing to kiss away her pain. Yet she took it in silence; Miss Task's belly heaved as she masturbated, panting close to a spasm.

The dark female took the last and forty-eighth stroke, her bare bum now a mass of purple and black weals, and sank to the grass with a long, low sob, just as Miss Task panted, 'Yes . . . yes!' and brought herself to a quivering, yelping climax. She was shielded by her sisters in lustfulness, some of whom fingered each other in quim, or embraced with teats and thighs pressing; Miss Crouch, heaving in her own exertion, wiped the sweat from her eyes and ignored them, as she surveyed the shaking body of her victim, a grim smile playing on her lips. She sighed.

Her fingers hesitantly pawed at her own crotch and the spreading patch of damp at her quim, as the Ladies began to openly frot, standing over the naked body of Mrs Holbein as before an altar. Denton and I no longer bothered to conceal our fully erect penises; our presence, as mere male drudges, seemed somehow irrelevant to this lustful female celebration. Miss Crouch approached and she fumbled to put her cane away but, at the same time, lifted her skirt right over her thighs, so that I saw the lush tangle of her wet mink-curls; she was indeed knickerless, and her flogging hand delved within the swollen quim lips as she rubbed her clitty in joyful, savage celebration of her dominance.

Soon, the air was full of sighs and squeals as the women brought themselves, or each other, to climaxes, their naked thighs gleaming with copious torrents of juices from their gaping wet quims. Mrs Holbein wriggled and thrust her flogged bum in the air, as though a willing offering to lust, and parted her thighs to show her own wet gash, where I saw her ebony fingers tickling herself like the others. Her flogging had made her lustful! And it was not long before she too moaned and sighed and her bottom squirmed in her spasm, as though caned anew. Suddenly, she leapt to her feet, rubbing her flogged nates casually, as though at a mere bee-sting.

'My, that was tight, Miss Crouch!' she cried. 'No hard feelings, eh?'

'No hard feelings, Madam,' said Miss Crouch uncertainly.

I felt as though Mrs Holbein had orchestrated the proceedings all along! She ordered Denton and me to plunge into the cold water, to reduce our cocks, then to dress properly. When we emerged, softened, we were fastened into our restrainers by Miss Crouch, and told to dress again. Thoroughly ashamed, we did so, and Mrs Holbein said pleasantly that the drudges had a debt to repay.

'Fancy my taking a dozen each for those worthless whelps!' she said. 'It must have been the sun. At any rate, they shall suffer for it.'

In the distance, there was the gong for luncheon, and the Ladies began to gather their things.

'Since you are here, Miss Crouch, I am booking these drudges for tomorrow. They shall serve me tea in my chamber at four precisely, and I shall want their attendance for two hours. I intend to do the business properly. Especially the new boy . . .'

She parted her quim lips very wide and retrieved from her slit a jewelled leather purse, with a golden clasp in the shape of a saddle and riding crop. The leather shone very wet from her quim; from the purse, she extracted a pound note and reminded the glowering Miss Task of her five shilling debt. With a sneer, Miss Task parted her own buttocks and withdrew two half-crowns from her bumhole!

She handed them to Mrs Holbein who placed them coolly in her little purse.

'You wish to discipline the males over tea?' said Miss Crouch.

'Of course. It is more civilised. Let me see . . . they shall take a dozen with cane, for what they owe me, so that makes one shilling and sixpence each, or three shillings.'

She proffered the pound note.

'But I have no change for such a large amount,' said Miss Crouch.

'I didn't say only the cane,' said Mrs Holbein, fixing me with her gaze. 'Or only a dozen . . .'

It was obvious that Mrs Holbein intended to birch us! Because we were 'booked' for chastisement in excess of a dozen cane-strokes, the rules excused Denton and myself from further caning that day. During the afternoon, I received a vigorous spanking of a hundred slaps from Miss Task and a slightly less harsh one from Mrs Chomley; in neither case did they suggest that I should unlawfully remove my restrainer, even though both beatings made my cock obviously excited. Miss Task smiled at that: I think she relished my discomfort as part of her chastisement.

Mrs Chomley begged to be allowed to take photographs with her pocket Kodak of my crimson bum, and of my bulging cock too, for her scrapbook. I had no objection, and even found her snapping mildly stimulating; afterwards, she admitted that Mr Chomley liked to see she was getting good value at Mrs Norringe's. In each case, the sum of one shilling was duly noted in my paybook, and Mrs Chomley tipped me sixpence.

With our shared experiences, Denton and I seemed to have become friends. He said shyly that he hadn't really minded being beaten by me at Mrs Mantle's, and had even rather enjoyed it.

Mindful of his seniority, I casually asked him if he had been in the Great War, perhaps as a boy soldier, and he replied, yes indeed, as a boy soldier he had been 'at the sharp end', but assumed a stoical expression which forbade further enquiry. The other fellows were quite secretive, and

I wondered how many of them had experienced discipline outside the confines of Mrs Norringe's. I was curious about Egham, where Ladies 'took fearful whoppings on their bare bums, and titties too', according to Denton; we agreed on a vague plan to sneak over there one evening and spy. Later, after a plentiful tea, we played cards or ping-pong, or read, until it was time to proceed to the dormitory at nine-thirty.

Our dormitory was spartan and spotless, with half a dozen metal beds arranged in two rows, and each provided with a cupboard, chair and chamber pot. Miss Owsley and Miss Crouch, canes in hand, supervised our retirement. On each bed lay a nightgown, which proved to be a rather pretty girl's nightie with frilly purple bows. Miss Owsley unlocked our restrainers, and on our final visit to ablutions we washed them before setting them on our folded uniforms on our bedside chairs. Denton had the bunk next to mine.

He whispered that he envied my spunk in wearing women's frillies that day at Mrs Mantle's, and had never dared go so far himself – our nighties, or drudge's skirts, meant for shame, were the nearest he got. I told him robing as female was easy, once dared, and provided a profound and serene satisfaction. Miss Crouch swished her cane and commanded silence.

Then she ordered us to lie on our backs and lift our nighties. She took a long thin chain with clasps at intervals, and draped it across our prone bodies, fastening the balls of each drudge. Each clasp had a little cowbell attached to it, and the end of the chain led to Miss Crouch's own chamber, so that any abnormal noise in the night would warn her of impropriety; I was lulled to sleep by the discreet tinkle of cowbells.

I awoke to the sun streaming through the dormitory. There was a gong, and a fierce tug on our ball-chain, so that we were obliged to hop from our beds and line up, our bells tinkling. Miss Crouch appeared, attired in a black rubber garment like a swimsuit, a rubber bathing cap, and a thick wooden paddle hanging from her belt. She signalled us to remove our nighties, then, naked, we padded down the stone corridor to the ablutions, the chamber being divided into washroom and shower area, separated by a stone partition.

Still chained, we were allowed into the cubicles to evacuate, then marched under the shower, where Miss Crouch opened a freezing jet of water; she then joined us. We hopped and slapped ourselves under the icy spray, shivering and crying out, until Miss Crouch announced roll-call; she called a name, and the first drudge stepped forward to the partition wall, where he pressed his loins to a large aperture about a thigh's breadth. Denton whispered that this was ploughing, and I realised that the fellow's penis was being rubbed by hand, or hands, unseen, on the other side of the partition.

While the naked drudge trembled at his morning stimulation, Miss Crouch belaboured his wet bum with spanks from her wooden paddle, whose cracks echoed above the noise of the shower. I heard Ladies giggling beyond the wall, and one of us cried out to the ploughed male that he should hurry up, as we were all freezing. Miss Crouch was protected from the shower by her rubber costume, tight as a second skin and outlining her breasts and bum with beguiling clarity as the droplets trickled down her smooth fesses.

At length, there was a whimpering yelp and a clinking of his cowbell, and his ploughing was completed. His spanking ceased, he rejoined us, shamefaced, his cock raw and half-erect. He was followed by each of the others, and lastly myself, so numb with the cold that I wondered if my penis would rise at all. Miss Crouch's paddle slapped my bare bottom with a wet, painful crack, and I pressed my balls and cock obediently through the aperture, urged on by impatient cries. The appearance of my flaccid penis was greeted by giggles from a number of female voices, and aah's of interest as she began to stir.

Miss Crouch's spanks rained very hard on my bare, and I was so ashamed at my humiliant situation that I felt my cock harden perceptibly. My balls were cupped by a soft palm which began to stroke me, then moved up my shaft, and a fingertip began to caress my peehole. The palm rubbed my shaft quite vigorously and, despite the numbing cold, my organ became halfway stiff. Now the fingers had my prepuce tugged back, and a palm rubbed round and round on my thickening glans and peehole. Suddenly I felt sharp claws scratch my balls – the hand could only belong to Mrs Holbein! At once, my cock thrust to full stiffness, and she purred.

'Come on, Roger,' I heard her whisper. 'Come for me . . .'

Her rubbing grew more and more vigorous, almost businesslike. I began to groan; the spanks to my bare seemed to rain harder and harder; and, to my joy, I spurted with almost unseemly haste and force into Mrs Holbein's caressing palm. Unleashed, dressed, and filing in for our breakfast, I was aware of a grudging respect from my fellows: I had shortened their ordeal by spurting the fastest of any of them. Denton whispered that a ploughing first thing in the morning certainly gave a fellow a hearty appetite.

My second day proceeded in humdrum fashion, with some minor drudgery such as sweeping floors or attending to the laundry – dressed in a frilly skirt and apron – and with only two relatively mild spankings from Ladies new to me; playful rather than cruel, and the spankings not exceeding fifty.

Four o'clock approached, and I met Denton in the common room. Apprehensively we ascended the staircase to Mrs Holbein's rooms. She greeted us with a crisp smile, and we were admitted to a spacious chamber overlooking the lawns and river; it was richly decorated with paintings and figurines, most of them erotic, of nude males and females with endowments of mythic proportion. Prominent in the corner was a rack of corrective implements.

Mrs Holbein wore a flimsy black silk peignoire, whose frilly hem swirled above her knees, scarcely covering her fount; with a mischievous smile, she said this was her ‘teatime gown’. Her long brown legs were sheathed in white silk stockings, with white suspenders and garter belt, plainly visible through the peignoire, and delicious against her ebony skin. She wore no panties. I gasped at the lushness of her pubic wig, though I knew it to be a ‘falsie’. Her head too was draped in the perruque of her own black tresses. Her shoes were white like her stockings, with very sharp toe-points and high heels. To my surprise, she said Miss Crouch might be joining us, as she wished to audition for a part in one of Mrs Holbein’s dramatic productions, or ‘playlets’.

‘Being in charge of play-acting gives me a certain influence,’ she said, rather haughtily. ‘Vanity is so powerful in our female breasts! I believe you are acquainted with Miss Porritt, the solicitor, Roger – she, too, has theatrical aspirations.’

I said that I should make her acquaintance in a few days’ time.

‘Profitable, I trust. Well, I dare say Miss Crouch is tied up somewhere, so we may proceed with our tea, and . . . other business. Gentlemen, you will please strip naked.’

‘You mean to beat us at once, Madam?’ I said.

‘Why, no – you shall be properly dressed to serve me tea, and then you shall be beaten,’ she replied.

We stripped, and stood nervously as Mrs Holbein produced a key – holding her finger to her lips in secrecy – and unlocked our restrainers. Her eyes widened in mock dismay as she saw both our cocks spring to attention. Then she handed us maids’ uniforms, just like Grubb’s, and told us to don them. Denton’s eyes sparkled, though he blushed. We had silk stockings and frilly skirts with aprons, blouse and corset – very tight – but no panties, and perilous high shoes that pinched most painfully. Then she crowned us with lush black wigs, which she said were made of her own mink-hair. I breathed in her smoky perfume and felt my cock rock-hard and, looking at Denton’s frilly apron, I saw his own bulge. Mrs Holbein applied dabs of paint and lipstick, and said we looked as blushing and pretty as any virgins.

In her little pantry, the tea things and cakes were already arranged, and all we had to do was infuse the tea. We served her at a little occasional table and were obliged to crouch before her as she supped, with our skirts riding over our bare bums, which she stroked. She unconcernedly allowed her own garment to ride up, revealing her bushy false mink, and knowingly teasing us, for her hand occasionally slipped below my furrow to caress my straining balls and the stiff base of my erection. She asked me if my costume was comfortable, and I replied truthfully that it was not.

'Good,' she said. 'Now you know what a Lady feels like all day.'

With trembling hands, we at last cleared away her tea things, and readied ourselves for our correction. Suddenly, I blurted that I was sorry for her shameful beating by the river, and was merited the harshest chastisement; she put her finger to my lips and smiled.

'A Lady's will expresses itself in different ways, Roger,' she whispered.

Then she sighed.

'I have whipped so many young males on the bare, and taken such delight in their squirmings, sometimes I feel guilty, but envious too, and desire to feel their pain myself. And when I lash a male in female things, it is as though I whip my own bottom. Now – I'll take you both over the sofa, if you please. Drop skirts and blouses, and I'll take you bare bum, with stockings and heels and corset, for your extra humiliation. Though I see that your robing has done nothing to soften your stiff cocks – perhaps thrashing will make you modest. Legs apart and bums well up, please – you may hide your heads in the cushions, but no biting however much you smart.'

Mrs Holbein shrugged off her peignoire; it slipped down her silky body to the floor, and she stepped out of it, nude but for her white stockings, heels and suspenders. She threw off her perruque, and her gleaming shaven head made her seem female dominance nakedly incarnate. She murmured that she loved to flog *innocent* males, to exercise pure power. She said she would cane us in sets of five to each bum, with no pauses.

'I have a pound's worth, not just a feeble dozen, don't forget,' she said as she raised her cane, a good four feet in length. 'I don't expect you to keep still as I beat you, and I imagine you will squeal for me most theatrically as your weals deepen. In fact I insist on it: blub and squirm all you like.'

The cane whistled and lashed my bare nates, and I jerked, unable to restrain my cry of pain. I gasped, yelping, as my bum took five strokes in the space of as many seconds, and my eyes brimmed with tears as I panted, listening to the cruel 'whop-whop-whop' on Denton's bum beside mine. Then the second five, and by now I was hopping in my uncomfortable shoes, my legs jerking straight and my buttocks clenched tight.

Whop-whop-whop-whop-whop!

'Ooo . . .' I gasped. 'O, Madam . . . O! O! O!'

Whop-whop-whop-whop-whop!

'Aah!' cried Denton, his buttocks red and squirming, 'Ah, no, no . . . please, no . . . aaah!'

She seemed to relish our cries of pain, which spurred her to still harder stroking, although I was powerless to keep from crying. Her beating took me artfully with two or three strokes all on the same ridge, then the next strokes to a different place, but always visiting each welt repeatedly, until my bottom felt lashed by molten iron. The shame of being caned in maid's frillies was quite forgotten in my unspeakable smarting agony.

'Mercy, Mistress!' sobbed Denton as we took our third set.

She laughed, and said he might as well demand sweet salt as gentle caning.

'Squeal for me, girls!'

I did; I begged and sobbed as my bottom squirmed, and I thought I should melt with pain. And gradually I began to feel a fierce, shamed pleasure in being able to sob and squeal openly like a girl, and not have to maintain a gentleman's reserve in my degradation. The dancing of my haunches seemed in a strangely sensuous way to be mimicking the gestures of copulation, and I no longer felt shame at my erect penis being visible to my fellow-victim, as though our flogging by a stern Mistress was a manly bond between us.

I thought I had never been flogged so expertly nor so painfully. Perhaps it was Mrs Holbein's strength, or the thickness of her rod, but when she ceased our beating at the fortieth stroke – eight sets of five – I felt my smarting buttocks had taken three times as much, and that I should never sit again.

'There!' she said brightly. 'I have had ten shillings' worth . . . forty each, at a penny ha'penny a stroke. But I gave Miss Crouch a pound note. It is time for the birch, my girls. You are lucky: the birch is twopence a stroke, so that is a mere thirty strokes each.'

'O, Madam,' groaned Denton. 'I beg you . . . not the birch. I don't think I can take it.'

'Sixty are paid for, and sixty must be given,' she said reasonably. 'You may watch, if your friend will take the full sixty, unless Roger is only a whimpering girly like you.'

'I'll take your sixty, Madam,' I heard myself whimper.

'Do not rise, either of you!' she commanded. I peeked and saw her fetch from her cabinet two statuettes of antique goddesses, many-breasted and quaintly endowed with enormous phalluses, large enough for the sternest dildo.

'The goddess Obispos shall embrace and cleave you for the birch,' she said gravely. 'And if unbirched, you must still be cloven, Denton.'

I heard Denton groan as his arse-cheeks were parted and the huge tool inserted into his anus, with orders that he was to hold it tight. I saw that Mrs Holbein was oiling my own obispos with juice from her own quim – her mink-wig was quite sodden with her love oil. Then I too gasped as the heavy shaft seemed to sear my trembling anus, pushed all the way to my root so that I wriggled and squealed; yet I widened my buttocks to take the engine as deeply as she could thrust, and with a strange new thrill in my balls, as though I had an extra zone of pleasure inside my arse-shaft.

Denton was ordered to squat in the corner like a dunce, to watch, clasping his buttocks to keep his dildo in place. He walked stiffly then crouched in position, thighs awkwardly spread and with a blush of shame on his face that matched the puffy crimson of his wealed bare bum. There was a crackling swishy sound as Mrs Holbein lifted a huge and fearsome birch from her cabinet, as delicately as if it were a bouquet of roses.

'There is much drama to the application of the birch, Roger,' she said, 'which is why I like it. It shall, of course, hurt you awfully, but I don't want you to cry out and squeal like a girl, as you did under the cane. Rather, you should grunt, and gasp deeply, for the birch is a man's punishment; so you shall strip entirely and kneel to take it naked, your head and elbows on the floor and your bum well raised.'

Groaning, and needing no encouragement to do so, I crouched, and gasped as Mrs Holbein dealt my dildo a scornful kick, driving it painfully up my anal shaft. She laughed quite cruelly, and tickled my fesses with the birch, to tease and frighten me. It was very heavy. Then I felt her sharp claws scratch me deeply in my welts.

'You are nice and puffy,' she said thoughtfully, 'with some fine ridging. The birch will give a nice overall effect, like a mosaic. Birching is art, and can be surprisingly gentle and ticklish, *or* . . .'

She lifted the birch and began to beat my bare bottom. I gasped as the heavy rods seemed to knock my breath from me and slam me forward on to my head and elbows.

'Hurt much?' said Mrs Holbein.

'Gosh . . . yes, Madam! O, how it smarts!'

'We'll skin you nice and slowly, I think,' she continued. 'We have plenty of time till your supper. Sixty, or rather, fifty-nine now, won't seem too bad, stretched over an hour, will it?'

I could not answer because her second stroke made me gasp and wriggle as though my bottom wanted to burrow right into the carpet, to escape my pain! And yet, I was proud – *wanted* – to take pain from her.

The pressure of the dildo in my filled anus made my cock remain at full stiffness and, moreover, each giddying stroke of the birch made my balls tickle and my helmet throb, as I felt the honey gather inside me; the birching came in sets of five, like the cane, but with decent pauses between, to let me sob and squirm and catch my breath. By the fourth set, my croup was a cauldron of molten agony, yet my balls and cock were aching to spurt! The pressure of the obispos in my anus added to my agony, and my shameful joy. Mrs Holbein remarked on my stiff cock with pleasure; Denton groaned in distress at the huge prong in his bumhole, his cock stiff too.

The room swirled around me; time dissolved, and I was alone with my hideous pain, worse than anything I had ever imagined. I knew I had endured birching at Virginia Lodge; but I could not believe Dido or Miss Florence had ever made me smart as savagely.

'O . . . O . . . how many, Madam?' I gasped.

She said I was past the halfway mark, with thirty-five taken and twenty-five to go. I wailed in despair, regretting I had asked, and clenched my fesses for the next set. Now she began to mark the sides and backs of my thighs, and the tender portion at the very top of my fesses. I did squeal horribly, like a pig, or a girl, or a hundred girls . . .

'O, please . . . please . . .' I begged, not knowing what I begged for.

'Do you want to spurt, Roger?' she said calmly.

'Spurt, Mistress? O! O! That was hard! O . . . spurt *now*? O!'

'Why, I believe you do,' she purred. 'I believe you would like to spurt in *me*, in my quim or even my bumhole. I have seen submission in your eyes. Admit it, Roger.'

'O, Mrs Holbein,' I sobbed, 'it is true . . . I long to worship you.'

And I blurted and gasped the truth of my submission to Ladies.

'Well! Having seen you ploughed this morning, I should

love your cream to spurt again, in true submission, as you watch another male fuck me . . .'

My heart leapt; she fetched Denton from his corner, pulling him by his stiff cock, and parted her thighs to insert his penis in her bumhole. Denton grinned and began to poke vigorously, and Mrs Holbein writhed and cried out in delight as she was buggered, bending over for her arse-fucking, and continuing to flog me with renewed force, squirming lustily as her anus was filled by my friend's cock. At her command, I twisted my head to observe – tears of shame filled my eyes, yet mingled with horrified delight: to witness the buggery of an adored Lady, and be flogged for my impudent peeking.

I saw that Mrs Holbein was joyously masturbating as she flogged me. And at her next birch stroke, I could not hold back, but to my anguished surprise, cried out very loudly as my sperm spurted in a hot jet from my bucking shaft. Three more strokes, which I scarcely noticed, and my birching was over. Gasping and sobbing, I collapsed on the carpet, and buried my head in my hands. Mrs Holbein continued to accept her buggery from the lad, grinding her heel on my cock and crushing me quite painfully, with harsh cruel laughter at my shame. Then, drawing Denton's pumping loins with her, she sank to her knees with her thighs apart, and flicked her stiff, swollen clitty right in front of my eyes; her gash was thick and spread wide, showing her tender moist slit.

'Give me your spunk, Denton,' she commanded, 'right in my bumhole, boy, while Roger watches . . . submitting like a girl!'

Denton groaned and trembled as he spasmed triumphantly inside her, shaming me as I watched his bucking thighs slapping her fesses.

'Aaah . . .' she gasped. 'So sweet, buggered by a real man's cock, and my bum filled with hot cream . . . I'm coming!'

She brought herself smoothly to a convulsive orgasm, her hands clutching my birched bottom in jerking, staccato caresses as she came . . . and I sobbed in my shame.

Grinning, Denton withdrew from her anus with a loud squelching sound; he wiped his glistening cock on her buttocks, slapping her bum with his limp flesh. She giggled in pleasure.

Abruptly, she rose and opened the door of her bedroom; both Denton and I started in surprise, for there was the figure of Miss Crouch! She knelt right by the door, at the keyhole, where she had been observing us. Miss Crouch said nothing, for she wore a thick rubber thong at her mouth. Her eyes were wide and frightened as she contemplated our chastised bodies; her body was sheathed in a tight rubber corselet, like her morning wear for ablutions, except that it fastened her legs tightly together and covered her whole body, leaving bare only her breasts, buttocks and fount. Her arms were strapped to her sides by rubber cords, and her wrists bound behind her back in heavy studded rubber cuffs.

'Miss Crouch!' cried Mrs Holbein gaily. 'Already in costume! I had quite forgotten you were with us. Well, you have seen our play-acting. Can you cope with a proper rehearsal of your own part?'

Miss Crouch eagerly nodded yes! I was stung, that my agony and shame should be deemed mere play-acting! Suddenly I felt vengeful . . .

Mrs Holbein lifted her captive, her bare arms rippling like whipcord, and deposited her face down on the carpet; she fetched a thick rubber cushion, like a sponge, and placed it under Miss Crouch's loins, then delivered a savage kick to her bare bum.

'Vanity, dear girls . . . It is amazing what women will do to gain exposure,' she said. 'I have the idea of a play about a vicious dominant Lady, who lures innocent victims to her chamber under false pretences, in order to humiliate and chastise them.'

Miss Crouch stirred and twisted her head, her eyes staring wide. She tried to speak through her gag, but shuddered as Mrs Holbein silenced her with a kick to the bumhole. The dark Mistress held her still with her instep across her neck, and said she must see if Miss Crouch was as keen an actress as spectator. She picked up her cane and brought it down hard across the woman's bare buttocks, holding her still with her crushing instep. A pretty pink blush appeared on the naked skin, to be followed by another, and another, the blushes darkening and puffing as Mrs Holbein caned her victim with hard, whistling strokes, and Miss Crouch's jerks of pain grew frenzied. Her rubber sheath squeaked as she wriggled and sobbed helplessly.

Mrs Holbein pulled Miss Crouch's head up by the scruff of her neck, so that her face was in front of Mrs Holbein's naked quim. With her flogging arm, she continued to lay hard strokes across the woman's bare bum and squelching rubber-sheathed shoulders.

'Think you can do the part, Miss?' she murmured – and Miss Crouch nodded her agreement!

'Tongue me in obeisance,' commanded Mrs Holbein, and squashed Miss Crouch's face hard into her sopping mink-wig.

Her nose was pressed above the fount-lips, and her flickering tongue found the hard swelling of her chastiser's clitty, which she licked and chewed avidly, with little moans of pain and pleasure mingled. When she had taken a good forty strokes on bum and back, her latex sheath was scarred and shredded, and her naked bottom was blackened crimson, puffed in harsh ridges; the carpet beneath her was pooled with a dribble of juice from her bare gash.

Mrs Holbein said her wealed bum must be soothed with cream, and ordered me to squat right over the grovelling woman's buttocks, as though to evacuate. I did so, and my Mistress began a fierce buggery of my filled anus, thrusting the figurine of the phallic goddess in and out of my bum so that I squealed and sobbed in my own pain. Yet I felt a delicious sensation of pleasure, as my insides trembled like my balls and the tip of my cock, where I saw a drop of sperm appear at my peehole. I groaned, knowing deliciously that I was going to come, and, as Mrs Holbein buggered me with the harsh dildo, I spurted my cream all over Miss Crouch's wealed bare buttocks.

Our chastiser knelt and began to lick my sperm from

Miss Crouch's fesses, her tongue delving into her furrow and tickling her moistened bumhole with long, lustful strokes. She licked her lips, and said that Denton was not to be excused his duty; my friend was obliged to take my place, and a few ruthless thrusts of his own dildo brought his cock to quivering stiffness, accompanied by his cries of distress. But as Mrs Holbein buggered him too, Denton blushed and trembled as his own spurt came.

Mrs Holbein licked up every drop, then pushed Denton aside, but ordering him to retain his obispos full in bumhole. Then she calmly squatted over Miss Crouch's glistening buttocks and made a stream of golden water, all over her wealed bare. Miss Crouch sobbed in her shame, more bitterly than at any cane-stroke, but made no move of protest at this degradation. The liquid was sopped up by her sponge blanket, and Mrs Holbein pronounced herself refreshed and satisfied. She took my cock in her mouth, sucking her clean of spunk and causing me to harden again; then she sucked Denton's too.

She ordered me to expel my dildo, which I did willingly, and helped her fasten it to her own waist, where it rose like a penis, with the phallic body of the goddess thrust into her own gaping gash. Now she squatted again, and I spread Miss Crouch's buttocks to reveal the wrinkle of her anus bud. Mrs Holbein tickled the pink little pucker with the tip of the dildo, then with a sigh of contentment thrust it forcefully right into the anal shaft.

Miss Crouch writhed and groaned quite piteously, but Denton was ordered to squat on her head, holding her down, while I took the cane. Mrs Holbein leant well back as she buggered the Mistress of Discipline with the long shaft, to leave me a clear field for the imposition of further discipline. I was to continue the caning of Miss Crouch's buttocks, and I did so eagerly, filled with a shameful desire for revenge, to inflict on a Lady's bare bum what my own had suffered. Any Lady's would do . . .

I caned her wealed flesh with all my might, exulting in my new power. When I had given a good twenty strokes, Miss Crouch was squirming violently, both under my caning and the fierce buggery of her dildoed anus, but her tongue was eagerly licking Denton's balls. Mrs Holbein was trembling too, her eyes moist, and hoarsely demanded a taste of my medicine. I was aghast – she nodded that my cane was to be applied to her own fesses.

I hastened to obey, and my cock throbbed unmercifully as I lashed her bare velvet orbs, watching their chocolate silk darken to puce under the whipping of the heavy rod. My lashes increased the fervour of Mrs Holbein's buggery; I saw that Denton's cock stood rigid, and Mrs Holbein gasped that Miss Crouch was to attend to the boy and plough him with her lips. Denton rose and knelt before Miss Crouch, pulling her head up so that her lips fitted snugly round his engorged member, which she promptly began to bite and suck, thrusting her head up and down in time to her own arse-fucking. Rivulets of love juice cascaded on Mrs Holbein's velvet thighs, and over Miss Crouch's torn rubber sheath.

Then Mrs Holbein gasped that I was to approach her and flog her from the shoulders down, landing my strokes at a slant, so that the cane-tip should fall across her buttocks and catch the top of her thighs. I did this and, as my cane scored her soft thigh-flesh, she squealed and writhed, bucking furiously in Crouch's anus, and her lips opened to clasp the throbbing bulb of my own cock. Now she sucked me powerfully as I thrashed her; her loins heaved as she bum-fucked the writhing woman, whose moans of pleasure rose with those of Denton as his rigid pulsing cock glistened with Miss Crouch's saliva.

Two impulses fought in me: the shameful desire to vengefully hurt a Lady's body, and my longing to abjectly submit to her – to all Ladies . . . I watched as my strokes wealed the thrusting bare orbs of Mrs Holbein's quivering bum; suddenly I could restrain myself no longer and I threw down my cane, to straddle her croup with my own haunches. She cried out in surprise as I poked my stiff helmet into her furrow and found her own anus bud, much larger than Miss Crouch's, and darkly mysterious as a Lady's purse.

My peehole caressed the soft pucker, then was inside,

and, with a hard thrust, I penetrated her. She moaned in delight; her own thrusting continued in her victim's anus as I pushed the full length of my shaft into her elastic bumhole, which seemed to fasten on my penis with gripping, sucking claws as I began to bugger her with hard, sharp thrusts. My peehole touched her belly's root, which seemed to open for me, then clamp hard as though frightened that at each thrust I should not return. I fucked that squeezing tight bumhole until I felt my balls ache again with desire to spurt inside her writhing dark body.

I reached down, supporting myself on my elbows as my hands found her pumping cooze, the dildo firm between the lips and the clitty raw and throbbing above. My fingers began to dance on her stiff clitty, and she shrieked; only my weight prevented her from toppling over, so frenzied was her writhing of pleasure at my cock in her anus.

Both females groaned louder and louder – I felt Mrs Holbein's belly flutter, and suddenly she cried out in her orgasm, just as her buggery, and the spurting of Denton's own cream, caused the same pleasure to invade Miss Crouch. At that moment, I could no longer hold back my own climax, and came with a heavy spurt right at the root of the black woman's tight rubbery shaft, the velvet buttocks squirming to milk every drop of seed from me as I plunged hard into the mouth of their naked ripeness.

Miss Crouch was unbound, and stood flushed and nude, shivering in the aftermath of her pleasure-ordeal.

'I trust I have got the part, Madam,' she said.

'Well, I'll let you know,' said Mrs Holbein imperiously. 'Now, my next scenario shall be similar, but with a lovely slave boy – let me see . . . He shall be stripped and his croup flogged to the bone, and his face smothered by the bare bum and cooze of his implacable mistress, who forces him to drink her juices – all of them – while her eager slave girl buggers and spanks him mercilessly. The slave is reduced to quivering submission, as males deserve to be. I shall play the Mistress, of course – Miss Crouch might do as the slave girl – but I wonder who should play the male lead?'

'Me, Mistress!' Denton and I cried in unison. 'Please, me . . .'

13

Stage Direction

Soon it was time for my visit to Miss Porritt, the solicitor. I took the bus to Egham and had to walk some distance, so I was glad to be free of my restrainer for the outing. I was nervous and preoccupied about my future and got lost, finding myself in a rather dingy part of town, near some military barracks – Royal Marines, I think. The street was lined with Ladies, who I perceived to be of easy virtue, who cat-called and made lewd proposals to me. The sum of ten shillings was mentioned, or sometimes 'special price, seven and sixpence to a nice boy like you, dear'. There were low public houses and the side streets were thronged, for many Ladies eschewed the comfort, or expense, of a private salon, and entertained their rough clients with equal roughness in the open air. At the mouth of one street, I had to step into the roadway, for it was clogged with soldiery, swigging at their rum bottles. One of them told me not to be shy, and join the queue.

'This tart'll do anything you want, mate – Greek, French, whip her arse, the lot.'

Prurient curiosity got the better of me, and I peered to see this notable at her business. I saw the bared croup of a male, slapping energetically against a female's sumptuous arse-globes as he poked her anus from behind, with her skirts and pink knickers round her ankles. Her lips, framed by tousled but lush blonde tresses, were fastened on the cock of a second male, while a third, wedged beneath her, had his cock in her quim.

'We call her the bicycle,' said my new acquaintance, 'because she rides here on one, and she rides like one as well. Best three shillings' worth in town!'

I was dumbfounded that a Lady should degrade herself so shamelessly, and for so much below her market price. I indeed saw beside her a push-bike, chained to a railing, and was sure it looked familiar. I advanced, and peered more closely: I did recognise the bicycle, and I recognised its owner. To my horror, it was none other than my Mistress, Miss Florence Dark.

I was still trembling at my monstrous discovery as the maidservant admitted me to the chambers of Miss Porritt. I calmed myself in her office, whose leathery comfort exuded the reassuring majesty of the law. She rose to greet me: elegant, youthful and full-bosomed, her large croup sheathed in sensible, though alluringly tight grey tweed, and her black shoes shining like mirrors. Her shiny auburn hair was demurely short, and bobbed up in little moon-shaped curls that prettily framed her large horn-rimmed spectacles and wide sensuous lips. Her handshake was firm as she bade me sit.

'So, Mr Prince, how are you faring at Mrs Norringe's? You are involved in the drama? How I love the theatre. I do not get up to Shaftesbury Avenue or the Haymarket as often as I should like, but the law is a kind of theatre, you know: the stirring speeches, the cut and thrust of wit, the awful majesty of the court, and the dreadful punishments of confinement, whip or birch . . .'

She breathed in sharply, and there was a mischievous twinkle in her eye as she peered over her spectacles; I mumbled that it suited me well, and I hoped I gave satisfaction.

'O, I hear that you do,' she said casually. 'Are you upset? You shiver a little.'

I assured her that it was from my hearty walk. In truth, I was still upset, because I recognised that beneath my horror at my Mistress's willing degradation was my own thrill at the idea of her as a shameless public woman, her body writhing under the cocks of strangers . . . a subtle lesbic revenge on males, degrading those who degraded her. This abasement made her somehow more precious to me, and more than ever to be worshipped as my haughty goddess.

Miss Porritt said we should get to business and, with a sigh, opened a bulky dossier with my name on it. She said she found the matter very complicated – I found it a hundred times so – therefore I shall not burden the reader with overmuch detail.

'In a nutshell, Roger, your will and your trust fund are contested – in the *Staatsgericht* in Vienna! Your father, as you may know, was a very . . . vigorous gentleman and had many female friends, some more than friends. There are claims and counter-claims, alleged siblings, even a claim that he has fled to Uruguay. At all events, your trust fund, and your revenue from it, are provisionally frozen.'

'Does this mean I shall not be going up to Oxford?' I blurted.

'That is the least of your worries,' she said. 'It could be worse – happily, you have friends here in northwest Surrey . . .'

The upshot was – I held an Italian passport, but Trieste, the city of my birth, was not incorporated into Italy until after the Great War. Before that, it was part of the Austrian Empire, hence I was technically of Austrian birth. And since my principal litigant, a certain Signorina Sabina Richter, unknown to me, was herself Austrian, the Roman courts had surrendered jurisdiction to the Austrian.

'All very complicated,' said Miss Porritt. 'We shall fight, of course – but it will cost.'

My dismay was alleviated by the delightful appearance of the secretary-maid with tea things. She was a handsome young Lady, robed as for the law, with a pleated tulle black skirt that came down to midcalf, but had a lovely white lacy petticoat peeping coyly over her white silk stockings. Beneath her stern white blouse, I saw the hint of a black brassiere, very large in cup, to accommodate her truly magnificent udders, which matched her tightly sheathed bum in ripeness. Sensing my lustful gaze, she nervously flicked an ash-blonde lock from her flushed cheekbone.

'Thank you, Samantha,' said Miss Porritt, and Samantha began to serve our tea.

I sipped gratefully, but stammered that I was quite without the means to pay expensive legal costs. Miss Porritt smiled, and said she would be willing to take the case *pro bono et pro rata*, but that some small token *ex gratia* would be required of me. She said it could be in the form of services rendered, with my own person; mystified, I was glad to agree.

Our legal business thus concluded, Miss Porritt said there was no time like the present, and my service could begin forthwith. She drew from her desk a large manuscript, with the title: THE FRUITS OF CRIME, A PLAY BY MISS EMILY PORRITT, LL.B (CANTAB).

'You shall act for me, Roger!' she cried. 'I have written a brave, prescient play, set in a pure world, where justice is female, and males are guilty until proven innocent!'

We were to act a courtroom scene, there in her office. Miss Porritt was to play judge and jailer, Miss Samantha would be barrister and court official; I, of course, was to be the wretched felon in the dock. Eager to please, I watched her don wig and gown, and Samantha robed herself likewise. Both Ladies then coughed and shuffled a little, and Miss Porritt said that, as the prisoner, I was to be shackled. I agreed nervously, and then she whispered that in her ideal world of female dominance, male prisoners were tried naked, for their shame. I murmured that I seemed to have no choice if I wanted my own case to be pursued, and Miss Porritt beamed.

'Exactly!' she exclaimed. 'So if you would be good enough . . .'

Nervously, I removed my clothing, and stood naked, cupping my manhood but unable to hide the slow trembling as I stiffened under the open scrutiny of two sensuous Ladies.

'Well!' said Miss Porritt. 'A miscreant male indeed!'

Miss Samantha dressed me in heavy chains, with cuffs

for wrists and ankles, and a cup-restrainer for my balls, attached to the chains. Miss Porritt placed the script before me, saying that Samantha and she already knew their parts.

'We take it from page thirty-seven,' she said. 'The trial has been conducted and the defendant automatically found guilty. Miss Samantha, defending, shall make her closing speech.'

'My Lady,' said Samantha, 'I beg for mercy for this wretched worm. He is only a male, and knows no better.'

'Ignorance is no excuse,' intoned Miss Porritt, putting a very fetching black lace cap on her head, 'and the prisoner shall rise.'

She looked rather impishly at my stiffening bare cock but did not smile.

'Have you anything to say before I pass sentence?' she said.

Hereafter, I reproduce our playlet as best I can. I must say in my own defence that I entered into the spirit of things quite willingly.

PRISONER: Milady, you err – I have no disrespect for Ladies. I worship and adore them. My thoughtless remarks were merely excess of enthusiasm. But if I must be punished for calling a Lady's bottom a peach, then I humbly accept a Lady's chastisement.

JUDGE: *I*, a Lady, err! You compound your offence with contempt of a Lady's court. To make an example, I shall sentence you to the maximum punishment allowed. For the offence, you shall be flogged on the naked buttocks, with twenty strokes of the cat-o'-nine tails, young man, and then soundly birched for your contempt, with a further twenty strokes on the bare. Yes, the birch! Do not quiver like some girl, you shall do plenty of that when your bare bum is flogged. The sentence is to be carried out at once. Will the court usher please hold the prisoner ready for punishment.

Miss Samantha pinioned me and forced me down over Miss Porritt's desk, with my legs and bottom splayed. Miss

Porritt took from her cabinet the two implements: a shiny, oiled cat, the thongs over two feet long and steel-tipped, and a huge bushy birch. She placed the birch before my eyes on the desk, then lifted the cat, and I realised my *ex gratia* service in kind was to be more than just play-acting.

PRISONER: Milady, I gladly accept a Lady's just punishment, and beg you to take my numerous other offences into consideration.

JUDGE: Agreed! But the flogging shall now be at the court's pleasure, up to or including twice the forty strokes ordained. The prisoner will not squeal or clench his buttocks tight under the lash, or the stroke is not counted.

PRISONER: Milady, it is hard not to squirm when whipped on the bare by a merciless and beautiful Lady, and hard not to feel joy at her dominance.

Miss Porritt told me sharply not to depart from the script, though she gave me a little smile. Suddenly, the cat lashed my bare buttocks with agonising force.

JUDGE: One! Pretty stripes, but you flinched, prisoner, so that stroke is not counted. (The whip fell again on my bare, very painfully.)

PRISONER: O! Milady! You are so strong and cruel! I beg you to show mercy to this insolent worm, even though I deserve to be flogged to the bone.

JUDGE: There! And there! And there! I'll show you mercy, you cringing whelp!

PRISONER: (I was hopping on tiptoe in my agony.) O, Miss! Milady! That was so hard! My bare bum smarts so cruelly, and I can't take any more!

JUDGE: (leering) But you must, worm. The cat shall crimson your bare worthless nates, and then the birch shall make the shreds of your arse-flesh glow.

PRISONER: (without acting) O! O! How it smarts! O, Milady!

JUDGE: And again!

PRISONER: (I was gasping in real agony.) O! Milady . . . O . . .!
JUDGE: Another!
PRISONER: (sobbing and writhing in pain) O! O! O!
JUDGE: How I love to see a male's bare bum striped and glowing! Take that!
PRISONER: O! Miss Porritt! You are very strict!

We had all departed from the script; my welts, my abject humiliance, and the stiffness of my cock under whip were sufficient prompting for both Ladies.

SAMANTHA: How lovely to see a male arse properly chastised, Milady! I feel all hot and trembly just watching the wretch squirm under your whip. His weals and raw red skin are a work of art.
MISS PORRITT: Wait until his bum blushes under birch! I shall flog him to purple, every inch of his vile male bum-skin shall bear my Lady's mark.
ROGER: Miss – have pity –
MISS PORRITT: Pity! For a *male*?
SAMANTHA: Flog him to the bone, Milady! (Vip! Vip! Vip!)
ROGER: O! I can't take the pain! I submit to you, Miss, I am slave in your service for ever, but please stop the terrible whipping!
MISS PORRITT: That *is* your service, whelp! (Suddenly, she reached between my splayed buttocks and grasped my balls roughly, then squeezed the stiff shaft of my cock.) What is this insolence! To stand without a Lady's permission! (Vip! Vip! Vip!)
ROGER: I cannot help it, Miss. I humbly beg your pardon. O! Ooo!
MISS PORRITT: Request denied!

She continued to flog me with the cat for five minutes, well past the twentieth stroke and, I think, not bothering to count.

SAMANTHA: (feeling my cock) The prisoner is still insolent, Milady!

MISS PORRITT: Then Mistress Birch must teach him manners. (She picked up the birch and obliged me to kiss it, and then I felt its awful swish on my raw buttocks.)
ROGER: I beg you to stop! The birch cuts me like red hot fire!
MISS PORRITT: You have not understood, you stupid male. You must beg me *not* to stop . . .

Stroke after stroke of the birch branded my bare bottom. My fesses jerked and wriggled convulsively, and I could scarcely breathe for sobbing. The pain of the cat was nothing to the agony of Miss Porritt's birch.

ROGER: O! Ah! Miss, I beg you, don't stop. Flay my bum till I can take no more! Flog me raw with your sweet birch, Milady.
MISS PORRITT: That is what I like to hear. Squirm, boy.
ROGER: Yes! Yes! To the bone, Miss! I deserve it, every stroke.

At every lash of the birch, my cock slammed against the desk top. I twisted to see that Miss Samantha's blouse was ruffled, the top two buttons undone to show the firm melons of her teats, while her hand had slipped beneath the waistband of her skirt and was rubbing her fount. Miss Porritt's arm too was enveloped by her judge's robe. At length, after a further fifteen minutes' flogging, she put down the birch, leaving me still wriggling in the lake of pain that scalded my bare arse-globes. She grasped my balls and squeezed me, and there was no further pretence at acting a play: her anger was unfeigned.

'Still in contempt! Impudently stiff!' cried Miss Porritt. 'You wretched worm!'

I was forced to lie on my back on the carpet, whose wool tickled my raw bum quite uncomfortably. My arms were stretched behind me and my legs parted, with a loud clanking of my chains. Miss Porritt stood over my head and doffed her gown; then her skirt, and her knickers, which slid down her stockinged legs and and fell on my mouth.

I was filled with their delicious sweating aroma for a moment before she stepped out of them and kicked them aside, revealing the wide swollen lips of her cooze under its thatch of curly mink-hair. She squatted over my face, with her gash inches from my lips, and then suddenly her thighs pinioned me in a vice-like grip and her Lady's place was pressed to my lips and nose. I smelt her ripeness and tasted the hot juices that spurted from her quim as she squatted on me with her full weight. I almost choked as her luxuriant hairy mink wadded my mouth. She sat on me backwards, so that my chin pressed the hard bud of her clitty, and my lips and nose were at the fragrant wrinkle of her anus hole.

'How does it feel to be squashed by a peach, you maggot?' she snapped, not joking.

I struggled to breathe and, with every gasp, drew in the dank fragrance of her cooze and bumhole as she scornfully crushed me. Then I heard the rustle of Miss Samantha's robes; they fell to my thighs, and the tip of my cock was brushed by her wet quim lips. Suddenly, a cock-clip was fastened brutally to the base of my shaft, and Miss Samantha whispered that I should not spurt till she had taken her pleasure from my disgusting flesh; with that, I felt my glans and shaft bathed in velvet wet sweetness as her gash enfolded me, and I felt myself helpless under the full weight of two female bodies.

Both began to writhe heavily upon me and I felt the movements of their fingers as they pleasured their clitties and moaned softly. Miss Porritt's powerful quim muscle sucked my tongue into her, and squeezed it like a plaything against the wet slithering walls of her slit, while her anal pucker opened and closed on my nose, tickling me. My mouth was by now drenched with her copious oily fluid. At the same time, Miss Samantha bucked gently, her cooze squeezing my cock. I felt them lean forward, and heard their lips smack in a kiss.

'I wish we could take him to the Egham gala,' said Miss Samantha, 'and whip him raw, to show all our friends.'

Her bucking and writhing on my cock grew more

vigorous; she sucked my glans powerfully, her wet thighs slapping on my belly, and she gasped hard.

'You know that males aren't allowed,' said Miss Porritt sternly, 'not even to be flayed.'

'O . . .' said Miss Samantha, wriggling on my cock. 'O! Yes! I am going to come . . . with your permission, Miss Emily.'

'Come on him, Samantha, then go and fetch the bum-piercer. Leave his cock clamped – I think a little discipline in the hole shall teach the whelp to behave.'

'O . . .' said Miss Samantha faintly, her cooze gushing heavily on my haunches, and then she began to jerk and flutter, with little moaning gasps as she came to orgasm.

When her spasm had subsided, she slid off me and I heard her heels clicking on their way to the cabinet. My face was still squirming under Miss Porritt's own cooze and thighs, and I heard her hoarse panting, her juices flowing in a strong torrent, as she approached her own spasm. The clitty bobbed stiff and swollen against my face, and she squashed down on me to nuzzle it, crying out softly in little chirps of delight.

I heard the swishing of a leather strap and the click of a buckle, and then felt the scented warmth of Miss Samantha's body straddling me anew. Now, my ankles were lifted by their chains and placed right up at my breast, spreading my furrow wide. Miss Porritt's cooze continued to crush me, and I moaned into her swollen wet lips as the tip of some cold, monstrous engine nuzzled and poked insistently at my anus bud. It was metal, and huge; I gasped in pain as the device was pushed into my protesting anal shaft but, with a moan of despair, I willed my hole to relax and accept the shaft which plunged right to my root, stretching my bumhole to breaking.

Miss Samantha's thighs slapped my own as she began to thrust the dildo fierce and hard, fucking me mercilessly in my tenderest place, and I squealed in anguish, my voice muffled by Miss Porritt's soaking cooze-thatch. Miss Porritt's fingers were on the bulb of my cock, pulling back my foreskin to reveal the naked glans – and then her nails began to scratch my bulb-skin very hard, raking at my moon birthmark. She commented as she clawed me in painful rhythm that I was experiencing the device of pleasure that the Ladies of my crusader forebears used in their men's long absences, when they were obliged to lock their quims in the chastity belt.

'The chastity belt is a grille of iron, worn at the waist and securely covering the cooze, but permitting evacuation and other necessary functions,' she said dreamily. 'How thrilling to be a prisoner of a brutal male, one's loins encased and kept pure for his own pleasure! The garment resembled the athletic support of a male, that is, the waist-strap left the buttocks and furrow bare; thus it was that the noble Ladies developed a taste for bumming, and had devices like this one in your own hole. You will be pleased to know it is the real thing – an antique poking-rod, fully seven hundred years old, and once used by the Lady of Sir Rogier de Prince, of Chertsey. Our sunny, suburban countryside is full of such dark traditions.'

I squirmed and squeaked under my cooze-blanket as the dildo vivaciously poked my agonised anal passage, with Miss Samantha emitting grunts of vengeful pleasure.

'Does it hurt?' she panted.

'Mmm . . .' I moaned, attempting to nod my head.

Miss Porritt was masturbating with busy fingers, and her flow of quim juice was newly copious on my face and lips.

'Good,' said Miss Samantha, and strove to fuck my bum harder and harder, with little cries of triumph when a particularly cruel thrust had me squirming like a speared fish.

Yet, at this cruel bumming, I felt that tickling joy deep inside me, at the very root of my hole and somewhere behind my balls, and Miss Porritt's clawing of my glans made me shiver in pleasure. She stuck one sharp fingernail right into my peehole, to a depth of at least a quarter of an inch, thrilling me magically. As she vigorously buggered me, Miss Samantha began to spank my exposed buttocks and thighs, very hard, with a stiff outstretched palm;

though this was nothing compared to the birch, the smarting on my already puffed and wealed bare was too much for my aching balls. Despite the cruel pressure of my cock-ring, I knew that I had to spurt, and felt a droplet of sperm ooze at my scratched peehole.

'He wants to spunk for us!' Miss Porritt cried.

'No! Not yet,' panted Miss Samatha, poking my bumhole quite savagely.

I heard the two Ladies kiss again, and Miss Porritt whispered that Miss Samantha should squeeze her titties, and she would do the same. There was a rustle of clothing as breasts were bared, then a flurry of little slaps and kisses and cries of indignant delight. Now it was Miss Porritt who moaned.

'O, Sammy . . . you bite my nippies so hard, it hurts so beautifully. Yes! O, don't stop . . .'

'Mistress . . . O!'

I could not hold back; I felt my two tormentresses writhing in new spasms, and my own honey welled and spurted in a powerful jet, despite the pressure of my cock-ring. I cried out loudly, gasping at the flood of pleasure that engulfed me, for my flood, forcing its way up my shaft past the ring, spurted from me with intensified pleasure. The spurt, the glowing and smarting of my buttocks under Samantha's raining spanks, her frenzied buggery of my strained bumhole, and Miss Porritt's clawing of my bulb, all made me faint with joy, as the three of us spasmed together; Miss Porritt caught my spurt in her cupped palm. Then I heard little giggles as she rubbed my cream into her own and Miss Samantha's teats.

Yet my humiliation was not over. Both Ladies rose, and I blinked, seeing my body glistening and sticky with copious fluids. Miss Porritt said I needed a wash, and dragged me in my shackles to her tiny bathroom, where both Ladies proceeded to cleanse me with their golden evacuations, the powerful streams leaving not an inch of my face and body unshamed. I was permitted to dry; my chains were removed, and my clothes thrown in to me. When I emerged, wiping the tears of shame from my face, my two lawyers were prim and tidy as ever, shuffling through legal documents.

'Well, Roger,' said Miss Porritt, peering over her glasses, 'I think that concludes our business for today. I may say you gave excellent service, and no efforts shall be spared in pursuing your case – as long as you are willing to serve again whenever summoned.'

I knelt and kissed the feet of both Ladies, spending a long time in sucking and licking their toe-points, and my tongue straying to lick the soft stocking-silk as well, which pleased them, for Miss Samantha murmured that I had learnt some manners.

'One other thing,' said Miss Porritt as I departed, 'I request you to put in a good word for me to Mrs Holbein . . . now that you can vouch for my theatrical talent.'

14

Gala

I did not go into detail when Denton asked about my legal visit, changing the subject to Miss Porritt's dramatic ambitions and our reading from her play. Neither did I go into detail on our 'rehearsal', but Denton grinned slyly.

'I hope it wasn't too painful, sir,' he said. 'You never know with women when the play-acting begins and ends. I think the females round here are in league, like witches.'

'That, Denton,' I said, 'is part of their charm.'

I said that my hostesses had mentioned a forthcoming gala at our sister establishment in Egham, and we agreed it would be a good occasion for our snooping expedition. In the meantime, acutely aware of my financial embarrassment, I did my best to be obedient to Ladies at all times, and thanks to their obvious rivalries over my services, my paybook became pleasingly full:

Miss Task, forty-five minutes: clean shoes, and serve morning coffee, thirty strokes with bamboo rod (split end) plus hand-spanking of fifty slaps: four shillings and threepence, plus fourpence tip.

Mrs Chomley, one hour: wash underthings, clean shoes with tongue, dust ornaments dressed in maid's frillies (photographs taken); fifty with yew cane, and fifty with three-tongued tawse (photographs taken of bare bum, before and after treatment); twelve shillings and sixpence, plus shilling tip.

Miss Task, one hour and a half: clean shoes and floor with tongue, dressed in maid's frillies, with no knickers, and taking cane on bare during duty; do all laundry including smalls and intimate garments; dust porcelain; serve afternoon tea; eighty with ashplant cane (forked tip) and a hundred with tawse; one pound two shillings and sixpence, plus half-crown tip.

Mrs Holbein, three hours: a hundred with cane, a hundred with cat, hand-spanking between; washing-up, serving luncheon and doing laundry, including shampoo of head and pubic wigs, service to quim and teats with tongue; licking shoes and stockings; polishing nipple, quim and anus rings; hand-spanking Mrs Holbein's fesses a hundred times; buggery with double dildo; one pound thirteen shillings and twopence (Mrs Holbein paid a halfpenny per spank for my own spanking of her bum); plus seven and sixpence tip.

Mrs Norringe: mouth-worshipping of shoes and stockings, then removing same with my teeth and licking her dirty feet clean; cleaning her bumhole and quim with tongue; thirty strokes of the birch; five shillings, plus sixpence tip, and a homily that I must be a good and obedient slave and make Dido and Miss Florence proud of my submission. (It was rare, but thrilling, to hear myself referred to so casually as 'slave'; I wondered if Mrs Norringe and the others of the 'league' were aware of Miss Florence's own willing enslavement and self-degradation as whore.)

Miss Task: no duties; a very rapid and painful four dozen with cane (sixty seconds), followed by the Lady's fulfilment of her promise to bugger me; a full hour's buggery with strap-on dildo, with Mrs Chomley in attendance, photographing my buggery with a pocket camera for her 'scrapbook'; one pound fifteen shillings paid.

These entries were typical, and often repeated: Miss Task and Mrs Holbein, I sensed, expressed their rivalry in their fierce attentions to my bumhole, and I grew to relish my imaginative and deliciously painful buggery at their fragrant hands. My restrainer remained firmly in place during all these sessions, as I insisted on obeying the rules, and was wary of Miss Crouch's catching me: not that I feared chastisement, but did not wish to take beating unpaid. Although I confess my sore balls ached to release their sperm at the penetration of my squirming anus shaft.

On only one occasion was my restrainer removed, by the rule-defying Miss Task, and that was when she turned the tables on the photographic Mrs Chomley, and obliged her to take an arse-fucking from my cock, while *she* took photographs. Mrs Chomley endured and enjoyed her buggery; it seemed that the scrapbook was for the lustful perusal of both herself and her spouse. When Miss Task taunted her that Mr Chomley should enjoy *those* photographs, she replied sweetly that he would: the sight of his own wife buggered by a virile young slave would excite him very much, and she thanked Miss Task.

I told Denton of my growing conviction that a good 'seeing-to' in the bumhole, at the hands of a thoughtful and dominant Lady, was just as therapeutic as morning ploughing. After the first initial shock of one's first penetration, there is untrammelled joy in complete submission to the female. He admitted that it 'wasn't too bad' but said that in the army it was an unspeakable crime.

I pointed out that there was an absence of females in the army; moreover, that Nature had blessed Ladies with two holes for pleasure, but rationed our poor selves with only one, so that we might as well make the most of it, and that submission, especially anal submission, is a joy of the mind as much as the body. I advised him he would learn much from our peeking at Ladies amongst themselves, at the Egham gala.

Denton was very nervous as we clambered over the wall into the Egham School for Submissive Ladies.

'It doesn't seem so clever at night,' he quavered. 'The Mistress is a pal of Mrs Norringe's, but a lot stricter – a real dragon. You hear stories of fellows caught peeking . . .'

I did not mention my summons by Miss Owsley that morning; I arrived, prepared for an inspection and unpaid beating, to find her with Mrs Norringe and Mrs Mantle. I curtsied, and Miss Owsley told me to take my shorts off and show bare. I obeyed, fully prepared for the cane, but instead felt three hands touching my bottom.

'You have been thrashed a lot,' said Mrs Mantle. 'Mrs Dark shall be pleased to hear of your endurance. She sends her best wishes.'

I asked if there were any word from Miss Florence.

'Not exactly,' she said. 'Just that your worthless bottom could never be caned black enough for her.'

I shivered in delight.

'Well, we do our best here,' said Miss Owsley, 'and his training is almost complete.'

She told me to make myself decent again, and proceeded to warn me of the evening's festivities at Egham; that I must not let male curiosity overcome seemliness.

'It is natural that males should wish to observe Ladies undressed together,' she said. 'But any transgression invites the strictest punishment, Roger – and I do not mean just the birch, or the cane, but punishment which goes beyond mere discipline.'

The house of the submissive Eghamites was like Mrs Norringe's, and set in the same rolling lawns secluded by thickets of trees. It was just south of the town, where the Thames loops away from the main road, and was set by the river; our approach was up a winding back path, rocky and somewhat disused. We padded up to the house and concealed ourselves in the bushes by the side, where we had a clear view of the front lawn which was set out for the moonlit proceedings.

At the side of the house, we passed several lighted windows, only flimsily draped, or not at all. We witnessed Ladies at robing, with lovely silken underthings and frocks, or else, to my surprise, naked and bound, under stern chastisement from Mistresses clad in leather or rubber costumes of dominance, as though in rehearsal for the gala proper.

The Eghamites took silent whippings on bare buttocks, squirming only a little, and their faces knotted in grim smiles. One young Lady was held with limbs stretched wide under the attentions of a tattooist! This mature female was applying her art to the very lips of the maid's fount, and her tattoo needle made a buzzing sound like bees' wings.

The full moon, and an array of torches, lit the scene. The lawn was thronged with Ladies, clustered with glasses of champagne to view little playlets of dominance and chastisement, in a harmonious pattern as though choreographed, with every stage and variety of humiliant punishment being enacted.

There was a distinction between the Eghamite Mistresses and their submissive maids. Guests or witnesses to their friends' submission wore daring and luxurious robes. The submissives were clad in a fetching uniform, grey like our own, but in thin, almost translucent silk, loosely furled like a skimpy short toga with a belted waist, and a hemline swirling on bare thighs and scarcely covering the fount and croup. Their nude bodies were clearly visible through these gauzy sheaths, and many were adorned with rings at nipple or quim or belly-button, with piercings of their skin, even their intimate folds and crevices, and much vivid evidence of the tattooist's art.

These submissive Eghamites wore no panties, but they had garter belts, with a strap on only one side, for they wore a single silk stocking, black and shiny, and a single high boot, leaving their other leg bare and unshod, so that their gait was hobbling. The outside of each stocking was striped all the way down by the gash of a single ladder.

In contrast to the glittering pearls of their guests, their necklaces were heavy iron chains, and the hems of their dresses were adorned with little bows. The Mistresses were clad sternly in leather and rubber and high black boots, their waists well festooned with whips and canes, and pretty embroidered eye-masks; they would select a maid for chastisement, and with a cane tip would lift the maid's dress by her bows, fastening the hem to her neck chain, to bare her.

The maid stood stock still while her Mistress administered a severe bare-bottom caning, the punished female standing rigid and quivering only slightly under lash. Frequently, the caning Mistress did not even interrupt her conversation or put down her glass to deal out a bare-bum beating of dozens, with very fast strokes.

In the far corner of the lawn, I recognised Miss Porritt. She was stern in her wig and judicial robe, which was casually parted at the front to reveal a shiny corset and jarretière of black shiny fabric – leather, or perhaps rubber, as it clung so tightly to her body – with stocking tops that were a ring of cruel little spikes, matching her black collar, spiked like a pet's. Her knee-boots were spiked too, and glinted with sharp spurs.

She stood over the bared bottom of a miscreant maid who knelt in humiliance before her, the tunic pinned up to her neck at both front and back, so that, apart from her single boot and stocking, she was nude. A dozen gowned Ladies watched avidly, eyes bright beneath dark silken hoods. Miss Porritt was attended by Miss Samantha, also legally attired, but underneath her robe she wore a frock of frilly white muslin, the skirt pleated and flounced in tiers like a pretty ballerina's frock, with white shoes and stockings, and flowers in her hair. The melons of her breasts gleamed bare and unsupported at the carelessly unbuttoned top of her blouse, over which her legal necktie dangled unknotted.

The gowned and hooded Ladies solemnly raised their arms and on Miss Porritt's questioning glance, turned their thumbs down. This was the signal for leather-corsed Mistresses to seize the abject maid, their bare breasts flapping prettily with little silver daggers pendant at their pierced nipples. The maid was fastened in stocks, which pinioned her wrists and ankles, with a centre shaft that pressed on her belly and presented her croup for chastisement, so that she was bent over almost double. The end of the central shaft bifurcated into two smaller shafts, which were shaped as cocks. One Mistress pressed her back down while the other fitted these shafts into her bared quim and anus, as the maid trembled helplessly.

Miss Porritt took a cane in each hand and began to beat

the tethered maid on the bare buttocks, delivering a single stroke to each fesse at once. The maid squealed and writhed as her skin blushed dark pink, and her squirming of her bare bum under the canes drove the dildos in and out of her stretched holes; soon, her face was twisted and wet with tears, and her flogged body convulsed violently.

After a caning of over three dozen to each fesse, Miss Porritt stepped back and ceremoniously handed her canes to the first jurywoman. Then she blatantly slipped her hand inside her black panties and began to caress herself at her quim, observing the gowned Lady continue the caning with a dozen strokes on each bare fesse, before handing on the instruments to the next. The two sternly clad Mistresses then knelt before the maid's face and, to silence her, obliged her to take their daggered nipples one after the other in her mouth.

The hooded Ladies too began to rub themselves, frotting quite vigorously between their rustling silken thighs as the beating grew more intense; Miss Porritt embraced her girlish junior, kissing her lips and squeezing her fingers under the frilly frock. The flounces rose at Miss Porritt's caress, bouncing over Miss Samantha's quivering thighs, so that I saw she was knickerless; her senior's hand sank beneath her mink of tangled wet curls and began to frot her hard on clitty, while Samantha, mewling with little gasps of pleasure, feverishly served her senior's gash in return.

Their legs trembled; locked in a lustful embrace, they knelt, their faces inches from the whirring cane-strokes that striped the bottom of their victim, and watching her purpling bare skin with rapture. The hooded Ladies, emboldened by their anonymity, raised their gowns to flutter in the still night air, and reveal moistened knickers under which eager fingers delved and rubbed at the spectacle of the naked maid's humiliance.

'The headmistress has her sluts well trained,' murmured one, rubbing her companion's fount over her wet panties. 'I am proud of my niece.'

She cooed, and fixed her own hand on that of her

caresser, and then the panties were lowered, rustling silkily over smooth bare thighs, and two dainty hands frotted naked bushy founts, the hairs glistening in the moonlight with oily exudation.

I recognised Mrs Holbein, her velvet skin criss-crossed with gold chains: golden rings at nipples, quim and furrow, and otherwise nude. Her head and mound gleamed proudly unblemished by hair. As she turned, I saw that she was pierced in her buttocks and under her shoulders: from these piercings hung filigree golden chains of three feet in length, making a swirling petticoat for her buttocks and thighs. Otherwise she wore only black knee-boots, with a single golden spur on her left ankle, and she had a choker of black leather studded with diamonds in golden clasps.

She was directing one of her 'playlets'. Miss Crouch, stern and crisp in a nursing uniform – a short white rubber sheath which moulded her body atop studded stockings and spiked blue high shoes – wielded a cat-o'-nine-tails to the bared buttocks of Mrs Chomley, whose body was wrapped in copper wire, leaving only croup and teats bare for chastisement. Her face was twisted in agony and streaked with tears, for she was fastened to a spit, her squirming body's weight supported by two dildos of fearsome girth embedded in her anus and cooze, and two chains which stretched her nipples cruelly.

As she turned, moaning, Miss Crouch applied the cat to her buttocks, while a Mistress, sheathed like Miss Crouch in tight rubber, but in black, with piquantly contrasting pink shoes, applied a thin springy cane with vicious whopping strokes to the quivering jellies of Mrs Chomley's naked breasts. Suddenly Mrs Holbein crouched on all fours and directed her own chastisement. She mewled and quivered in pain as the masked and rubber-sheathed Mistress held her leashed by her choker, and flogged her bare ebony globes with a quirt of four whistling steel rods. I could not mistake her lithe body: it was Miss Task . . .

I saw one Mistress robed entirely in silver mesh, a tight sheath of armour like a crusader's, with a peaked nose on her sinister helmet. Ripe breasts and croup shimmering tight beneath her carapace, she scourged a nude maiden on the bare buttocks with a metal quirt of rods; her victim wriggled in suspension from a crossbar between two posts, to which she was clamped by nipples and quim lips, stretched like dough as they strained to take the weight of her squirming body. The meshed Mistress lashed her with strokes that took her cunningly from below, on bare bum and thighs. My cock throbbed hard. Denton whispered that Ladies left to themselves were shameless, to arouse a fellow so . . .

Some of the Ladies, lustful with frotting, lifted their skirts and frillies to offer their bottoms for playful spankings, continuing to pleasure themselves as their pink bum-flesh was slapped by eager palms.

Beyond the maid in stocks stood another luckless Eghamite: she was on tiptoe in a stout, forbidding pillory, and her naked body was flogged on her croup while her fount jerked helplessly at the rhythm of her caning, pierced by a huge obispos that protruded upwards from the pillory's shaft. Another maid hung by her fingers from a tree branch, looking out on the river twinkling distantly as three Mistresses at once caned her naked buttocks, shoulders and thighs, the long springy canes flashing yellow in the moonlight. I thought her bottom severely darkened by the cane, until I saw that her globes bore a livid tattoo in the shape of black roses spread across both fesses, the stem leading into her furrow and to her quim lips, with the tendrils of the root spreading down her thighs, swirled with the long dangling mink-hairs from the unkempt forest on her mound.

Her flogging was pitiless, and, after several dozen lashes, she gave a loud moaning gasp and went limp, only to be revived by a bucket of cold water from a large glass tank, curiously like an aquarium. Then her ankles were raised and fastened to the branch beside her hands, bending her in a U shape. Her pendulous breasts hung slack, revealing their own rose teat-tattoos, with the distended nipples poking through the blossoms like pink stiff buds. Two of the hooded Mistresses began to chew and bite on her nipples, while the third knelt and licked her bumhole and quim, till she moaned, now, in pleasure.

Then, from the water tank, a black-gloved Mistress took two shiny black squirming things, and fastened them with a snap to the nipples and the quim lips – I thought perhaps to the nubbin of the flogged maid's clitoris itself. She shrieked and struggled, and I saw a golden stream pour from her wriggling fount, over the device of her torment: she was pinched by live lobsters. Her tormentors writhed too, from voluptuous clit-frotting. I shivered as I thought of Miss Owsley's warning . . .

A striking young Lady suddenly appeared at the torchlit doorway of the main house. Even in silhouette, she was superb: her proud, ripe figure was swathed in a black velvet gown that demurely covered her ankles, but swept low at the breast so that, shrouded in darkness as she was, I could see the moonlight glint on the bare teat-skin. At her waist, she wore a black cane which sparkled, the whole shaft studded with jewels. She was masked in black velvet, framed by a cascade of honey-blonde tresses, and her haughty, disdainful poise told me that, despite her youth, this must be the Mistress of the submissive Eghamites. She turned her head slightly, so that I saw her lush lips curling in a smile – the dazzling teeth – and the profile. It was Miss Florence.

She descended from the steps, in fluid, regal motion, to be greeted with curtsies and bows from the Ladies. Just then, Denton said nervously that he was too worried to stay, and would leave me to it. Before I could reproach him for his timidity, he slipped rapidly away, and then I heard a clatter of hooves in the driveway. I turned to see Dido, in the seat of a jaunting car, clad in a cloak and tricorn hat like a highwayman, but beneath it the spilling of bare breast over the skimpiest scarlet corselage, black stockings and lovely gleaming thigh-boots.

She waved a long, springy cane at her ponies: two maids who snuffled and snorted in their tight harnesses, with gags and blinkers, their nude bodies gleaming whip-kissed in the moonlight. I recognised those bare bottoms and the bushy minks: the ponies were Grubb and Miss Bernice Mantle.

Denton clambered up in the pony trap, and took position at Dido's feet, covering them with obeisant kisses, while she flicked the cane smartly over Grubb's and Bernice's bare bums, and they trotted away, kicking high in their heavy iron shoes. At that moment, I heard a rustling of leaves behind me, and smelled Miss Florence's perfume.

'Well, well. A naughty drudge, peeking where he should not peek. Are you fond of lobster, you worm?'

I looked round, and fell to my knees, clutching the hem of her robe and her shoes; she kicked my lips scornfully away with a sharp toe-point.

'O!' I cried. 'I am your slave, Mistress. Do with me what you will – I gladly submit to your chastisement.'

'Then I shall have to think of a chastisement you *won't* accept gladly,' she drawled, pinching me by the earlobe. I rose to face her.

'Come along, you naughty boy,' she said.

'Yes, Mistress!' I blurted.

'It is proper for you to address me as Miss Florence,' she replied.

Then she ripped my clothes from me, snarling like a beast, until I stood shivering and naked. She grasped the bulb of my timid cock, which stirred at her touch, and led me thus into the throng.

'A male!' murmured the Ladies, chastiser and chastised alike. '*A male . . .*'

And the murmurs grew to a vengeful baying. The Lady in crusader's armour laid down her flogging tool, and confronted my Mistress.

'A male has no right here,' she snarled, her voice muffled and tinny. 'Especially not *this* wretch!'

I knew her voice!

Miss Florence squeezed my balls and brushed my peehole delicately with her forefinger – in an instant, my penis stood hard, and the assembled Ladies gasped, some putting hands to mouth to hide their lustful glee. Brutally, Miss Florence drew back my prepuce to reveal the swollen crescent of my moon mark.

'Is *this* what you fear, Miss?' she snapped.

'By what right –?' shrieked the Lady in armour.

'By this right,' said my Mistress. 'First, I am Mistress of this establishment. Secondly, this male possesses the title descended through centuries. He has the birthmark! He has come home to reclaim his ancestral property, as lord of this manor – *and he is my slave . . .*'

Everyone looked at me. I was in ecstasy – my Mistress had empowered herself over me!

'Yes, Miss Florence – *Mistress*,' I blurted joyfully, 'I am your slave.'

The armoured Lady threw off her helmet and blonde tresses flowed over her silvery breast. My guess was true – it was Miss Alice Arbiter.

'It is I who am Lady of this manor,' she spat at my Mistress. 'The boy is an interloper, a fraud. It is I who have the true birthmark. I have waited for this moment to reveal it.'

I saw Miss Porritt whisper to Samantha, who departed.

Suddenly, Miss Arbiter unsheathed herself – stripped off her armour and stood nude, her mound gleaming proudly in the pale light as she pulled aside the lips of her gash to reveal, deep in her pink gash, a moon mark.

Mrs Holbein approached us, carrying the water tank unaided.

'I believe the Lady is overheated,' she said. 'With your permission, Mistress . . .'

She curtsied to Miss Florence, who nodded solemnly, and Mrs Holbein suddenly upended the tank and its entire contents over Miss Alice Arbiter, drenching her in cold water. Miss Arbiter shrieked her outrage but, to my surprise, the water trickling down her breasts and belly was not clear: rather, a turbid yellow colour. Her blonde tresses were darkening rapidly to black.

'A shaven quim and legs and arms,' said Mrs Holbein drily, 'perfectly tasteful. But you neglected to forsake your head locks. Vanity, Miss, vanity!'

My Mistress suddenly cracked her cane-tip right into Miss Alice Arbiter's spread gash lips, catching her squarely on the moon, and the Lady howled in pain, cursing my Mistress.

'It is nothing but a tattoo,' said Miss Florence calmly. 'A deception.'

She lifted her cane again and whipped me right on the exposed glans of my stiff penis, the cane's tip touching only my birthmark. The shock of her lash made me giddy with submissive pleasure – but it tingled without hurting me at all.

'The true birthmark of the ancient lord of this manor,' said Miss Florence, 'is a nerveless adornment, and numb to all sensation. It may be whipped or scratched or bitten, without causing distress. I believe Mrs Holbein will testify to that. You don't think you were brought here by chance, do you, Roger?'

'But, Mistress,' I blurted, 'why the secrecy from me? Why my long servitude and submission to punishment?'

'We had to test you, Roger. By right, you are my master. This ground, and Virginia Lodge, too, and Mrs Norringe's and Mrs Mantle's, all belong to your estate. To think we were in thrall to the false sisterhood of the so-called Miss Arbiter! Abetted by that wretch Denton, who shall suffer for it. We needed time to train you to be an *obedient* master.'

I cried that I longed for nothing but submission to her, my true Mistress, and was about to plead for merciful treatment of my friend Denton.

'There is the proving test for you,' she said gravely, 'to show yourself true lord of the manor.'

At that moment Samantha returned, clutching a sheaf of photographs and documents, and Miss Alice Arbiter, shivering wet and naked as she was, turned to flee. She was quickly restrained by the Mistresses, and Miss Florence ordered her trussed and bound.

'But do not whip her . . . just yet,' she added.

'Mistress,' said Miss Porritt, curtsying in excitement so that one bare breast popped prettily from her corselage, 'you know of Master Roger's affairs: a mischievous lawsuit impeding his just assumption of his rights, by a certain Miss Richter. I have now got documentary and photographic evidence of her fraud . . . *This* is Miss Sabina Richter!'

She pointed dramatically at Miss Arbiter, now quivering under stout cords, and her bosom swelled as she drew herself up as though for the stage.

'She is one of these stateless people – a chameleon, belonging everywhere and nowhere – who has made a career of deception, aided by her undoubted physical charms. Would that males had more sense than to be swayed by female wiles! Happily, the law provides us with documents and title deeds, more powerful than any woman's charms!'

Miss Arbiter cowered and covered her face with her hands, so that only her bright, baleful eyes glowed in hatred at us. And suddenly I knew where I had seen those eyes before . . . It was but a few years, yet time and pain had clouded the memory until now. I saw Miss Arbiter swathed in a military leather greatcoat, and felt again the searing pain of her whipping on my innocent bare buttocks . . . and my shame at her theft of my precious load of documents. 'Just title deeds,' my father had said, to comfort me. Now I understood the importance of title deeds.

I was led to a large oak tree, whose trunk bore a curious, gaping knothole. This, said my Mistress, was the 'hallowed tree'.

Miss Porritt ceremoniously carried a massive obispos of old, carved wood decorated with little naked nymphs and impish fauns. She placed it alongside my erect penis and pronounced it a perfect match. She said this was the very tool left by my ancestor, Sir Rogier, to his Lady as he departed on his crusade.

The knothole was in the unmistakable shape of a female gash. I was pressed against the bark, with my penis at the hole, and my Mistress caressed my balls and shaft with a few deft and tender strokes to make sure I was fully erect. Calmly, she lifted her robe and placed her fingers at her cooze, which was at last shaven bare!

Her sumptuous hillock gleamed nude under the moon, its ripe swelling revealing the delicious harmony of her body, its firmness a joyous mirror of her croup and breasts.

She put her fingers in her gash lips and withdrew them glistening with her oils; then she anointed my cock until she was slippery. She clasped my buttocks, and pushed my oiled cock firmly into the knothole, and I slid in: the gash fitted me like a glove, and was soft and silky and moist.

She cried that here was the master, and my flesh must be kissed by my Ladies, in homage. Quickly, I was bound by arms and legs right round the trunk of the tree. My legs were splayed and my naked buttocks spread wide, and I felt the tickling caress of Ladies' lips on my balls and my anus bud, and on the wealed skin of my fesses. I began to sigh with pleasure, as the obeisant Ladies cooed their own, their chant echoing that of Dido, Miss Florence and Grubb, as they chastised me at the tree by the lake.

Suddenly, I jerked against the tree and cried out, for the kissing lips were replaced by the hard lash of a cane. Miss Florence's perfume assailed my nostrils as she caned my bare, to three dozen, the jewels that studded her cane-shaft making me squirm and gasp in dreadful smarting, and each lash slamming my cock into the tree-gash, as though I were poking a silky wet cooze. After three dozen, the kissing and licking recommenced, and I felt tender fingers stroking my fesses.

Then I took three dozen more. Now I sensed that my Mistress ceded her jewelled cane to others, and I think I took cane from every Eghamite, Mistress and slave alike. I squirmed and moaned, delirious in pain, yet joyful in my humiliance to many Ladies. I looked up: the moon beamed down like a friend or a greater, cool Mistress, and I felt my sap rise in my balls as I jerked in agony against the tree. And then my groans grew to cries of joy as I felt myself spurt inside the silky tree-hole, and heard the cheers as I spasmed. Sobbing, I was released from my bonds, and my Mistress withdrew from within the knothole her pink silk panties!

She knelt before me and took my cock in her mouth, licking and sucking my bulb until I rose stiff again. Now, Mrs Holbein came forward, to clamp me with a golden cock-ring, detached from one of her own nipples. I looked at the lawn, and saw it a sea of pale orbs rivalling the moon above: every Lady, Mistress or maid, knelt to present me with her bared buttocks.

Miss Florence handed me her jewelled cane and whispered instructions to the lord of the manor. Gravely, I dealt seven hard strokes to each bare bum before poking the Lady in her cooze with my throbbing member, my spurt-ring enabling me to bring each female to her climax without emission of my own juices. I recognised Miss Crouch, squatting beside Mrs Holbein and Miss Owsley: there was Dido and her two ponies, Grubb and Miss Bernice, and, further along, Mrs Mantle herself, her bare bum as firm and pretty, and as tempting, as her daughter's.

'O . . .' moaned the lesbic Bernice as I poked her, 'give me cock . . . master!'

'Fuck me hard, sir,' whispered her mother, quivering in pleasure as my cock slid into her sopping cooze.

The bound Miss Arbiter, or Signorina Richter, watched us balefully.

My cock was raw and numb with my exertions, but they were not at an and; again, I passed along the serried ranks of cane-flushed bottoms, and at my Mistress's solemn command, buggered each and every writhing Lady, their silky, elastic bumholes squeezing my cock to iron hardness. Still I was restrained by my clamp from spurting, until, finally, Miss Florence herself knelt, lifted her robe to reveal bare globes and fount, and I took her first in her cooze, bringing her to orgasm as she frotted her naked clitty; then in her bum, where I finally, and with loud cries of my pent-up pleasure, delivered my cream to the root of her squirming tight anus.

She rose, and faced Miss Alice Arbiter.

'Beat her,' she commanded.

The Mistresses, panting gleefully in their tight leather and rubber corsets, fell on her with whip and cane, and began Miss Arbiter's thrashing.

'Won't you stroke her, Roger?' said Miss Florence, 'before we proceed to your adornment?'

I thought of vengeance for that first, cruel beating, all those years ago.

'Yes!' spat the squirming Miss Arbiter, her lips a rictus of pain. 'Have your revenge . . . *signorina*! Nothing can spoil my memory of your bum glowing under my whip, and your male humiliation *in my woman's power* . . .'

'No, Mistress, with your permission,' I said, looking disdainfully at the flogged charlatan, 'I don't think I am worthy. That is Ladies' work.'

As she led me into the house, I saw Mrs Holbein vigorously buggering Miss Arbiter with my own ancestor's cock-dildo, her squeals muffled by my Mistress's gasmask; a sort of revenge. Yet her buggered cries were joyful, and I was pleased that my cock's likeness gave her anus pleasure, as my squirming bum had given her pleasure years before.

My Mistress said that I must be adorned as *her* property, if I were to fully claim my own. I did not demur as she led me to the tattooing chamber where, for an hour, I trembled in agony as the needle of the Lady tattooist pounded at the bulb of my cock, adorning me with a smiling sun to complement my moon.

Then my nipples and the flesh of my buttocks were pierced, and silver rings inserted, soldered shut so that I could not remove them. The same was done to the tender place between balls and furrow; a further silver ring was inserted right through the pierced bulb of my penis. Miss Florence said this was a slave-ring, and showed my submission to her. My earlobes and navel were pierced too, but no metal inserted.

Dido came, and together they took me into a bedchamber, and my Mistress said that she and Mummy had me all to themselves.

'Have you still some cream for us, slave?' she said, 'because otherwise, I shall have to whip you till your balls oblige me.'

I knelt and kissed her feet, then Dido's, and said that my correction had better proceed.

I was caned by each Mistress in turn with the jewelled cane, and so hard that amid my squealing and the clenching of my smarting purpled fesses, I heard the force of the lashes dislodge the jewels from the cane's shaft. Time seemed to drift as I writhed in sweet flogged agony. When I had taken full one hundred with the cane, dawn was beginning to glimmer.

'O, Mistress,' I sobbed. 'Why so hard?'

'Because . . . *because you are male*,' she purred.

Miss Florence took a diamond fallen from her cane, and fastened it with a silver clasp to my pierced navel, then did the same to my earlobes. I pressed my face to her loins, and she lifted her robe to reveal her moist shaven quim, into which I buried my tongue. Dido presented her own gash, and with my tongue and lips I pleasured the two Mistresses until their slits were streaming with love oils.

Then I mounted them, and fucked them in cooze from behind, one licking my anus bud and balls while I poked the other. They came to spasm well before I spurted in Dido's cooze; then I must pleasure her in her bumhole, and then my Mistress Florence demanded cream in her own cooze. Eventually I obliged, and we embraced slippery in fucking and buggery till the cock crowed.

'Despite Miss Arbiter's exposure, Mistress,' I said, 'nothing will rob me of the joy of believing all women to be witches, and in league, as Denton says.'

'Denton . . . you mean Greville. You must know eventually. The worm! He was never in Flanders, he was a medical orderly in Mesopotamia, where Daddy took a shine to him, and he used to arrange Mummy's nursing sessions. She told me he was very good, and it is true. So I got Mrs Mantle to give him a place whenever I felt my disgusting lusts for male flesh too strong to resist.'

'You mean, you and Dido . . . with Denton?' I gasped.

She smiled cruelly.

'Yes, Roger. And many others. I know you peeked at me when I was about my charitable works in Egham that day of your interview with Miss Porritt. It was Mummy who introduced me to . . . nursing. The liberating thrill of self-abasement to the male animal, indulging desire while punishing oneself for it. And getting shillings for it! In less humiliant moments, there is Denton's – Greville's – cock at my service. He is in my thrall, lest I give away his secret. One AWOL too many, in the stews of Port Said, poor lustful Greville! But he is very, very good, as Mummy will attest. Does it bother you that our coozes have trembled as cock after cock spermed in us? Some men, like dear Daddy, find it exciting.'

I said, truthfully, that her pleasure was her slave's greatest joy . . . that I should be happy to serve her as humiliant maid, in frillies and pink panties, and watch as male after male thrust his cock between her precious thighs, while Dido birched me for my impudent peeking . . .

She flicked my tattooed cock, so that my cock-ring slapped against the skin of my throbbing bulb.

'Yes, Greville is virile – though no master like you, my sweet slave. Now you may serve me with another fuck, before you serve us our breakfast, in maid's frillies.'

I performed in every position of lust: my Mistress rode me, with Dido's cooze and bum squashing my face; I buggered each of them, then was ridden by Dido; took both of them in cooze, and finally was vigorously poking my Mistress, her thighs bunched over her breast and my belly slapping their backs as I fucked her wet gaping quim. My cock was numb and rock-hard, and I brought each of them to climax repeatedly, but could not myself spurt.

'I want your cream, Roger,' cooed my Mistress, panting as I fucked her hard, with Dido's hand spanking my bucking bum-globes. 'Come in my cooze, slave.'

I gasped that she had quite drained my balls, but I would serve her like an obedient slave till I dropped.

'Mistress,' I said suddenly, 'you remember when you chastised me by the summerhouse . . . you Ladies together?'

'Our league,' she panted, but with a little giggle. 'Yes, I do.'

'You teased me horribly, threatened me with a Turkish birching.'

'On the balls . . . yes, Roger, I remember.'

'Would you have? Birched my balls? I mean, really?'

Miss Florence's fingers delved at her squirming gash,

and she began to fiercely masturbate her stiff clitty, her fingers darting between her gash and my belly. My bottom jerked in real pain, as Dido now beat me with a searing birch full on the bare. The birch can be a tickle, or white-hot agony. This was agony.

'Birch your balls? Why, yes, slave,' she gasped, beginning to heave in the throes of her climax. 'I believe I would . . .'

I kissed my Mistress's lips for the first time, and cried out in ecstasy as we came together.

Envoi

An English Gentleman

A slave must not feel pleasure, so I am forbidden to say that my life as lord of the manor at Virginia Lodge is one of untrammelled bliss. Gone are my foolish fancies of Oxford and a so-called education – what education does an English gentleman need, other than to be the slave of imperious and demanding Ladies?

I am obliged to share the servant's shed with Grubb, who oversees my household duties, such as laundry or 'mucking out', and has permission to whip me bare when I displease her. To prevent unseemliness, my cock and balls are enclosed in a restrainer, chained to the wall at night, and to which my Mistress has the key.

There is not one day when I go without beating on the bare: with cane, whip, or birch, often in a variety of painful bindings and restraints, and from each and every Lady of the house. The merciless Grubb, especially, delights in making my adornments jangle as she flogs my naked buttocks.

I must be available at all times to serve my Ladies for their pleasure, frequently observed by the Major, or for the pleasure of any of their friends, who vie to make my fesses squirm the most. Mrs Holbein has assured me I shall be troubled no more by Miss Alice Arbiter, or Richter, as she was given a shameful tattoo and 'whipped out of town' for good.

Sometimes I am permitted to serve as maid, and wear my Mistress's frilly things, and even her pink silk panties, and am afterwards bound in leather harness and cords, shackled and whipped to the bone for my impudence in wearing them.

Frequently, I am taken 'at stud' to Mrs Norringe's, or to the college of discipline at Egham, where I am whipped mercilessly if my cock fails to pleasure enough Ladies' holes, and whipped mercilessly if she does not fail. Sometimes I am accompanied by my good friend Greville, and we poke, and take our bare beatings, in playful rivalry, though he insists on calling me 'sir', happily out of earshot of my Mistress. We compare our flogged bums, and giggle, just like two thrashed schoolgirls . . .

At other times, Grubb permits me to wear her frilly maid's uniform, and my Mistress gives me her pink silk panties; thus robed, I serve her in her bed as she entertains a succession of young gentlemen visitors: a dozen or so brutal, lusty males, naked and fucking her vigorously in her precious cooze as she moans in her repeated ecstasy, permitting me a taunting smile every now and then. Afterwards, I must clean the bedspread sopping with her cooze-oils, and take down my frilly knickers to receive a birching on the bare for my impudent spying. And if I take four or five dozen, without protest, my own cock is permitted to taste her buttered bun . . .

After one such session, she rewarded me by giving me my mail, a postcard from my father in Uruguay! It was a photograph of him with a Lady in a revealing swimsuit, on the beach at Punta del Este, and she bore a striking resemblance to Miss Alice Arbiter, only she had red hair. His arm clasped her waist most affectionately. He said that business was good, and hoped to see me soon, and always knew I should assume my place as lord of the manor . . .

I shall always treasure the memory of my first visit back to Egham. It was a Sunday, the roads quite deserted, and we were to journey there by pony and trap. The Major asked if Dido would not prefer him to drive us in the car, but she said it was a fine day for a ride, and Roger was just getting things ready.

Dido, Miss Florence, and Grubb settled themselves on

the seat of the trap. I made sure my frilly maid's uniform – Grubb's kind loan – was smart and smooth, my stockings striped with a single sluttish ladder, and my iron shoes polished and shining. My corset was horribly tight, and my cock restrainer pinched: a double restrainer, that filled my aching bumhole to bursting. Then I positioned my bridle and harness correctly, adjusted my blinkers, and tucked my skirt up to present my bum, with the pink silk knickers drawn up tight. The reins flicked, and I felt the smarting of three canes together, cracking on my naked bum. At once, with a whinny, I jerked into trotting motion. Let no one deny that Ladies are sweet sorceresses!

'Giddy-up, master!' cried Miss Florence, as the cane whipped me.

Whinnying in pleasure, and proud at last to be an English gentleman, I obeyed my Mistress.

NEW BOOKS

Coming up from Nexus, Sapphire and Black Lace

Taking Pains to Please by Arabella Knight
June 1999 Price £5.99 ISBN: 0 352 33369 3
It can be a punishing experience for willing young women striving to please and obey exacting employers. On the job, they quickly come to learn that giving complete satisfaction demands their strict dedication and devotion to duty. Maid, nanny or nurse – each must submit to the discipline of the daily grind. In their capable hands, the urgent needs and dark desires of their paymasters are always fulfilled: for these working girls find pleasure in taking pains to please.

The Submission Gallery by Lindsay Gordon
June 1999 Price £5.99 ISBN: 0 352 33370 7
For her art, Poppy the sculptress seeks out and recreates the heights of submission and domination. Each sculpture she creates is taken from life – a life of total sensual freedom where she meets a strange cast of brutal lovers. From strangers in restaurants to tattooists, from a baroness to a uniformed society of fetishists, Poppy experiences rigorous obedience and tastes power for the first time. The result is her Submission Gallery.

The Handmaidens by Aran Ashe
June 1999 Price £5.99 ISBN: 0 352 33282 4
Tormunil can be an exceedingly harsh place for pretty young serving girls. Destined for a life of sexual slavery at the hands of merciless overlords, the chosen ones are taken to the Abbey – a place where strength is learned through obedience to those who follow the path of the Twisted Cross. Taken into this strange world, the young and beautiful Sianon and Iroise are allowed few privileges. Tormented to the peaks of pleasure, but punished if they seek release, their only hope of escape lies with the handsome young traveller who has fallen for their charms. This is the fifth in a series of Nexus Classics.

NEXUS NEW BOOKS

To be published in January

KNICKERS AND BOOTS
Penny Birch

When Stephen Stanbrook consults therapist Gabrielle Salinger about his yearnings towards sexual dominance, her girlfriend, Poppy, is intrigued. Determined to find out more, she traces his exploits on the net as he seduces two young submissives, Nicola and June, known in the SM community as Knickers and Boots. Before long she's put through her paces by him, together with them, and all in uniform. Meanwhile, Gabrielle's old playmate Jeff Bellbird is stalking them in the hope of something even more perverse.

£6.99 ISBN 0 352 33853 9

THE PUNISHMENT CLUB
Jacqueline Masterson

Twenty-year-old Fudge and her mistress, Clarissa, join a club devoted to traditional discipline and the 'training' of attractive young women. They discover a whole network of quintessentially English societies dedicated to bondage, domination and spanking. The fun becomes ever more competitive and arduous, however, and Fudge finds that she must help the club take on its great rival 'The Church of the Birch' at its annual summer fete and sports day.

£6.99 ISBN 0 352 33862 8

CONFESSION OF AN ENGLISH SLAVE
Yolanda Celbridge

Introduced to the joys of bare-bottom discipline by lustful ladies, naval cadet Philip Demesne, posted to the far east, painfully learns true submission from the voluptuous dominatrix Galena, aboard her private carriage on the Trans-Siberian Express. Escaping from her lash, he is kidnapped to serve in an English school of female domination, transplanted to the emptiness of Siberia to escape do-gooding restrictions on corporal punishment. His male arrogance utterly crushed, Philip gladly submits to total enslavement by women with unlimited flagellant discipline.

£6.99 ISBN 0 352 33861 X

To be published in February

PRINCESS
Aishling Morgan

Princess follows the (mis)fortunes of Aeisla, her compatriot Iriel, and their ad hoc band of nubile, amazonian warrior women as they are forced to flee their native Aegmund or face bizarre and public erotic punishment. Their passages worked copiously, they arrive by ship at the kingdom of Oretea. Political scheming, slavery and perverse punishments ensue in this, the fabulously inventive final part of Aishling Morgan's *Maiden* saga.

£6.99 ISBN 0 352 33871 7

THE SMARTING OF SELINA
Yolanda Celbridge

Blonde journalist Selina Rawe eagerly infiltrates Her Majesty's Prison at Auchterhuish, where corporal punishment is mandatory for wayward girls, along with more specialist treatments from a gorgeous resident nurse, while the lustful Hebridean mariners provide little – or perhaps too much – relief. Sapphic governess Miss Gurdell worships the bottom beautiful, and Selina is horrified to learn that hers is the tastiest of all. A novel of craven submission from the author of *The English Vice*.

£6.99 ISBN 0 352 33872 5

THE INSTITUTE
Maria del Rey

When Lucy is sentenced to be rehabilitated in a bizarre institute for the treatment of delinquent girls, she finds that the disciplinary methods used are not what she has been led to expect. They are, in fact, decidedly perverse. By the author of *Dark Desires*, *Dark Delights* and *Obsession* – 'The Queen of SM' *Caress*. A Nexus Classic.

£6.99 ISBN 0 352 33352 9

NEXUS BACKLIST

This information is correct at time of printing. For up-to-date information, please visit our website at www.nexus-books.co.uk

All books are priced at £6.99 unless another price is given.

THE ACADEMY	Arabella Knight 0 352 33806 7	☐
AMANDA IN THE PRIVATE HOUSE	Esme Ombreux 0 352 33705 2	☐
ANGEL £5.99	Lindsay Gordon 0 352 33590 4	☐
BAD PENNY £5.99	Penny Birch 0 352 33661 7	☐
BARE BEHIND	Penny Birch 0 352 33721 4	☐
BEAST £5.99	Wendy Swanscombe 0 352 33649 8	☐
BELLE SUBMISSION	Yolanda Celbridge 0 352 33728 1	☐
BENCH-MARKS	Tara Black 0 352 33797 4	☐
BRAT	Penny Birch 0 352 33674 9	☐
BROUGHT TO HEEL £5.99	Arabella Knight 0 352 33508 4	☐
CAGED! £5.99	Yolanda Celbridge 0 352 33650 1	☐
CAPTIVE £5.99	Aishling Morgan 0 352 33585 8	☐
CAPTIVES OF THE PRIVATE HOUSE £5.99	Esme Ombreux 0 352 33619 6	☐
CHALLENGED TO SERVE	Jacqueline Bellevois 0 352 33748 6	☐

CHERRI CHASTISED	Yolanda Celbridge 0 352 33707 9	☐
CORPORATION OF CANES	Lindsay Gordon 0 352 33745 1	☐
THE CORRECTION OF AN ESSEX MAID	Yolanda Celbridge 0 352 33780 X	☐
CREAM TEASE	Aishling Morgan 0 352 33811 3	☐
CRUEL TRIUMPH	William Doughty 0 352 33759 1	☐
DANCE OF SUBMISSION £5.99	Lisette Ashton 0 352 33450 9	☐
DARK DESIRES £5.99	Maria del Rey 0 352 33648 X	☐
DEMONIC CONGRESS	Aishling Morgan 0 352 33762 1	☐
DIRTY LAUNDRY	Penny Birch 0 352 33680 3	☐
DISCIPLINE OF THE PRIVATE HOUSE	Esme Ombreux 0 352 33709 5	☐
DISCIPLINED SKIN £5.99	Wendy Swanscombe 0 352 33541 6	☐
DISPLAYS OF EXPERIENCE £5.99	Lucy Golden 0 352 33505 X	☐
DISPLAYS OF PENITENTS £5.99	Lucy Golden 0 352 33646 3	☐
DRAWN TO DISCIPLINE £5.99	Tara Black 0 352 33626 9	☐
AN EDUCATION IN THE PRIVATE HOUSE £5.99	Esme Ombreux 0 352 33525 4	☐
THE ENGLISH VICE	Yolanda Celbridge 0 352 33805 9	☐
EROTICON 1 £5.99	Various 0 352 33593 9	☐
EROTICON 4 £5.99	Various 0 352 33602 1	☐
THE GOVERNESS ABROAD	Yolanda Celbridge 0 352 33735 4	☐

THE GOVERNESS AT ST AGATHA'S	Yolanda Celbridge 0 352 33729 X	☐
GROOMING LUCY £5.99	Yvonne Marshall 0 352 33529 7	☐
HEART OF DESIRE £5.99	Maria del Rey 0 352 32900 9	☐
THE HOUSE OF MALDONA	Yolanda Celbridge 0 352 33740 0	☐
IN FOR A PENNY £5.99	Penny Birch 0 352 33449 5	☐
THE INDIGNITIES OF ISABELLE	Penny Birch writing as Cruella 0 352 33696 X	☐
INNOCENT	Aishling Morgan 0 352 33699 4	☐
THE ISLAND OF MALDONA	Yolanda Celbridge 0 352 33746 X	☐
JODHPURS AND JEANS	Penny Birch 0 352 33778 8	☐
THE LAST STRAW	Christina Shelly 0 352 33643 9	☐
NON-FICTION: LESBIAN SEX SECRETS FOR MEN	Jamie Goddard and Kurt Brungard 0 352 33724 9	☐
LETTERS TO CHLOE £5.99	Stephan Gerrard 0 352 33632 3	☐
LOVE-CHATTEL OF TORMUNIL	Aran Ashe 0 352 33779 6	☐
THE MASTER OF CASTLELEIGH £5.99	Jacqueline Bellevois 0 352 33644 7	☐
MEMOIRS OF A CORNISH GOVERNESS	Yolanda Celbridge 0 352 33722 2	☐
MISS RATTAN'S LESSON	Yolanda Celbridge 0 352 33791 5	☐
NON-FICTION: MY SECRET GARDEN SHED £7.99	Ed. Paul Scott 0 352 33725 7	☐
NEW EROTICA 5 £5.99	Various 0 352 33540 8	☐
NEW EROTICA 6	Various 0 352 33751 6	☐

THE NEXUS LETTERS £5.99	Various 0 352 33621 8	☐
NURSES ENSLAVED £5.99	Yolanda Celbridge 0 352 33601 3	☐
NURSE'S ORDERS	Penny Birch 0 352 33739 7	☐
NYMPHS OF DIONYSUS £4.99	Susan Tinoff 0 352 33150 X	☐
THE OBEDIENT ALICE	Adriana Arden 0 352 33826 1	☐
ONE WEEK IN THE PRIVATE HOUSE	Esme Ombreux 0 352 33706 0	☐
ORIGINAL SINS	Lisette Ashton 0 352 33804 0	☐
THE PALACE OF EROS £4.99	Delver Maddingley 0 352 32921 1	☐
THE PALACE OF PLEASURES	Christobel Coleridge 0 352 33801 6	☐
PALE PLEASURES	Wendy Swanscombe 0 352 33702 8	☐
PARADISE BAY £5.99	Maria del Rey 0 352 33645 5	☐
PEACH	Penny Birch 0 352 33790 7	☐
PEACHES AND CREAM	Aishling Morgan 0 352 33672 2	☐
PENNY IN HARNESS £5.99	Penny Birch 0 352 33651 X	☐
PENNY PIECES £5.99	Penny Birch 0 352 33631 5	☐
PET TRAINING IN THE PRIVATE HOUSE £5.99	Esme Ombreux 0 352 33655 2	☐
PLAYTHINGS OF THE PRIVATE HOUSE £6.99	Esme Ombreux 0 352 33761 3	☐
PLEASURE ISLAND £5.99	Aran Ashe 0 352 33628 5	☐
THE PLEASURE PRINCIPLE	Maria del Rey 0 352 33482 7	☐

PLEASURE TOY £5.99	Aishling Morgan 0 352 33634 X	☐
PRIVATE MEMOIRS OF A KENTISH HEADMISTRESS	Yolanda Celbridge 0 352 33763 X	☐
PROPERTY	Lisette Ashton 0 352 33744 3	☐
PURITY £5.99	Aishling Morgan 0 352 33510 6	☐
REGIME	Penny Birch 0 352 33666 8	☐
RITUAL STRIPES	Tara Black 0 352 33701 X	☐
SATURNALIA £7.99	Ed. Paul Scott 0 352 33717 6	☐
SATAN'S SLUT	Penny Birch 0 352 33720 6	☐
THE SCHOOLING OF STELLA	Yolanda Celbridge 0 352 33803 2	☐
SEE-THROUGH £5.99	Lindsay Gordon 0 352 33656 0	☐
SILKEN SLAVERY	Christina Shelley 0 352 33708 7	☐
SISTERS OF SEVERCY £5.99	Jean Aveline 0 352 33620 X	☐
SIX OF THE BEST	Wendy Swanscombe 0 352 33796 6	☐
SKIN SLAVE £5.99	Yolanda Celbridge 0 352 33507 6	☐
SLAVE ACTS	Jennifer Jane Pope 0 352 33665 X	☐
SLAVE GENESIS £5.99	Jennifer Jane Pope 0 352 33503 3	☐
SLAVE-MINES OF TORMUNIL	Aran Ashe 0 352 33695 1	☐
SLAVE REVELATIONS £5.99	Jennifer Jane Pope 0 352 33627 7	☐
SOLDIER GIRLS £5.99	Yolanda Celbridge 0 352 33586 6	☐
STRAPPING SUZETTE £5.99	Yolanda Celbridge 0 352 33783 4	☐

THE SUBMISSION GALLERY £5.99	Lindsay Gordon 0 352 33370 7	☐
TAKING PAINS TO PLEASE	Arabella Knight 0 352 33785 0	☐
THE TAMING OF TRUDI	Yolanda Celbridge 0 352 33673 0	☐
A TASTE OF AMBER £5.99	Penny Birch 0 352 33654 4	☐
TEASING CHARLOTTE	Yvonne Marshall 0 352 33681 1	☐
TEMPER TANTRUMS £5.99	Penny Birch 0 352 33647 1	☐
THE TRAINING GROUNDS	Sarah Veitch 0 352 33526 2	☐
UNIFORM DOLL	Penny Birch 0 352 33698 6	☐
VELVET SKIN £5.99	Aishling Morgan 0 352 33660 9	☐
WENCHES, WITCHES AND STRUMPETS	Aishling Morgan 0 352 33733 8	☐
WHIP HAND	G. C. Scott 0 352 33694 3	☐
WHIPPING GIRL	Aishling Morgan 0 352 33789 3	☐
THE YOUNG WIFE £5.99	Stephanie Calvin 0 352 33502 5	☐